Parts per Million

Finalist for the PEN/Bellwether Prize for Socially Engaged Fiction

"*Parts per Million* effortlessly weaves the personal with the political in this relentless page-turner. Part psychological thriller, part hard-boiled noir, the characters are fresh, real, and alive. With a lightness of touch and an uncanny ear for great dialogue, Julia Stoops tells the story of four activists in a time of war, their moral and emotional conflicts, their betrayals and their small acts of heroism. *Parts per Million* reads like the bastard offspring of Graham Greene and Naomi Klein."

—Robert Newman, author of *The Fountain at the Center of the World*

"Deftly layering humor with strong rhetoric, *Parts per Million* is inspiring with its fights against the status quo. . . . [The characters are] intense, committed, and uniquely flawed, and their actions and relationships give *Parts per Million* an impressive depth beyond its social messages."

—Meg Nola, reviewer, *Foreword Reviews*

"While Julia Stoops documents activism of the early 2000s, *Parts per Million* couldn't feel more relevant today. The struggle to remain faithful to the ideals—and hard work—of activism, the thrill of the rare, hard-won victory, and the navigating of personal politics, gives this book a thrilling narrative and makes it an inspired wake-up call to all of our inner activists."

—Ben Parzybok, author of *Sherwood Nation*

"*Parts per Million* is a cry for justice and a journey through the heart. Julia Stoops brilliantly conjures the social and political unrest of the early 2000s. The war drums, the resistance, the secretive birth of the surveillance state—all lit by deep emotional honesty. Stoops's keen eye sweeps us into the lives of three Portland activists—separate souls shakily united by a cause, a house, and a radiant artist/ex-junkie named Deirdre, who simultaneously illuminates and complicates their struggles. Compelling and deeply compassionate, *Parts per Million* takes us to a time and place we thought we could forget, but can't, and shouldn't. Reading it may be the surest way to understand who we were then, and—in the tumult of our times—who we need to be today."

—Scott Sparling, author of *Wire to Wire*

"Through the fully alive and magnetic characters in this book, Stoops captures our most serious global issues with her uncommon insight, wisdom, and humor. A remarkable, page-turning feat."

—Karim Dimechkie, author of *Lifted by the Great Nothing*

"The little-known history of West Coast, Left Coast eco-activism in the early aughts bursts to life in this timely and important book, full of finely drawn characters and outrageous intrigues. Eco-fiction at its finest, *Parts per Million* is one of the origin stories of the resistance, and a primer for the fight to come."

—Susan DeFreitas, author of *Hot Season*

"In her carefully thought-out debut novel *Parts per Million,* Julia Stoops gives us a team of young and not-so-young political activists at the beginning of the twenty-first century, working overtime to correct what they see as dangerous if not disastrous forces at work in the American political status quo. Stoops's adroit involvement of digital technology in the story gives a lively real-world edge to the presentation. Like a heartbeat against the center of the novel's environmental and war concerns is a love relationship laden with hopes, dreams and challenges familiar to the times. *Parts per Million* is a timely and stimulating fictional look at the difficult and too-often thankless task of defending the planet."

—Harold Johnson, author of *The Fort Showalter Blues*

"The page-turning plot would be reason enough to read *Parts per Million,* but Julia Stoops gives us characters so fully developed the novel feels like theater-in-the-round. The questions they ask themselves are central to our times–how do we live ethical lives in the face of so much institutionalized greed? If the personal is political, how can we turn away from anyone in crisis? Stoops takes us on a joyride through the political turmoil of the early twenty-first century, bringing anti-war protests and direct-action environmentalists vividly to life. Her characters may wear their political hearts on their sleeves, but it's their internal struggles that capture our attention and make this story such a rich and timely read."

—Stevan Allred, author of *A Simplified Map of the Real World*

PARTS PER MILLION

A NOVEL

JULIA STOOPS

FOREST AVENUE PRESS
Portland, Oregon

This is a work of fiction. Any resemblance these characters have to actual persons, living or dead, is entirely coincidental.

Cover design: Gigi Little
Cover art: Julia Stoops
Illustrations: Gabriel Liston
Interior design: Laura Stanfill

Library of Congress Cataloging-in-Publication Data

Names: Stoops, Julia, author.
Title: Parts per million / Julia Stoops.
Description: Portland, Oregon : Forest Avenue Press, [2017]
Identifiers: LCCN 2017041263 | ISBN 9781942436355 (softcover) | ISBN 9781942436362 (ebook)
Subjects: LCSH: Interpersonal relations--Fiction. | Communal living--Fiction.
Classification: LCC PS3619.T689 P37 2018 | DDC 813/.6--dc23
LC record available at https://lccn.loc.gov/2017041263

1 2 3 4 5 6 7 8 9

Distributed by Publishers Group West

Printed in the United States of America by United Graphics LLC

Forest Avenue Press LLC
P.O. Box 80134
Portland, OR 97280
forestavenuepress.com

For environmental activists of every stripe.
One day you will be considered heroes.

This the car Franky told me about? Looks like an old banger.
85 Oldsmobile Toronado. Last of the G3.

PART ONE

1: NELSON

NELSON IS STANDING FIVE hundred miles from home, surrounded by sagebrush, waiting for this to be over. There is no moon, only the sweep of the Milky Way.

Next to him Fetzer is just a shape in the dark. Fetzer whispers, "They're using napalm. To get the beams going. I hate the smell of napalm in the morning."

Nelson grapples for a sympathetic reply. Eventually he says, "I can imagine."

"Camera on?"

"Yeah," says Nelson. He's glad for the small talk. "It wasn't focusing. But Jen turned on her flashlight and I got it locked in on that."

Fetzer grunts in reply.

The Earth Freedom Brigade certainly chose a lovely night for a firebombing.

It had never occurred to Nelson, as he was studying the science of the natural world, that he'd end up being a part-time cameraman. He's a better writer. It would be nice if the Brigaders asked him to write their communiqué. He'd refer to data and present a cogent argument for the release of the horses. Instead, some kid will pen some hyperbolic paragraph, and Jen will think it's great, Fetzer will cock an eyebrow at it, and Nelson will sigh as he uploads it to the website. But at least being a cameraman at a sabotage action isn't as nerve-racking as being an actual saboteur.

The soft sounds of horses float over from the corral. Nelson closes his eyes. He sees himself and the others as tiny figures on the vast, high desert plain. Tiny people doing big things to put the world right. All this risk, all this danger, the worth of it. He expects the familiar jolt of purpose, but it doesn't come.

It's been nearly six years since Nelson turned his back on the Forest Service. Jen and Fetzer had sought him out, asked him to listen. They'd opened his eyes to what was really going on, and after that, sitting at a desk making bureaucratic decisions about forests lost its meaning. He'd tumbled out of his desk job and into an exhilarating, terrifying life with them, disrupting development projects and blockading forest roads. Until one day a fellow activist sent them a VHS tape of some folks hanging a banner over a freeway. The video was so bad it made the action look like a joke.

Nelson and Jen and Fetzer had been sitting on a ragged sofa, late at night, the TV the only light in the room. Jen had said, "I'd be embarrassed to show that," and Nelson and Fetzer agreed. Then Fetzer crossed his arms and smiled at an idea.

"Wouldn't it be great if there was some team of journalists that specialized in direct actions? They'd travel around the country and document all these things that nobody ever hears about."

It was one of those spear-through-the-heart moments. Nelson had turned to Fetzer and Jen and said, "We could be that team."

How clear it all seemed back then.

"Done," says a voice, and Nelson opens his eyes to the dark. One of the Brigaders walks in front of the corral, snapping twigs on his way over to the van.

Nelson really wants this to be over. He shifts his feet, but bumps the tripod. Repositions it. Wipes his damp palms on his pants. There's a scraping sound, and a guy near the van says, "Quit spilling it on my fucking shoe."

"Shhhhh," says another guy.

Fetzer's voice is a close-by murmur. "And they're using aluminum-sulfur for the igniter."

It occurs to Nelson that Fetzer, with nothing to do right now, has chosen to stand beside him instead of Jen on the other side of the barn. If Nelson asked, Fetzer would probably shrug and say something like his feet hurt and he can't be bothered picking his way over there in the dark. But they both know that Jen is in her element, surrounded by these Brigader kids on the cusp of a firebombing. The energy coming off her the past few days has been palpable. They both know, even if Fetzer won't articulate it, that there's a comfort in each other's company.

"We're like the Three Musketeers," Jen once joked, and Nelson had to explain that it wasn't a good analogy because the Three Musketeers didn't share their urgent need to save the planet.

"But still," Jen had said, and she wiped the cuff of her plaid shirt under her nose. "They rode around and did rad shit."

Nelson imagines the three of them on horses, and it makes him smile. For a moment it seems marvelous, beautiful, that they've stuck together all this time.

Fetzer was drunk the one time he told Nelson, years ago, about napalm bombing. It was like the end of the world, he'd said. He'd witnessed it burning through to bone. It burns bone. Keeps burning.

Bones. Barns. Paint it on the heavy beams to keep them burning. Nothing more pathetic than an arson strike that fizzles because your incendiaries are weak.

The barn is black against the starry sky. A flashlight swings a slippery beam, making grasses, shrubs, and feet surreal, then the light bobs and bounces with footsteps that crunch across the dark. Maybe it's Jen.

Nelson turns on his headset mic. "Camera two?"

"Forgot my water bottle," Jen's voice says in his ear.

Earlier, in the dusk light, Nelson saw a patch of Sierra Valley ivesia, just starting to bloom. Those tiny yellow flowers! *Ivesia aperta var. aperta*. A Species of Concern, according to the Feds, and too beautiful to lose. Last time he visited this area he was a grad student researching the genus. Now he's about to film an arson by a bunch of people who are stomping all over the place. Jen better not be stomping on any Sierra Valley ivesia.

Nelson tips back his head and the night sky fills his vision. The silence of the stars. If he'd carried on with his normal life, right now he'd be asleep in bed with Lise.

His neck hurts, and he brings his gaze back down. Over a decade ago it was hard work looking for that plant, eyes on the ground for hours. Finding one was like finding a jewel. It was only his thesis, but it felt like he was writing a book of jewels. Now, here in the dark under the watching stars, he's pointing a camera at a barn in the last minutes of its existence. Back when Nelson was doing his thesis, he would have despised who he is today.

Fetzer's profile changes, listening. There's a faint rumble in the distance.

"Helicopter?" says Nelson, and already his heart is thumping louder than the faraway sound. There's a guy in the van with a police scanner, but who knows if he can pick up aviation communications.

Fetzer's inhalation makes a quiet whistle in his nose. "That's—not a helicopter," he says, like he's not sure. He holds still. "That's a semi truck. Compression braking on the freeway." The sound fades. Nelson breathes in deep and pulls his hands out of his pockets. Squints to the viewfinder. Battery's full. Manual focus is on. Just like it was five minutes ago.

Fetzer murmurs, "That girl Emma was giving you the eye earlier."

Nelson puts his hands back in his pockets. Last thing he needs right now.

"She's pretty cute, don't you think?" Fetzer adds.

"She's what, nineteen? Twenty?"

Fetzer sighs.

The horses are pacing. One of the Brigaders, Brian, whisper-shouts, "Ignition in five minutes!"

Nelson looks over to where Jen should be in the dark. "Camera two?" he says into his headset.

Jen's voice comes into his ear. "Locked and loaded."

Brian stage-whispers, "You camera guys ready? This is it! Where are you, Jen? Wanna make sure the horses don't run you down."

Jen's flashlight clicks on, small in the distance, and waves an arc in the dark.

Brian checks in with the Brigaders one by one, and when he gets to Emma she calls out, "I'm doing another check for small animals." Her flashlight blinks through cracks in the barn wall. Stomping sounds, and her high, young-woman voice. "Fuck, it stinks in here," she yells.

"Quit holding us up, Emma," Brian says, and there's a note of contempt that makes Nelson's heart twinge for the girl. "Wanna burn this fucker down."

The flashlight turns off, and there's the crunch of Emma jogging away.

"Everybody ready?" says Brian. "You, ah, the other camera guy?"

Irritation sparks through Nelson. He says, "Yeah," but his voice disappears into the dark. He clears his throat and checks the viewfinder. *Other camera guy.* Sheesh. He drove five hundred miles to be here. Least the Brigaders could do is remember his name.

People always remember Jen's name. She's a large enough woman with a square enough face that in those flannel shirts she sometimes gets mistaken for a guy. Even with the long hair. So the name helps clear up the ambiguity. And people remember Fetzer just fine, being so short and with his shaved head and his black combat boots. He looks like a little thug, until you realize he's a really good guy. But everything about Nelson must be average and ordinary to these Brigader folks. Forgettable.

Horses snort. They're not being released until the barn is on fire.

Nelson, Fetzer, and Jen had argued with the Brigaders about it earlier that evening. Brian had declared the order of events would be fire first and horses second. "It'll drive them away," he'd said as he tossed a dreadlock over his shoulder. "And good video. Horses in firelight!"

They'd explained that the fire would frighten the horses and they should be released beforehand, but Brian just grinned and said, "Think of the footage!"

And Nelson had decided right then that Brian didn't deserve to be cell leader. In the supposedly leaderless structure of the Earth Freedom Brigade.

"Besides," Brian argued, "fire's a natural part of their ecosystem."

When Brian had stepped away, Nelson muttered after him, "Think this is a movie or something?"

Now Brian calls through the dark, "Emma? Got the second gate?"

"Yeah," she says, sulky. Nelson can't blame the supporting actress for feeling unsupported.

"This is it, guys!" says Brian, his voice shrill with excitement. "Ignition commences."

Faint crackling sounds come from inside the barn, then Brian is crashing through the sagebrush, going, "Oh wow oh shit oh wow!" Then everything falls quiet.

Nelson's heart starts to thump again. Above him float constellations, but through the viewfinder there is only black. Nelson presses the record button until it gives way with a tiny click. It's a negligible movement under the magnificent wheel of the sky.

The horses shouldn't have to run past fire, for god's sake. Sure, they'll be free. But already their social structures are messed up from being captured and corralled, and now they'll be extra traumatized on top of it. And here he is, standing in the desert, nameless to these people whose intentions are so noble and whose tactics are so messed up.

The crackling in the barn gets louder, and the first splinter of yellow appears through the wall. Then the smell of smoke hits Nelson, and the oily diesel smell of napalm. The fire's in the viewfinder now, a flower on the side of the barn, then *whoomf* it goes, and it *is* like something in a movie, bursting flames and roiling smoke, and metal hinges squealing, the Brigaders whooping and yelling, and the horses galloping, pounding the ground, dust clouds billowing, horses black on yellow, light fracturing through their legs.

Nelson is breathing fast. He pulls back from the viewfinder. The world is hot and lit up like an orange circus. The air stinks and roars. The smell of sage and dust and horses and napalm stings his eyes, fills his hair, invades his clothes. Nelson's sleeve is orange. His hand is orange. His fingernails are orange. Beside him, Fetzer is standing clear and sharp head to toe. His shaved scalp shines in the firelight. His head is down like he's searching—searching the ground for a jewel, but his eyes are closed tight.

Oh god, the smell of napalm. This must be a nightmare for him.

Nelson reaches to put a hand on Fetzer's orange shoulder, but Fetzer turns away and heads for the car. Nelson lifts his face to the smoky copper sky. Heat presses on his bare throat.

This isn't how it's supposed to be. His life. Not like this.

A single star blinks through the smoke. Then the star is obscured, and a tear slides onto Nelson's hot cheek.

"Fucking amazing!" says Jen in his ear. "Burn, baby, burn!"

2: FETZER

THE MARYVILLE FIREBOMBING WAS the start. But what blew up in our faces that year was bigger than that blaze.

It was early June 2002. In our cheap motel room at dawn, we were sitting in the dull light of the TV and the one lamp that worked. Through a chink in the curtains the new day was coming with no sleep to mark it from the old one. Jen was repairing a headset, and Nelson was at the desk with a camera plugged in, playing his tape over. I had my tired ass on a bed, leaning up against pillows, flipping channels till I found the news. The firebombing wasn't news yet. Probably someone had seen the smoke and driven up there, but it wasn't on TV.

Jen cut a tiny piece of electrical tape. "That was one fine burn. My-tee fine."

"Pretty sure it was my last," I said.

Jen looked at me from under her hair.

"Tired of doing favors for them." I said. "About time they figured out how to document their own goddamn actions."

Jen put down the headset. "Dude, seriously? You trust EFB kids to produce quality video?"

I was not in the mood for Jen's perfectionism. "Right now, I ache all over, I can still smell napalm despite the hot shower, and I spent all last night being told what to think by a jerk who was in diapers when I was founding co-ops. Either we stop doing this, or we do it our way."

Jen and I had this argument from time to time. A few years earlier we'd agreed to step back from direct action in order to devote ourselves to reporting it. Achieve a little distance, as it were. Me, I was ready to get out, anyhow. Direct action is best left to the young and energetic. And Nelson, he was never a confident saboteur. Jen, though, I knew she missed the excitement.

Jen muttered, "We're so fucking detached. Always watching, never doing."

Nelson stared down at his hands. Mr. Clean, as we sometimes called him, had uncharacteristic black under his nails. His tie hung over the back of a chair. At least he hadn't worn the damn thing to the firebombing, but it was highly likely to be going back on after he took a shower. He unplugged the camera and started packing it away. In a tired voice he said, "We're journalists. We are trying to effect change, but we're doing so as journalists."

I wasn't really listening to Nelson; at the time I was more interested in arguing with Jen. I said, "What do you mean, 'detached'? We're at every damn action we can afford to travel to."

Jen rolled her eyes.

I pointed the remote at her. "And I'm not putting up with that kind of crap again. Ever."

"Jeez," said Jen. "Let it go. Those guys were noobs. We'll probably never see them again."

"Bullshit like keeping those poor goddamn horses there till the fire was going."

"Well, yeah," Jen conceded. She grabbed her hair the way she does, like grabbing an orange cat that's trying to get away. "That did suck." She wound her hair into a knot, picked up the headset stem, and went back to wrapping tape around a wire.

Nelson looked at me with those big and gentle eyes. "The napalm didn't help, huh?"

I turned back to the TV. "We're all tired. Let's just drop it." But I could feel those eyes on me. He reminded me of Father Mulcahy on *M.A.S.H.* right then, like an earnest young chaplain, wanting to make things right.

We'd documented an arson, sure, but I mark that day as the beginning of the year everything went up in flames. So when I look at Nelson today, aiming those sincere eyes out at the world from a press conference, or sitting with his tie loosened and his shirtsleeves rolled up at the dinner table on his rare evenings at home, I can hardly believe that year happened. And sometimes to remind myself I look for the crooked fingers on his left hand.

"War wound," I'd said once, and he snapped at me that it was disrespectful to soldiers who'd seen real combat. I reminded him I'd been in Vietnam, so was entitled to make the judgment.

But anyhow, back in the motel in Maryville, actual sun was coming in through the chink in the curtains and Jen was throwing her CD player and her magazines and her underwear into a bag. She's a big girl, but not in the feminine areas. She wore these sports bras that had a flattening effect on her already debatable chest. I got up off my butt and started picking up the burrito wrappers and banana peels. The words came over the TV and we all stopped and turned.

"... first articulation of a doctrine of preemptive strike," the anchor said. Then a clip of el Presidente's speech at West Point the day before, dropping the quiet bombshell: "Our security will require all Americans to be forward-looking and resolute, to be ready for preemptive action when necessary to defend our liberty and to defend our lives."

He meant Iraq, of course.

"No way," said Nelson. "That's against international law. He'd have to get it past the House. The Senate." Nelson's betrayed eyes looked up at me. "The U.N. wouldn't let him. Right?"

"Let's hope the hell not," I said.

Jen stabbed her toothbrush into her bag and announced, "The Empire strikes first."

WE WERE HEADING NORTH out of Maryville, and there was a cop parked near the freeway on-ramp. Just a speed trap, but it stopped our conversation. Eyes forward, I eased on the gas like we drove up that particular ramp every day of our lives, three oddballs in the front bench seat of an '85 Oldsmobile Toronado. At least that's what the exterior would have you believe: inside it was biofuel and custom electronics, but you wouldn't know it by looking.

Big inhale. Blinker on to merge. Big exhale when we were around the curve, then we set out for real—across the flat, dry landscape of northeast California.

"Good thing we put on the Californicator tags," said Jen.

"Good thing," I said. I got the needle to 70, and sagebrush and rocks and the occasional saltpan passed us by as we barreled north toward the

Oregon border. We were sleepless, and that damned oily burnt smell hung around even though we all had on clean clothes. The ones from the op were in two layers of black plastic bags in the trunk. If we were smart, we would've dumped the bags, but we were too poor to throw clothes away, and anyway, we'd have to be super smart to deal with dumping. Fingerprints on the bag, buttons, zippers. Too much to deal with. Could've burned them, but fires in a flat, dry landscape tend to attract attention. Like the one we videotaped. It was hitting the news right then on the car radio.

"Arson was the probable cause"—Jen turned it up—"of a blaze at the Bureau of Land Management's Wild Horse and Burro facility near Maryville, California, says Lassen County Sheriff Craig Griffith. No one was hurt in the early morning attack, but a barn, office trailer, and part of a corral were destroyed. Gates were opened, a fifty-foot section of fence was cut, and all one hundred and forty-eight wild horses escaped. Initial investigations indicate the attack was deliberate, with remains of incendiary devices found on the scene. Authorities suspect a radical environmental group carried out the attack. At this time no one has come forward to claim responsibility, and police have no suspects in the case."

Nelson sighed. "It has got to go in the next show."

Jen said, "Uh, *yeah*? Or did I miss a memo? Are we now documenting actions for the sheer ebullient fun of it?"

Nelson waved an annoyed hand. "No, I mean that thing from Bush about a preemptive strike."

Jen and I agreed. Problem was, our radio show was then like it is now: last Saturday of every month. We'd have to wait nearly four weeks to discuss it on the air.

Cars passed us. Trucks. I kept the needle just under 70.

OUR HOUSE WAS EMPTY when we got home. We were sitting in the kitchen and grumbling about where was Franky when he was supposed to be watching the place. Turned out he was getting groceries and sweeping the streets for strays. Franky was a good kid—helped us out with food and computer discs and toilet paper, bless his generous trust-fund heart—but he took some management. While he was picking up soymilk and cans of beans, somewhere in his pretty-boy head he made the decision to pluck Deirdre off a bus bench and bring her back to our place. Franky thought she'd only stay a night. But if you knew how many locks we had on our door and how hospitality-challenged we were, you'd understand why we weren't at all happy with him when he showed up smiling and contrite with a skinny Irish girl in tow. Despite the brown paper bags bulging with gifted groceries.

3: JEN

So unbelievable. We get home from a big firebombing only to play host-with-the-most with some random stranger. What the hell was Franky thinking? He's a goddamn house sitter, not a hotel manager. Of course Nelson, being ambassador from planet Dork, is into it right away. And Fetzer caved in like five minutes! Bunch of rescuers.

The woman Frank so generously invited into our headquarters stands in the doorway, looking around like she's hungry and there might be a buffet conveniently laid out somewhere among the filing cabinets and desks.

"Stay there," I tell her. Last thing I need is her snooping through our stuff.

Fetzer stands in the middle of the basement with his gut sticking out and his hands on his hips. "She can go over here," he says, and walks down to the end, like we're supposed to follow. There's that old camp cot against the wall. He eyes the pipes along the ceiling and strokes his chin. "We could string wire, rig up curtains. Out of sheets."

"What for?" I say.

His voice goes quiet as I get closer. "She'll want privacy. I have a feeling she'll be here more than one night."

"Nope. No way."

He picks up a stack of folders off the cot, then looks back at her leaning in the doorway with her arms folded tight. "She's sick, see?"

His Dorkiness comes over all cow-eyed with concern. "Franky's making tea. Does she seem kind of unwell to you?"

I yank the folders out of Fetzer's hands. "What the hell is wrong with you guys? She could be a fucking Fed."

Fetzer yanks them back. "Keep your voice down. And I seriously doubt even a Fed would go to the trouble of faking that sweaty pallor."

Nelson whispers, "What's wrong with *you,* Jen? Have some compassion for people for a change."

"What? You think 'cause I'm female I should be all nurturing? Well, let me fill you in, guys. 'People' doesn't include foreign total strangers who follow Franky home. For all we know she staked him out while we were away, and this whole thing's a set-up."

"Listen," says Fetz. "She didn't follow him, he brought her. I don't like this any more than you do, but she's sick and alone and I don't feel right sending her back out there."

"Seriously? Doting on this girl just 'cause she's weedy looking? If I turned up on the doorstep, think you'd wanna rescue me?"

Nelson bends down to pick up a pile of *Forest Alliance* back issues. His stupid tie drapes across the magazines. He says, "Of course we would. Now, she needs a pillow and some bedding. And a lamp would be nice."

"Dude," I say. I am lost for words. "Sometimes—I wonder what planet you're on."

But they rig up the sheets and put blankets on the cot, and I have to admit it looks seriously cozy. Kind of like a fort when you're a kid.

Fetzer heads upstairs. Franky gives the woman a mug of tea and brings her over. Her hair's really greasy—she gets credit at least for not being gorgeous. She looks at the fort and says, "It's grand," in that accent.

Nelson gives her a dorky smile and says, "I hope it's comfortable."

This is such a waste of bandwidth. I grab the flashlight he's holding and point it at the dark end of the basement. "Bathroom's down there. Provided as is, without warranty. The light switch is hard to find, so you'll need this."

I toss her the flashlight and she fumbles it against her bony chest. Physically, you could not find a girl more opposite of me. Short. Thin. Straight black hair.

Nelson shoots me a pissy look. "We'll be upstairs. Top floor. Let us know if you need anything," and before he and Frank leave me alone with her, I go around and shut down the Crusher and the PowerBook. The other computers are off already, but the servers have to stay on. She better not mess with the servers. I also lock the filing cabinets and the archive cupboards, and grab the Maryville tapes and the big box of discs. Notice how the guys leave it up to me to take care of the security of our data? Fuck this annoying shit.

On the top-floor landing Fetzer's waiting for me. He grabs the tapes that are slipping off the box in my arms. "This is the last damn thing we need."

I want to drop the box on his foot. "Then why'd you say yes so fast?"

"C'mon. What else could we do?"

"Say no."

Franky comes out of the spare room and pushes past us into the bathroom. "Don't be mean, guys," he says. "She's nice."

Fetzer lifts an eyebrow. "Girl looks like Wednesday Addams. Don't tell me you're into her."

"Hmm, not like that," says Franky. "I can stay again tonight, huh?" He concentrates on squeezing the toothpaste tube in the middle.

"Course," says Fetzer. Then he points a tape at him. "But listen, Saint Francis, no more bringing home strays, okay?"

Franky just whales on his teeth. Keeping them super white must be part of the job description. This is worse than that Mexican kid he brought home last year. Turned out the guy was expecting sex. Fetz gave him twenty bucks and told him to scram.

"I mean it," says Fetz. "The wrong person in here could seriously jeopardize some folks."

"Seriously," I say, "our files have people the FBI would love to get to know. Those people trust us."

Franky pulls out his toothbrush and whines through foam. "Oh, come on. She's harmless. You'd do the same. She just got into Portland, and half her stuff was stolen." He stares down at his toothbrush. "Sitting there with that one little backpack. She looked so sad."

Fetzer heads for his room. "Unteachable," he says. The door closes behind him.

WE SHOULD'VE LEFT FIVE minutes ago. Franky's at the gym, and nothing's stirring behind the fort sheets.

"Maybe she bailed," I say.

Fetzer peeks through the fort sheets. "Still asleep."

"Well, don't wake her up," Nelson whispers. "She obviously needs it."

I say, "No way she's staying here alone. She could smash the servers."

There's a sound behind the curtain, and Fetzer peeks in again. Then he yanks the sheet back, and the girl's leaning over the edge of the cot, puking on the floor. Which is pretty much the grossest thing you could witness at eight in the morning. The puddle engulfs a rusty paper clip. She coughs. Fetzer tosses trash out of a metal wastebasket and gets the rim of it under her chin just in time for another hurl.

We're supposed to be deep in the Willamette National Forest by lunchtime. The room reeks. This is *so* unbelievable.

Fetzer looks up at me. "Jen!"

Nelson's got his hand on her back. She heaves again. Fetzer keeps holding the wastebasket.

"What?"

"Get a towel, for chrissake!"

After they clean up the mess and bring a glass of water, the girl wipes her mouth with her sleeve and says, "Making a hash of this. Sorry."

Nelson, pathologically polite, says, "Don't worry about a thing."

In the distance the railroad crossing bells start up. The girl says, "And I'm such a gom with computers, I couldn't find your bleedin' servers if me life depended on it."

Which is almost funny considering they're right over there in the ceiling rack.

Nelson shoots me his classic shitty look. The train roars past, and the girl sits up like an old woman in pain. A piece of her greasy black hair falls forward. The train dies away.

Fetzer says, "You going to throw up again, Deborah?"

"Deirdre," she says and holds the glass in both hands to take a sip. "Bleedin' hope not."

Fetzer lifts his chin and stares into space. "Franky's back."

The guy's got radar ears. Then I can hear it too, Frank's car on the gravel outside.

"Good," says Fetzer. "Let's go interview this tree-sitter."

Finally.

4: FETZER

DEIRDRE CAME TO US because of Franky, but she got to stay because I kept my mouth shut the afternoon Jen and Nelson and I got back from the tree-sitter interview in the forest.

The basement door swung open before I even got the last key in the lock. "Guys, I am *so* glad to see you," said Franky.

Deirdre had gotten sicker. The mess of her black hair on the pillow shifted, and she turned her head enough to look at us out of watery eyes. She drew her knees up under the blanket, and I was thinking, *man, she needs a bath,* but then it hit me like a punch in the gut. She wasn't some poor sick kid; she was a stupid druggie using our place as a detox center. Standard operating procedure would've been to throw her out.

But something stopped me. Maybe it was how much restrained misery was lying on that pathetic camp cot. At least the poor kid was trying. Trying counts.

She pulled the blanket around her neck. "It's just a tropical thing. Got it in India."

Nelson's eyes bugged out. "Malaria?"

She shook her head.

While Nelson murmured platitudes and Jen peered down like Deirdre was a squashed animal on the road, I folded my arms and stared at her until she figured out I'd figured her out—and that what happened next was going to be up to me. I kept my eyes on her till she turned her head away.

"Know anyone in Portland?" I asked.

Her eyes closed. "No. Please don't toss me out."

Nelson went to sit beside her but I stopped him.

"I've seen this with buddies of mine when they got back from 'Nam." I didn't mention it was one particular buddy, Ron, who sweated in my bed for a week while I slept on a sofa. "She just needs to ride it out." I nudged Nelson until he was past the curtain.

Nelson stepped back in. "How do you know it's the same thing?"

"Get outta here," I said, and shooed him and Jen and Franky away like turkeys.

I rolled a chair into her cubicle, pulled the curtain, and waited till there were no more footsteps going up the basement stairs. Her eyes opened but she didn't look at me.

I folded my arms. "Jesus, girl, you're an idiot. Coming here like this. Fuck this."

She rolled over to face me and drew her knees up again. "I'm sorry," she whispered, then she closed her eyes again. "Forgive me, Blessed Mother, forgive me. Oh, dear God, it hurts."

My arms relaxed, unfolded of their own accord. The urge to yell at her was gone.

She cried silently for a minute. My hand lifted without me making a decision about it. Knuckles touching her forehead, slipping on the warm sweat. Her skin was soft where I pushed the sticky black strands off her cheek.

"I know, kiddo. I know."

THEY DIDN'T NOTICE ME come up the stairs, and I paused and watched them. Franky was at the sink, washing dishes. Nelson was lying on the kitchen sofa—this big brown velvet behemoth we had—and staring out the kitchen window. Jen was at the kitchen table with headphones on, frowning at a green sound wave spiking across her laptop screen.

She and Nelson were ticked off about the tree-sitter interview because Samuel, who occupied the platform, wasn't inclined talk to anyone in a tie. I'm way past the point of being able to climb a rope, so Jen had hoisted up that tree and muddled through without Nelson. Who even back then was the best interviewer I've ever known. And in the meantime, wind gusts played havoc with the sound quality, and Jen's safety. And now she had to pull the raw material into radio-quality shape.

Deirdre's sour smell hung around me even at the top of the basement stairs. Jen was saying, "We gotta redo it, Nelse. He's like um-ing a lot, and spitting into the mic. And this wind—shit."

Nelson kept staring out the kitchen window. Jen pulled off her headphones. "Nelse?"

"Hmm?" Nelson turned to Jen, his eyes polite and there-for-you.

I almost said, *There's something you need to know about our guest.* But I didn't. Because by then Deirdre had me disarmed.

She'd looked up at me from that sweaty bed and whispered, "Promise you won't tell them?" She took my hand, held it tight. "I've got to get away from that shite. Fresh start. No one even thinking it about me." She'd squeezed harder. "Please, Fetzer?"

Everyone deserves a fresh start.

I stepped into the kitchen and Jen looked up. "Hey Fetz, listen to this." She tapped a key, and Samuel the tree-sitter's voice said, "—scientists say, uh, we've entered a period of catastrophic species extinction." Wind rumbled in the mic. "And there's this giant, uh, gap, you know? Between mainstream eco-consciousness and this totally dire situation faced by the planet. It's like, recycling soda cans just isn't going to—"

I agreed the sound quality was bad, but Nelson and Franky quickly diverted the conversation to Deirdre. Nelson insisted we take her to an urgent care, and Franky said he'd pay for it.

A day's stubble on my head was like sandpaper under my hand. I told them it wasn't an infection. I told them it was more of a viral type of thing. Antibiotics wouldn't help.

And there it was. The lie that bought me time. I couldn't bring myself to throw her out, but I knew letting her stay was a risk. Just not the kind Jen was worried about.

"And I need a sponge," I said, "and a bucket. Franky, can I get in under there?"

Franky stepped aside so I could open the cupboard under the sink.

"She threw up again," I said into the silence.

NEXT TIME I WENT up to the kitchen, Franky was spooning mac 'n' cheese onto plates.

Franky supported several causes, but we were his favorite. He didn't just write us checks, he put in time, and I always appreciated it when he stayed the night. It meant a break from lentils and rice. It meant comfort food.

Franky handed me a plate with two mounds of orange chow.

Jen sat sulking at the table. "You know how carbon-intensive cheese is."

My mouth was watering. "I do. But Franky was kind enough to cook, so stop being a brat."

Jen stabbed at her slippery olive-oil macaroni. "She's gone by tomorrow."

Nelson put down his fork. "You can't be serious."

Before it turned into an all-out argument, I mentioned an upcoming protest at UW. Students were planning to turn their backs on Madeleine Albright during the commencement ceremony, for saying it was "worth it" to sacrifice a half a million Iraqi children for the sake of foreign policy. The ensuing discussion distracted them enough to get through the meal. And when we were done eating, I told them I was going back downstairs to check on Deirdre.

Nelson shrugged. "If you're tired, I'll go."

I didn't pick up on the studied nonchalance of that shrug. "Nah, I'm fine," I said, and headed down to the basement.

5: NELSON

NELSON FLICKS ON HIS bedroom light, and across the room his reflection stares back from the double-sash window that looks over Novi Street—looks north, except with the light on at night he can't see out, just his reflection alone with the bare walls. His reflection hand pushes the reflection door shut, cutting off the energy of the household, the roommates, the relentless bickering.

Hardly anyone goes down their dead-end street, except for the homeless guys. But still, it feels exposed with no curtain. It's for a good cause, though: the blue sheet that usually hangs there is now part of Deirdre's private area in the basement.

Nelson places the laptop on his desk. He sits down, and out of habit he reaches to turn on his lamp, but that's also with Deirdre.

Journals? Or the website? He's behind on the journals. And site updates, too. He pulls the *BioAgriculture Quarterly* from the top of the stack and opens it to an article about soil movement on the high plains.

Without the lamp, his head casts a shadow on the page. The wall in front of his desk is pitted and painted a sticky ivory semi-gloss. Years ago in another life he and Lise had their own house, with smooth matte walls. And real curtains. And plenty of lamps.

Okay. Soil movement on the high plains.

Two floors down and behind the threadbare blue sheet that used to cover his window lies Deirdre, shivering. Her teeth chatter in him, chatter in his chest, until he takes a deeper breath.

Right. More than a thousand farmers in Montana have given up in the drought. That's a lot of failed farms. Only one percent of tallgrass prairie—

He places his palms over the article, stares at the backs of his hands. He noticed how small Deirdre's hands were.

He turns his own hands over. Through the gap between his wrists he reads "experts predict another dust bowl."

This is unproductive. He should work on site updates instead. He opens the laptop and balances the journal on the edge of the desk as a reminder to look at it again before he goes to bed.

At least the laptop screen is easier to see.

What if Fetzer's wrong and she needs antibiotics?

Nelson enters his password and the website admin system opens. Spotlight on Big Oil, Politics and Elections, Energy Alternatives, Species in Danger, Environmental Racism, Global Extreme Weather Watch. Every single section needs work.

The Actions Archive is always good for inspiration. Already Jen's started the Maryville Wild Horse entry. The EFB communiqué is in place, but it's still waiting for the video clip to be edited. Then there's that lousy mink liberation clip they got last week from Sweden. He clicks it open and the video is jerky and dark. Blurred people move around with flashlights. Small white blobs appear, then disappear—they might be mink escaping, but the camera shakes so much it's hard to tell. Animal squeaks and whispered Swedish. Yep, it's lousy.

The Pigeon Terrorism one is always good for a smile, and he clicks it open. There's Jen's hand, throwing breadcrumbs into a gray sidewalk doorway. The camera pulls back and catches Fetzer's boot getting out of the way. Pulls back more to reveal the red-and-yellow McDonald's logo. Next shot shows the doorway filled with pecking pigeons, and McDonald's patrons milling around, wondering how to get past the excited, dirty wildlife.

Oh god, there's the V&B Logging Company one. They'd gone to Idaho for the Forest Witness folks.

He shouldn't watch it. He really shouldn't.

He clicks, and it opens.

There's the eight protesters sitting cross-legged in a circle in the company lobby, holding hands with their arms locked together inside metal tubes. They're chanting, "Not one more ancient tree." Nelson fast-forwards to where the police show up and threaten to pepper-spray.

But the protesters want the company president to agree to meet with them. The police pull out their cans, aim jets of OC point-blank. The protesters close their eyes tight; they cry out. They writhe, still joined at the elbows. They yell, "This is a peaceful protest!" They plead for the torture to stop.

The police stop. Ask them if they're going to leave. The kids' backs are slumped, their heads are bowed. They are in shock. One of them mumbles something, and a cop steps forward, pries open one of his eyelids, and sprays again. The screaming escalates, and Nelson clicks. The video closes.

The air in his room has gone gritty and hot.

Sounds downstairs in the kitchen, talking. Maybe Fetzer's coming up to say, *Nelson, she's worse. We need to take her to urgent care.*

Nelson places his hands flat on either side of the laptop and pulls in a deep breath that stretches his lungs and presses his tie against the edge of the desk. The strain inside feels like he's swallowed a stone, but he holds the breath for one. Two. Three. Then lets it out: "whhhhh," like a yoga teacher showed him years ago. Back when he lived in a house with smooth clean walls, and took classes like that.

The talk downstairs turns to laughter. Fetzer's probably just getting a snack.

Then it's the sound of Jen taking the stairs two at a time, and Nelson's door bangs open, and the energy of the household flies into his room. He yanks his hands into his lap, and the journal falls on the floor.

"Dammit, Jen, would you please knock?"

"Catch you jacking off?"

"I'm doing site updates." He picks the journal up and unbends the corner. Outside a train is coming.

"Perving over the *BioAg Quarterly*," says Jen. "Whatever spins your fan. Here." She throws him a can. He catches it, the cold metal a shock in his hands. The window rattles from the train.

"I don't want a beer right now," he yells over the noise.

Jen snaps the tab off her own can, and waits till the train passes. "You gotta help me get through this crap Frank bought. Besides, you need to relax." She tips her head back and chugs.

The can is freezing in Nelson's fingers. He pulls the tab, leans forward, and slurps to stop the foam from dripping onto his pants.

Jen wipes the back of her wrist across her mouth. "You look like crap."

"Thanks for the helpful feedback. I'm tired, okay?"

Jen examines him. "Not *tired*, more like deer-in-headlights."

Nelson pushes his fingers up under his glasses and rubs his eyes. "Been reading about Montana. It's tragic. They say it's going to be another dust bowl."

Jen drops her head and her long hair falls forward and bobs for a while, then she flips her hair back and smiles to herself. "You're a case, John."

He turns his face away. The room is too—anyone could see in. Deirdre is so sick. The trains will keep her awake. Breathing deep hurts. He wants to curl up in the dark. They might have to redo the interview.

"We really need to redo the interview?" says Nelson.

"Nah," says Jen, "I fixed it."

"Oh, good. Thanks."

Jen drinks from her beer. Nelson takes a sip. Bitter. Cold.

"Once again," says Jen, "Jen Owens saves Omnia Mundi Media Group's ass."

"Yeah. Thank you."

Nelson sips again. The energy of the house pours through the door, roaring rivers of it. He stares at a spot near his clothes rack and listens to the roaring.

"Boy, you're fun," says Jen, and then she's gone.

"Could you close—?"

The doorframe is empty. The universe pours through. Nelson gets up to close his door, and in the hall coming from Jen's room is the sound of typing. No doubt she's in that chat room that seems to go 24/7. He turns off the overhead light, but the room doesn't go completely dark because of the streetlight. Now no one can see in, but there's not enough light to work by. He has to get through his share. No excuses.

He turns the light back on. Picks up the beer from its puddle of condensation. A memory bursts in from nowhere: Jen running ahead of him into a gully, panting and grunting. All of them running, stumbling, tripping on roots, branches whipping them in the face.

He shouldn't think about it.

He turns the can in his hands. His shirt cuffs are frayed. Shirt's so old it used to share a washer and dryer with Lise's things.

He tips his head back and drinks. There are cracks in the ceiling, and droopy lines of cobweb. The beer is bitter in his throat.

Jen, stumbling through a gully, a dark stain of urine spreading down her pants. Those good people in Idaho, tortured, screaming. The slap of fright when a flashlight caught him with freshly pulled survey stakes in his hand. He shouldn't think about these things late at night.

Nelson rotates the can in little twists, gathering wet on his fingers.

Deirdre probably thinks they're pigs. The basement's so cluttered it took him three tries to find a place to put down the *Forest Alliance* back issues. And when he moved the bag of hats and wigs, there was mildew underneath.

This isn't how it's supposed to be.

He could be working for a successful research institute. Managing one, even. Working just as hard, but at least the work would have currency.

Nelson sets the can down on the desk. He breathes in and holds the pressure against the sore place in his chest. Sometimes it feels like a small rock is lodged in there.

Who is he kidding? If he returned to the industry he'd be sucked back into the groupthink.

He breathes out: "whhhhhh." He picks up the journal and turns his chair around so he's not casting a shadow. He finds the article on soil movement on the high plains and starts to read.

6: FETZER

JEN MADE IT CLEAR she didn't want Deirdre upstairs. But Deirdre needed company—being alone made her weepy. Franky, bless his heart, offered to stay, so we took turns, him and me and Nelson, sitting with her in her sheeted cubicle. The first couple of days meant lots of trips to the bathroom. Girl nearly turned herself inside out. Then that slowed down, and the anxiety attacks set in. She tried to hide it, but I could tell.

Even with Franky helping it was hard to get work done. Lunchtimes would find us still laboring on our morning task of going through the papers, looking for environmental stories for the archives. What we gathered were typically cookie-cutter pieces off the AP wire; you had to go to the alternative media online for anything different.

A few days into it Franky came upstairs and stood by the kitchen table. "Hey, guess what?" he said to me and Nelson. He bounced on his toes like he was waiting for a starting gun.

I kept reading the paper, perturbed as I was by an account of a guy arrested for refusing to leave a New York mall. Reason they wanted him out? His *Give Peace a Chance* T-shirt. Which he'd just bought at the same mall. Strange times.

Franky grinned. "She's better."

"Good. Now get some sleep." I went back to my paper.

"Really?" said Nelson. He stood up and adjusted his tie.

"For chrissake, let her get some sleep too," I said.

But we did go down to say hi. She lay there smiling in the bunched greasy sheets, and her hand squeezing mine was small and weak.

"Thank you," she said with the staring gratitude of the convalescent. "All of you."

She slept through dinner. Later Nelson took a pillow and a blanket down to the basement.

"Going to crash on the sofa," he said, "in case she relapses."

It made me stop halfway up the stairs, wondering if he knew. Nelson arranged his pillow on the vinyl sofa below. That sofa had a straight back and metal arms. It was clammy, hard, and crap to sleep on, but Nelson's capacity for self-sacrifice was mighty. He looked up, gave me a crinkle-eyed smile, and I was reminded why women find him attractive.

"She's not heading for a relapse," I said.

Silence from behind Deirdre's curtain. Nelson spread the blanket along the sofa, gave the pillow a couple of light punches. He glanced over at her curtain and then it struck me: he wasn't just being his usual uber-gracious self. He liked her.

I headed up to the kitchen, then up to the top bathroom. That bathroom drove me nuts. We've had it renovated since then, but there used to be this one little mirror above the sink. It was the right height for Nelson and Jen, but I had to stand on my toes if I wanted to see anything below my nose. So I was ignoring the mirror and scrubbing my molars and wondering what to do. I'd told Deirdre she was under our roof on one condition: she had to be one hundred percent honest and one hundred percent clean. "One fuckup," I told her, "of any kind, and you're out."

She'd taken my hands in both of hers and told me she wasn't that person anymore. And I felt proud of her. Wanted her to succeed.

But now I was worried about Nelson. The guy'd had lousy luck with women since he'd left his wife to join us six years earlier. He'd dated a little, but it was always women with some agenda other than him, and sooner or later things fell apart. So now I was intrigued, but torn. He'd grown isolated, and Deirdre, well, she was the first woman he'd shown any interest in for a long while. And she was newly clean in a strange town, away from whatever bad scene she'd fallen into. And there was something different about her, different from my 'Nam buddy Ron, the way she smiled so hard, so full of a humble kind of joy. And she'd be on her way, soon. Maybe a quick fling would be a distraction, I told myself. Enough to take Nelson's mind off the suffering world, I told myself.

That bathroom had this hundred-year-old sink, the whole thing a network of gray cracks. They looked lacy on a good day, unhygienic the rest of the time, and I used to whack my toothbrush on the edge of that sink more than just to get the water off, because I wanted to see the whole thing collapse. Just the right angle, just the right pressure, and maybe that sink would drop into a pile of little cubes at my feet the way things fall apart in cartoons.

7: NELSON

"... TIME OF DAY it is with the bleedin' windows covered up?"

Nelson jolts awake. Vinyl sofa. Basement. Deirdre.

"Sorry," she says. "You were yakking away. Thought you were awake."

Her curtain is open and she's sitting on the edge of the camp cot. "I mean, it's so dark in here it's fierce hard to tell if it's morning or evening."

"It's morning," says Nelson. Lise used to complain about his sleep talking. The taste of a dream falls into a hole and is gone. He sits up, puts on his glasses, and the basement comes into focus. The concrete floor is inhospitably cold under his feet. Deirdre's wearing Jen's big red *Stumps of Mystery* T-shirt—Fetz must have snuck it out of Jen's room.

Public persona. He straightens his back and smiles. "You look better."

She smiles back. It gives her a mischievously starving look. The green LED equipment lights dot the dark corners of the basement. His lost dream is like a word on the tip of his tongue.

"Those are grand pajamas," she says.

Behind Nelson's eyes strings of tension pull tight. "My pajamas?" He looks down at his legs. Fine blue and white stripes. His only pair. Rarely worn. But sleeping down here in underwear wasn't an option. He shrugs. "They're just ordinary pajamas."

Her smile stretches on. "They're delightful."

He has never considered his pajamas delightful.

"Nelson, more than anything I want to get cleaned up."

"Of course. Yes." He slides his feet into his slippers. "Thing is—"

She's going to have to come upstairs sooner or later. But if he takes her to the top bathroom and she bumps into Jen . . . she looks so happy. Now's not the time to start a fight.

"Would you mind using the shower down here?" he says. "Oh, but you'll need things." He gets up from the vinyl sofa, heads past the dehumidifier, past the copier and the server rack, past the maps, up the narrow basement stairs—there's no one in the kitchen yet—and up the main stairs.

When he comes back down, she's leaning against the clippings cabinet. The red T-shirt hangs off her like a caftan.

He hands her his old navy-blue robe and a gray towel. "It was folded, so it should be clean. And here's some soap. Sorry it's a little small, I couldn't find a fresh bar."

The piece of wet soap slides around in the jar lid. That smile again, making a V in her face. Her eyes are a light, light brown.

"It'll do the job," she says.

The bathroom's tiny window is caked with grime. The toilet bowl is mottled with gray and ochre stains. He can smell mildew off the shower curtain.

Deirdre brushes off his mumbled apology. But it's truly gross. He and Lise once had an en-suite bathroom with celadon-green ceramic faucets, with matching soap dish and mirror. And through a second door was the nursery. They'd painted it pale yellow with white trim, and spent the year before he left trying to get pregnant.

He backs out of the little bathroom. "Oh, and we did your laundry. I hope you don't mind."

Her eyes slide away. "You're a thoughtful lot, aren't you." She lays the robe and the towel across the sink, then closes the door.

On his way upstairs he wonders if she was being sarcastic just now. The Irish accent makes it hard to tell.

Still no one in the kitchen, and no sounds from the top floor. He likes being up before everyone else. Before the bickering and the distractions.

He fills the kettle at the sink, puts it on the stove.

Last week when Deirdre was lying sick and in pain, Jen had the nerve to say, "Even if she's not an infiltrator, she could still do something stupid, like leave a window open." Then Jen walked off, adding, "There's people seriously trusting us not to compromise their identities."

Nelson had retorted with, "I think if we explain the delicacy of our situation she'll understand and behave appropriately."

"Based on what?" Fetzer had said.

Nelson had almost replied, *Instinct,* but he wasn't sure, and then Jen came back with Deirdre's day pack. "Asleep. No clue."

"This is nuts," Nelson had said. "How can we expect her to be trustworthy when we go snooping through her stuff?"

"Dude," said Jen, and she squished her heavy face into that sneer. "Be honest, we don't know a thing about her."

And Nelson had to admit Jen was right.

Jen unzipped the daypack and pulled out a battered notebook held together with a rubber band. She dangled it by a corner. It looked like a diary. There were others in there just like it.

Fetzer took the notebook, flipped off the rubber band and thumbed through pages. Nelson yelled, "Hey!" and grabbed it off him.

In his hands the diary's cardboard corners were swollen and eroded to rounds. He picked the rubber band off the floor, stretched it back over the cover. Deirdre's private thoughts in there.

Jen then scooped out a ball of clothes, and Fetzer went through each item, holding it up, shaking it out. Nelson had protested, but when Fetzer suggested they do her laundry, it seemed like a considerate thing to do.

Then Jen pulled out a three-ring binder. Large black-and-white photos in plastic sleeves. Fetzer had put down a blouse and Nelson had put down the diary and they'd stood either side of Jen while she turned the stiff pages. Photos of people in streets, people in cafés, in bedrooms. Sad people, laughing people, tired people. They didn't look like strangers; they knew her. Deirdre's life.

"These are good," Fetzer had said. He pointed at a girl sitting on stone steps. She stared back, hugging her knees, and Nelson realized the girl was missing two fingers.

Jen had quickly lost interest, so Nelson took the binder and turned more pages. There was something dark about the people. Even the smiling ones looked like they were on the edge and didn't want to look down. He'd almost said, *Interesting,* but that's a cop-out when you're talking about art. He'd tried to think of something more intelligent to say, but nothing came.

The kettle whistles, and Nelson swings it from the stove and pours his cup full. The tea bag struggles and brown swirls from it like dye. He isn't sure if he likes Deirdre's work. Landscapes are more his thing. He should dig out his Ansel Adams prints and put them up. He never bothered after this last move, but maybe it's time to decorate a little.

Nelson dunks the tea bag. He was so irritated when Jen had looked around at Deirdre's strewn possessions and said, "Least she ain't no counter-hacker babe."

But he was curious when Fetzer found her passport. When he opened it, a credit card clattered on the floor. Nelson had picked it up. The bank was called Westpac. *Deirdre A. Sutton* was embossed in the red plastic.

Fetzer turned the passport sideways. "Deirdre Assumpta O'Carroll." He raised an eyebrow at them. "Would it be possible to have a name that was more Irish Catholic?"

"But here it's different," said Nelson, and he held up the credit card. "Here it's Sutton."

Fetzer shrugged. "Married. Not married." And Nelson knew, because he had checked, that she wasn't wearing a ring.

Fetzer kept reading. "Born Edenderry, Republic of Ireland, April 1972. So she's thirty."

It had been a surprise. She seemed younger.

Fetzer flipped pages. "Huh. Traveled some. Really was in India. Australia, too, for a few years. And her US visa expired three months ago." Fetzer had snapped the passport shut and dropped it in the daypack.

And when Deirdre's laundry was done, Nelson looked through the binder again. The photos made him anxious. And they made him want to know her.

So now Deirdre has clean clothes. Nelson sips his tea in the quiet kitchen and watches red-breasted house finches out the window. They're making a home again under the eaves. They're pretty birds.

He should shower, get dressed, and go back down to see how Deirdre's doing.

8: JEN

*** THEJENERATOR HAS JOINED #rezist

<schrodingers_cat> I checked in versioning yesterday.

<TheJenerator> are you three really here this early, or am I hallucinating?

<schrodingers_cat> hi Jen

<VioletFire> you're hallucinati

<VioletFire> ting

<ignite> Hi Jen

Well isn't this just great. That's Sylvia's car pulling up outside.

<TheJenerator> Hi Ig. Been a while.

<ignite> How ar you Jen?

<TheJenerator> Good. Cept its gone fucking insane around here.

<schrodingers_cat> Vi, Sal has a sandbox model with clear instrucitons.

<VioletFire> Caper2 versioning?

<schrodingers_cat> Caper3 versioning, even better.

<VioletFire> What's up, Jen?

<TheJenerator> This sick GIRL showed up. And now shes staying.

<schrodingers_cat> a GIRL?

<TheJenerator> YEAH! She just showed up and my lame roommates let her stay.

<VioletFire> don't you have like a million locks on your door?

I can hear Nelson downstairs, undoing the million locks to let Sylvia in.

<TheJenerator> Affirmative. And suddenly it's ok to have a stranger in the house

<ignite> Jen's jealous she's not teh only girl anymore.

<TheJenerator> And now someone *else* showed up. It's breakfast time, for christ's sake.

<VioletFire> joy joy joy

<ignite> poor Jenerator is inundated with actual people

<TheJenerator> It's this other nutjob we work with. She just came over, no warning. Sigh. later, dudes

*** TheJenerator has left #rezist

Sylvia says, "Good morning, Jennifer," right behind me, and I slam the laptop closed and stand up.

"Sylvia."

Her hair's close-cropped and she's all done up in a dark red suit. Her eyebrows are plucked tight. Women like her make me feel shaggy. "We had an appointment?" she says.

"Nope, don't think so."

Sylvia raises those tightbrows.

"Jen." Fetzer has his hand up. "I asked her to come by to share what she knows about the Bluebird timber sale, then I forgot."

"Well that's just great," I mutter. But I have to admit, I am curious about Bluebird.

Sylvia murmurs, "That's not like you to forget, Irving," and I snicker at his first name.

She looks around the living room like there's nowhere clean enough to sit. "Let's talk in your sunny parlor," she says, and clacks her high heels on over to the kitchen table.

"What's with the scary outfit?" I say.

"I had a breakfast meeting," she says. In those shoes she's my height.

"Who with, Donald Trump?"

She puts on a simpery smile. "Entrepreneurs who eat vegans for breakfast."

Fetzer comes between us. "Cool it, ladies." He sets two coffees on the table. Asks Sylvia if she saw Nelson downstairs, and has she met Deirdre yet?

Sylvia sits at the table and crosses her pantyhose legs. Sunlight off the green Formica makes her face glow like a hologram. "Indeed I did. She seems charming."

I can't help the snort.

Sylvia sips her coffee. "You don't think so?" she says, more curious than arguing, and I sit down.

"I just don't get it. Franky literally found her on the street. I mean, I'm all for saving the world, but not one indigent at a time."

Sylvia pouts like I said something mean.

"This is seriously eroding our security culture," I say.

Her eyes widen. "Oooh. Security culture."

"You're not helping," Fetzer mutters, and he sits down with us. Right then Nelson and Deirdre appear at the top of the basement stairs.

"Hey!" I say, "I thought we agreed she wasn't—" But Fetz is grinning, and everybody's going "Hi!" like it's some damn reunion, and I know I won't win this one. They come over, and Nelson holds the back of a chair like a waiter, and Deirdre sits down between me and Fetz. Table's crowded with Sylvia here too. But for once chicks outnumber dudes—three to two.

Nelson heads for the fridge and starts rummaging. Deirdre gazes around like she's arrived at some tourist destination.

"The light's gorgeous," she says. "So bright. So different from downstairs."

Except she says "brate" and "daff-rint" and "doan-stairs."

She seems thrilled to hear from Fetzer how we moved in a year and a half ago, how it was a commune in the sixties and they took out the walls to make it open plan. And he seems thrilled to be telling her. Now that's she's cleaned up she's almost what people call pretty. Fragile, though. Just the kind of woman guys get all chivalrous over.

She turns to Sylvia. "It's me first day out of bed, you see. Was sick as a small hospital." Before Sylvia can reply, Deirdre swings her gaze around again. "And it's so *tidy* compared with your basement."

Sylvia smirks.

Deirdre points across the living room to the main stairs. "And you sleep up there?"

Fetzer says, "Yep. Four bedrooms and a bathroom."

"Is that Franky still asleep?" she says, playful like she's caught him out.

Fetz says, "Franky's gone home. He just house-sits now and again. Stayed a few extra days this time."

She doesn't even register that it was for her. Instead she looks at the sunlight on the floor and murmurs, "It's so bright it's singing. Resurrection and the light."

It's just our crappy old kitchen. Countertop and sink under the window, white cabinets, old stove, roll-cart full of dishes and plates. Not sure what she's seeing. Maybe she's clinically insane. Great.

She nods at the jars of beans and rice and flour. "Those shouldn't be sitting in the sun."

"Write that down, will you?" I say to Fetz, and get up for more coffee.

"Your hair!" says Deirdre. "It's on fire!"

"Huh?" I grab my hair but no one's exactly throwing a blanket over me. Deirdre stares. "Most gorgeous hair I've ever seen." Except she pronounces it "garr-jiss." Girl's giving me the creeps.

"It does look extraordinary in the sunlight," says Nelson, and Sylvia's nodding, too.

"Whatever." Time for another cup of joe.

Nelson says, "Deirdre, how about eggs?" He holds one between finger and thumb as if she wouldn't know an egg unless he showed it to her.

Sylvia watches like it's theater.

I pour myself more coffee and murmur, "Pretty sure they're called eggs in Ireland, dude."

"Eggs would be lovely," says Deirdre, and Nelson starts whirling around the kitchen like an ice skater, getting a frying pan from the cupboard, a plate from the roll-cart, and spiraling the end of a stick of butter around the pan. Gross. God, I wish they'd all just go vegan.

"So, Deirdre," says Fetzer, "you're a long way from home. You heading back there?"

"Uh, hello?" I say. "Sylvia's here to tell us about Bluebird, and she's probably in a hurry." I sit back down and sip coffee to get the smell of frying chicken embryos out of my head.

Sylvia looks at her watch, smiles at Deirdre. "I've got time."

Apparently enough time to listen to Deirdre's story about how she's heading home by way of LA, by way of Portland, then one of her bags gets stolen. The one with the plane ticket, money, and camera. I have no idea why this is supposed to be interesting.

And I need a break from this table. The dishes are piling up out of control and I start running hot water. I'm sort of in Nelson's way, and I sort of don't care. Fetzer asks Deirdre about the photos. They're very good, did she print them herself, yadda yadda. Yes, she did. And what's she been doing in the US? Waitressing, mostly.

She babbles on. My hands are red from the water. Makes the freckles disappear.

Fuck, this is annoying. Wish we did more rad shit like the Maryville action. Christ, if the EFB finds out we let strangers stay, they'll never ask us again.

"So, you need a new plane ticket?" Fetzer asks.

Deirdre says, "Franky said maybe, um, Jen could make me one?"

I drop a crusty cereal bowl into the water and turn. "Franky said what?"

"That you'd know how to make a fake plane ticket. You're a hacker, right?"

"That *idiot*. He should *so* not be telling people shit like that."

"Oh, come on," says Nelson, "it's Deirdre." Like we've known her for years. He shimmies the eggs onto a plate, sets them in front of Deirdre, and sits down.

"No!" I say. "We've been through this before with modelboy. If his tongue flapping gets me or any of us in trouble, I swear I will crack every database he's in and erase his existence."

Stupid Sylvia is smiling to herself again.

Fetzer rolls his eyes. "It's not like it's a big secret with other people."

"You needn't be worrying, I'm not telling a soul," Deirdre says.

"That's so reassuring," I say. "I am now at peace." I wipe my hands on a dish towel and sit down next to Nelson.

"So you *can't* make me a ticket?" says Deirdre. She pierces an egg yolk with her fork and yellow oozes out.

I grab some toast off the pile in the middle of the table. "Could if I put my mind to it. Transactions get batch-processed in the middle of the night. Avoid the website, crack the backend database. Audit trail happens on the interface side, not the data side. The cracked file's edits won't get logged until—"

"Really?" says Nelson, incredulous. Sylvia's raised her tightbrows, too.

I shrug. "Yeah. Probably."

Deirdre says, "On second thoughts, it sounds dodgy. I'm not keen on adding a nicked plane ride to me list of confessionable sins."

Nerdiculous gives her a lingering glance. Figures. He digs women with principles.

Damn. Sounded like a decent challenge, too.

They carry on about ways she could find an under-the-table job, and what about that credit card? Maxed out, of course. And yes, we know she's an overstayer.

Finally I get everyone to focus so Sylvia can tell us about the Bluebird timber sale.

She uncrosses her legs and leans her forearms on the table. "Okay. So, the highest bidder was Glendale Group, right?"

"Hold up," I say, and nod in the direction of Deirdre.

Everyone just looks at me like, WTF?

"Private conversation?" I say.

Sylvia gives me a pitying look. "I'm hardly divulging state secrets. So anyhow, Glendale threatened to back out unless the old-growth logging that was included in the original BLM sale got put back in. It turns out Glendale is owned by a holding company—"

Deirdre puts down her fork. "I need to lie down." There's a mess of egg and toast still on her plate. "Sorry. Me eyes were bigger than me stomach."

"That's perfectly fine," says Nelson. She's gone pale, and leans her hands on the table to push herself up. The table wobbles and we all have to grab our coffees.

After she's back downstairs, I whisper, "See how she reacted?"

"Jen," says Fetzer. "An infiltrator would act cool. She's exhausted, that's all."

"Why? She's been lying down for days."

Fetzer points his fork. "You're pissing me off."

"She obviously needs to stay a little longer," says Nelson.

I shake my head. "No way."

Fetzer says, "He's right. She won't make it out there. She couldn't fend off a mosquito."

Nelson chimes in with, "She's homeless. And she's illegal. She could get deported."

"So?" I say. "Free trip back to Ireland. Sweet!"

Sylvia's shaking her head.

Fetzer sighs. "You trust the INS to take care of her? She could be detained for years. They're backlogged with Muslims already."

"Oh c'mon. We're not Amnesty International." I point to the basement stairs. "Who knows what the hell she's poking her nose into right now. We're completely vulnerable."

Fetzer rubs a hand over his bald head. "She should stay."

"What? You're acting like this is already decided. Sylvia, tell them this is crazy."

Sylvia shrugs. "She seems charming. What's the problem?"

Before I know it I'm on my feet. "So I'm the bad guy now? Where's the goddamn security standards, huh? Flying out the goddamn window soon as a girl with the stomach flu shows up. Fuck this, I'm making an executive decision for the safety of Omnia Mundi. She is *out* of here."

Sylvia looks up at me with her chin in her hand. "If you kick her out and something bad happens to her, you'll never forgive yourself."

Quiet fills the kitchen. Nothing but quiet from downstairs. I head on over to the dishes. The sun's so bright I have to squint. The water's tepid now, but the cereal on the bowl has softened and swirls away under the scrubber.

Goddamn Sylvia's right, of course. I cannot turn a sister out on the street.

9: FETZER

JEN'S CONCESSION THAT MORNING to let Deirdre stay was a big deal, but we didn't make a big deal out of it because she'd hate that more. Sylvia gave us the inside dope on some upcoming timber sales, then left to go back to her corporate world. We called Deirdre up to the kitchen. Told her she could stay longer. She gave me a hug but I got out of it quick. Because by then she'd switched from being a sick and sweaty piece of humanity to being a woman: not my type, but I liked the shine on her hair and how her clear olive skin stretched over her cheekbones. Her light brown eyes made me think of tree sap and amber.

She stood with her hands clasped at her chest, looking like she wanted to put her arms around Nelson, too—I was watching—except that he kept his hands in his pockets and his eyes on the floor. Demons raging as usual, like a kind of white noise. Strange life for a guy like Nelse, living with us weirdos. He needed something warm to wrap his arms around. And I figured she wasn't staying long, not with that expired visa.

Jen ignored Deirdre's huggy vibe and started pulling recording equipment together for our two o'clock. She looked up quick when Nelson suggested we cut Deirdre some keys.

"She gets *keys*?" said Jen, and we were off on another round of argument that ended with Deirdre promising "on the Blessed Virgin" that she'd never lend them out.

Once Jen calmed down, Deirdre asked, "So who's that Sylvia, anyway?" I told her about Sylvia's strategic consulting business, how she hobnobbed with executives and fed us tidbits on the side. How it let her believe she was being subversive in a Robin Hood sort of way.

"She's no subversive," said Jen. "She works for the dark side. Besides, most of the stuff she tells us we could research ourselves. She just saves us some time."

And by "research" Jen meant "hack databases."

"We appreciate our sources," said Nelson. "Most people in the mainstream won't talk to us."

And if it weren't for the fact that Nelson dressed "normal" and spoke well, nobody would've talked to us at all. Jen and I liked to snicker at his wardrobe, but we understood its tactical value.

I invited Deirdre to go with me to get the keys. Poor girl headed across the living room to the front door. I let her pull on the handle, jiggle it. Her frowning face turned to us.

I said, "Sorry, Deirdre, it's nailed shut. We have to go out the basement."

"But why?" she said.

"Security," Jen muttered. "Not that there's much point anymore."

Deirdre ran her fingers down the jamb. "What if there's a fire?"

Jen snorted. "You planning on starting one?"

Nelson sent me a wary look. I sent back a shrug that said, *Jen's just going to have to learn to hang.*

Strange how easy it was to take sides.

"C'mon," I said, and Deirdre followed me down to the basement. As we were exiting the one working door, she paused at the threshold and said, "All the world?"

For a second I didn't know what she was talking about, then I remembered the sign. 'Omnia Mundi Media Group' was on a small plaque by the doorbell. Went by it so often I'd stopped seeing it. "That's our name, yeah."

Her smile was faint. "Seems rather all-inclusive."

"Yeah, huh. It was Nelson's idea. How the hell did you know what it means, anyhow?"

She looked at me straight on. "I picked up a wee bit of Latin on me way through university, didn't I."

Tucked inside her diary I'd found a piece of burnt foil and a toilet paper tube squashed flat. I took some satisfaction in adding Latin to my mental list of what made her different from that. And hopefully able to escape that.

She followed me down the narrow cracked path along the side of the house, through the smell of warm earth and mold. The early-summer weeds were already tall, and when I turned around she was grazing her hands across the tops of the stalks and smiling, in love with life.

"I feel like a snake," she said, "all fresh and rubbery in a new skin." She squinted up at the strip of sky between our house and the warehouse next door. "I can smell roses."

"Over there," I said, and pointed at the climbing rose over the front porch. "We neglect it, but it puts out flowers every year."

Deirdre went to the rosebush, pulled down a stalk covered in the small pink flowers, and sniffed. "Mmm." Then she held her arms out in the sun and watched a green leaf-hopper crawl across her wrist. She turned, and her smile melted any residue of doubt. I wanted a breath of fresh air in our stale, cynical household. I wanted her to stay.

Then she saw the Toro parked on the street and said, "This the car Franky told me about? It looks like an old banger."

I put my hand on the warm white paint. "'85 Oldsmobile Toronado," I said. "Last of the G3. Front-wheel drive. V8 diesel. It was a luxury car back in the day. Converted it to run on biofuel seven years ago. It's got nearly two hundred thousand miles, but the transmission's still strong, so it's got a few more good years."

She checked out the interior. "Funny front seat."

"Means all three of us can sit up front."

"He said you've got computers in there?"

"Ah," I said, and I unlocked the trunk. There were few things I was more proud of than the work Jen and I had put into that car. "Got the power distribution block and the PC in here. And a dual-battery setup under the hood. The second battery lets us draw power even when the car's off, without draining the startup battery. Put in a high-output alternator, too." I pointed to the wires exiting the back of the trunk. "Then we've got an inverter to convert it to 120. Then circuit breakers connect to outlets throughout."

Deirdre laughed and pointed through one of the windows. "You've got wall plugs in there!"

"Beautiful, huh? The whole thing is plug and play. And check this out." I opened the passenger door. "Old cars like this? You can mess with the head unit and not screw up the seat belts, brake sensors, and whatnot. This is a whole new one. I distressed it a little so it doesn't look too slick. But open this up aaaand—satellite radio, CD changer, it's nice. Then there's a central console, and look at this—" I opened the fold-out screen on the dash and booted up the system. "It'll read emails out to you. Plus it's got a GPS system. Plays DVDs, too."

"But how do you get emails?" she asked.

"Easy. We keep track of networks we know and intercept them as we pass through. And when that doesn't work—" I pointed to the Ear, which is what we called the Pringles-can Wi-Fi antenna we kept on the back seat.

She says, "That thing? It looks like a chip can on a tripod."

"Looks are deceiving. Aim that right and you can pick up Wi-Fi from miles away."

"Jaysus," she said, her hands pressed to her cheeks. "I have no bleedin' idea what Wi-Fi is, but it sounds impressive."

The sun was getting hot, and our shadows were sharp on the gravel. She looked around, smiling at the windowless warehouses, the pallets stacked up against the building across the street, and our own unused porch with its climbing rose and its missing front step that led up to our nailed-shut front door. The peeling paint, the cracked blinds, and the pieces of tacked-up cloth in the windows. In the distance, there was the beeping of a truck backing up. Deirdre grinned and I grinned too.

"You people are bleedin' deadly," she said.

10: NELSON

NELSON STIRS HIS COFFEE. He isn't much of a coffee drinker, but he's been sleeping badly and tea just doesn't deliver the caffeine he needs right now. Next to him at the kitchen table, Jen is reading on a laptop, and Fetzer's marking up the newsletter draft. Deirdre's been gone all afternoon, but that must be her coming up the basement stairs.

Jen arrived home furious about losing a collection of video editing log notes, and Fetzer's been grumpy all day. Deirdre's smile is like sunshine. She steps around the embarrassing coffee table and comes over to the kitchen. She sets a brown paper bag onto the kitchen table and says, "This is for you lot. I got meself a job!"

"That was fast," Nelson says.

Fetzer unrolls the top of the paper bag and peers inside. Smiles for the first time all day.

"At the diner on the corner," says Deirdre.

"Mr. Nguyen's?" says Nelson. "He's great. We go there all the time."

"So to celebrate," she says, and with a magician's flourish she reaches into the bag, pulls out a smeared chocolate donut. "Ta-da!" She takes a white plate from the roll-cart and places the damaged donut in the center. Then she pulls out an apple pastry, and finally a maple donut.

Fetzer stares at the pastries like they're wads of money.

Jen's mouth hoists into a sneer. "Why'd you bring us this crap?"

Deirdre's smile drops. She's hurt, and Nelson's neck prickles with anger.

Fetzer helps himself to the chocolate donut. "It's free food. Quit complaining."

Nelson says, "I think this calls for a glass of wine."

Deirdre's smile returns, slowly, and just for him. "That'll do nicely," she says, and suddenly he sees her naked—head back, mouth open, hair across a pillow.

He turns away. In the top cupboard, upside-down, stands his crystal-cut stemware. The only wedding present he kept. Was allowed to keep. He takes four goblets down and sees the big parties, bright kitchen, halogen lighting, computerized oven. Lise's gushy guests. He didn't want any of it; he just wanted the family they were going to have. The goblets are dusty, but he doesn't want to interrupt the flow of the moment by washing them. He rights each one on the table. "We haven't finished off that case Mrs. Krepelter donated," he says, and pulls a bottle of Pinot Noir from the cupboard at the end. He uncorks it—deftly, because Deirdre's watching—and usually would let it breathe, but not now. The leathery fragrance curls into his nose. The crystal twinkles; the wine is like garnets.

"Here," Nelson says to Deirdre, careful to hold the goblet by the stem.

"Lovely," she says, and gives the glass a quarter-turn. "Pretty pattern."

Nelson scratches his ear. It's been years since anyone's noticed his stemware. "Thanks. They're, uh, Waterford, actually."

Deirdre sips and closes her eyes. "Oh, that's good. Just what I needed."

Her eyes open on him with that topaz gaze, and warmth sweeps into his chest. He hands the second glass to Fetzer, who swishes it around, breathes it in, and nods like he's agreeing to some complicated plan. Jen takes hers and mutters something about wishing it was a cold beer.

They sit at the kitchen table and the talk turns to telling Deirdre about their monthly broadcast production schedule, the eleven stations they're syndicated on, how they started with nothing but a newsletter and a mission to disseminate environmental news. Fetzer lifts his glass. "And look at us now!"

Nelson stares down at his wine. *Look at them now. Three misfits and a goofy part-time model with a trust fund who helps out. They left behind direct action to become a media group. The free press is supposed to be the linchpin of democracy, right? But what good is it doing when so few are listening—*

Deirdre winks at him. He wants to reach out and touch her hair where it rests silky and dark across her collarbone. Instead he reaches for the apple pastry.

They open another bottle, and Jen's telling them about how her backpack zipper failed as she was cycling across the Hawthorne Bridge and a wad of her video log notes fell out and flew everywhere. Nelson tries not to grin. He hasn't eaten since breakfast, and the wine is going straight to his head. Coffee, sugar, and wine, breezing through his limbs, tumbling inside his skull.

Jen burps. Then her mouth twitches into a smilish sort of shape. "Cars were running over them and everything."

And then they're all laughing, Jen too, at the image of her scrambling around on the bridge, fifty feet above the Willamette, grabbing at pages peeling away in the wind.

Deirdre smiles and says, "Okay, so if you're such keen environmentalists, why would you be driving such a big old car? It's brilliant on the inside, but you could've done all that to something that uses a wee bit less petrol."

Fetzer nods. "Good question. You know when I go out to the shed in the mornings? What do you think I do out there?"

Deirdre looks out the window at the backyard shed. "Um. Run on a treadmill?"

Nelson's laugh kicks so deep he gets a cramp. Wine sprays out of Jen's nose.

After they quiet down, Fetzer folds his arms on the table. "No, dear. I make the biofuel. The Toro runs on Mr. Nguyen's used fryer oil."

Deirdre's topaz eyes sweeten with delight.

She's beautiful. She is so beautiful.

11: FETZER

THE IRONY DIDN'T DAWN on me till much later: it was Nelson who offered her that first glass of wine. I was selfishly enjoying the fun that evening, and not thinking through the implications. What struck me at the time was the way she relaxed her arm next to his on the crowded kitchen tabletop. The way she leaned closer to him when she laughed. The way they tried to look like they weren't looking. A girl wants to get back to being a normal human being and who better to hold her hand through it than Nelson, an entire first-response team rolled into one human being.

But the day she got the job at Nguyen's diner I was just enjoying the lightness of the moment—unusual for us—as we sat together at that green Formica table and laughed. As the afternoon drew on, Deirdre got tired and went downstairs to her cubicle to crash. Once she was gone, Nelson pushed his chair out from the table and stretched his legs. He'd eaten the apple pastry, and there was just the maple donut on the white plate. Jen shoved it away. "Bunch of addicts."

"Quit acting superior," I said, and I cut the maple donut in half. I was feeling lazy from the wine, and the permission it seemed to be giving me to take an evening off. Topsy-turvy lazy from wine and having a girl laughing next to me. And it was a really good maple donut. I slid down in my seat. Dragged the point of the knife through some frosting on the plate.

Nelson pushed his fingers up under his glasses and rubbed his eyes.

Jen said, "I'm surprised at you, Nelson. I figured you'd go for someone smarter."

Nelson straightened his glasses. "Excuse me?"

My plans for Nelson and Deirdre aside, I couldn't resist having some fun, and that was my cue. Lifted my hands up all flippy and camp. "Deirdre," I said, "like my fancy wine glasses? They're *Waterford*." Jen tilted back in her chair, snickering on a slow idle. I flapped my wrists and batted my eyes. "You spilled some? Don't get up, Deirdre, I'll get the dish sponge. Oh, and while I'm standing here, Deirdre, would you like to suck me off?"

"Shut up," said Nelson. His face was red. Jen and I laughed so hard Dee must've heard us downstairs.

He snatched up the plate, dumped the amputated maple donut in the compost, and circled the plate under a blast of water.

Jen said, "I thought your next one would be an intelligent, nerdy type. After, you know, the last couple of prima donnas."

Nelson scrubbed the plate. Steam from the hot water billowed around his shoulders.

"Like one of those diehard biologists," said Jen. "Wears socks with sandals. Ponytail. No makeup. Finds coyote scat exciting and knows every fucking detail about the sex life of some insect that lives in caves."

The plate looked clean, but Nelson kept scrubbing. "I'm just trying to make up for the bad manners she has to put up with. So mind your own damn business." He angled the plate into the dish rack. Turned to face us. Folded his arms. "Besides," he added, "she *is* intelligent."

Jen and I started debating the likelihood of crazy sexual scenarios and we just about asphyxiated from laughing, until I mentioned levitating tantric sex and Jen's chair bumped upright. "Shit," she said. She had a slight frown. "That reminds me. I found this press release from the Cascade Graduate Institute about getting federal funding to test this, like, hovercraft thing. Something amphibious, for the military."

Nelson looked relieved that the conversation was no longer about him. "Military R&D at Cascade? That's weird."

"I know," said Jen. She went over to the coffee table—it was this hulking wooden thing from the seventies, with a cinderblock standing in for its missing leg. She opened the laptop. "Yeah. A SEALION craft with modular capabilities. So then I checked out some other local colleges, and Willamette College of Tech and Northern Oregon U? Turns out they're suddenly getting federal R&D bucks for military shit, too. Three million to Willamette Tech to develop infrared and thermal imaging equipment. And NOU's getting two mil to develop approach-system software for military planes."

Nelson asked, "How deep did you have to dig for this?" He disliked it on principle when Jen hacked, not that it stopped him from using the information it brought. But after 9/11 and the passing of the PATRIOT Act, it added an extra layer of worry.

"Surface scratch," said Jen. "Communications departments love to crow about this kind of thing. Okay, NOU's isn't public yet, but their intranet security is made of, like, twigs and string. And it's due for release next week anyhow."

I said, "Can we put an environmental angle on any of this?"

Jen looked up, her face pallid from the light off the laptop. "Sure. But, you know—times like these—I think it calls for expanding our beat."

"Absolutely," said Nelson. He lifted his hands in exasperation. "This preemptive strike thing is bullshit. The corporate media's screeching about Iraq being a threat, even though there's zero evidence they've got WMDs anymore."

So two things were set in motion that night. Deirdre found her new poison, and we found a thread. We picked up that thread and followed it, not realizing it was a lit fuse.

This feels good!
Sure does.
BUSH'S
AMERICA
ONE NATION
ILWU

PART TWO

12: JEN

<TheJenerator> when are you going to be done, Ig?

<ignite> im almost ready. just need to make room on my home dir

<schrodingers_cat> there are two things we need to cover:

<schrodingers_cat> 1) reviewing tasks in the collector and 2) making our own sandboxes.

<TheJenerator> since Vi's here, i suggest we start with (2)

<ignite> Q: how much space do i need for a sandbox?

<TheJenerator> aw CRAP, here she comes.

<ignite> that girl that mpved in?

<TheJenerator> yup. She got a job but unfortunately it's not one of those 16 hour a day ones in a maquiladora.

<VioletFire> New girlfriend, Jen? Didn't know you swung that way.

* TheJenerator does not swing.

<ignite> hahahahaha

<TheJenerator> brb

Fuck, it's noisy. I'm trying to get some work done here, people. As in, shut up? It's not like her day at the diner's the most interesting topic in the world, Nelson, you chocolate-milk-drinking freak. I saw you with that bottle of Nesquik she brought you yesterday. No, don't come over here, Deirdre. Please. Don't. I am trying to work.

Shit.

"This time I have veggies," she says, and pulls a cucumber out of her paper bag like she expects a medal. The cucumber looks ridiculously phallic in her hand.

"Organic?" I say, knowing the answer.

She drops the smile. "Don't think so."

Nelson says something sappy to her and she goes upstairs. What a waste of bandwidth.

`<TheJenerator> Okay, she's gone.`

`<TheJenerator> If folks want to build a sandbox, note that I've copied the README out of the sandbox buildout stuff.`

"Jen?" says Nelson.

"What?"

`<TheJenerator> Aaaarg! My roommates are driving me inSANE. Brb.`

"We can use the help with the food," says Nelson, "with an extra mouth to feed."

"What are we, an orphanage?"

Fetzer says, "You've been typing for two hours, Jen. Take a break."

The #rezist window scrolls up without me.

He's right. I need to pee.

`<TheJenerator> People, sorry, but this is turning out to be unworkable. Back later.`

`*** TheJenerator has left #rezist`

WHEN I GET UP to the kitchen she's sitting on the velvet sofa writing in that diary. Probably "journaling" about me. What a crock. But by now I am pretty sure she's harmless. Like Fetzer said, if she was an infiltrator, she'd be doing a better job of fitting in.

She closes the notebook with one skinny finger between the pages.

I say, "Hey, uh. It's cool that you can bring home food."

She doesn't look up. "I'm not staying long. I'll keep out of your bleedin' way in the meantime."

"No. Fuck, it's not like that. I was just busy, okay?"

She lifts her eyes. Funny colored eyes. Like Pabst.

I say, "It's just weird having someone else around. Who isn't tuned into how we do things."

She lays the notebook down. "Okay." Then she checks out her nails. Who knows why, they're all bitten.

The fridge turns off. And as if to make up for it, the crossing bells start up.

"So," she says, "how long've you lot been together, anyway?"

"Omnia Mundi? About six years. We used to be with this bigger group that did more direct-action stuff. But then we split off."

She shifts over from the middle of the sofa. Guess that means sit down.

Whiff of sweat—mine or hers? I want to sit back, but somehow this isn't the time to lounge. Elbows on my knees. Next to her I feel giant.

She says, "Split off?"

"Yeah. The sabotage and shit was awesome, but we got tired of some of the other guys' accountability issues. That's when we started the Omnia Mundi Media Group."

Funny how where you end up is less about what you want and more about what you're not willing to put up with.

She asks me how old I am and her eyes widen when I say twenty-eight.

"But I'm barely adult, yeah, I know."

The train comes, honking loud, vibrating the house. My feet look big next to hers. Hers in tan laceups. Weird shoes to wear with a skirt. Last time I wore a skirt was eighth grade. Her profile's beaky. If I didn't know she was Irish I'd think Italian. Or Jewish. The train passes and it goes quiet again.

Her face swings around, eyes too pale and too close. "Let's start over and be friends, okay?" She holds out her hand.

"Deal," I say, and take it. It's small. And way warmer than mine. She's smiling now, but I can't look right at her. Then her thin arms are around my back, squeezing. There's dust bunnies under the roll-cart. Looks like a spoon's stuck under the fridge. I'm just getting my brain to coordinate whatever's involved in hugging her back when she lets go.

Whoa.

Silence drops like a damn theater curtain. *Try to be nice. Try to be nice.*

"Hey, um," I say. "You been to the river? The sunset's pretty cool over the river."

THIS FENCE IS GETTING looser. I do a bent-kneed jump onto weeds and grass. A path like a deer trail runs beside the fence. It's from the homeless folks, though, wider than a deer trail. Deirdre's slow and I have to help her over. Fence rattles as she comes off it, thumping into the weeds.

We step over the train tracks and head down past the A-1 Tire & Brake

Co. Taking this walk is always cool, heading toward Ross Island Sand and Gravel poking above the trees by the river. Thinking of Tre Arrow. Thinking of those cement trucks burning in the night. I miss that guy. Stay safe, man. Keep low.

Down the next street, across the parking lot, down the alley that goes under McLoughlin Boulevard with the trucks roaring overhead like airplanes. Past Mattresses by MacElroy, and Ron's Vending Machine Sales, with rusting vending machines in the back lot surrounded by razor wire.

Can see the Willamette now, between warehouses. It's one cool river. Love this place.

Where'd she go? Guess I walk fast. Man, she's like nearly a foot shorter than me.

We get to the end of the parking lot for Seymour's Construction Sealants and stop at the ragged crust of pavement. Down the riverbank it's all weeds and bushes. Plastic binding and beer cans. Setting sun makes the water sparkle. I usually go down the track to the water, but it's narrow and steep and she's still not a hundred percent.

She shields her eyes and looks across at the city on the other side. "It's so different over there."

"Yep," I say. All chichi'd up with bike paths and non-native trees and riverfront condos. Looks like a whole different town. But it's better here. Something about it, even with McLoughlin's noise and the litter and everything. Best place to get away and think.

Underbellies of the bridges all concrete and girders. A tourist boat eases past, guide's loudspeaker voice drifting over in snatches. Tourists gobbling up the BS.

"What's it called?" she asks.

"The boat?"

"No, the river."

"This is the Willamette. I can't believe you don't know that."

"Do now," she says to the water.

"You really aren't from around here, are you?"

She lifts her pointy chin higher. "Beware. There are more of us out there than you think."

I laugh but don't know what to say. A caller on the show once said I was insular. But how many people bother to care as much as I do about the big issues? And it's great being a left-coaster. A best-coaster. Wouldn't trade it for anywhere else.

"You from Oregon?" she asks. Her hand still shading her eyes.

"Yep. Born in Roseburg. To redneck parents. Got out of there soon as I finished high school."

She nods like she understands. "I grew up surrounded by bloody bogs, would you believe. Left home at seventeen. Left Ireland."

"Peat bogs? Awesome. Peatland ecosystems sound amazing. Sequester a lot of carbon, too."

Her eyes stay on the other side of the river.

"So where did you go?" I say.

"London."

"Cool."

She snorts. "Not when every second parson you meet suspects you're IRA."

It takes me a second to figure out she said "person."

"Holy shit. Yeah, there was all those bombings in the nineties."

A breeze pushes a strand of her hair around.

"So—were you?" I ask.

She looks at me like I just kicked her. "Yer fockin' kiddin' me. They're awful! Bombing innocent people who had nothing to do with the Orangemen."

I swear her accent's ratcheted up a notch. "Uh, sure. But didn't the British army do pretty similar shit in Ireland?"

Her eyes get a desperate look. "They're awful, too! Violence never fixes a fockin' thing."

My hands up like *whoa*. "Understood."

She turns back to the water. "Besides. I'm from the Republic, not the North."

"Yup. Understood."

She stares across at the condos for a while. Tells me she waited tables. Saved her money, went to Australia, went to college. How good it was to get away from home. Then she asks me what "Willamette" means.

And I have no idea.

Deirdre's eyes do a circle around my head, checking out my hair again. People fucking fixate on my hair. If I was pretty they wouldn't notice the hair so much.

"Maybe it's means something about fire," she says, and her eyes return to the water. "It looks like it's on fire, dunnit, flames dancing on the water."

•••

THE BED SAGS UNDER my back. Maple leaf shadows on my ceiling from the lamp in the parking lot on Taggart. It's leaf shadows in summer, twig shadows in winter. "Willamette" is from the French pronunciation of an Indian village called Wal-lamt, which looks like Wal-Mart—gross—but probably meant "spillwater," according to the interwebs. Good to have that squared away.

She doesn't tell you much. People who travel a lot usually bore you to death with stupid stories, but not her.

A breeze twitches the shadow-leaves.

Weird how I never think of Roseburg anymore. Mom and Dad down there, rotting away on junk TV and junk food and junk ideas about what's worth fighting for.

Deirdre's hug—that threw me.

And her fingers on my arm when we climbed over the fence. Digging in, letting go, leaving white marks under the freckles for a second. Then she was stepping onto the train tracks, looking down them one way, then the other, like a little kid hoping to see a train. And on the way back, she goes and slips her hand under my hair like she owns it and asks what kind of shampoo I use and says it's beautiful.

"Not you, too," I said. It's bad enough having modelboy Franky nag me about "hair care."

But she told me that when she was a kid she prayed every night for curly red hair. And that they'd called her japhead in school, and said her mom bonked a Chinaman.

"Bloody racist where I come from," she said. "It was good to get far, far away."

Fuck. I was glad to leave home, but imagine wanting out of your whole country.

She stroked my hair across her palm. I didn't know what to say. Sometimes think I should just let it dread up. That's such a scene, though.

Can't stand scenes. Even ones I like.

Deirdre's so scrawny. Who knows what Nelse sees in her.

Poor Nelse. Last girlfriend he had went off with a guru, and the one before that was getting heavily into the sabotage shit right when we were getting out of it. Then before that was his crazy-ass screaming wife. The guy is kind of a loser.

Like I can talk.

13: NELSON

NELSON'S WATCH SAYS QUARTER to four. All around is sweet summer green and sunlit pavement. A drop of sweat trickles from his armpit, but his shirt today is white, which doesn't show so badly.

He found one of Deirdre's house keys on the path this morning. He should mention it to Jen and Fetzer, but she was so happy when they told her she could stay. No point jeopardizing it now. He rolls up his shirt sleeves and turns the corner.

The bells on the diner door tinkle and he steps into the linoleum cool. Deirdre comes out from the back and her face jumps with happy surprise.

The door hisses closed on its pneumatic buffer, and the sound of traffic on Division fades. A few people sit, absorbed in their food. The small stone is lodged back in his chest, back in the sore place. He shouldn't have come. What's he going to say? But when he steps across the sunlight spotting through the elms it calms him. The counter is pink Formica, worn down in patches to the brown underlayer where decades of customers have rested their arms. The rush of juice filling a glass makes him look up. That pointy smile tweaks Deirdre's mouth and she drops in a red straw.

The juice is pink. "Here," she says. "It's grapefruit. It's really good."

"Thanks." The straw is silly but he doesn't want to seem rude so he leaves it in.

Across the counter from him she fills napkin holders. "For the evening shift," she says. Her face is soft and unhurried and he can't think of a thing to say. They're right. He's into her, and he's not handling it well. Thank god Mr. Nguyen comes out front. That big gray-toothed smile under his Bart Simpson baseball cap.

"Hello, Mr. Nelson, nice to see you today." His cap reads, *Don't have a cow, man.*

"Hi, Mr. Nguyen."

But Nelson can't take Mr. Nguyen's cheerful nodding, and he looks down at the counter. He's a freak. He hasn't been in a real relationship for years. He has no idea why this woman is so attractive to him.

He says, "How's business?"

Mr. Nguyen mops toward the espresso machine, slight and sharp and quick. "Good. Since Miss Deirdre, more customer here."

Deirdre gives Nelson a sideways look. "Nooo," she says, the way she does, drawing out the syllable in disbelief. "And which customers would they be?"

Mr. Nguyen balances the mop handle in the crook of his elbow and counts on his fingers. "More real estate lady. More bike messenger. More college student." He winks at Nelson. "Every day now she here."

Behind Nelson's eyelids, the strings tighten. It hadn't occurred to him she was meeting other people. Maybe it's already happened. Maybe she's about to mention that she'll be home late tonight because she has a date.

Mr. Nguyen mops around the drinks fridge. "Always leak." His head ducks with the quick movements of the mop. "But Miss Deirdre, fate bring you. You good luck. I give you raise."

"Oh!" she says. "Thanks, Mr. Nguyen."

"No problemo," he says, and steps through the doors into the kitchen.

Deirdre giggles. She takes another napkin holder into those small hands and asks, "So, what brings you to the humble diner?"

Nelson pulls the key from his pocket, slowly lays it down on the counter. Her eyes widen. Keeping his finger on the key, he slides it across the pink Formica toward her. "I won't tell if you won't."

Smiling, she snatches up the key and drops it in a pocket. Then she pushes a wad of napkins through the hole and tugs them straight from the other side. "That's bleedin' good of you," she says to the napkins.

"No problemo."

He drops his eyes and sips the juice. And it is good.

A snicker comes from her, small and musical. "You're sweet," she says.

He doesn't dare look up. Sweet-tart juice darkens his red straw.

"Oh look," she says, and her gaze is on something past his shoulder. "It's lovely when it does that."

Nelson swings his stool around. A breeze is shaking the elms outside and circles of dappled light shudder across the pink tables and the gray linoleum.

Of course she'd notice that. She's sensitive to beauty.

There's a simple shock in his chest. His head fills like a rising summer tide. He turns back to her, and the wonder in her face brings tears to his eyes.

ON THEIR WALK HOME, Deirdre stops at the weedy lot behind the diner. "I'd love to watch," she says. "Got the day off tomorrow."

The thought of having her as an audience is exciting, but he tries to sound blasé as he tells her they'll probably put in an all-nighter to produce the show. It's a community radio station, and the equipment is old and breaks down a lot. "So ask Franky to give you a ride there. And if you get bored, there's always volunteer work to do," he says. "Stuffing envelopes and so on. That is, if you don't mind."

She snaps off a stalk of dried grass. "I haven't done anything useful in ages. It'll be good." Then she drops the grass and sighs. "I do like weeds."

"Me too," he says, even though the biologist in him is supposed to despise invasive species on principle. "I love it when they reclaim unused urban areas like this. Reminds me how tenacious and resilient nature is."

She touches a shaft of dock. "And how quickly the remnants of our bolloxed-up civilization would be engulfed if we humans disappeared."

Apocalypse delivered with a touch of whimsy.

"Let's hope not," says Nelson. Then, "That's curly dock. *Rumex crispus*," and there's a question in her upturned face with its sudden smile. *Guess Latin's going a little overboard.*

She looks back at the dock and says, "Are they flowers?"

"Apetalous. Just sepals and a calyx. The leaves are edible." Further down is a small *Rubus parviflorus*. "Look," he says. "This is a thimbleberry. Prefers to live under forest canopy. I don't know how it's surviving here."

"Funny name. Can you eat them?"

The berries are still pale, and he says, "Couple of weeks they'll turn red, and they're delicious. Intense flavor."

The tip of her tongue licks her upper lip. "Mmm," she says. "I'll keep an eye out."

He doesn't mention that they'll also be covered in vehicle pollution. Not enough to harm her, though, and he doesn't want to spoil the good mood.

She points along the sidewalk. "Are those poppies?" she says, and walks toward the glowing yellow flowers.

"Yeah." *Eschscholzia californica.*

She folds down, sitting easily on her heels, and sets the bag of pastries on the sidewalk. Another excuse for Jen to complain. Fetzer will be happy, but he shouldn't eat that stuff. He's put on a lot of weight since 9/11, and on his short frame it really shows.

Deirdre cradles a poppy flower in her fingers, and Nelson wants to stop this moment in the sun and keep it.

"Can you smell them?" he asks, and squats next to her. He lifts one of the fire-colored cones and she leans forward, holds her hair back with a hand, and sniffs.

"Spicy," she says.

He sees himself dropping poppy petals on her black hair, laying poppy petals on her smooth belly.

She looks up from the poppy. Her shadow is dark and solid on the sidewalk, and her face is translucent with reflected poppy-glow. Obsidian hair, topaz eyes. And before he can kiss her pale mouth, here, crouching right here on the sidewalk on the corner of Division and Twelfth, with a brown bag of day-old pastries, and traffic going by, and crows calling in the haggard cherry tree across the road, here on the corner of Division and Twelfth, where he's balancing on his heels with the sun hot through his shirt and one palm crunching on the sidewalk grit, before he can kiss her here, she stands up and stretches sideways. She goes, "Ooh," and stretches the other way.

Opportunity lost.

Her pale mouth smiles from far away. "Still getting used to being on me feet all day."

He stands, brushes the grit off his palm. Small pink dents are left behind.

She picks up the bag, the paper glassy with circles of grease. "Mind if we make a wee detour?" she asks.

HE FOLLOWS HER PAST the house. Down the block to where the road's cut off by the chain-link fence and train tracks. Along the dirt path beside the gray warehouse. Blackberry vines catch at his jacket. Then they emerge onto Taggart. Just like she said, there they are, sitting in the shade under the overhang of an abandoned loading dock: the three homeless guys who push their carts down Novi sometimes. Older, harmless looking. Nelson was embarrassed to admit he didn't know their names. Chuck, Eb, and Sinclair, apparently. The men watch him and Deirdre cross the street and enter the shadow of the overhang. One of them says, "Incoming."

Deirdre holds up the bag. "It's a full one today."

The big white guy in a filthy camouflage jacket jumps down, takes the bag in his stained hands, and unrolls the top. His grin is sudden.

"Thank you, hon."

She sends Nelson a glance. "Not organic, I'm afraid."

The man climbs back onto the loading dock. "Least of my worries, lady, least of my worries."

"I've seen you around," says Nelson. "You live here?"

The rail-thin black guy says, "Cops leave us alone here."

The third man, small and trembling with disease, reaches for the bag, looks in. "God bless you, sweetheart," he says.

"Hah," says Deirdre. "I need all the blessings I can get."

Camo-man ducks his head. "All of us do, lady, all of us do."

They set to eating. No more words. Deirdre and Nelson return to the heat and light, and walk the dirt path beside the gray warehouse. There's a flattened glove on the path, and a used condom and a dead bird. It's one of the finches, ruby feathers on its chest, triangle of wing. Must have been a sudden death for it to be out in the open like that.

"You do this every day?" Nelson asks.

"Yes." She's walking quickly, her hands in her pockets. They approach the house, and it's all happening too fast. Then she stops and looks up at the broken porch and the two front doors. Neither of which ever get opened.

"Anyone on the other side?"

"Of the house? No, it's empty. The landlord offered the whole duplex for a discount if we renovated, but we're too busy. Besides, we don't need that much space."

Then she's moving again, and he follows her along the side path, then down the half-stairwell to the basement door. It's a private space, not visible from any windows.

"I had no idea," he says. He wants to stall her. "Thank you."

She looks at him. "Pardon?"

"You've solved three problems: Mr. Nguyen needs to know his old pastries aren't going to waste. Those guys need food. And Fetzer needs to stay off the sugar."

She smiles that V-shaped smile, and before he can say anything else, she unlocks the door.

"Hey, Nelson," says Jen from the map wall.

"Yeah?" he says.

"Gotta start prepping for the station retreat."

Oh, for god's sake.

Nelson flings out, "Why?" He reaches for Deirdre, but she's walking toward her sheeted cubicle and doesn't notice. Opportunity truly lost.

"Uhhh," says Jen, enunciating as if to an idiot, "'cause we've only got a week after tomorrow's show?" She turns back to the map of southern Washington and sticks in a pin.

"I know," says Nelson, wishing he didn't sound grumpy. He likes the annual radio station retreats. "That it?" he asks when he's closer. The pin is in the green patch of the Gifford Pinchot National Forest. One of his favorite places.

Jen traces a spidery line through the green. "If I'm interpreting this forest road right."

"How about we take Deirdre, show her a real old-growth forest?" he says, but Jen flatly replies, "No room."

Damn you, Jen, and your equipment that takes up the whole back seat.

14: JEN

THEME MUSIC, UP. STEADY. And—we're rolling. Good-fucking-bye to the worst night of production ever.

Fetzer adjusts his headphones and looks over his notes. Nelson's tie is gone and his shirtsleeves are rolled up. I fade the music down and Nelson brings his mouth to his mic.

"It's that time again, folks. Welcome to the June edition of *All The World*."

"Good Saturday morning to our listeners in Portland," says Fetzer, "and hello to our listeners around the nation on our sister stations, and around the world streaming on the web. I'm your co-host, Irving Fetzer, and our show for you today is jam-packed with news and surprises."

So far so good, considering we're running on zero sleep. Fetzer pulls away from his mic, Nelson leans into his. Dude better remember to credit me.

"It certainly is. Hello, I'm your co-host John Nelson. And our engineer, the genius of all things technical, is Jen Owens."

Thank you. Now if only you'd remember to put the toilet seat down.

"Today's program will knock your socks off," says Fetzer. "In the American segment, we have the Bush Administration's plan to open up Alaskan Rainforest to logging, and the congressional debate on Yucca Mountain."

Nelson picks up with, "Our direct-action segment features an interview with tree-sitters trying to save a stand of the Willamette National Forest. We also have a report on the Earth Freedom Brigade's recent firebombing of a wild horse facility in Northern California. I know we'll get calls about that one."

Finally Nelson has his focus back, after the last few days mooning over Deirdre.

"And that's not all," Fetzer says. "In international news we have an exclusive interview with Annie Ekine, spokeswoman for Niger Delta Justice, on their ongoing conflict with oil companies. Plus a report on the debate over GE organisms in the European Union, and an update on indigenous groups' efforts to protect ecosystems in Brazil. Stay tuned for more after the news headlines. But first, a word from our sponsors."

Fetzer pulls away from the microphone and scratches his nose. The background music runs along. Nelson stares into space. Pay attention, dude, we've got three hours to go.

"That's right," says Nelson, "we don't have any sponsors. Omnia Mundi operates independently of any organization—"

"—governmental or otherwise," Fetzer growls.

"Our mission is to collect, archive, and disseminate information from all positions within the environmental and ecological movements. All means all. Visit us on the web at Omnia Mundi dot org."

"And now," says Fetzer, "environmental headlines from around the planet."

Track 082, and—it works! Thank you, Jesus.

Fetzer stretches. Nelson yawns, then he jumps up so fast his chair almost tips over. Huh. Deirdre's here. Grinning through the porthole. He lets her in, and I turn the studio mic on to hear. She's brought a cardboard tray of espressos and a bag of something from The Bread Line on Burnside. Nguyen's a good guy, but his coffee sucks. It's bagels and cream cheese. Bet she didn't bring any vegan spread.

Nelson points me out to her and she waves.

"Hi," I say into my mic.

Nelson says, "We're live again in a minute, but you can hang out in there." He points through the big window to Studio 2. "Wanna help stuff envelopes? Talk to that woman with gray cornrows, she's Isobel, the station coordinator."

"Sure." Deirdre's checking out the chili sauce stain on his shirt. The half-eaten muffins. The empty coffee cups. Fetzer's already got cream cheese on his chin and he's licking it off his fingers. Doesn't take much to win over the bald dude, just some food. He's like a dog.

"Ten seconds," I say. Nelson's closing Deirdre out into the hall. Okay, she's found her way to Studio 2. Isobel's doing her usual over-the-top warm welcome, and good old purple-haired Beverly is sitting her down. There's a Rasta guy there I don't know, with super long dreads.

Now is anyone going to bring me one of those espressos?

Oh joy. She's sitting across from me. Sure, there's twenty feet and two panes of plate glass between us, but way to make me feel self-conscious, Deirdre.

TWO HOURS DOWN, ONE to go. Top of the hour—station identification—and—"You're on."

Fetzer leans in to his mic. "Welcome back to *All the World* . . ."

Ugh. How hard would it be to find a different segue?

". . . In this month's BullyWatch we examine the military academic complex . . ."

Nelson's staring at Deirdre through the glass. Deirdre's stuffing envelopes and nodding at something Beverly's saying. Two of the phone lines are blinking. "Nelse," I say, and he jumps, looks guilty. "You've got two already." He gives me a thumbs-up.

". . . brings to mind West Point, the Coast Guard Academy and a few others. But what about civilian institutions . . ."

Someone must have cracked a joke 'cause everyone in Studio 2 is laughing. Kinda wish I wasn't stuck here in the engineer's booth on my own.

". . . it doesn't take a rocket scientist to figure out that with that kind of cash flying around, the Pentagon is going to exert some pressure . . ."

Now they're listening. Deirdre catches Nelson's stalker stare—hah!

". . . Pentagon threatened to pull all 300 million of Harvard's federal funding if its law school denied access to military recruiters. Well, Harvard caved, and . . ."

Aww, look at that. His little hidden finger-wave. But I can see you, Nerdiculous.

". . . Omnia Mundi has learned that recent local recipients of Pentagon millions to develop military technologies include Northern Oregon University, the Cascade Graduate Institute, and Willamette College of Technology . . ."

Fetzer's sagging with each sentence, but Nelse is sitting up straighter. Something about a good show just pumps energy into the guy. Uh-oh, Fetzer's flubbing. It's thermal *imaging,* dude, not thermal visioning. Oh, come on, no. Not landing equipment. Jeez, the military's figured out how to land the fucking things by now. *Approach* systems. For bad *weather*.

"Precision approach systems for bad weather," I murmur, and he lifts a hand to show he's heard.

Three phone lines blinking now.

Fetzer says, "By the way, I meant to say aircraft approach systems for NOU, not landing equipment." He pushes the button for line one and says, "You're our first caller, welcome to the show."

"Hi, guys, this is Maybell." Sounds like a fifty-something mom. I bet she's afraid for her kids. "I listen to you every month," she says, "and I always learn so much. But this time I just had to call. I—this is—I don't know what to think about this. I had no idea. One of my sons is at WCT doing computer science and the other's at Cascade, in engineering."

Bingo.

"We've always been a peace-supporting—a family that supports peace," she says. "We raised our kids to value life, and peace, and, well, I just hate to think my boys could be working on weapons. That could get used in a war, you know?"

Fetzer says, "I understand your concern, Maybell. Are your sons grad students?"

"My older one is. My younger one will be next year."

"Find out what they're working on," says Fetzer. "Find out if they even know the big picture of what they're working on. Drop us an email. We'd like to know."

"Oh, I will," says Maybell. "I'm looking at the details on your website right now, I'll show them this."

"Thanks, Maybell. And keep talking peace."

"Hello, caller," says Nelson, "you're on the air."

"Hi. Thanks for taking my call. This is Dan, and I'm calling from Austin, Texas." He sounds retired. Bet he's going to bring up something from before I was born.

"I remember way back in '61 Eisenhower warned about the influence of the military-industrial complex in civilian life—

Bingo again!

"—I remember that speech, it was his farewell address. That was more than forty years ago. What's wrong with this country? Why don't we learn?"

"Dan from Austin," says Nelson, "good point. This has been happening for decades. But the scale of funding and intensity of influence has escalated in the past two years . . ."

Fetzer starts tidying up. Gathers the muffin pieces and the extra bean burrito they gave us. Okay. So the trash can is not the burrito's destination. Dude, quit eating that, it's been out of a fridge for hours. Besides, you've put on, like, a spare tire in a matter of months.

Nelson's gesturing like he's in front of a crowd. ". . . and with the *relentless* rhetoric about protecting America from terrorists, we tend to forget that the *overwhelming* majority of people who die in war are *ordinary citizens,* and their deaths go largely unreported in the US . . ."

Well, look at that. The envelope stuffing has come to a halt and now Deirdre's the one staring.

ONLY TWELVE MINUTES TO go. Fetzer's got his head in his hands, and this is the fourth call Nelson's taken in a row. Where does Mr. Mild get his energy? Ooh, and it's a ticked-off caller, too.

Nelson says, "For example, what makes the Earth Freedom Brigade's property destruction different from that of, say, the Boston Tea Party, where enraged Americans dumped forty-five tons of tea into the harbor?"

"Well, it was different back then," says the guy.

"So you said, but I'm asking what makes it different."

Heh. Go, Nelson.

"Well, they weren't risking lives of innocent people, for starters."

Nelson folds his arms on the table top. "So you think eco-activists endanger people? Can you give an example of someone who's been injured by the actions of an eco-activist? Any example at all?"

The line is silent. Everyone in Studio 2 is watching. The guy with dreads is nodding at Nelson. Then the caller says, "There was that police officer. He was acting as a security guard. Got killed when they bombed the building."

Huh? News to me.

"When was this?" says Nelson.

"About four years ago. In Alabama, yeah."

"You're mixing it up with an abortion clinic bombing. Birmingham, 1998, and yes, the officer died. But can you give me an example of a person injured by environmental activists?"

This is why Nelson is on air and not me. He's going to have his own show one day. I can just see it.

"Must happen a lot," says the guy. "They've been blowing things up for years."

"My point is that there *are* no examples. The Earth Freedom Brigade are *scrupulous* about preserving life, both human and animal. They sabotage property and systems they consider dangerous to life on earth, and in the process they go *out of their way* to avoid causing bodily harm. So if you wanted to make a comparison, the American revolutionaries' tarring and feathering of tax collectors in the 1770s looks downright brutal."

Dude's like a terrier, won't let go.

"Well, okay," says the caller, "but these eco-terrorists, they're just a bunch of spoiled kids. They need to grow up and face facts."

"That's pretty much what the British thought of Americans back in the 1770s," says Nelson. "Rioters. Savages. Spoiled children. Good thing those spoiled children kept their vision intact, otherwise we'd still be bowing to the queen of England."

Through the window to Studio 2 comes silent clapping from Isobel and the others. The lines are full. We're not going to get through them all in ten minutes.

This has turned out to be a damn good show.

DEIRDRE RUNS UP TO us in the hall. "That was bleedin' fantastic!" She grabs Nelson's arm. "The woman from Niger was heartbreaking. And that bit about the Alaskan rainforest—you've got me caring about every bloody tree in that forest."

Pain ricochets up from my knee and my water bottle rolls under the stupid church pew. I kick the pew. "Why the fuck does this thing have to be here?"

We have been awake for thirty hours.

Nelson sits on the pew with a thud. Fetzer leans against the wall and pinches the bridge of his nose. The cell phone rings in his pocket. He frowns at it, flips it open.

"Omnia Mundi Media Group," he says, then starts going, "Yeah, uh-huh . . ."

"And I loved the bit from Shakespeare," Deirdre says.

I wish she'd shut up; I want to know who's calling.

"Oh," says Fetzer into the phone. He ducks his head and smiles. "Thanks."

Nelson gazes up at Deirdre with those big eyes all full of lust. He lifts one hand and says, "'O pardon me, thou bleeding piece of earth, that I am meek and gentle with these butchers.'"

Deirdre presses her hands together like praying. "It's perfect. What's it from?" Except she says "parr-fact."

"Can we make it tomorrow?" says Fetzer. "Yeah, we're, uh, booked up the rest of today."

Who the hell is he talking to?

Nelson looks sheepish. "Well, actually, *Julius Caesar*. Mark Anthony says it over Caesar's corpse, so it doesn't really have anything to do with the earth."

"Oh, that doesn't matter," says Deirdre. "It works."

Fetzer shuts the phone with a click. "That was Kate Simms. *Oregon Herald.* She wants to run the Pentagon cash to local colleges story."

I say, "Cool."

"Yup. Providing it gets past her senior editor. She's hoping for a front page above the fold."

"She's not bad for mainstream," I say. "I'd trust her with it."

"Kate Simms?" says Fetzer. "She's the best one there. She is a true, truth-seeking journalist. Old school."

"It's always nice to be noticed," says Nelson.

Jeez. The look Deirdre sends him is giving me diabetes.

15: FETZER

I THINK DEIRDRE FELL in love with all of us, in a way. I remember the evening she stood in the kitchen and looked around at us with a moved little smile. Thing is, she had a beer in her hand, one of Jen's she was helping herself to, in exchange for pretending to be interested in Jen's lectures on organic microbrewing. I saw what I wanted to see. Her happy. Jen adjusting, even trusting. Best of all was Nelson stepping out. Slow, like he was in a space suit and he wasn't sure there was enough air, but for sure.

And, I must admit, it was damn nice to have a decent cook in the house. I told her so, and she laughed and tossed her hair back as she reached into the fridge. Then she handed Nelson a bag of purple beets, and said, "Would you mind peeling these?"

Nelson took off his jacket, rolled up his shirt sleeves, serious and honored. Me and Jen got to watch the Dee and Nelson show as they made dinner.

She got the jar of brown rice (which she had earlier moved, along with the lentils, flour, and beans to the bottom of the roll-cart, out of the sun) and measured some into a pot.

"You have any relatives in Portland?" To Nelson, not to us.

Nelson was flaying strips off a giant beet into the sink. "No," he said. Peel, peel. An evening's worth of story there, with his dad who hasn't spoken to him since he left the Forest Service, and his neocon brother. "My father lives in Florida," he said, "and Mom passed away when I was in college."

"That's terrible," said Deirdre, and she crossed herself over the pot of rice.

"Hah!" I said. "Haven't seen anyone do that in decades."

Nelson looked up from his beet. "Do what?"

"She crossed herself."

"It's the least you can do," said Deirdre, and she stirred the rice to wash it. "When someone speaks of the dead."

Nelson stood back to let her drain the water. Science guy wary in the face of her superstition, his hands were magenta, and he held the beet like some wild and holy orb. For a second I thought of a heart pulled from a living chest, which was such an un-Nelson-like image I almost laughed. They'd raised him Lutheran, pale and plain, and even that he turned his back on.

He should have just handed her his heart and said, *Here, chew it up now, get it over with, save me some time.*

She ran more water. "Any brothers or sisters?"

"A younger brother. In Malaysia. He's vice president of a mineral resources company."

"Do you see much of him?"

"Not much."

His hands looked dipped in dye. She set the pot aside and started washing lettuce, crowding him at the sink.

"That's no good," she said. "I know what it's like, though. Didn't know me da, and me ma died a few years ago." She crossed herself again, a gesture so quick you could miss it.

"Sorry to hear that," said Nelson. Right then the phone rang, and he turned, and his white shirt was dotted with pink beet juice. He'd forgotten the apron.

"Avoid contact with skin," said Jen, and she reached for the phone. "Omnia Mundi Media Group." She grabbed a pad, scrawled on it, and held it up for us. "EFB."

Finally: the Earth Freedom Brigade was getting back in touch.

"'Kay," said Jen. "It'll go up tonight."

She hung up. "That was Brian. They're ready for the video to go live."

"'Bout time," I said.

"You doing a film?" said Deirdre.

Nelson gestured with the peeler. "It's some work we did a few weeks ago. Right before you came, actually. We filmed an action, and it's going on our website."

"An action?" said Deirdre, then her eyes bugged out. "You've got beet juice on your shirt!"

"Yeah. And my tie."

"And you know nothing about this," said Jen.

Deirdre turned. "What? Why not?"

"For your safety," said Nelson. "Better if you don't know anything."

She frowned in confusion.

We'd discussed it earlier, what we'd tell her when the inevitable questions came up.

I said, "This is how it works, Deirdre. People do things for a better world. We document them, usually on video. Some of the things they do are technically illegal. We don't draw the line at technicalities. But when we put the documentation on our website, we say it was sent to us anonymously."

It took a second for her to connect the dots, then her hand went to her mouth. "Jaysus Christ, you mean like that arson you talked about on your show? You were there?"

Nelson looked down at the damn beet. "We were there."

Deirdre pressed her hands against her apron. "Holy Mary. You light fires?" She glanced at the door. The nailed-shut door.

"It's not what you're thinking," I said. "We're not arsonists. Think of us as part of the fifth estate."

"The what?"

Nelson said, "Non-mainstream media. Unconstrained by gatekeeper institutions."

She shook her head like she was driving off a gnat. "But that kind of violence," she said. Her eyes skittered to the knife on the chopping board. "Why even support it?"

"The point is the wild horses were set free," said Jen. "Weren't you listening?"

"But why were you there?"

Nelson said, "We're independent journalists. We're building archives. The whole environmental movement."

Deirdre's voice got squeaky. "But why burn it *down*?"

Jen pulled herself up straight in her chair and unfurled her thick arms. "To repeat. The BLM's management of these herds is a fucking joke." She gave Deirdre the stare. "They're supposed to protect the horses, but they get a shitload of money from letting cattle and sheep graze public land, so they say it's being overgrazed by the horses and round them up. Which is bullshit. The horses are outnumbered fifty to one by livestock. So what do they do with these amazing wild animals? Adopt them out." Jen's smile was smarmy. "Isn't that just adorable? People adopting and taking care of wild horses? Well the adoptions are a sham. Ninety percent end up as pet food. The BLM eliminates a third of the horses they're supposed to be protecting."

"Oh," said Deirdre.

Jen sat back and laced her fingers across her stomach. "Sucks, doesn't it?"

"But isn't 'action' a bit of a euphemism for burning down someone else's bleedin' building?"

Jen's mouth tweaked in a half-smile. "Three buildings."

"We had nothing to do with the planning or execution of it," said Nelson. "And action is just standard terminology. Covers, you know, tree-sits, protests, barricades."

"Action figures sold separately," said Jen.

Deirdre put a hand to her forehead. "There are other methods for getting your point across."

Jen looked at Deirdre through slits. Her hair was wild around her head. "You have no idea what we're up against, do you?"

And I said, "Let she who has not sinned cast the first stone."

The look Deirdre gave me. Reproach, and fear.

Nelson, in his best gentle-but-firm voice, said, "The purpose of eco-sabotage is to take the profit out of exploitation. The Earth Freedom Brigade takes a lot of risks, makes a lot of sacrifices, because they're committed to a cause they think is right."

Deirdre snorted. "I've heard that kind of nonsense before." Then, "Aren't you afraid you'll be implicated?"

"Nope," I said. "Got the video in the mail, remember?"

"But it'll get traced to you. You were there at the same time."

"Change the tags on the car," said Jen. "Pay cash for gas and motel. None of us has a regular job. Frank answers the phone and says we're out. Only person who might blab is you."

"And if we were worried about that," I said, "youda been out on your ass weeks ago."

Deirdre rolled her eyes. "Don't worry. I won't say a thing. It's just a bit of a surprise, that's all." She put her hand on her forehead again. "Mind if I have another beer?"

The kitchen fell quiet. The light was yellow and warm. Jen went to the fridge and handed Deirdre a bottle. "Try the Creekbed Porter. It comes out of a nearly zero-waste operation."

A FEW DAYS LATER we were camping in the Gifford Pinchot National Forest at the radio station's annual retreat. Franky house-sat, and I was glad he had Deirdre's company. Jen had joked about them getting it on, but Franky responded that while he thought Dee was "super awesome," he wasn't "into her like that, you know?" Because even though she was "like, really nice," she was also, "like, ten years older."

Good, I thought. *My plan is working.*

It was early July and still cool in the forest. Jen and I were hiding in the tent, despite which I was slapping at my neck. "Fucking mosquitoes driving me fucking crazy."

Jen, protected by all that hair, ignored me. She laid a piece of Plexiglas on the tent floor and set the laptop down, sat cross-legged, and wound her hair into a knot. Sometimes I'd wonder what it must be like to have all that wavy stuff growing out of your head. I'd rub my scalp, prickly with a day or two's growth, and envy her mosquito cover. But it got tangled in branches, trapped in car doors. That hair also got the attention of the girls, the guys, and the ones in between. But Jen preferred people at a distance, regardless of gender. Sometimes I wanted to push her out the door in the mornings and tell her to go play with other kids.

Jen flipped the laptop over and took to the battery slot with a coin.

I said, "Hey, that Zoe's something else, huh?"

Jen eased out the battery, put it in a plastic bag. "She's all right."

I said, "Great legs, great ass, and proud of it."

"That's sexist. Quit sounding your age, old man."

"Gotta love the scantily-clad hippie chicks," I said.

Jen pulled a new battery out of another plastic bag. "Hey, I found a place where the Ear works. Got a line of sight from the top of the ridge."

"Good. You check the news? On second thought, maybe I don't want to know."

"Just the usual depressing shit." Jen clicked the new battery into the laptop.

"Yup," I said. "But that Zoe? She was all over you at that program committee meeting."

Jen pressed her freckled fingers down on the battery even though it was already in. "She was all over Nelson, Fetz, and you know it."

Jen's middle name is Victoria, but I figured that was a clerical error at the Health Department's Vital Records Office. It was really "Victim."

"She left him alone soon as he said he had a girlfriend."

Jen turned to me. "He usually says that to keep girls away, but now it might actually be true, huh?" Then she flipped the laptop over, booted it up. "It could get weird, you know, if they do hook up."

"Hell no," I said. "Already he's easier to live with, and he's not even getting laid."

Jen snickered. "He's easier in some ways, but he's, I dunno, lost focus. Could get worse when he finally remembers he's got a dick."

"That's sexist," I said, and Jen snorted.

The tent flap zippered open and Nelson poked his smiling head in. I thought he'd heard us, but his face showed only simple joy. That and wearing an old T-shirt and jeans instead of his usual jacket and tie made him look younger than his thirty-four years.

"There you are," he said. "It's nice out. What are you doing hiding in here?"

Jen said, "Maintenance. Close the flap. We're trying to keep bugs out."

Nelson said, "Zoe's here. She wanted to know where our tent was."

Zoe's cute face poked into our tent. "Hey, guys." She was about twenty-five, light-brown skinned, and she reeked of pot. We said hi. She said, "Hey, Jen, wanna take a walk to the overlook?"

Jen stared down at the laptop, and I swear if she'd said she was busy I would've slammed it shut on her fingers. But she said, "Sure," and Zoe said, "Cool," all squeaky, and Jen angled her large limbs out of the tent.

Nelson climbed in. He had a touch of sunburn on his nose and forehead. "Wow," he said, "that hike to the next crest is fantastic. I wish Dee could've been here." Then he flopped down on his sleeping bag and went on about how great the retreat was and how amazing the energy was and aren't those direct-action people inspiring?

I said, "Yep. Plenty to see and do."

To be honest, I was feeling jaded about the return-to-nature shit that the youngsters kept shoving in my face. For one thing, it doesn't scale. There are six billion souls on the planet. A solution that won't work for the global population isn't a solution. And if there's going to be some huge social restructuring that forces a return to a nontechnological lifestyle, who'll get the good, fertile land? The white people with guns, that's who. Everybody else will starve on the margins. We've got to be smarter than that.

Nelson gazed at the ceiling of the tent. "Rainier looks incredible today, huh? And oh, man, go down from the ridge a ways and there's a patch of hemlock, about three dozen trees, and they're huge. I'd say seven, eight feet across at the base."

I stretched out my shrapnel knee until it clicked. "Old, huh?"

"Yeah." He laced his fingers over his chest and sighed. "Then about halfway up there's a waterfall. Drops about a hundred feet, maybe more. Wish Dee could've seen it. I'm gonna use it as a starting point for an essay."

I didn't sleep too well the night before—mostly due to him sleep talking—and I was ready for a nap. "Great," I said.

"You know?" he said, with a small, thoughtful frown, "streams and rivers aren't just any old water moving along." His hand lifted and traced a slow line above his head. "They're this thread of energy, you know?"

Uh-oh, I thought. *Here comes the essay.*

His arm followed a wide curve. "Circling through ecosystems in their own time dimension, like they have for millions of years. And everything we do is so temporary, you know? Like even if you dam a river up, it's really just biding its time, because in a million years the dam'll be eroded away, or simply bypassed." Nelson sat up and opened the laptop. "Hey, did you hear what that guy Willow was saying? That Independence Day should be renamed Inter-dependence Day?" Nelson shone his lit-up eyes in my direction. "You know, because we're all dependent on each other, and the earth and systems and so on."

"Yeah," I said. "I get it."

He gave a self-conscious smile and watched me stretch out on my sleeping bag.

"Happy Inter-dependence Day," I said, and turned my back to him. "In case I forget tomorrow."

THE MORNING AFTER WE got back from the retreat, Jen and I were up long before Nelson—bizarre enough. But in that morning's papers we were learning something even more bizarre: a proposed new Department of Homeland Security. First of all, who the hell since the Nazis names where they live "Homeland"? Internal Security, sure. Domestic Security, okay. But *Homeland* Security? Second of all—ironic, much? It was a bunch of other peoples' home-land for millennia before the US even existed.

That morning, Jen and I shared a wary look over the tops of our papers.

"Unaccountable to the public," I said. "Exempt from FOIA disclosure."

Jen nodded. "Massive reorganization of the federal government. And more armed federal agents with arrest powers than any other branch. I'm getting a laptop."

Nelson plodded down the main stairs. His eyes were puffy and his hair stuck out.

"Velcom to ze new verlt orter," said Jen. He ignored her and sat down at the table.

Jen set the laptop in front of me, open at the ACLU's website. The new Department of Homeland Security planned to deny its 200,000 employees whistleblower protection. "Way fucked up," said Jen, then she gave Nelson's chair a kick on her way over to the fridge. "Party party party. She's turning out to be pretty wild, huh?"

We'd returned late the night before to a rainstorm, and to Joe Cocker blasting and Deirdre and Franky dancing around the kitchen. The place smelled of booze and sweat. There were open bottles, and hardened candle wax puddled on the kitchen table.

The smile on Dee's face when she'd noticed Nelson. And Nelson frozen, staring, watching her dance.

Jen had yanked the boombox cord out of the wall, which made Franky and Deirdre collapse, laughing, but not touching—I noted they weren't touching—onto the brown velvet sofa.

"Remain seated until ride has come to a complete stop," said Jen. Then we went upstairs to bed, and Franky followed. There was just the sound of the rain outside and the clink of Dee gathering up wine bottles.

And now it was morning, and Nelson was picking at a lump of wax on the table.

Jen dropped her butt on a chair next to him. "Looks like someone didn't get much sleep. Probably didn't even stay in his own bed."

Nelson's head snapped up. "What?"

Jen raised her hands in mock surrender. "Whoa! It speaks."

"Maybe now's not the time," I said.

Jen kept her hands up. "Guess you won, Fetz. Unless he's bullshitting us."

I wanted to slap her. "You're not helping, Jennifer."

She smirked. "We had a bet going about whose bed you'd wake up in."

Nelson's eyes bulged.

I said, "It was just a joke, dammit. A stupid joke, didn't mean anything. Quit taking everything so goddamn seriously."

Nelson folded his arms on the table and stared at the wax. "Leave me the hell alone."

Jen sat back, snickering.

I should have been taking Nelson more seriously. Instead I said, "Now you listen to me, dumbasses. We agreed to let Deirdre stay because it made for a pleasant change, remember? Breath of fresh air. But not if it turns this place turns into a fucking soap opera."

I turned the laptop around so they could see the ACLU page. "Hell in a handbasket, kids. *Hell* in a handbasket." Jen and Nelson watched my jabbing finger. "We've got work to do, and we've got years invested in it, and it's getting even more critical that we stay on it."

They said sorry and we went back to work. For the next couple of weeks, I noticed Nelson avoided being alone with Deirdre. But we got through the backlog of site updates, a long-delayed book-editing gig, and we put out a damn tight newsletter.

Then we got a call from Kate Simms, the *Oregon Herald* reporter who'd run our "Pentagon Cash to Colleges" story. She had some follow-up questions. We made a date to meet at Nguyen's diner.

DEIRDRE PLAYED OBSEQUIOUS WAITRESS with us, but when Kate turned up I shooed Dee away. Kate came with a baby in a sling. Some deal about the sitter was sick. The baby burped, gurgled, and fussed. Kate somehow maintained focus despite swaying him back and forth and jiggling him up and down. Nelson gazed at that kid, and I knew what was going through his head. When we first met him, he and his attorney wife were trying to start a family. We'd turned that couple's world upside down.

Kate was plump, pretty, and chin-up-confident. Everything Deirdre wasn't. She had light brown curls and a blue silk blouse with faint stains that I attributed to baby puke.

After the introductions and chitchat, Kate said to Nelson, "I enjoyed your essay on water."

Nelson dropped his eyes and tweaked a smile. "Thanks."

"Really. It was beautiful. Poetic."

"Yikes. I hope it came across as more practical than that."

Kate bounced the baby. "Perhaps you're a practical poet."

Made me wish I'd written an essay about water.

Then Kate said, "Anyhow, I need to find out what's up with the Harry Lane omission."

Nelson and Jen looked as puzzled as I felt.

Into the silence, Kate added, "Rumor has it you left Harry Lane out of your exposé because you're leftie snobs."

"Harry Lane University?" I said. "What's up with them?"

Kate said, "A research assistant at NOU complained that I picked on them even though Harry Lane's Pentagon contract was bigger."

"For real?" said Jen. "But, Harry Lane's, like, a private liberal arts school."

"Liberal arts and sciences," Nelson corrected.

Kate paused her baby-rocking. "You mean you really don't know?"

"Uh, no," said Jen. "Do you?"

Kate sighed like we were tiresome morons.

Jen whacked her hand on the table. "Harry Lane! Hah! How fucking rich is that!"

"Seems incongruous," said Nelson. "Bastion of progressivism and all."

We looked at Nelson, who had done an honors year at HLU during his undergrad days—the inherent elitism of which Jen loved to tease him about. "I guess we need to look into this," he said. "Good tip. Thanks."

"You're welcome," said Kate. No smile. Then she had to go. But first she had to use the restroom. Would Nelson mind holding him? Nelson's eyes stretched wide, and he took the child like you'd take an egg yolk that was being handed to you.

"What's his name?" he asked.

"Adrian," said Kate over her shoulder.

How seldom you recognize the start of things.

16: JEN

CAN HEAR HIM AND Deirdre coming in downstairs.

"Hey, *Nelse*!" I yell. "Harry Lane University! You gotta hear this!"

Nelson's voice floats up: "Hang on."

"Do I detect a note of irritation?" I ask Fetzer, and he nods.

Nelson climbs the basement stairs with the enthusiasm of a tired snail.

"Dude. Get your ass up here," I say, and when he emerges at the top, I add, "Apologies if this is interrupting something important. 'Cause this is, like, *more* important?"

"Get a load of this," says Fetzer, and he grins, quick and triumphant. He hands Nelson the document.

"What is it?" says Nelson. And do I detect a note of reluctance?

Fetzer says, "Well, if you read the *words*, Nelson, you'd learn all about HLU's shiny new contract to help the Pentagon distinguish suspicious activities from ordinary body movements."

I point to the third paragraph. "Pentagon's got so much spy video to go through, they need software to help."

Nelson reads from the document. "Video and Image Recognition and Analysis Software—VIRAS? The ability to search existing video data and monitor real-time video data for specific activities or events will provide a dramatic new capability to the US military and intelligence agencies . . . to identify and catalog cases of gathering, moving in a group, shaking hands, kissing, exchanging objects, kicking, carrying together . . ." His eyes scan the page. "Harry Lane's doing this for them?"

"Developing algorithms," I say, "to identify human activities and evaluate whether they justify a military response."

Nelson pushes his hair off his forehead. "God, this is awful. Where's it going to be used?"

Fetzer says, "Afghanistan. Maybe Iraq, if it comes to that. But you know they're gonna use it on civilians in"—he makes air quotes—"the Homeland."

Nelson gazes across to the kitchen window like he'd rather be somewhere else.

"Thing is," says Fetzer, "there's been no press release. They're keeping it under wraps."

"I mean, shit," I say. "It's *so* not Harry Lane. Can you imagine?"

Nelson shrugs and says we should just go straight to HLU's chair of Engineering and ask. A move that did not occur to me, I must admit, but then I don't carry the privilege of the well-educated white male.

"You think he'll deign to talk to us?" says Fetzer.

"You're assuming the chair is a he," says Nelson.

"Big assumption, Fetz," I say.

Fetzer says, "I guess worst that can happen is he—or she—says no."

WHEN FETZ AND I get back, Nelson's already made an appointment for us to see Dr. William Reynolds on Thursday.

"Cool," I say. "Your chai latte."

Nelson takes the latte, sets it aside. "His secretary was really helpful. Said she was a fan of the show. I mean, she was like, I'm-moving-another-meeting helpful."

Fetzer starts eating that nasty scone he bought. "Fans are good. But see, I was right: he's a he."

Nelson sighs and goes, "Yeah." Closes the calendar, starts tidying shit up.

"What's up?" I say. "You bummed about your alma mater?"

Nelson shakes his head.

Fetzer softly asks, "How's things with Deirdre?"

"Hah. Too much else to do. Like you said, we can't afford distractions."

Fetzer puts a hand on Nelson's tan corduroy shoulder. "I didn't mean be a monk. Buddy, you need a life."

Nelson gathers pens, drops them in the pen cup. "I get anxious around her," he says.

"Just come right out and ask her on a date," I say.

Of course nobody says, *Jen, you need to get out more too.*

Fetzer says, "You know she likes you."

"It's pretty fucking obvious," I say.

Like last night when she brought him a cup of tea. "Whatcha reading?" she asks. "Article about timber companies," he replies. "Looks bloody dull," she says. And he tells her about how he's fascinated with the "tapestry of it all." The history, the law, ecology. "You have lovely hands," she non-sequiturs. Disbelieving, he holds them up to check. "Oh. Thanks." Then he tucks them under the desk. I was staying quiet 'cause I wanted them to keep going. Then she gestured at his desk. "Why do you do all this?"

And Nelson stopped acting like he was in a bad dream. He looked right at her and it rolled out of his mouth like only Nelson can get away with: "I try to defend what is defenseless. One day I realized I had to try. And then I knew I couldn't do anything else."

Which is why Fetz and I picked him, as I must remind myself from time to time.

17: NELSON

"I'M TAKING A SHOWER," Nelson says, "and that's final."

Deirdre's curtain is open, but she's at work. He pulls his tie loose and unbuttons his shirt on his way up the basement stairs. No way he's going to meet Dr. William Reynolds unwashed.

Jen says from below, "Downtown's jammed this time of day."

Nelson's sick of the nagging. He leans over the banister. "There's time for me to shower."

Fetz says, "We haven't even rehearsed."

God, they've been interviewing people for years. Surely they have it down by now.

Empty kitchen. Dishes are done. Deirdre's put three dandelions and two small Cecile Brunner roses from the front porch in a glass in the middle of the table. He sees her dancing the night they came back from the retreat: twirling, hair flying. His heart aches.

FETZER DRUMS HIS FINGERS on the steering wheel. Jen logs in at the console, checks email. Nelson lets his shoulder lean against the car door. The sky is windless blue and the city sparkles. The message from Reynolds's assistant at eight this morning: Could they come in earlier? Dr. Reynolds is flying out of town tonight. He would appreciate it.

To supplement their internet research, they'd left for the public library so early that he'd missed seeing Deirdre, and they'd spent the morning in a dark corner, digging through obscure journals, feeding coins into a photocopier, getting hungry.

They ate through a box of crackers, and an orange they'd found in the car. Nelson was too nervous to eat much. But now he is clear and calm. Clean shirt. Flossed teeth. A folder on his knees full of evidence—enough to convince him now—that Dr. William Reynolds, former Research Fellow in Defense Policy Studies at the Heritage Foundation, and a regular and generous contributor to the Republican party, has no business chairing a department at Oregon's most liberal independent educational institution. At least not if it means bringing in stinking war business.

IT'S STRANGE BEING BACK on campus. The old Sci and Eng building has been replaced by a steel-and-glass structure called Hewell, and Engineering lives on the fourth and fifth floors. Reynolds's assistant turns out to be a heavy black woman in a tight yellow suit and dangly earrings.

"I am so pleased to meet you," she says, and her voice is deep. "I'm Nancy. My daughter and I, we listen to your show religiously. She's going into twelfth grade, and she is a science *nerd*." Nancy's laugh is big, and her manicured fingers rest for a moment on the closest shoulder, which happens to be Fetzer's. But Fetzer's holding up one hand, saying, "Don't tell me, don't tell me— Nancy Washington? the co-op? On Thurman?"

Nancy gives Fetzer's shoulder a push. "I was wondering if you'd figure it out!"

Fetzer grins, slaps his thigh.

Turns out in the seventies Nancy lived with some activists above a store that did exchanges. Fetzer was a regular. He'd bring in kitchen appliances he'd fixed and leave with 8-track tapes.

Fetzer rubs a hand over his scalp. "So, you listen to the show but you never got in touch? Jeez, Nancy."

Nancy flips a hand. "Oh, you know. You get busy."

"Wait. So, your daughter, she's in twelfth grade, she's born in '83, '84?"

"'Bout five years after I left, uh-huh."

Fetzer spreads his hands wide. "And you never told me?"

Nancy glances at her feet. "It was hard, Irving. Having a kid makes you practical. Just focusing on surviving, you know. I kinda—" Her hand drops off her hip, hangs loose at her side. "Went to school. Got some office skills. Been working ever since."

Fetzer looks at the ground and nods. Nelson knows what he's thinking, how hard it is to stay on the margins as you get older. How hard it is to not cave under the survival pressures of neoliberalism. And what a shame it is each time they learn of another friend whose radical energies have been diverted by circumstance and necessity.

Nancy touches Fetzer's shoulder again. "But I listen to your show, oh yes." Her smile is enormous. "And I feel like I know you, John, and Jen. Well, sorta. And I do what I can for the environment," she says as she moves away. "Except I can*not* stop using paper towels, know what I mean?"

They follow her down the hall and into an office, where she hovers her hand—with matching yellow nail polish—above a speakerphone. "And I'd like to do biofuel in my car, like you all use? But without the infrastructure—" She leans toward the phone, presses a button, and says, "Dr. Reynolds? Mr. Nelson and his party are here." She straightens up and drops a hand on her large hip. "And no way am I going to make it myself. I have enough to do, working and raising a daughter. You have any idea how much laundry a seventeen-year-old generates? Just because she's a science nerd doesn't mean she doesn't go through clothes."

The phone says, "Send them in."

Nancy goes over to a door, opens it wide. The inner office is huge and wood-paneled. One wall is filled with photos of Portland's bridges, each taken from the air. Apart from being late-middle-aged and white, William Reynolds doesn't look like a typical engineering chair. Athletic and tanned, he looks like a man who's made lucrative decisions and knows how to be in charge. A man who's arrived. He looks a little like Nelson's dad.

Reynolds says, "Have a seat."

Three leather-trimmed chairs sit in a semicircle in front of the massive desk. Reynolds shakes Jen's hand, Fetzer's, then his grip is tight around Nelson's. Nelson suddenly feels shabby and tugs his jacket sleeve over the frayed cuff of his shirt. He knew HLU had a big endowment, but this big?

"Thanks for, ah . . ." Reynolds sits in the executive chair behind the desk, spreads his palms. "Coming in earlier. Got called away at the last minute." He smiles with his lips closed.

The bridges have been shot at different angles and at different times, and for a moment they seem to be tumbling together under an impossible gravity.

Nelson replies, "Thank you for taking the time to speak with us. We appreciate how busy your schedule is."

Reynolds leans back in his chair. "Sure. Now, what can I do for you?"

Nelson says, "As I outlined in the email, we are a media group called

Omnia Mundi, and we run an informational website about environmental issues, and we also have a monthly radio—"

Reynolds waves a lazy hand. "Nancy showed me your site."

"Cool," says Jen. "Our operation's all Linux based, of course."

Behind Nelson's eyelids strings pull tight.

Reynolds looks straight at Jen for the first time and smiles faintly. "Idealists."

Jen says, "Well, sure. Aren't you guys into peer production?"

Nelson clears his throat.

Reynolds rests his elbows on the desk and hunches forward. "We're, shall we say, rather uncomfortable with products that don't come with a large degree of accountability on the part of the vendor."

Jen fidgets. "I don't mean necessarily office environment, I mean R&D—"

Reynolds's mouth hooks up at both ends in another thin smile. "I hope you didn't come here to preach open source to me, young lady."

"I'm an alum of Harry Lane," Nelson cuts in, and Reynolds shifts his eyes away from Jen. The strings pull tighter.

"It was, um, an honors year in botany."

Reynolds's face is the face of a man who is waiting for nothing in particular. Nelson almost adds that he was on a full merit scholarship, but he hates to brag. And by now Reynolds is no doubt wondering why the hell Nancy didn't screen this meeting better.

"Anyhow, it's come to our attention," says Nelson, and he wishes he didn't sound so officious, "that Harry Lane University was awarded a contract from the Pentagon—"

Reynolds brings his hands together on his desk.

"—to develop software to interpret surveillance video—"

Reynolds says, "That's an interesting theory. How did you come up with it?"

Fetzer holds up the VIRAS document. "Here's the RFP from the Pentagon."

Reynolds's smile has become permanent. The meeting is dangling by a thread. With contempt he says, "The DOD doesn't send out RFPs for something like that."

Fetzer checks the document. "Okay. It's a 'Broad Agency Announcement.' Whatever. Our point is—"

"I'm curious to know how you came across that document."

The bridges on the wall are tipping, tumbling.

"Fell off the back of the interwebs," says Jen.

"Jen," says Nelson. Wishes he hadn't.

Fetzer says, "It's actually freely available at"—and he holds the document at arm's length to read out the small-print URL.

Reynolds's eyebrows go up. The meeting is in the toilet. "Well, this is interesting," he says, "but I'm afraid I have another commitment."

"Dr. Reynolds," says Nelson. "We have just a couple of questions if you would oblige us a moment or two longer."

Reynolds presses a button on his speakerphone. "Nancy? We're done."

Nelson tosses a look at Fetzer. Fetzer holds up a picture of an aerial drone. "These MQ-1 Predators fly video surveillance missions in Afghanistan and—"

The door opens and Nancy stands, smiling blandly, professionally. Reynolds says, "Escort them out, please."

Nelson, Jen, and Fetzer stay in their seats. They won't get another chance. Nelson holds up the maps of surveillance camera locations in Manhattan and Portland. "We're concerned about the exponential growth of—"

Reynolds looks at his watch. "I have a schedule."

Asshole. Nelson stands. His back is straight and he breathes in deep. The sore place isn't sore. He says, "Congratulations on securing such a lucrative contract."

Reynolds maintains that wire-thin smile.

"Thank you for your time," says Nelson. He follows Jen and Fetzer over to Nancy with her hand on the doorknob.

"I'll show you to the elevators," she says, one hand out, and those manicured nails curl into her palm. They follow her ample yellow form down the hall. Near the elevators she stops and turns. Now she's frowning.

"What the hell was that about?"

"Besides being a train wreck?" mutters Jen.

Fetz says, "Did you know this department's creating surveillance technology for the Pentagon?"

Nancy's face screws up. "Seriously?"

Nelson says, "Not officially, but, yeah."

Nancy mutters, "Holy shit. I knew something was up." She shoves a card between the covers of Nelson's folder. "My home number's on the back. We need to talk. But none of you are going to be coming back around here, that's for sure." She shakes her head. "When he smiles like that? He wants you dead. I'd bet money you're going to get banned from campus."

Nelson's shirt is sticking to his skin. "Harry Lane bans people?"

"This guy?" she says, and jerks her head in the direction they came. "He gets what he wants. There was some communists tabling during Political Fair? And they painted this big 'Eat the Rich' slogan on the floor? Okay, dumb move, but he made a stink about it, and they got kicked out for good."

Jen grimaces. "Shit."

Nancy says, "I know. I got transferred here spring semester, and I tell you, it's not like Linguistics. It's weird."

"This is not the Harry Lane University I know," says Nelson. "But good to meet you, Nancy. We'll be in touch."

Nancy says, "Please do." She touches her cheek and murmurs, "Look at that. I think I just reconnected with my old angry side."

Fetzer tips her a salute.

THE UNDERGROUND GARAGE IS cool and smells of fumes.

"That was terrible," says Nelson. "What a waste of an opportunity."

Jen has her hands in her hair. "We *told* you we should've rehearsed."

Nelson snaps, "Well you weren't helping. *Linux* based? What's that got to do with anything? And who the hell cares?"

Jen drops her hands. "Who the hell *cares*?"

Fetzer says, "No plan survives contact with the enemy," and gets in the driver's side.

Typical. Jen can't see past her personal agenda, and Fetz just sidesteps.

But when they emerge from the garage into sunlight and the shady trees of downtown, something in Nelson softens.

He says, "Even if we were coordinated, I doubt we would've gotten anything out of him."

Jen says, "Yeah. It was bizarre."

Fetzer says, "It certainly was, young lady," and Jen huffs.

Nelson is sticky, but all the windows are down and the breeze is a godsend. As they cross the bridge he says, "It didn't go the way we hoped, but hey, we met an ally."

"Allies are good," says Fetzer.

"Allies are good," says Jen. "Allies are good."

Fetzer turns onto Division. Nelson says, "Hey, could you drop me off at the diner? I want to grab a juice."

"Got juice at home," says Jen.

"Not grapefruit." The diner has a carbonated kind now.

"Dude," says Jen. "We've got, like, things to talk about?"

"What, that it was a bust? We know that already." They pass Twelfth Avenue. "I'll just be a minute. Can I get you guys anything?"

No one replies. Fetzer turns onto Thirteenth and pulls over. Nelson gets out. The car pulls away. Rounds the corner into Novi. Disappears.

He should have gone home with them. They'll be discussing what to do next. But as he approaches the diner, through the plate glass window there's Deirdre, wiping a booth table. She leans into each wipe, tired. He sees himself walking in and putting his arms around her, but when he does push open the door, she's heading back to the kitchen. Mr. Nguyen looks up from behind the cash register.

"Hello, Mr. Nelson!" he says. His ball cap depicts Homer Simpson in tighty-whities. "Beautiful day! What would you like today?"

Right now a strong drink would go down well, but Nelson says, "I'm actually here to see Deirdre."

Mr. Nguyen gets a knowing smile. "Second one today," he says, then steps into the kitchen and calls out, "Miss Deerdra! Mr. Nelson here."

Second one?

"Hi," says Nelson as she comes through the swinging doors. But there's something urgent in the way she steps out from behind the counter.

"Hi," she says. "So, what would you like?" Even though she's now on the wrong side of the counter to get him something to drink.

To put my mouth all over your skin and bite your hair between my teeth and push into you until you laugh and cry at the same time.

"You must have had a busy morning," she says. She clasps her hands in front of her chest. A second ticks by. She's squeezing her knuckles to the color of bone. His hug is stuck and won't come out. She says, "You missed Sylvia by half an hour."

"Sylvia?" He hopes he doesn't sound as relieved as he feels.

Deirdre nods. "She dropped by for coffee. How about you? Want something to drink?"

"I can't stay long. We're busy."

"Oh, just a wee glass?" She smiles, and warmth suffuses his chest. His hands feel naked, but he holds them toward Deirdre anyway, palms up. He looks right into her pale eyes, and she unties the bony knot of her own fingers and lays her hands on his. Her skin is hot.

"It's good to see you," he says, and rubs his thumbs across her knuckles. Her shoulders relax. The day is redeemed.

When they're sitting down with glasses of grapefruit juice, he racks his brain for the list of conversation topics he'd written out in an earlier moment of determination. College—did she go to college?

She stirs the ice in her juice with a straw. "Got me master's in classical studies."

Nelson sits back. "Wow. I had no idea."

Her smile is wry. "You were thinking I was a wee bit dense, were you?"

"No, no, not at all."

She murmurs, "Just because I don't know about computers and North American flora."

"No. It's not like that. You're just so quiet about yourself."

She looks sideways out the window. Parked at the curb is a red pickup with a plastic American flag on its antenna.

"I touched on the classics," he says. "In undergrad. An ancient history survey, and a course in Greek drama."

Her face opens out like she found a photo of an old friend. "Oh," she says, "that explains the Denman's *Greek Plays* in your bookcase. The playwrights said it all, didn't they?"

Of course. That time she helped him take laundry upstairs. His collection is motley and lacks balance. He wishes she hadn't looked through it. But how to explain the attrition from all the moves and the mildew? And there's no time anymore to just browse in bookstores and explore.

"I used to have more books," he says. "That one's a survivor."

"Oh, I know what you mean," she says. "It's hard to keep a decent library if you're not settled."

The kinship is a blessing, and their eyes meet for a few seconds before she looks away. He leans back against the cool vinyl. "So, what got you interested in the classics?"

She lifts out her yellow straw, licks it. "The Greeks weren't Catholic. I loved how they told such big stories without Jesus or Mary."

Catholic. Near the window a little sugar lies spilled on the tabletop. He's seen her cross herself, heard her evoke Mary.

Her voice is slow, casual. "Who was your favorite playwright?"

He sits forward. His mind won't give up any names. He scratches his nose. Anything. Please. He wants to say *Oedipus*, but that's a play. Something that sounds like *Oedipus*, with an *S* in it. *Oesipus?* No. *Aespilus?*

He looks up. "Aeschylus."

It must be the right answer because she says, "Oh, he was brilliant," and she lifts her arm in an arc. "'Well I know that men in exile make of Hope their daily food.'"

Exile. "Is that from *Oedipus*?" he asks.

Her fingers encircle her glass. "*Agamemnon*. Sophocles wrote *Oedipus*."

The ways she says *Sophocles*, it's like she's in love.

"To be fair," she continues, "I remember more from the Oedipus trilogy than from *Agamemnon*." Her hands lift, and her chin lifts, and she is beautiful. "'So, you mock my blindness?'" she quietly chants. "'Let me tell you this. You with your precious eyes, you're blind to the corruption of your life, to the house you live in, those you live with. All unknowing, you are the scourge of your own flesh and blood, the dead below the earth, and the living here above.'"

Nelson sits back. "Wow. That's intense."

Her eyes snap onto his. "As is life, don't you think?"

The pink of the table reflects under her chin, and her pupils do a tiny searching quiver back and forth on his face. An image of her against his chest, of their bare chests, pressing together.

She murmurs, "You've hardly touched your juice."

He picks up the glass, pulls out the straw. Grapefruit bubbles bitter-sweet in his mouth. He gulps, and he can take more. He's going to drink it all. His head tips back, throat stretching. He doesn't need to breathe, he needs sweet, bitter pink juice.

She has one eyebrow cocked when he puts the empty glass down. "Thirsty lad."

He wipes his smile with the back of his hand.

"John," she says, and the electric shock of it jolts him back to earth. "Why don't you use your first name?"

"Oh," he says, "Silly habit. Fetzer hates his first name, and he insisted on his last name when I met him, and so as a joke I said he had to call me Nelson, and it stuck."

She smiles. "John's a grand name," she says. "Strong. Clear."

"Thanks. I can't take credit for choosing it. But you can call me John."

Please call me John. I want to hear my name in your mouth.

"John," she says, and her gaze slides over to the spilled sugar. "I should get back to work."

•••

SHE'S NOT LOOKING SO tired any more.

"It's just canned tomato soup, with extra spices and tofu," she says, and ladles some into Fetzer's bowl. "No veggies from Mr. Nguyen today."

Fetzer says, "Bummer if we can't go back on campus. I want to look at the project firsthand."

"I'm sure it's delicious," says Nelson.

"You kidding?" says Jen. "It'll be classified. But seriously, can one guy get us banned?"

Nelson says, "It's a private institution. They can reject whomever they want."

Deirdre sits down next to him. Her eyes check the place settings, the bread, the open bottle of wine. Fetzer is salting his soup, and Jen is slurping spoonfuls already. They don't see how much she cares.

Nelson wants to say grace. Anything to slow the moment, shine attention on it. But it seems pretentious to stop them for a ritual that's never been invoked in this household before.

He tastes the soup. Full-flavored and garlicky. Amazing what she can do even with something out of a can.

"It's really good," he says to Deirdre. Her smile is warm and private.

"We need to figure out a way to get back in," says Jen.

Deirdre says, "Why don't you wear those disguises?" She stares at the side of Fetzer's head. "I'm dying to see you in one of those wigs I found in the basement."

"You saw no disguises," says Jen.

Deirdre opens her mouth, then smiles. "Must be imagining things."

". . . WAIT TILL FREE from pain and sorrow he has gained his final rest."

Nelson sits shivering on his bed. For the past few hours an abject universe has rumbled through him. Now it's back to paper and words, and the open-mouthed mask sings at him off the cover. The red numbers on his clock say 2:46 a.m. He should've been working, but he opened *Oedipus Rex* and read it straight through, and now it's heavy in his hands like a bowl of blood.

Nelson stands up and puts Denman's *Five Greek Plays* back into his bookcase. The journals he brought to bed last night sit on the desk. There's work to be done.

18: JEN

I TURN AROUND AND tell Nelse and Fetz, "You realize how easy this is going to be?"

Nelson shrugs under his nerdwear jacket. "Jen, let's try and figure something else out. I mean, come on, we've probably been banned from campus." He looks at Fetz. Fetz stares at my screen and rubs his dome.

"Best way I know," I say. "Colleges are pretty vulnerable. Security's often pretty chaotic, like, they're a bunch of little fiefdoms, you know? So it's hard to enforce standards."

Deirdre's footsteps creak over our heads in the kitchen. Fetzer glances at the ceiling. "If they have a whole engineering computer department or whatever, surely they know what they're doing."

"Don't be so sure." I crack my knuckles, type *users/secret/mole_scan_harrylane.edu*.

"So you know a way in?" says Fetzer.

Mole launches. "Starting a port scan as we speak."

Nelson whines about risk, and I say, "Yeah, yeah, makes me a terrorist. Hardware firewall's blocking access to just about everything, of course. I'm looking for a machine that's less well defended. Like maybe a server set up without IT oversight—set up wrong, you know?"

The status screens show the host names being resolved into an IP pool. I switch to performing a scan. "They're running HTTP servers out of a few places," I say, "and everything's connected through them, but I'm looking for one with a weak spot that'll let me onto the network. Then once I'm in on the ground level, I can do a password crack." I swing the chair around. "By the way, this will take a while."

Fetzer says, "Why would a university let a computer be vulnerable like that?"

Mole chugs away on the first batch. "Just need one virus stuck on a dumb downloadable game some doofus in HR likes to play, and you've got a Trojan opening up an exploitable port."

Nelson says, "Seriously?"

"Don't I tell you to never open attachments? Anyhow, you guys should go do something else. Only thing more tedious than doing a port scan is watching someone do one."

MOLE PRINTS "COMMON EXPLOIT DISCOVERED!" Music to my eyes.

I yell, "Hey guys, get your asses down here."

The workstation's identity is *admin26.harrylane.edu*. Soon you'll be owned, admin26.

Nelson looks like the poster child for National Worry Week.

Fetzer says, "What happened?"

"Penetration, boys. And I know you'll be all over that."

"That's sexist," says Fetzer. Without conviction.

"Right. I'm in on the ground level. Going to start with an OS detection."

Mole menu option four. "Okay, Harry Lane's administrative offices are running Microsoft IIS. Which is pretty common for organizations, and the unpatched versions are so fucking vulnerable you almost feel sorry for them."

Nelson says, "Why?"

"Oh, you know, the Ukrainians."

"What Ukrainians?"

"The Ukrainian hackers? Had a field day with that particular security hole last year. Sixty reported break-ins in thirty-two states, which means way more in reality. Institutions tend to keep their yaps shut about breaches."

While Mole's checking the server version, I check for the Trojan that let me in. Sure enough, the Solitaire virus. Love this.

"And guess what." They peer over my shoulder.

"Do I have to spell this out?" I say. "Look, HLU's is still unpatched."

Fetzer says, "HLU's what exactly is still unpatched?"

"Operating. System."

They back off.

"You know what this means?" I say. "They're morons. Because they never applied the patch."

Nelse and Fetz give each other a look. "So what now?" says Fetzer.

"I got in through this desktop machine. Some administrator. Got to start identifying valid user accounts and crack a password."

Fetzer sits one thigh on the edge of the desk and keeps his eyes on the screen. The Crusher starts the crack, and generates seven dictionary words within seconds.

"I'm not even going to push further," I say. "Obviously they don't enforce strong passwords. Look at this: 'binky'? And 'madonna'? Come on."

"So where to now?" says Fetzer.

"So these passwords might get me access to trusted systems, you know, beyond user-level access. But for now the VNC is giving me a back door into this machine."

I dig around for the data file. "Hey, while I'm here, maybe we should enroll in some courses. Then give ourselves As."

"That's not funny," says Nelson.

I thought it was pretty hilarious, but whatever. "Okay, this machine belongs to Douglas Heinrich. Deputy Director, Communications and Marketing. Now I need to find the way to Reynolds's."

"Dinner's ready," Deirdre yells down the stairs.

Nelson goes to the bottom of the stairs and yells back, "We'll be up soon, we're in the middle of something."

She yells, "Are you hacking into that university?"

"Ah," he yells, looks across to us, looks back up the stairs. "Yeah."

"Maybe you could each take a bullhorn," I say, "and go up on the roof?"

Nelson holds up his hands. "Sorry."

"Hah! That was so fucking easy. Okay, see this? Reynolds's directory tree."

Fetzer points at the screen. "Can you download those interoffice memos?"

"I'm on it. Know what? I'm going to look for the mail archive, too."

Fetz can't keep the grin off his face, and even Nelson nods with satisfaction.

Fetzer then pats his stomach. "But first, dinner."

19: FETZER

THE THREAT OF ANOTHER war was blossoming on the news, and even the so-called "liberal media" got busy interviewing retired generals and war analysts. Bush had some explaining to do, and when he came to Portland that August, we and a few others went downtown to greet him.

We crossed the river and had to park in Old Town because the city was jammed with buses trapped nose to tail by protesters. The sound of drumming led us to the crowd as it swept east on Alder. The street was wall-to-wall with gray ponytails and fresh mohawks and short-back-and-sides, holding signs and walking and dancing and clapping to the beat. Made me proud to be an American right then. Prouder than I'd felt in a long time. We got near the marching band at the front and let the noise take us over: nothing to do but step along in the Mardi Gras of it. Stern-faced kids thrashed hard on Bush's "what-me-worry?" face in the middle of their big drums. Thunder came out of them, bone-shaking syncopation, a sound I'd never heard downtown amid the office buildings and parking lots. On the corner of Fourth Avenue cheerleaders bounced up and down as we passed. Striped and skinny and plump with green hair and no hair and long hair flying with the pompoms. Behind us was a bunch of buttoned-up guys who looked like accountants figure-eighting a set of large upside-down flags. A woman with giant blue clown glasses skipped by. There was a group of unsmiling vets going the speed of their buddy in a chair. I slowed down and considered saying hello but Jen tugged my sleeve because the drummers were getting away from us. We passed elderly ladies in slacks holding signs with *Bush's government: One more corporate scandal* and kids in black with *ENEMY COMBATANT* patches pinned to their backs. They made me do a double-take. Even Congressmen—a group I'd normally classify as among "the powers that be"—weren't getting away with criticizing Bush anymore. In this context the enemy-combatant half-joke seemed riskier than it would have even a few weeks earlier.

"This feels good," Jen yelled into my ear.

"Sure does," I yelled back. I was hoping to run into Nancy. She was a firebrand back in the day, and even though it had been a surprise to see her in a mainstream environment, I figured she'd be at the protest. But then the realization struck me: despite the lifestyle diversity of the crowd, there wasn't a single black person in sight.

The mood shifted when the march reached Second Avenue and a set of bike cops swooped around and cut us off from the Morrison Bridge. We were surrounded. The drums kept up, pounding loud, and the crowd pressed closer.

"What's happening?" yelled Nelson. Jen was clapping and shuffling to the beat. "Dunno," she yelled back, but then she rolled her eyes. "Check it out."

Behind the cycle cops a dozen men in black had appeared. Feet spread, pants tucked into shiny boots, identical pairs of gloved hands on identical nightsticks. The helmets, the visors. You could see the crowd become aware of them. The drumming got louder. Kids whacked their skateboards on the ground. Banged on hubcaps. Blew on whistles. The cops kept us hemmed in, and I was getting claustrophobic. Every time I stepped backward it was onto someone's foot. I needed to be on the perimeter, but I didn't want to get any closer to those robocops. When a guy tried to push his way past, the cops wouldn't let him leave. Nelson took out a notebook and started writing. This was turning into a story.

A chant rose up of "*Whose* streets? *Our* streets!" Then three teenagers staggered toward us, two girls and a guy, flushed in the face and gasping like they'd been held underwater.

"Tear gas?" said Jen. She snapped photos.

Strangers put arms around the kids' shoulders, sat them down.

"We'd be smelling it," I said. "It's OC."

Nelson scribbled faster. Two white thirtysomething guys in polo shirts groped toward us, eyes screwed shut and coughing into bandannas. Jen got one by the elbow, and Nelson tucked his notebook into his jacket pocket ready to help, but right then two Black Cross medic girls appeared. They sat the stricken guys down, pulled drink bottles from their frayed knapsacks, and poured what was probably diluted Maalox into the guys' streaming red eyes.

Something was happening on the other side of the intersection that we couldn't see for the crowd, and couldn't hear for the noise. A woman yelled, "This is a peaceful protest," her voice shaking with shock and hurt. The riot cops had disappeared without us seeing them go, but the bike cops leaned on their handlebars and stared straight ahead like there was nobody there. More pepper-sprayed folks stumbled toward us. "What the fuck are you doing?" screamed the woman. "You can't trap people then pepper-spray them!" The crowd picked up a chant of "*Peace*-ful *pro*-test" that swelled around us. We were trapped, they were using tactics I hadn't seen before, and Jen, Nelson, me, we were pumping our fists and chanting our lungs out. Then a clean-cut Toyota-and-Chablis couple broke through, staggering in pain, and in their arms two beet-faced shrieking children.

Now how do you explain pepper spray to a toddler?

"*Peace*-ful *pro*-test, *peace*-ful *pro*-test," shouted the crowd. Nelson gripped his pen so hard his knuckles were pale. Bodies pressed close. The chant got garbled, mixed up with new words taking over. The Black Cross medic girls got the family on the ground and started their ministrations. The crowd was turning outward, facing the bike cops, jabbing their fingers at them, and the new chant cleared into a rhythmic, "Shame! Shame! Shame!" The cops didn't blink. "Shame!" yelled the crowd.

Jen's finger jabbed the air. Nelson's notebook jabbed the air. A short white guy with dreadlocks shoved a video camera into one cop's face. "Fucking fascists!" he screamed. "This is a peaceful protest!"

"Hey, is that Brian?" Jen yelled in my ear. "From the EFB?"

The officer stood unflinching, his hands loose on the handlebars, one foot on a pedal and the other on the ground.

Jen added, "So he has his own camera now, huh."

"I think it is," said Nelson. "Oh god. This isn't going to end well."

"Fascist bastards," screamed the guy. I was pretty sure it was Brian, even though we'd only met him once before, and in the dark. He bounced on his toes like a boxer, brought the camera within inches of the cop's face. "You like hurting little kids? You like it? Huh?"

The cop dropped his hand to his belt, brought up an aerosol can the size of fly spray, and shot a jet of oleoresin capsicum right into Brian's face.

Brian wheeled away, but turned back like an enraged hornet, screaming incoherently and holding up his shaky camera. Not a flicker on the cop's face, and Brian got another blast of point-blank OC that knocked him to his knees.

He rocked and gasped. The Black Cross girls were busy with the family. Nelson ran toward Brian. Jen and I followed. The cop turned. He looked right at me and mounted his bike, and on some invisible cue all the cycle cops mounted their bikes. I felt it in my guts. I was sure they were about to ride through the crowd, spraying OC indiscriminately as they went, but next moment they were yelling, "Move back, move back," and there was a tire shoving my shin and I was caught between sleeves and necks and faces and there was nowhere to go but backward. Nelson, bless him, grabbed ahold of my shirt, and together we grabbed Jen before she got separated. But as we moved the crush lessened, and a cheer went up from the other side of the intersection. The cops were freeing us northward.

"What happened?" said Nelson. "What changed?"

Brian was left behind, along with the other stricken folks lying in the intersection. The Black Cross girls had mercifully been allowed to stay, and as we crossed Third, one was kneeling beside Brian, holding his head.

"No idea," I said. We spilled around trapped cars like water. Despite being inconvenienced, some of the immobilized drivers clapped and flashed V signs at us, and after a while we took up the new chant, "*Not* my president, *not* my war." The pride I'd felt was gone, but little by little the hope trickled back. Hope that maybe there were enough people against attacking Iraq, and that maybe, despite the war on citizenry in defense of Empire, maybe if we all got behind it, we could avert the looming atrocity.

BACK HOME WE PORED over the reports on Indymedia. Turned out we never made it to the main protest outside the Hilton. And they had it worse, with armed riot police, rooftop snipers, and helicopter gunships overhead. The police declared a state of emergency and pushed people back with so much tear gas, rubber bullets, and pepper spray that they hit old folks, kids, and even reporters. The TV news was all over the "state of emergency" because those words are gold to them. But they painted the crowd as out of control. And they ended with a clip of the mayor claiming the police actions that day were in line with current policy on safety.

20: JEN

"THAT'LL BE SYLVIA," FETZ says to me.

I'm so buzzed from the protest I don't even care!

The sound of her heels up the stairs and she comes into the kitchen, Nelson following.

"See tonight's news?" I ask her.

Sylvia gives Dee one of those girly half-hugs, then takes a seat at the kitchen table. "Yes. Very dramatic."

I open the fridge. "It was awesome. Till the cops got violent." Huh. There were six Creekbed Porters in the fridge last night, and now there's four.

"They pepper sprayed *babies*," says Nelson.

Sylvia frowns. "Pretty thoughtless bringing kids to a protest, though."

"You're kidding, right?" I say, then, "Anyone want a beer?"

Fetzer says, "I want something better," and he's on his knees, pulling one of Mrs. Krepelter's bottles from the cupboard at the end. He stands up and announces, "We fucking exercised our fucking First Amendment rights today. Loudly."

"Damn right we did," says Nelson, and he stands on his toes to get down the good glasses. They're made of, like, lead crystal and they make me nervous, but whatever. Jeez, that fight he had with Lise in our old kitchen, when he first joined us. She actually came over to try and get them back. "All your stupid new hippie friends'll just break them," she screeched. "Take something you can use, like some blankets." But for some reason Nelson loves those glasses. And maybe it's because I'm afraid it will mean I'm a hippie, I am extra careful not to break them.

Fetzer brings the bottle to the table. "Why the hell shouldn't you take kids to a protest?" He points a finger. "Every single person has the right to protest without fear of retribution. There were old people there, families, and everyone in between. Just like it should be."

Sylvia says, "I wouldn't take a kid. Crowds can be unpredictable."

Dee puts the salad on the table. There's a lot of grated carrot, which I like 'cause of the way it soaks up the dressing. And some kind of casserole thing with green beans and tempeh—excellent. "I wouldn't take a child, either," she says.

Fetzer pops the cork and sets the bottle down. "It was a march, not a riot. The cops were the ones being unpredictable."

"They were fucking insane," I say, and reach for the bottle.

Fetzer yanks it away. "Gotta breathe. This is a '97. Show some respect."

"You're full of shit. It says '99."

Fetzer looks at the label and his forehead scrunches. "Shit."

"Huh," says Nelson. "She must've given us a mixed case."

Fetzer goes to the cupboard at the end and kneels, pulls bottles out one by one. "Guess so. We've got one '97 left, the rest are '99."

"Well," says Dee, "let's just drink what's open."

Fetzer comes back to the table. "It's not like this one's terrible. But the '97? It's a sweetheart." He starts pouring the wine, and it's dark in the fancy glasses.

"To the First Amendment," says Nelson.

"What's left of it," says Fetzer. We're all standing around the table and our glasses clink above the food. Mine extra gently.

Nelson's tie is off. Is it my imagination or is he loosening up a little the last few days? He says to Sylvia, "We'll do a story about the police response for the next show."

"Uh-uh," says Sylvia, like she doesn't think it matters all that much. Then she pulls a box out of her giant purse and hands it to Deirdre. "This is for you, darling. You need a connection to the outside world."

Deirdre turns the box over in her hands.

"A cell phone?" I say.

Sylvia looks smug as hell. Turns out the fucking thing has a built-in *camera*.

Fetzer grins. "Haww. That's cool. That is very cool."

Nelson says, "That's really generous, Sylvia."

"You never give *me* a phone," I say. Only half-joking, 'cause I could sure as hell use a camera phone way more than Dee.

Deirdre pulls it out of the box, and it's all silver and smooth. She touches the small square that houses the lens. "I can take photos," she says, like it's only just dawned on her. She looks up into Nelson's eyes, and they're staring at each other so hard I'm getting uncomfortable.

21: NELSON

THE BASEMENT STAIRWAY IS a black hole tugging at Nelson, pulling him downward. His hand is on the banister, measured, silent, like defusing a bomb. Not that he's ever defused a bomb, but it probably feels like this, with the sweating and the churning. Bare toes slide forward to find the edge. One step down, and the dark fills with the thrumming of his heart.

The violence today. Meted out so casually. And strong, young Brian, felled like a tree.

Nelson breathes in on the sore place. Inches his foot to the next edge. Steps down.

It's way too easy for one person to hurt another. Way, way, way too easy. It doesn't make sense. It's never made sense.

In a slow-motion dance, he grips the handrail, feels for the edge, reaches his toes down. His heel down. Pause. The air is cooler. The handrail is sticky. The photocopier hums.

He'd hurt Lise. He hadn't meant to, but it was a side effect of his decision.

Lean forward, grip the handrail.

He would've hurt her more if he'd stayed and pretended.

His heartbeat rises like a flood, and when he ducks his head below the basement ceiling, he is engulfed. Deirdre's curtain is closed, but there she is, awake, her cross-legged silhouette on the cloth.

Just as quietly as he came down, he will go up again. Yes. He will tiptoe through the moonlight in the living room, creep up the main stairs to the top floor, close his bedroom door behind him without even a click, and crawl back into his bed.

The dehumidifier gurgles. But there's another sound. A sniff. A small hiccup. She's crying.

No turning back now.

He steadies his hand against the wall. Toes down, then heel. His body sways around his thudding heart. Another step. Another, then the shock of cold concrete at the bottom.

The basement is like the sea after a wreck, full of debris. This debris happens to be at right angles to one another and mostly arranged in piles, but in the nearly-dark there's a lot to navigate. Luckily the power LEDs on the electronics are like tiny lighthouses. The floor is freezing. He stops a yard away from the dim blue fabric of her curtain, and breathes in sharp against the sore place, trying to edge it out. The ferocious hard-on he had in his bedroom is gone.

Why is this so damn difficult?

Lise in his head says, *Too much doubt makes John a dull boy.*

"Deirdre," he whispers, pointlessly, since there's no one to wake up, "are you okay?"

Her silhouette jumps. "Jaysus." Her silhouette hands pull at blankets. "Aye. Come in."

He opens the curtain to muted brown light. They should get her a better lamp. And a floor mat. Her oversize gray T-shirt reaches baggy to her elbows and covers her bottom. She has a plastic cup of wine in her hands.

He says, "Sorry I startled you."

She doesn't look up. Pats the cot. He sits. Her obsidian black hair almost touches her knees. He bends down to peer up into her face, but where the T-shirt stretches across her thighs he can see her panties. He makes himself look away. On her cardboard-box nightstand is a cheap clock and a book of T. S. Eliot's poems. A charming surprise. The box is on its side and holds small piles of underwear. She probably keeps her notebooks under the cot, with the photos. Clothes hang like ghosts from a pipe along the ceiling. Heartbreakingly, third-worldly simple. The skirt she wore today, and her jeans, and the frilly sea-green top she had on dancing that night.

He says, "What's wrong?"

Her face rises, puffy and wet around the eyes. She hands him the cup of wine. "Nothing."

He takes the wine, and a laugh falls out of him, nervous and absurd.

"Please. You're going to have to do better than that." He sips. It's strong. He's sharing her cup. His lips are touching where hers have touched.

She looks up at the ceiling, sighs, and says, "It's just very hard."

"What is?"

"Being here."

Behind Nelson's eyelids the strings are about to snap. "Really? Why?"

"It's just hard, okay? It's hard to be settled. You guys are brilliant, but it's hard."

"Are you homesick?"

"Homesick?" She snorts. "No."

"Can we make it easier?" he says. "Would you like to move upstairs?"

She shakes her head.

He forces himself to ask, "You want to move out? I can't blame you, we're not the best housemates you could find."

"No," she says, still shaking her head. "And that's just it."

"What's it?"

Her face is shadowed on one side. "I've become attached."

He's not sure if she means attached to him, or to all of them.

"Well," he says, and it's like negotiating a treaty in a dialect he doesn't fully understand. "We're really glad you're here."

And "we" especially means him.

Her voice squeals, whispery. "But it's all so bleedin' tenuous."

She's so close. It's so quiet. "You mean, staying here?" His heart slams in his chest. "You can stay as long as you want, Deirdre."

"Everything." Her hands lift, then drop like dead fish on the blanket. "It can all go," she whispers, "in an instant."

He wants to say, Yes, it can all go. In our lifetime we may see total environmental and social collapse. But that's not really what she means. He's sitting rigid as stone, but like a slow cog, something inside him begins to turn.

"Jaysus Christ," she says. "Stop looking at me like that, I'm a right mess."

The turning cog bends him closer to her. He sets the cup of wine on floor. Echo of his breath off her skin. Touch of her cheek to his lips, her lips to his lips. He holds there, his heart walloping, his mind spinning, every muscle in his back holding him in this awkward tipped-forward position so he doesn't fall on her.

Her hands press against his shoulders. Slowly push him away. She sits loose and still, her eyes closed like she's meditating.

He has done the most absolutely dumb thing of his whole life, and he can't retract it. From now on, this moment will be the division. Everything after this will be tainted by his error, and everything before will be imbued with innocence.

"So," she says, her voice like dry paper, "it's really scary, falling in love with you like this."

His limbs flood, adrenaline but smoother. The room swings, he shifts into her outstretched arms, pulls her tight. Warm body through thin cotton. Her knee digging into his side, her skull pushing his glasses into his temple. They rock back and forth and he could cry but he kisses her neck instead and tells himself to breathe. The cot bumps like a raft on choppy water, and she's up on her knees—no, don't push away, no—but it's her wet mouth and hot thigh and grasping hands, and there under the pipes along the ceiling, with the photocopier humming in the sea of debris, and the city sleeping all around them, there on the creaky metal camp bed that can barely fit one person, he tumbles under the surface of his life.

IN HIS HAIR. IT'S her hand. He spreads awake.

"I have to pee," she says. The cot wobbles as she gets up, and his elbow knocks the wall. She's in the air he breathes, she's in his mouth, she's on his skin.

He rolls onto his back and laces his fingers behind his head. He's floating in a spring sky. On the cardboard box sit his glasses where she'd placed them. He doesn't put them on. The toilet flushes in the distance. He needs to go, too, but he can't imagine ever moving from this bed. That jewel smile when she comes back. It's where he will live out his days.

THIS TIME HE WAKES with a bump, and he's knotted and gritty. She has to look at him like that again. She has to take him back up into the spring sky.

"Hey," he murmurs.

She breathes, her eyes dozy slits.

"You awake?" he says. Her eyes open, then she props her head on her hand. "Do you always leave the light on?" he asks.

"Mmm." Her face dips down until their foreheads touch, and it's like she has only one eye. Her finger traces a line down his sternum.

Maybe there is nothing to say, after all.

"What's up?" she whispers. Atoms collide and scatter with no sound.

In the emptiness left behind, his heartbeat rises. She pulls back and gazes at him. "Tell me. I think you need to tell me how you came to be here."

LEDs shine pinpoints of green in the night sea beyond her curtain. Beyond that is the broken trajectory of his life.

He breathes in against the small stone, the pressure in his chest.

"I used to be with the Forest Service," he confesses.

"Mmm?" she says.

He smooths a corner of the sheet against the thin mattress. "Should be called the National Timber Industry Service."

"Why'd you work there?"

"Joined right out of grad school. Considered myself a reasonable sort of conservationist, you know? Rational, pragmatic, able to make compromises."

She strokes a finger along his wrist. "What did you do there?"

"Desk job. Dealt with state and local governments, forest industries, private landowners. God, this makes me uncomfortable."

"Now why on earth would it be doing that?"

"Because I was ignorant. And dishonest. Told myself I was doing a good job of managing the land, you know? Till I met Fetzer and Jen. They approached me after a town meeting. Pretended to be with the *LA Times*."

Deirdre's smile almost makes him smile.

"Yeah, I was flattered. Until they were sitting in my office and it turned out they ran a newsletter for the old Northwest Forest Alliance. They'd been up at the Enola Hill protests. They spread photos and statistics across my desk and told me what they'd seen. Filled some gaps in my reality."

Deirdre keeps smiling like the words *Enola Hill* are merely pleasant syllables.

It was a dry summer day when Fetzer and Jen stepped into his Salem office. They sat in his two extra chairs and spoke reasonably. Gathered up the photos and the printouts at the end. Shook his hand and thanked him for listening. Said they had a feeling he'd be open to listening.

They may as well have pushed over his bookcase, tipped his desk up, emptied the drawers on the floor.

He breathes in against the sore place.

"You see, we managed this forest called Enola Hill as part of the commercial timber base. I didn't like the idea of cutting it, but I took it for granted that if you don't agree with the law, vote someone in to change it, and until then put up with it, you know?"

"Ah," she says. "Faith in oligarchy."

"Yeah, huh. Clinton passed the salvage logging rider. A judge declared logging Enola Hill was legal, and it was my job to support it. At least in principle. I didn't personally issue the road-use permit, but I could have. And I would have."

Deirdre strokes her fingers in small half-moons behind his ear.

"Enola Hill was bad, Deirdre. Very bad. Old-growth hemlock and Doug fir. Lynx, cougar, spotted owl, all under the saw."

He places a hand over her heart. His life, her life, meeting here.

"The Yakama and Umatilla were devastated. The Nez Perce had used it as a vision-quest site for centuries." The sound out of his mouth is nearly empty. "It was like destroying a cathedral."

The sore place burns. "I couldn't believe what an idiot I'd been. Twenty-eight years old, and naive as a stupid kid."

Deirdre's hand is on the back of his neck, massaging, forgiving. "No." Her voice is like velvet. "You opened your eyes."

He shakes his head. "The cathedral still came down."

Outside the crossing bells start clamoring, breaking the still night. He waits for the shrieking train to pass.

"Fetzer drove me up there," he says. "Jen came, and this other guy, Ralph. Fetz took us up in the Toro. It was a really hot day."

He twines his fingers with Deirdre's and thinks of upended roots.

"Worst ride of my life. Ralph despised me on principle, said they should dump me in a gully. Luckily Fetz had just converted the Toro. Gave us all the step-by-step details. Kept Ralph from pushing me out of the car and abandoning me in the forest."

Knotted roots.

"Six years ago, almost to the day."

He closes his eyes.

"Fetzer stopped at a trench blockade. Some women were trying to keep it going. You could see down the hill, bald spots. They call it selective logging, but that's a joke. Some elders from Warm Springs came by. It was like a funeral. People kept looking over at me, like 'What's *he* doing here?'"

The branch he's holding onto won't let him go. The sun is slanting through the evening trees and birds are gathering in the canopy. A dump truck fills the trench in seconds, and the logging convoy drives over, shaking the ground where he stands. A woman in a green T-shirt whose name he wants to know but doesn't dare ask lifts her arms to the forest and she calls out, "Your last night." Insects flit around her in the clearing like flecks of golden light. Huge sweat stains on her shirt from digging all day. She keeps her arms up, does a slow circle. "I'm so sorry," she cries. She starts sobbing, circling and crying "I'm so sorry," over and over until it's wailing and not words anymore.

A leaf touches his face, but it's Deirdre's hand.

"That night"—with his eyes still closed, he takes Deirdre's hand and presses her palm to his lips—"I wrote my letter of resignation."

The skin of her hand grows damp from his breath.

"Joined the Northwest Forest Alliance. Left my wife."

Deirdre's hand twitches. "Your what—your wife?"

He opens his eyes. "Her name was Lise. Is. She's still in Salem. Last I heard."

Deirdre's lower lip is between her teeth.

"It was really hard," he says. "Took them weeks to trust me."

"Jen must've given you a rough time," says Deirdre.

"She was okay. Mostly. But the monkeywrenching was terrifying."

Nelson lets go of Deirdre's hand. "I never even lied on a tax return, and there I was, prowling around at night pulling out survey stakes, hoisting supplies up to tree-sitters. There's this thing called a dragon, used in blockades." He gestures a mound. "A big pile of cement with a pole in it, you make it in the middle of the road, and activists chain themselves to it." He drops his hand and mutters, "I got good at mixing cement."

Deirdre says, "It's a bit bloody hard to picture."

"I can hardly believe it myself."

She rubs his hand. "Then what?"

"It wasn't right for me. I mean, it was fantastic and liberating. But some of the people were too angry. No, rightfully angry, but too provocative. It scared me, but I didn't know where else to go, you know? I'd walked away from everything. Friends, career, family."

"They thought you'd gone off your nut."

"Yeah. Pretty much."

His best friend, Craig, was teaching science at their old high school in Maryland. They'd been best men at each other's weddings, and kept in contact for years. A message from Craig happened to arrive soon after Nelson resigned from the Forest Service. It was full of banalities and exclamation points. Remodeled kitchen, son's soccer practice, upcoming vacation. How can you be so excited, Nelson thought, when water tables are being poisoned by gasoline additives? When five hundred children die of poverty in Africa every hour? When butterflies that once thickened the air are almost extinct? Nelson wrote back that he'd left his job, and left Lise. He wanted to do the right thing, he wrote, and he wasn't sure this was it but it was a start. He was on a journey, he wrote, and he was scared. Craig must think he's crazy, right? He'd visit Craig when he got his finances sorted out, but right now he was out of a job and the divorce was expensive. It would be great if Craig managed to squeeze in a visit to Portland. Nelson needed to talk all this over with a friend. Nelson sent the email twice, a week apart, in case the first one had gotten lost in cyberspace, but Craig never replied.

Nelson sighs. Deirdre lifts her hand in her quoting mode, and says to the pipes above them, "'Men would say of him he went up and down he came without his eyes; and that it was better not to even think of ascending.'"

"That's good," says Nelson. "Let me guess, Sophocles?"

"Plato," she says.

"I could have used it in '96."

The copier hums. The lamplight is drab and brown. "So I realized I had to leave the Northwest Forest Alliance," he says, "but I'll be honest with you, by then I was in love with a woman in the group."

Deirdre says, "Ah."

"She was pure dedication. Fiery, passionate, courageous. Everything I wasn't, with my spongy misguided conservation, my cushy Forest Service career"—he sweeps a hand out—"my unquestioning faith in the—" His hand clips the lamp, it lands with a crash and the light goes out.

"Sorry," he says, and he fumbles in the dark. The sheet tangles around him and he kicks her. "Sorry!"

"You big oaf," she says, laughing.

"But I'm sorry." He reaches down and touches shards of lightbulb glass on the floor. "About the mess," he says. He pulls his hand away. "I'm such a goddamn mess."

"Yeah, well, me too," she says. The flat of her hand smooths a slow circle on his back. It wells up, how much he's missed being touched like this, wells up like water in the desert.

If it means marrying sexy nerd boy...

PART THREE

22: JEN

ON THE LAPTOP I connect to the network. *My* network. There would *be* no network if it wasn't for me. The only other person in #rezist is the German script kiddie who won't take a hint. Lame lame lame. "Ciao" I type, and sign off.

The bed bounces under my back. There's a balled-up T-shirt digging into my shoulder and I throw it across the room. It hits the wall and catches on the antenna sticking out of the bookcase.

No Nelson at breakfast. So he finally found his way into Deirdre's panties. Let's hope he's smarter than the average lobster and can find his way out.

Fuck, I can't stand being kept out of the basement. Should just go down there. Walk in on them. Who the fuck cares.

But noooo. Give them their priiiivacy, says Fetzer.

Back to the laptop. Yesterday's work.

Now this makes me feel better. The stuff we found in among the shit I downloaded from Reynolds's workstation.

Okay. Harry Lane prez to Reynolds, chair of Engineering, first memo: *No, we will not entertain defense contracts. Does not jibe with Harry Lane's mission, yadda yadda.* Second memo: *No defense contracts, dumbass.* Third memo: *Pleased to begin negotiations for the defense contract.*

Big fat WTF on that one.

Then a lot of back and forth hammering out details. Fucking five million clams worth of details. To me that seems kind of generous in exchange for some algorithms—heh, I'd be happy with fifty thousand, but then the Pentagon's not asking me, are they? And for good reason.

Then there's the extended project description: *The US military and intelligence communities have an ever-increasing need to monitor live video feeds and search large volumes of archived video data for activities of interest.*

Sure you do, Big Brother. And now you've found some obedient Thought Police technicians.

Well, we're going to blow you open, you pricks. Fucking fascists and your fucking cronies, your fucking greed and your fucking unaccountable neoliberal empire.

FINALLY NELSON EMERGES FROM the house and comes down the path. He opens the driver's door, nearly sits on Fetzer's lap. Fetzer facepalms. Nelson walks around the front of the car, climbs in on the other side of me, and does a wallet-checking pat on his nerdwear jacket. Fetzer starts the engine and swings the dull white nose of the car onto a lurching U-turn. "So, Nelson." He grins and whacks the wheel. "You son of a bitch. You finally got some action."

"Eyes on the road," I say.

Nelson holds up both hands. "Let's just focus on what we need to do today."

Fetzer spits out a laugh. "Come on, admit it, you are now one happy camper."

"Deirdre isn't 'action,' all right? I love her."

Fetz rolls his eyes rather elaborately for someone in control of a two-ton vehicle. He whines, "'Deirdre isn't action,'" then he reaches past me and pokes a grubby finger at Nelson's jacket. "We want details."

Nelson snaps, "No."

"Jeez, I don't," I say.

Fetzer stops at a light and gives me a look. "He bombed."

Nelson folds his arms. "You're not going to manipulate me, Irving Fetzer."

"And I'm not in the mood for titty-talk," I say.

Fetzer steps on the gas and we all lurch backward. "Yep. You bombed."

Time to take abrasive action. I reach over and roll Nelson's window down a couple of inches. "Need some air." Nelson's hair blows around.

"Okay, okay," Nelson says to the dashboard. "It was wonderful. Happy now?"

"Wonderful?" Fetzer waves him away. "You sound like Franky."

Nelson closes his eyes and laughs.

Me, I'm going to barf on the folders in my lap.

23: FETZER

IT GOT ANNOYING, BUT the upside was Nelson wasn't depressed anymore. He was, however, distracted: he and Deirdre couldn't be in the same room without being next to each other. And breakfasts got off to a slow start with him coming upstairs late. But I was thankful he put up with that tiny camp cot instead of bringing her up to his room. The walls upstairs were thin.

One day when we were all at the breakfast table, Franky came by during his morning run. He dropped a fat handful of mail from our P.O. box on the kitchen table. "From your fans," he said.

"We could use the affirmation," muttered Jen.

That morning we'd found out about Operation TIPS, the Terrorism Information and Prevention System. Truckers, letter carriers, and utility workers would be recruited as spies because their routines made them "well-positioned to notice suspicious activity" generated by the rest of us.

I, too, was eager to think about something other than my country's giddy slide into overt fascism, and I sorted the mail into piles. Bills, junk, and hand-addressed. Hand-addressed was usually the best. Sometimes it was cool surprises like obscure newspaper clippings from a friend, or a supportive letter from some elderly radical. That day there was only one hand-addressed. It wasn't bulky. "One of these days girls'll send us naked pictures," I said.

Franky poured himself coffee, pulled the comics from the stack of papers on the floor, and sat down. "Keep the hope alive, Fetz."

Nelson opened an envelope addressed to him, and it turned out to be from a sustainability conference in San Francisco that wanted him to submit a proposal.

Jen said, "Wow. They want you to give a talk? That rocks."

"Congrats," I said, and wondered how on earth he was going to focus on such a task.

Nelson said, "Yeah. It's an honor." But then his eye caught the logo on another envelope. "Oh, look where this is from." It contained a single sheet. Reading it made him hold his breath, then let out a sigh. "Well, at least we had some warning. It's official. Members of Omnia Mundi are no longer welcome on the Harry Lane University campus."

"That arrogant prick," said Jen.

"Why?" said Franky. "Are you guys, like, banned?"

"Long story," I said, "Let's read something else." I opened the handwritten envelope. Portland postmark, ink-jet paper, word-processed font. Except there was no greeting, and no signature. Just three short paragraphs. I scanned them fast.

"Hey, uh, we got some hate mail." I smoothed the paper flat and read out loud. "'How low will you and you partners in crime the SOCIALISTS go to brainwash the people of America? Well evidently there is no limit to how low you will go.

"'We're BLESSED with the opportunity to contribute to the safety and security of our great nation. America is great and our best days are ahead. You are disgusting for sowing the seeds of despair and undermining our country. You all deserve to die.

"'You think you can get away with this but we're watching your every move. You're going to slip up, and we're going to get you. You will get what you deserve.'"

I looked up at their stares.

"Fuck," said Jen, and she took the letter. "Is that a death threat? Wow, our very first."

"It's not funny," I said.

Under Jen's elbow was an Operation TIPS story, and I could see the words . . . *higher percentage of 'citizen spies' than the former East Germany had under the Stasi . . .*

"You should take that to the police," said Franky.

Jen sneered. "The who?"

"He's right. We should," said Nelson.

But after an hour or so the surprise wore off, and we started joking about our "partners in crime the SOCIALISTS." We brought it up a couple of times after that, but we were busy, scattered, and no one got around to running that particular errand.

24: NELSON

NELSON HAS HARDLY BEEN able to concentrate on the morning papers. Fetzer carries his bowl and cup to the sink. "We're working on the House and Senate report this morning, you and me? And Jen's taking care of that broken web forum."

"Yeah," says Nelson. He watches Fetzer head down to the basement, then he glides his hand up Deirdre's arm. "The House and Senate report is the last thing I feel like doing."

She gives him her alone-at-last smile.

"I've been thinking," he says.

"Mmmm?"

In this morning light, under this soft sky over this house, over this shining city he calls home. This kitchen sink and these red-breasted finches and this warehouse next door. In here, out there, the trajectory of his life. This is where it gets righted, set on a new course.

He traces the back of her hand. "Been thinking about our future."

She flips her hair back. "The future is out of our hands."

"Well," he says. Hope has frothed through him these past few weeks. A delicious sense of possibility. "I like to think it can be anything we want."

Another smile. "Typical American optimist."

He sits back. "Really? Didn't realize I represented the national character."

She scrapes butter across her toast. "Yer a typical Yank."

"Riiiight," he says, then, "Thing is, what do *you* want, sweetheart?"

"A better camera than the one in me bloody phone."

He laughs. "Besides that. In the long term."

"Long term?" The knife pauses in her hand. Her topaz eyes. The sharp V of her mouth. "*Now* is fockin' brilliant."

"Oh, I know. It's fantastic."

She's so much happier than when she first arrived. They both are. He's never felt this way about anyone. It's obvious: they're right for each other. They need each other.

He rubs her shoulder. "But. Well. What about the future?"

"You know I'm not legal."

The perfect opportunity to bring it up. But she stands and takes her plate and uneaten toast to the compost. He comes up behind her, puts his arms around her, and watches her hands rinse the plate. He mimes her actions until she giggles.

"So we could, you know. Get married. Problem solved."

Deirdre balances the plate in the rack, then picks up the sponge, wipes around the edge of the sink. Her bottom is soft against his crotch, her neck is smooth against his cheek. Downstairs Fetzer's no doubt looking at the news online. Upstairs Jen must be taking a shower because the pipes are whooshing.

If they knew what he'd just said, they'd think he was nuts. But they don't understand. They never have.

He slides his hands under Deirdre's T-shirt, drifts around her belly, brushes over her small, soft breasts. "It's very soon, I know. To be talking about it. But I'm happy. You're happy. So why even pretend there's anything else we'd rather do?"

Deirdre arches her spine. Lets go of the sponge. Far away a lawn mower drones. She's trembling.

He rests a slow kiss on her neck. "You never talk about your previous marriage."

Her bottom presses against him. She whispers, "I don't ask about yours."

"I'd tell you everything if you did."

"What would be the point?" she murmurs. "We're here, now."

"I love you," he says into her ear. Her head turns until her cheek is under his mouth. He kisses her cheek. Her face comes around. Between kisses she says something, it sounds like, "Here," and her hands are digging under his clothes.

The stainless steel of the sink is warm in the morning sun, and she's so warm in between. He bites her hair. A spoon gets knocked into the sink. Shuffly, giggly, gaspy, pressing against her so hard her hand gets jammed down there, making her laugh. Never stop laughing, sweet Deirdre.

Zippers. Buttons. Stupid underpants! Hot skin.

Fetzer's downstairs. Jen's upstairs. For god's sake, nobody move.

More laughing, hurry-up-soft this time. Up you go. Edge of the sink. Oh yeah. Her thighs around his waist. Lucky lucky lucky. Oh my god.

Her mouth opens; her eyes, body, throat, all catch in a soft high sound.

25: FETZER

I WAS TAKING A break during the August show, hanging out with Jen in the engineer's booth, when Sylvia dropped by. She'd never visited us during a show before, so it was a surprise. She brought a tray of iced coffees, and the three of us sipped and watched through the glass as Nelson carried on alone.

". . . minimum of four percent of Americans will be recruited into the TIPS program," he said.

"That was quite a story about the Bush protest," said Sylvia. "You might even get a call or two."

I waved at the call board. "There's people on hold already." There were two coffees left. "Who's the fifth one for?" I asked.

Sylvia stirred her straw through her ice. "Is Deirdre around?"

"She's working," said Jen.

". . . TIPS informant reports will be available to local police forces . . ."

"By the way, you go to Harry Lane?" I asked.

Sylvia picked up a folder to fan herself. "No. Columbia."

". . . targeted individuals will remain unaware that reports are being made . . ."

"Why?" she said, "Do I look like a Laney?"

In those kitten heels and tailored red dress, she looked nothing like a typical Laney.

"Just wondering." I said. "We're about to out their sordid little affair with the Pentagon."

Sylvia's eyebrows went up and she stopped fanning.

". . . cable installers and telephone repair workers will report on anything in private homes deemed suspicious," said Nelson.

"Do tell," said Sylvia.

Jen said, "Harry Lane U got this mega Pentagon contract to make software that reads surveillance video."

"Reads it? Automatically?" The fanning resumed.

Jen faded in the music as Nelson wound up his segment. "No need for human eyes."

Sylvia said, "How can software interpret video?"

Jen shrugged. "They don't even have software that interprets human faces or speech a hundred percent, let alone complex movements."

"You just know there's going to be mistakes," I said. "People will get killed."

"Huh," said Sylvia, filing the information under "mildly interesting." Jen pressed a button, the "Music of Dissent" segment started, and Nelson took off his headphones and rubbed his hands over his ears.

"So is this Harry Lane Pentagon thing a secret?" said Sylvia.

"It wasn't super secret," I said, "but they never announced it."

Sylvia sipped her coffee and gazed at Nelson. "Don't take offense, dears, but are you sure anyone's listening?"

Jen and I shared a quick smile. "Quite sure," I said. "Classes started this week. We made a cryptic announcement to the student association. And Jen posted another on the student forum. Laneys have been bugging us with questions all day."

"Ninety seconds," said Jen.

"I need to get back in there," I said. "Oh, and FYI, the chair of Engineering? Guess where he used to hang out."

Sylvia indulged me by looking up at the ceiling as if in thought, then said, "I give up."

"The Heritage Foundation!"

Her grimace was mild, even elegant. "Now *that's* a bad fit for Harry Lane U."

Jen said, "Fetz, sixty seconds."

I picked up my coffee and another for Nelson. "Thanks for bringing these," I said on the way out.

Naively.

26: JEN

I TYPE "LOSERS" BUT it appears in the IRC window a nanosecond after Violetfire and ignite sign off.

2:17 a.m. and it's just me and a blinking cursor. Crap. I hate being the last one left.

Everything's quiet. Like the world's slipped into a coma.

Maybe I could edit the calls we got today on the show. Best call-in ever, so many angry post-Bush-protest Portlanders, so many pissed-off Laneys, so many excellent points. Good idea of Nelson's to make a downloadable file of the highlights.

But audio editing's the last thing I feel like doing.

There's the folder with Dee's cell-phone pictures. Heh. Me and Nelse eating breakfast. Mr. Nguyen wiping a table. Blackberry vines in the back yard. She was so excited to see them on the screen, and soooo disappointed when she saw the prints. "They're blurry," she said.

"Well it's 72 dpi," I told her. "What do you expect?"

She'd looked up at me. "I have no idea what you're bleedin' talking about."

"Think of it as the ideal resolution for electronic storage and delivery."

She looked at the prints, looked back at me. Frowned. "Pardon?"

Told her she could donate the phone to me, but she didn't like that idea.

I open the Maryville firebombing clip on the site. For some reason I keep watching it. A good job, if I may say so myself. Split widescreen, simultaneous views from my camera and Nelson's. The horses are fucking amazing, even at this size. People must think so 'cause it's getting hits on the site.

I close the laptop and it makes a fat click.

Under the stack of *Infiltration* is the stencil.

And it's warm out. And everyone's asleep.

Backpack. Two cans: red and white. Roll them slowly to keep the ball bearings quiet. Folded aluminum foil. Black T-shirt. Wallet out and on the desk. Keys front pocket. Hair up, cap on, black bike helmet, time to go.

I RIDE AROUND LAURELHURST park and shake the cans, then head back down to Hawthorne. Thank you Jesus, Deirdre and Nelson were asleep as I snuck past them in the basement. The clock on the corner of Thirty-Ninth says 2:38. A single car at the intersection, then the light turns green and it moves on. Clock says 67 degrees. No breeze. No cops. No one in sight. The lights on in Fred Meyer but nobody's home. Still straddling the bike, out comes the virgin stencil, out comes the white can. Shake one two quick and spray. The hiss of it loud in the night, the smell of enamel catching in the back of my throat. Stupid nozzle dribbles white on my finger, but there it is shining bright and true on the TriMet bus stop plexi.

t h e y
p e p p e r
s p r a y e d
b a b i e s

Damn, that feels good.

The foil crackles orange in the streetlight as I wrap the stencil. No cops to the east, none to the west. North and south are clear; let's go reclaim some more of the commons.

Empty streets make it easy, flying with the summer night on my face.

This time it's in red, on the sidewalk at Hawthorne and Thirty-Fourth. Reality hacking. Making a place in the system for *my* response, fuckers. Belmont and Thirty-Fourth. Take this unit of cultural information and fucking let it into your brains, damn it. Belmont and Forty-Fourth outside Movie Madness, good foot traffic here. Spread it around, folks. Back to Hawthorne at Twentieth, then Division at Twenty-First. Subvert the message. Change the message. Division at Eighth, another bus stop. Let the message loose.

•••

THAT WAS MAYBE A knock.

Another knock.

"What, dammit? I'm trying to sleep."

Through the door Fetzer says, "It's after nine. Even Romeo's up."

"So?" Got to change these sheets today.

"We're interviewing the woman from Save the Cascades at ten."

"Oh. Yeah. Crap." My ass is reluctant to haul. White and red enamel all over my hands.

Damn, it's on my pants, too. The doorknob starts to turn. "Hold on!" My room stinks of spray paint. I open the window, pick another T-shirt off my floordrobe, and squeeze out through the smallest possible opening in the door.

Fetzer tries to peek in. "You got a, uh, friend in there?" he says, soft and surprised.

Hands in pockets. "Nah. Just cataloging my stash of enviro-porn. I gotta powder my nose—I'll see you down there."

He sniffs the air, then one side of his face creases with a half-frown. "Right."

27: FETZER

WE'D PICKED UP THE mail from the P.O. box, then stopped for coffees on the way home. No hate mail that day, but we did get our first issue of the *Harry Lane Gazette*. Being banned from campus had spurred Nelson to sign up for the monthly alumni newsletter. And as Jen skimmed the rag she noticed a call for artists for Harry Lane's photography gallery.

"This could be our way back in," she said.

It took me a moment to get her point.

"She means Deirdre," said Nelson. "And it's ideal. No one there knows her."

"Hah, that is true," I said. "What do they want, a resume?"

"Portfolio," said Jen. "Call for an appointment."

"You think she'll mind?" I asked.

"I'm sure she'd be happy to," said Nelson. Smug.

I got out the phone and made the call.

But when we got home Sylvia's Audi TT was parked outside the house. She had one of the gray ones. I secretly coveted it.

We could hear them cackling from downstairs. They were sitting on the velvet kitchen sofa, a bottle of wine between them, Sylvia with her legs crossed and her arm along the sofa back.

I sternly greeted Dee with, "I told you never to open the door when you're alone." Dee and Sylvia gaped at each other, then they held up their matching cell phones and took pictures of us standing there like idiots.

Despite the camera phone being a disappointment, Deirdre couldn't stop using it.

"Don't tell me we had a meeting," said Jen.

Sylvia shook her head. "Just dropping by."

I told Deirdre we got her a show in a gallery, and she lowered her phone. "You what?"

"Harry Lane University has this gallery devoted to photography!" said Nelson. "Well, we didn't exactly get you a show, more like an appointment to talk to the curator."

Alarm jangled in Dee's eyes. "When?"

Jen looked at her watch. "Three."

Deirdre jumped up. "You're bleedin' joking. You think I'm going in for an interview like that with no flippin' preparation? You're out of your tiny minds! I don't even have a portfolio together. How am I supposed to pull a portfolio together so fast?"

Nelson gestured meekly in the direction of the basement. "We thought you could just take that binder you have."

"Then you didn't think too clearly, did you?" She paced. "It takes *time* to get ready for something like this. I can't just *waltz* in there with a stack of photos under me arm. I have to do research. Find out what they're looking for. Edit me pictures down to fit." She whirled around. "Jaysus Christ, you think it's easy, don't you, just pick up a few snaps you have lying around and have a wee chat about them and you're flyin' it. Well it's *not like that*."

"Holy cow," said Jen. "Girl's got lungs."

Nelson said, "Deirdre, please, could you keep still a minute?"

Hands on hips, she stopped in front of me. "You *could've* asked."

"Look," I said, "Don't sweat it. The main thing is to get you on campus. Doesn't matter what your portfolio looks like."

Nelson winced.

Deirdre crossed her arms. "It doesn't matter what me *portfolio* looks like?"

I apologized. Nelson persuaded her back to the sofa, sat her down. Calmed her down. Suggested she exhibit her work more. That she treat this like a trial run, and that he'd help her find other venues.

OUT FROM UNDER HER cot came the heavy binder. She turned pages and muttered, "I'll have to choose them in the car. Shit. Shit. They're all mixed up. There's Stuart from last year. Sal in New York, and Sal again with Rico and Janey. And there's that famous fountain."

"Deirdre," I said, "you can do better than a show at a college. Nelson's right, this is just practice. You should get these out. In a magazine or something."

"It's amazing any of them's survived," she murmured.

I said, "They were made by a survivor."

The smile she gave me was watery and grateful.

I reached down and touched a picture of an old woman in what looked like a city park. Shadows from some object out of the frame covered her in unplaceable, confusing shapes.

"Something about them," I said, "kinda grabs at you."

28: JEN

"HERE SHE COMES," SAYS Fetz to the rearview.

"Finally," I say. "Thought she'd been swallowed by the Ministry of Truth."

Deirdre waves at us through the window as if waiting forty-five minutes for her in this stinking underground garage hasn't been a giant waste of our time. Nelson flips the seat forward and she climbs in the back. "Nancy's gorgeous!" she says. Then she goes on about meeting the curator, seeing the gallery space, and that Reynolds is apparently "cheesed off" that there's posters up all over campus protesting the Pentagon contract.

"You get photos of them?" I ask.

"A few." She giggles. "I felt like such a spy. And Nancy loves your hair, by the way."

"Huh?"

"She said, 'I've never seen such fine hair on a white girl.' And I got a show! In December! But the thing is, the curator doesn't want the work I have, she wants new work. Images that 'speak to the local or regional culture.'"

"You must be present to win," I say.

They fall into a discussion about how she'll need a real camera, and a darkroom, and Dee whines, "I have no idea how I'm going to pull it off."

I say, "What would you take photos of?" I'm thinking the bridges, trilliums in Forest Park, roses, the usual stereotypical Portland images.

She leans forward, and I can smell the mint on her breath. Girl eats a lot of mints. "You."

"Me?"

"The lot of you."

"Aie," says Fetzer, "I don't like that idea."

"Can't," I say. "Security."

"I don't mean while you're hacking or setting fires, I mean just around the house. You know, dinner, watching TV and so on."

Nelson huffs. "For the record, we do not set fires."

I flip around and say, "For fuck's sake, Deirdre. We just wanted some help getting inside this stupid campus. Don't tell me this is going to turn into some long-term art project."

But she's smiling in a conspiratorial way that makes me pause. "Ah. But Dr. Reynolds would be a collector of fine-art photography, wouldn't he. And he attends the openings."

Fetzer strokes his chin. Nelson slowly smiles, and I have to admit, the idea of that prick seeing our mugs all over his swanky gallery walls is pretty funny.

29: FETZER

THINGS UNFOLDED PREDICTABLY FOR a while. Dee fretted about her exhibition. Jen and I worked. Nelson occupied himself with Dee.

Thanks to Kate Simms at the *Oregon Herald*, our Harry Lane/Pentagon story got more traction. Her angle was somewhat questioning, but one of her editor's conditions (unstated, she told us later, but implied) was to balance that with a "local liberal institution does its part for national security" slant. Nevertheless, from there the story migrated to the noon news, evening news, made it onto the AP wire the next day. Our inbox filled up, and the phone rang a few times—mostly independent sites, but a couple of mainstream dailies, too. No doubt Reynolds's phone rang itself off his desk, what with the daily anti-Pentagon protests at the university, and the Students for Peace invasion of the Department of Science and Engineering that made the local news. Dozens of folks danced like crazy, while others locked themselves to furniture, big U-locks around their necks. Four fire trucks and twenty po-po cars on the scene. Took them two hours to get the kids out. No tear gas because the press was there, shaky footage on the evening news of Students for Peace making one hell of a joyful noise unto the planet.

Free Speech Radio News requested a follow-up story, and Nelson narrated it in one take, with a shine in his eyes and his voice so clear and smooth that Jen had almost no editing to do. Within a week of that we got offers from three more stations to pick up the national syndication, which took us to fourteen.

We saved the letters to the editor at the *Herald* for a while. About half were critical of surveillance culture and the Pentagon, and the other half wondered what the crazy lefties were thinking, letting terrorists wander around under our video cameras unnoticed. And that anyone who thought differently was unpatriotic, including Kate Simms, and the *Herald* for not firing her. Kate Simms said she wasn't worried. I wasn't worried.

Well, I was worried, but not about the stupid *Herald*.

On the domestic front, Jen and I decided Dee had to go. It was intolerable giving those two their privacy in what was essentially our office, and the only route in and out of the house. And Jen and I didn't want Dee moving upstairs. So one day I waited until Dee was at work and I grabbed a big orange extension cord and went looking for Nelson. Found him in the basement bathroom taking a leak with the door open and the lights off. Perpetual twilight through the grimy window. I let him zip up, then I said, "We need to talk about you and Dee."

He turned into the shadows to flush. "Yeah?"

Two-day-old head stubble under my hand. "She needs to get her own place."

When his face came back around it was the betrayed boy.

"Hey," I said. "It's not the end of the world. She can move in to the other side of the house."

"But it's not hooked up. You're suggesting she go without electricity?"

"Nope. She can use ours." I held up the extension cord. "Couple of these and we drill holes in the wall and run them through to power strips."

I told Nelson I'd snuck over there earlier and checked out the top floor, which had probably once been a dance studio. The interior walls had been removed, making it one big space, and there was broken mirror all over the floor. I also told him Dee was welcome all hours, all days, and that to be honest I was hoping she'd keep up with the cooking.

Once Nelson saw the place he was into the idea. It had a separate entrance via a metal staircase on the outside of the building. The staircase led to a small foyer with a window that looked out over Novi. We spent fifteen sweaty minutes getting that window unstuck.

Later that afternoon Nelson stood on the balcony at the top of the stairs that was more like a fire escape grating than a balcony. When he saw Deirdre walking down Novi he called out, "Got something to show you."

Her feet clanged up the metal stairs. "I didn't know this was yours," she said.

"It's not," he said. "But come in anyway."

She flapped a hand in front of her face. "Whew, it's stifling." Nelson looked nervous, because if she didn't like it, she was going to end up somewhere farther away.

"Yeah, it faces west," said Nelson. "Nice sunsets."

"Sunsets?" She looked around the empty foyer. "What did you want to show me?"

"Through here," I said, and led her into the main room. We'd cleaned out the broken mirror and swept the floor. The long wall where the mirror had been was blotchy from the glue. Dust motes hung in the air, and the light coming through the tall sash windows on the west side just about scalded your eyeballs.

Deirdre looked around. "This is huge."

Nelson said, "We were wondering if you'd like to move in."

"Here? Jaysus, really?" She threw her arms out and spun in a circle. Then she hugged us both.

It was always a shock when she got close like that. She was small and big and dark and bright at the same time, like she could morph right there in your arms, and you'd be left holding onto something else.

"Glad you like it," I said, and extricated myself.

We showed her the bathroom at the other end. Just a tub, and not even a clawfoot we could've sold for cash. A rusty cabinet over a sink as cracked as ours, and a stained toilet. Through the window you could see the big silver maple in the back yard.

"Hot water," said Nelson, and he opened the closet like it was a game-show prize. "Once Fetzer gets it hooked up."

"We'll rig up a shower head, too," I said.

"We can help you get whatever you need," said Nelson.

"Yeah," I said. "We know the best dumpsters."

WE HAD A GOOD time, fixing up her place. Even Jen helped. Business as usual was set aside as we pulled that big room into something habitable. Franky's muscles bulged like yams getting the furniture up the narrow stairs. Deirdre still didn't have a camera or an enlarger, but it meant a lot to her that she was getting a space that could accommodate her photography. Personally, I didn't like the idea of my mug up on some gallery walls, but I went along with the plan because it meant a lot to me, too, to see her so happy.

I never told anyone, not even afterward, that I went through her stuff sometimes. The first time I didn't find a thing, so I left it alone for a few months. But toward the end I snooped a couple more times. I wasn't proud about running my own Department of Homeland Security, but I just had to do it. I never read her diaries—the musings of a thirty-year-old drifter weren't interesting to me—but I'd go through her clothes and shake out her books. Checked the nooks and crannies of the bathroom. Never came up with what I was looking for. And because I thought I knew what I was looking for, when I found glasses smelling of booze and tacky on the inside, it didn't mean much. By then we were drinking wine with dinner every night, and I figured it was just leftovers.

It was a contractor who found her stash, when we converted her place into the archive a couple of years ago. Her clothes hamper must have sat over that laundry chute trapdoor, barely visible in the grimy bathroom floor. A shelf in there, and lots of dusty bottles. Gin and wine. One from Mrs. Krepelter's case of '97 Pinot Noir. Putting two and two together, I figured Dee must have stolen the '97s early on and replaced them with the '99s when she realized we'd notice.

The contractor thought the stash was funny, but I made him promise to keep his mouth shut.

30: NELSON

NELSON'S SKIN SMARTS IN the sun. His nails are dirty, and he's sticky with sweat. The trees hang still. The front garden weeds are the color of straw. On days like this he can close his eyes and imagine he's walking across a pale Pacific island, or standing in a desert in Nevada ringed with distant mountains. Somewhere scoured clean by heat and light, where mold and mildew can't grow, and neither can regret or fear. But today his eyes don't close on a desert vision because he's heading for the diner. Squint-bright light, and the smell of dry grass and hot pavement.

A truck backs into the tiny parking lot of the bindery on Twelfth. Fumes and dust and the driver watching his mirrors so he doesn't clip the sign. A dime shines from the gutter, and Nelson smiles back. He thought he'd be fixing up Deirdre's place alone, but the others have been great.

"CAN'T WAIT TO SEE IT," she says, and she leans across the counter for a kiss.

"The water heater's ready," he says, "and Franky and Jen found some furniture, which they're repainting as I speak. You're getting a brown chair with red rungs and a red chair with brown rungs. Because that's the paint we have."

"Grand. And a sofa?"

"Found one. It's kind of a pistachio green color. But a bed's going to be harder to find."

She says, "Can't we use yours?" and he explains it won't fit down the basement stairs. And Jen refuses to unseal the front door. The camp cot will still have to do.

He adds, "It's a great place, but boy it's hot in the afternoon."

"It'll be good practice," she says, and points to their favorite booth, "for when I'm burning in hell. Can you stay a bit?"

SHE SETS THE JUICES down, and they slide into the seats.

There's more color in her skin than three months ago.

She says, "What?" to his gaze.

He sips his juice. He gets grapefruit every time now. "What went wrong, sweetheart?"

She frowns. "When?"

"You were so thin when you arrived. So down and out."

She flips back her hair. "Told you. I was hitchhiking. Lost me money. But look how far I've come. And I'm getting a darkroom soon! I can't wait to print photos of you."

He says, "Why didn't you just find an Irish consulate?"

She laughs, then pauses. "It didn't occur to me. Anyway, if I'd done that, I wouldn't have met you, right? It was fate."

"Fate?" The word sounds nonsensical. "But weren't you afraid?"

"Sometimes. But that's to be expected, isn't it? What are you most afraid of, John?"

"Like, a phobia?"

"No, not like that. An existential fear."

His thighs are stuck sweaty to the vinyl. "Fear. Um. Well, I suppose I'm always afraid of what's happening to the planet."

Her eyes wait.

"That we'll reach a point of no return. Environmental collapse. Disasters, starvations, enormous suffering."

Her eyes wait more.

"Not that there isn't enormous suffering already," he adds. "But what a tragic waste it would be. When we have the freedom and ability to make things better, and instead we destroy everything that's so beautiful."

She plays with her straw. "Maybe it's inevitable."

"Excuse me?"

"Perhaps," she says, "it's our fate. To destroy ourselves and take everything down with us. Except for the cockroaches, of course."

She's been replaced with a strange twin. "You're joking, right?"

She drops her eyes to her glass, brings them back up. "No."

"Kind of an outdated concept, don't you think? Fate?"

"It's timeless."

He smiles, shakes his head, and crosses his arms on the table. Leans forward. "Deirdre," he says, trying to keep the condescension out of his voice. He peels one thigh off the vinyl seat. "Scientific revolution? Past couple of hundred years? It's liberated us from ideas like that, right?" He gestures around. "Look at what we've achieved now that we've gotten out from under the idea that we have no control over our future."

"This diner?" she says.

"You know what I mean. Communications. Medicine. Travel. The social freedoms that come from being emancipated from superstition."

She shakes her head and smiles. "Ah, it's all temporary. And control is just an illusion."

"An illusion?" He says it too loud and he brings his voice down. "And what about responsibility? If you believe in fate, you can't take responsibility."

She drops her chin into her hand. "Maybe it's not like that. Perhaps we're a monstrosity. Perhaps nature will let us destroy ourselves, so it can start over."

"No." He shakes his head. Across the room the cappuccino machine hisses steam into Mr. Nguyen's stainless-steel jug. Three girls are at the counter, midriffs showing, the flares on their jeans printed to look like sixties embroidery. The exuberant self-expression of a generation ago co-opted, mass-produced, and fed back to today's willing consumers.

Nelson's eyes are gritty. "No." He turns back to Deirdre. She's staring at him.

"Oedipus," she says.

"What about him?"

She takes her chin off her hand, sits up straight. "He was wise, right?"

He jiggles his foot under the table. "Uh, I guess so."

"He used his wisdom to defeat the Sphinx and save Thebes."

"Okay. Yeah."

"Well, his wisdom's a crime."

"A crime?"

"It's his undoing. That's the whole point of the story. It disrupts the natural order. Then comes patricide and incest. Nature won't tolerate it, and the time comes when his fate is revealed, and he is plunged into a living hell."

"What? What's that got to do with—"

She says, "We think we've gotten the upper hand, you see, that we've subdued nature and fate. But nature and fate bide their time, then they bite back."

The sore place is awakening in Nelson's chest. He peels his arm off the tabletop.

Deirdre shrugs. "Too much knowledge is a crime, see? Better to stay ignorant." She taps a finger on the table, then points. "In fact, as Silenus said, best not to be born at all."

"Christ. How can you even *say* that?"

Diner patrons look up, stare for a moment, look away.

Tender Deirdre, who makes Garden of Eden love, makes him cups of tea, takes pastries to the homeless guys—it's like a fissure has opened and strange goo is oozing out of her head.

"Sorry," he says, quieter. "I'm just surprised, that's all. You're being so—so nihilistic."

"Hmm," she says, and looks out the window. Squints in the sun. "More of a pessimist, really."

"Whatever. It's—it seems too cavalier. Too carefree."

Her laugh is sour. "Hardly carefree." She glances back at him. "Death's the big thing, isn't it. The one place we're all heading."

"So this is your big fear?" he says.

Her eyes follow cars along Division Street. "Don't want it to be."

"But it's normal to be afraid of death," he says.

She leans toward him and her face goes wide and bright. "Hey, you know that part in *Peter Pan* where Peter is marooned on a rock, and the tide is rising and he knows he's going to drown?"

The table's pink Formica swims with overlapping swirls. How does she make him feel like he's never read a thing? "No."

"Ah. It was probably left out of the Disney version. So he's standing there and his heart is pounding and the water is lapping at his toes. And it suddenly occurs to him, 'To die would be an awfully big adventure.'"

The points of her smile are like blades. The sore place swells in his chest.

"Isn't that brilliant?" she says. Her face is full of reflected pink. "What if you could live like it were true?"

Burning damp stings his eyes. She takes his floppy, confused hands in hers. "You all right, love?" She passes him a paper napkin. It's dry and comfortable against his face. "Forget it, okay?" she says. "It's just silly talk."

The screwed-up napkin is damp in his hand. Out the window an afternoon breeze shudders the elm leaves. Her face has gone soft with concern. He breathes in deep, and the sore place cools like a coal dropped on snow. "It's okay," he says.

As long as he can hold her hand. As long as they love each other, it's all going to be okay.

THEY'D SET UP FANS in two of the windows, but it's still ninety outside and an oven inside. Everyone's being a trouper, trying not to complain. Nelson is grateful.

The fans thrum the air, and the tiny fridge Fetzer picked up outside a house on Belmont whines as it tries to keep on top of its task. It makes it hard to hear the music, a John Coltrane CD they'd bought her, along with the boombox, as a housewarming present. And Jen had made Deirdre some business cards and handed them to her in an envelope with a shrug. "Since, you know, you're having that show."

Just her name, address, phone number. Black on white. A simple design, but it looks good. Deirdre had laughed at the cards like they were quaintly absurd. Then she put a hand over her mouth and mumbled, "Jaysus. I'm really staying, aren't I?"

"That's good of you," Nelson had said to Jen.

Deirdre's phone rings and she sits down on the red chair with brown rungs. "Sylvia! Come over! We're having a housewarming. Me new place."

Of course. He should have thought to invite Sylvia himself.

Jen splits a bag of ice and tumbles it into the cooler.

Fetzer brings in another fan, an old standing rotary. "Bathroom door," he says to Nelson. "To pull cooler air from the shaded side."

Nelson helps him set up the fan. "Thanks," he says to Fetzer. "Really. I appreciate it."

FOUR BEERS, AND NELSON has to hold on to the back of the sofa. "Must be the heat," he says, and he starts laughing.

"Whoa!" says Franky, and he catches the rotary fan before it hits the floor.

Christ. Tripping over the cord already. Now that he's up, his bladder is urgently full. "Back in a minute," he says.

The sound of heels clangs up the metal stairs. Must be Sylvia, finally.

"Least no one can get up here unnoticed," says Fetzer.

Nelson closes the bathroom door and unzips. Fetzer's always worrying about ambushes.

He lifts the toilet seat. "PUT ME DOWN!" is lettered in sharpie underneath, and he laughs.

It's quieter in here, and not as hot. The air smells of bleach, and a cool light glows off the new aqua-blue shower curtain.

When he comes out there's a new microwave perched on top of the salvaged fridge, and Sylvia's sitting in his place on the pale pistachio sofa. Franky's taking a phone photo of her and Deirdre, arms around each other, lifting their beers in a toast.

"Oooh, let's see," says Dee, and Franky hands her the phone.

Jen's lying on the floor, her head on a cushion, a beer balanced on her stomach, chatting with Fetzer. Fetzer's on the brown chair, his feet up on the red one. The music's easier to hear now that they've turned off one of the window fans. Franky takes a bite of his raspberry popsicle, sits back down on the cot, and it squeaks like crazy. Gotta oil the thing. Sometimes it squeaks so much when they make love, they burst out laughing.

Things are so much better. When Nelson joined them six years ago, it wasn't like this. There was no resting. No sweet times. It was anger and fear and sleepless nights crawling around with black on his face. It was striving to prove himself. It was arguing about tactics. And sometimes it was pure, simple panic. And things coming out of himself that made him wonder what sort of person he'd be if he was pushed to the edge.

Like the last time they were helping build tree-sit platforms. Getting ready to send two comrades up into hemlocks as wide as upturned buses. Nelson was carrying heavy coils of rope down a gully. Jen was fifty feet in front, and Fetz was uphill on the other side of the gully with the others. Jen had reached the stream at the bottom when the guy appeared from behind a giant root ball. Suspenders, no belt, frayed pant legs. A logger. The guy grabbed Jen's pack, pulled it off. Then the second guy appeared. With a rifle. They turned her pack upside down. Tools fell out. "Fucking greenies fucking everything up" echoed through the forest. The coils of rope tumbled from Nelson's arms. He knew this was how it was going to end. This was what Lise would read in the papers. What they'd tell his dad when they broke the news. What they'd tell Craig.

Jen was running, but the rifle was already balanced on a shoulder, an eye to the scope, and the futility of it all was pulling at Nelson's knees, sucking him down.

The forest filled with the sound of the others crashing through the undergrowth, and the loggers roaring ". . . fucking idiots need to be taught whose forest this is . . ." Then someone shrieked, "John!" and next thing he knew he was moving. The wrecking sense of futility was gone, and he only knew a pounding need to get between Jen and that rifle. The bang was so loud he almost fell over, but he wasn't hit, and when he looked up she was still ahead, panting and grunting. Roots tripped him, the stream's bank slid away under his feet, branches whipped his face, but he gained on her till she wheeled around and lifted a broken branch over her head. She threw the branch sideways. "Fuck! Dude! I thought you were one of them." She grabbed his hand and together they stumbled all the way to the road.

Everyone made it to the van alive. "They were just trying to scare us," Fetzer had said. He was the only one not shaking too much to drive, so he drove, even though it was Ralph's van.

Nelson still wonders if Fetzer wasn't just saying that to calm them down.

And later that night when they huddled together and drank soup and gave each other backrubs, Nelson said he couldn't understand why the sorest place was between his shoulder blades. Everything else hurt, but his back felt like someone had stood on him in heavy boots.

Corynn dug her thumbs around his scapula. He had a huge crush on her, but she hadn't entered his mind when he was running. Strange what the body does when the brain can't think.

"You were bracing for a bullet," said Fetzer. And everyone went quiet. Having a vet on board with jungle experience wasn't just sorta interesting anymore.

"Nelson!" says Deirdre, and she's patting the space that's opened up between her and Sylvia on the sofa. "You dreamy ninny, come sit down!"

"And congratulations," says Sylvia. She also pats the sofa.

Nelson just smiles and pulls another beer from the sloshy ice in the cooler. He pops the cap on his way over to Dee and Sylvia and their welcoming faces.

There's a lot to be grateful for.

31: JEN

THE BALD DUDE HOLDS open the basement door and gives me that look.

"Forget it," I say, "I've got to finish this blog post."

"We need the extra pair of hands," he says.

"Building her stupid darkroom is not on my to-do list."

Fetzer's outline is portly against the light. "The sooner this gets done, the sooner I'm back on the newsletter."

He has a point. I grab my coffee and a paper and follow him out the door.

But—no one's at the car. "So where are they?" I ask.

Fetzer stomps up the metal stairs. He bangs on Deirdre's door, yells, "We said *nine a.m.*," and stomps back down so hard the stairs wobble.

"I told him we'd give them an hour to get this lumber." He holds up a forefinger. "*One* hour."

Mug of coffee in my right, *Seattle Times* upside down in my left. "I'm sick of him sleeping in. We're not getting through the papers."

Fetzer leans his butt against the Toro, folds his arms. "I noticed."

Used to be if we got behind on shit Nelson would start nagging. Now it's like he doesn't even care.

Deirdre's door opens, and I hate the way Fetz and I look up like a couple of baby birds, so I flip the *Times* in the air and catch it right way up. *BUSH VOWS VICTORY IN WAR ON TERROR.*

Two pairs of feet on the stairs, syncopated and light and hollow, and Nelson says, "Sorry," in a breathy voice. But he isn't. He doesn't give a rip 'cause he gets to flatten her into the mattress whenever he wants. Squeak squeak *squeak* through my bedroom wall. Aie.

Nelson spins his keys on his finger and says, "I'll drive." Breezy, like he's James fucking Bond. Dee flips the seat forward and climbs in the back.

Great, and I'm in the middle. Could go in the back with Dee, but—crap. She's brought that fucking camera, too. The thing's as heavy as a brick, and almost as big. Some obsolete analog piece of junk she found on eBay.

"Leave it at home some time, Deirdre."

"Now why would I want to do that?" she says, and smiles like I made a joke. She murmurs near my ear. "No need to be shy." That mint on her breath again.

The camera shutter clicks then the springs squeak from her bouncing back on the seat. No, don't remind me, please.

"I know you love it," she says, all soft and flirty, and my heart lurches and my coffee almost tips over.

"Know how I can tell?" she says, and I'm about to say I'm a heavy sleeper and I have no idea what you're talking about, but she says, "You're brushing your hair more."

"Am not," I say, and swat her hand off my damn hair.

Ugh. I *so* should have banged on the wall the first time I heard them.

Fetzer sinks into the seat next to me, slams the door and says, "Did you notice *I've* been brushing my hair more?" He slides his hand over his shiny dome and Deirdre giggles.

"We all in?" says Nelson. He switches on the GPS, turns the car around with one hand lazy on the wheel, and heads for Twelfth.

Used to be if he was late for anything he'd at least apologize.

Newspaper on my knee. "Listen up, people." I say. "'President Bush vowed victory in the 'first great struggle of the new century' today as he led the nation in marking the shattering terrorist attacks of one year ago.'"

The Chimp-in-Chief looks out at me. His stupid ears, the wrinkles of fake sincerity on his brow. There's the snap of breaking paper and my finger is through the photo. Poke, rip, finger severs jugular. Up the through the face, through the headline, separating "Seattle" from "Times."

"You got some kind of problem with the guy?" says Fetzer. Nelson snorts. And Dee's been clicking the camera the whole time.

"Can't a citizen," I say, and turn around to her, "deface a photo of the unelected *resident* in peace?"

"I love it," she says, and clicks another one. Lowers the camera. That sharp smile.

The car in front has a bumper sticker with an outline of the towers and an outline of the Pentagon, and it says, *Never Forgive Never Forget*.

"Give it a rest," I say.

Nelson checks her in the rearview. "You bring the list?" he says, and they all start talking about her fucking darkroom. Crazy idea, shutting yourself up in total darkness to make pictures. And in the bathroom, no less. Seems vaguely gross, working in a bathroom.

Dee sits forward again. "You're all brilliant for helping out, thanks."

Her minty breath.

This is *such* a waste of bandwidth.

"No problem," I say. "We've got plenty of time. We're only trying to save the planet. It's not like there's any urgency or anything."

32: FETZER

IT WAS A COOL morning in early fall when she came prancing up to the kitchen with the thing still wet. It sticks in my mind, because Franky had come by and brought in the morning papers. From which we learned of Tony Blair's dossier of so-called evidence of the Iraqi arsenal of chemical and biological weapons, and Saddam's plans to use them.

"Me first print!" Dee said, and waved it in our breakfasting faces. It was a black and white of Nelson of course, with the light just right on his face as he gazed out one of her windows, his eyes searching the world for an answer. It's a nice piece. I still have a copy.

"Five more rinsing in the bath," she said. "That system with the siphon? It's brilliant."

I'd taught her about hydrostatic pressure, and to shove the hose down the sink pipe far enough that it was below the top of the bathwater. Good thing the sink's strainer was missing.

"Isn't he beautiful?" she said.

"Cool picture," said Franky. "Black and white makes it look, you know, classic."

Jen turned down her mouth and nodded. High praise.

Nelson said, "I don't remember you taking that."

She kissed the top of his head. "You were watching Chuck and Eb and Sinclair wheel their carts down the street."

He took the photo from her. "For Christ's sake, you can see my wrinkles."

"Smile lines." She snatched the photo back and headed for the basement. "I loooove my new enlarger," she sang as she went down the stairs.

"You've been traded," I said.

"Yup," said Jen, and she snapped her paper straight. "She looooves her new enlarger."

Nelson rubbed a hand over his eyes. "She started at six. Wouldn't let me into the bathroom."

"Aww," I said. "Missed your morning blow job. Too bad."

"Shut up," said Nelson.

Franky said, "It's breakfast time, guys. Keep it decent."

The headline on page two was *PLAN EMERGES FOR SHORT, INTENSE WAR.*

A COUPLE OF WEEKS later we were surprised by a visit from Sylvia. Deirdre jacked her within ten minutes, took her over to the "studio," as it was by then called. We followed, and that's when we got our first inkling of what Deirdre was up to. And when I say "we," I'm not including Nelson, who spoke daily about how hard she was working and how great the show was going to be. We'd pretty much ignored him until we saw for ourselves that he wasn't just blowing hot air. Half of Dee's long, glue-stained wall was filled with a patchwork of glossy black-and-white photos. Nelson. Franky. Jen. Me. The car. The diner. The homeless guys. Even the damn shed.

"Hey," said Franky. "That's me." Like he'd never seen a photo of himself. Or more like he'd never seen one he hadn't posed for. He was at the sink, and she must have been on the kitchen sofa to get him from that angle. She really was a master of natural light, and the way it played on his face was perfect. But he looked sad. Concentrating, I guess, on the dishes that were out of the frame, but his eyes were downcast and there was a sag in his mouth.

"I look like crap," he said. "You're not putting that one in the show. Please say you're not."

Deirdre just smiled. Sylvia stepped up to the photo. "You should definitely include it."

"But it's horrible," said Franky.

Sylvia pointed at another photo and said, "This one's good." A sentiment she didn't express lightly. It was a shot of Jen and me, pouring fuel in the shed. Again, the light. Catching the big glass flask. It must have been late afternoon with the sun raking across each slat on the shed wall, and me and Jen looking like a couple of pioneers oblivious to the larger world.

"And this one," said Sylvia, pointing at a photo higher up. She turned to Nelson and said, "Darling. Almost *too* darling."

Nelson looked embarrassed. Dee must've leaned out her foyer window as he was taking out the recycling. He was looking up at the camera, his face full of that joy and surprise that you see almost exclusively in the pure of heart.

"Oh, that's profound," I said when I spotted one with my boots sticking out from under the Toro. "That one really speaks to the human condition."

"More like the Toro's condition," said Jen. But I had to hand it to Dee for the composition. Somehow, without me knowing, she'd gotten near enough that my boots were up close, taking up most of the picture. The bottom of the chassis was way in the background.

Jen cracked a smile at a picture of herself, her hair and shoulders lost in the clutter of the basement, her hands on a keyboard.

Sylvia stepped back and surveyed the wall-of-us. "This is going to be a knock-out show."

Deirdre smiled and hugged her shoulders.

Then Sylvia realized the camp cot was Deirdre's bed, and she offered her pillowtop because she was getting a waterbed.

"Wow," said Nelson. That's very generous of you."

And, naively, I agreed.

IT WAS NOT LONG after that we got a call from Nancy at Harry Lane University.

"It's sure getting crazy around there."

"The protests?" I said.

Nancy had told us earlier, after the first Students for Peace takeover of Sci and Eng, that she'd befriended the campus activists. A few words about Angela Davis visiting the co-op in the eighties seemed to win their trust, and she corresponded with them through a home email account.

"Uh-huh. There's a daily vigil outside Science and Engineering. It's like a gauntlet."

"Interesting."

"Uh-huh. And Engineering's split. A third of the kids are against the contract. They're boycotting classes. The other two-thirds are pissy that they can't work in peace."

"How's Reynolds?"

"He's on the phone all the damn time. Now that he's gotta walk through that vigil any time he wants to go someplace, he pretty much stays in his office and does his business by phone."

"He okay to you?"

"Oh sure. He has no idea I got a brain between my ears that harbors opinions, so we get along. How's that little Deirdre, anyhow? She taking pictures for the exhibition?"

"Like gangbusters."

"She should come back here. There's going to be a die-in next Tuesday morning at nine. Students are gonna lie all over the quad like the place has been bombed." Nancy dropped into a snicker. "It's secret, okay? But she might want to take photos."

I said, "Admit it, you're having fun."

Nancy laughed so loud I had to hold the receiver away from my ear.

Thing is, we were distracted. With a war on the horizon and a peace movement picking itself up and dusting itself off after Vietnam, there was even more to do than usual. Part of me resisted getting involved in Harry Lane U again. We'd outed them, and now important stakeholders—the students—were protesting. We'd done our job, let them do theirs.

But when I returned to the breakfast table and told Jen and Nelson about the divided student body, the vigil, and the die-in Dee could photograph, I got interested in that damn university all over again.

I said, "Thing I don't understand is, how does Reynolds get to throw his weight around? He's the head of one department. The university has, what, dozens?"

"Yeah," said Jen. "Why's this one guy got so much privilege and influence?"

Out of habit we looked at Nelson to provide the next morsel of information, make a clever connection, remember some nerdy detail. But he was glazed like a donut, so full of Deirdre he could barely see straight.

"Maybe we should all go see the die-in?" he mumbled instead. "Undercover."

33: NELSON

NELSON TUGS AT A chunk of russet hair above Fetzer's ear. "It's crooked."

"It's *fine,*" says Fetzer, and swats his hand away. "*Quit* it."

Jen turns the car around and heads for Twelfth. She says, "Can't the guy wear fake hair in peace?"

Dee sits forward from the backseat. Lays her hands on Fetzer's shoulders. "You don't want to be walking about looking gormless, do you?" she says, and Nelson smothers a laugh. Eight thirty a.m. and already he's punchy. They really need to get more sleep.

"It does need a wee bit of adjusting," Dee says, and Fetzer submits to her tugging.

"You brought your camera?" says Nelson, and Dee whacks his shoulder. Because of course he asked her that already. He reaches over the seat and pretends to whack her back and she ducks, then slumps across the back seat with a giggle.

Jen sighs.

"Sorry," says Nelson, and he faces forward. Jen's been so touchy lately.

NELSON LOOKS UP AT the sleek white structure. "This wasn't here when I was here. It was an old Victorian house. I think it used to be Philosophy." They all cup their hands around their eyes and peer through the glass. The gallery walls are empty, and a small ladder sits in the middle of the shiny wooden floor.

"Dear God, it's bigger than I remember," says Deirdre.

Nelson says, "I can't wait to see your work in there."

To think he used to be ambivalent about her style. Now he can see how good she is. And watching her print—the ghost images burning their way onto the paper—it's like magic.

He's never been so close to someone so creative.

Jen looks at her watch. "We need to get to the quad."

PEOPLE HAVE STARTED LYING down. The ground is wet, but they're just lying right on top of it. In all sorts of positions.

"That the vigil?" says Jen, and she points across the quad to a clutch of people in coats. A handful of chairs. Signs leaning up against the steps to Hewell. Coffees are being handed around.

"See the lady giving out coffees?" Nelson says to Deirdre. "She works in the cafeteria. I think her name is Claris. We used to chat about perennials."

Deirdre lifts the camera, zooms in, takes a picture. Then another shot of the growing die-in.

But of course he can't walk up to Claris and say hello because he's wearing a longish blond wig, and if anyone asks he's a Dutch exchange student studying violin for a semester.

"I want to get a shot from above," says Deirdre, and they all look up at the buildings framing the quad.

"Funnily enough, your best bet might be Hewell," says Fetzer.

"Gah!" says Nelson. "Okay. Then let's go to the top floor so we don't bump into Reynolds."

But when the elevator doors open there's Reynolds. Nelson's effervescence vanishes. Reynolds is talking to another guy. They're waiting to get on. Nelson's limbs stall. Fetzer steps out and to the right, and he manages to follow.

Only when they hear the lift doors close do they stop.

Nelson's heart is thumping on his ribs. "That was the guy," he whispers to Deirdre, and she goes, "Ooooh," and looks back at the elevator, smiling behind her hand.

Jen clutches her cloth cap. "Seek shelter and cover head."

Fetzer rolls his eyes at the universe. "Got that over with, at least."

Large windows line the hall, and spectators have gathered to look down at the quad. Nelson squeezes in between students and guides Deirdre in front of him. The quad is now full of bodies. The bodies lie horribly still. Dozens and dozens of dead. It's hard to watch.

"Check it out," says Jen. Nelson follows her gaze to a photographer with a giant camera and a black camera bag over his shoulder. He crouches to take a photo. "Maybe the *Herald*?" she says.

"That's exactly what they want," says one of the students between Nelson and Jen. "Exhibitionists that they are."

"Fucking lame," says another. "Lying on the ground like a bunch of retards."

Nelson catches Jen's eye. The crowd around them is thickening, and he has to brace to avoid squashing Deirdre against the glass.

"Shut up," says someone else. "This is awesome."

"Is this a dance thing?" says a woman. She's standing on tiptoe to see and cradling manila folders to her chest. Maybe a teacher, maybe not, it's hard to tell.

"Are you kidding?" says Jen. "They're protesting a possible war against Iraq."

A voice behind Nelson mutters, "Gay bitches."

"Really?" says the woman, like she's never heard of the buildup to war. "But what's it supposed to *be*?"

"Like lying down's gonna stop a war," says a voice.

"Douchebag hippies."

"It does make you think," Nelson says, "what this place would look like if it was bombed."

"So?" says a guy. "Who's gonna bomb Harry Lane?"

Nelson says, "Well, what *any* place would look like if it were bombed. The point is, modern warfare kills a huge number of civilians—"

"Isn't this about that Pentagon contract?" says a voice.

"Should nuke the fuckers for harboring Bin Laden," says another.

Nelson says, "Iraq isn't harboring Bin—"

"Five million to make spy machines or something."

"Four and a half million. To develop software."

That voice behind Nelson was older. Male.

"I think it's actually five," says Nelson.

He can't see Jen or Fetzer anymore. The bodies in the quad below are packed tight, and some of the building entrances are blocked.

"It's four and a half. I should know," the man says, but when Nelson turns, he can't tell who spoke.

A fight breaks out in the quad below.

Nelson whispers to Deirdre, "I'm going to guide you backward, okay?"

and he wraps his arms around her and pushes back against the press of bodies. The last thing he sees out the window is campus security breaking up the fight.

EVERY QUAD-FACING WINDOW IS packed with people, and for a moment Nelson imagines the building tipping over under the uneven weight.

"Christ," mutters Jen. "I thought this was a liberal school."

"It is," Nelson insists. "It's like it's been infected."

"Let's look around," says Fetzer. "Since folks are so preoccupied."

Lecture rooms are empty, just book bags and coffees left behind like some academic Mary Celeste. In one lab a video is on pause, the chemical chain reaction diagram stopped in its tracks. Office doors are open, with nobody at the desks. A printer spits paper onto the carpet.

"I reckon we should drop in on the fourth floor," says Jen.

"Just for fun," says Fetzer.

"Just for fun," says Nelson, and the lightheadedness returns. He winks at Deirdre and together they all slip into the stairwell.

NANCY'S OFFICE IS EMPTY. The door to Reynolds's office is open.

"Who's going in?" says Jen.

"What are we looking for?" says Nelson. The wall beside him seems to come closer, then moves away. He puts his hand out to steady it. "We haven't thought this through."

Fetzer says, "I'll go, you three keep walking."

"I'll go," says Deirdre. "He doesn't know me."

"I'll go," says Jen, and next second she's crossing Nancy's office. She peeks around the doorframe, then she gives a thumbs-up, steps into Reynolds's office and out of sight.

"Shit," says Fetzer. "We don't have a plan." He looks up and down the hall. "You two walk. I'll guard." He gives Nelson a push, and he and Deirdre amble toward the window crowded with spectators at the end of the hall.

"Ohmygod," says a woman nearby. Her hair is stick-straight blond and her eyes are wide on him. Who the hell is she? Oh, please don't let this be some girl he dated. No, too young.

"Oh. My. God." she says again. Her hands cup her face, then press against her thighs. "You *so* look like Kurt Cobain!"

"I do?"

Deirdre squeezes his hand hard. "Excuse, please," she says. "Not good English."

He's supposed to be Dutch!

"Hel-lo," he says, and holds out his other hand to the stupid woman. "I am not Kurt Cobain. I am Jacob Meertens."

"Oh, but you soooo look like him," the woman gushes, and she takes his hand in both of hers. "Like back from the dead, you know? Kaylee!" she calls, and she points down at Nelson's head. "Come meet this guy! He totally looks like Cobain!"

Heads turn, eyes look him up and down, slide away. Kaylee appears and studies him. "Kinda," she says. "But friendlier. With glasses. Awesome."

There's movement behind him, then, "*There* you are, Jacob," says Fetzer. "You need to quit wandering off like that." Fetzer scoops them up without breaking his stride.

IT'S NOT TILL THEY'RE in the car and Fetzer is pulling out of the parking space that Nelson asks, "Find anything?"

"Not sure," says Jen. "I got this." She tugs a wad of folded papers from her back pocket. "The file on his screen? I sent it to print. Plus there was this note in the middle drawer of his desk."

It's small. In pencil. On Harry Lane University note pad paper.

"You took the note?"

"No," says Jen. "I made a hologram of it which I am now holding in my hand."

Fetzer's shaking his head. "A note he keeps in a drawer? He's going to miss it for sure."

"There were other notes in there that looked the same. Sheesh, it's not like I took them all." Then Jen pats her hip and goes, "Wait, I did take them all!"

Nelson's heart does a flip. "Please tell me you didn't."

Jen digs around, elbows him in the ribs, pulls out Deirdre's phone. "You forgot this, darlin'."

"Me phone!" Deirdre's hand reaches from the back seat, but Jen snatches the phone away.

"I need to keep it till I download the photos. I only grabbed this one 'cause it's so faint I thought the camera wouldn't pick up the writing."

Nelson leans his head back until it's resting on the firm leather of the seat. He lets out a moan that turns into a laugh.

Fetzer smirks and shakes his head. "Well, what's on the note?"

"It's just numbers. By the way, Sylvia called for you, like, twice."

"And what's the printout?" says Fetzer.

"Numbers, too."

"Me? What did she say?" asks Deirdre.

Jen shrugs. "I didn't answer."

Nelson would like to take the rest of the day off. Except it's only ten a.m. He gazes sideways at the printout in Jen's hand. "Looks like the department budget."

"What a waste," says Jen. "Wish he was drafting something resignable. Like a dirty email to a teenage boy."

"YOU KEEP LOOKING AT that one," says Deirdre.

"It keeps pulling me back," says Sylvia. Nelson glances up. They're talking about the one of him on the sidewalk. Everyone says it's so great, but it makes him look young. Looking young has plagued him his whole life.

Sylvia winks at Nelson, then turns back to the photos. The ice clinks in her glass. "None of me, darling?"

Nelson returns to the budget. Something about it. And something about the note. All the notes, which have been downloaded from Dee's phone and printed out, the handwriting a little fuzzy, but readable. Columns of numbers, often the same numbers over and over again, in different order.

"Course there's some of you," says Deirdre, "Here. From when you came to dinner."

Sylvia makes a tiny startled sound. "When did you take those?"

"You and Fetzer got into that conversation about hydrogen cells and I snuck me camera out."

Nelson knows the ones she means. Four photos of Sylvia on the brown velvet kitchen sofa. Legs crossed. Arm along the back. Arm off the back, gesturing. Twisting around to say something to Jen, who's out of the shot. She looks regal.

He envies Sylvia, sometimes, her relentless confidence.

Sylvia and Deirdre giggle. The air smells of lemon and gin, and Nelson reaches for his glass. It's like a spot of snow in a field of heat.

It was nice of Sylvia to bring the gin. And the bucket of ice. And the tonic and the lemons. The gin is some hand-made kind he'd never heard of and is apparently expensive. Deirdre was impressed enough for both of them. He takes a sip of the bitter, complex fluid, then sets the drink back on the desk. The desk is from Sylvia, too, along with the queen bed. Which is so comfortable after the camp cot it's become even harder to disentwine himself from Deirdre each morning.

Now they're looking at the one of Nelson with his apron on, at the stove. Like that first morning when he made her eggs.

Sylvia bumps Deirdre with her hip, and makes a hollow sound laughing into her glass. "How can you stand being so fucking happy?" Then, "Girl, I shouldn't get you drunk. You need to work."

"Don't be worrying about that," says Deirdre. "The prints come out better after a few."

"Yeah, right."

But it's true. Somehow it all just flows. But she does get forgetful. Like when they got back from St. Johns the other day, and he found her door unlocked. Anxious, he let himself in, and when he went down to the end and around the corner, he was relieved to hear her humming behind her bathroom door. He knocked, because it's important not to open the door while she's exposing paper. But he had to pound on the door before the humming stopped. The door creaked open, and there she was: her happy face, a pair of tongs in one hand, the other hand pulling off headphones, the wires tangling in her hair. He squeezed her so tight she yelped. Then the boozy smell hit him.

"It's good to be home," he murmured into her ear. In the bath, prints turned gently in the water dribbling from the tap. She hung off his neck and hummed.

"You're drunk off your ass!" he said, and held her at arms length. It was funny, with her big smile and sleepy eyes, her chin tipped back on a lazy neck.

"I'm *print*ing," she said, and laughed like she'd played a practical joke. She turned in his arms and pointed the tongs at prints hanging from the wire. "Picture of you. Picture of you. Picture of—"

He wrapped his arms across her belly, sank his nose into her hair. "Please don't leave your door unlocked." They shuffled out of the bathroom. On their way over to the bed, the tongs clattered onto the floor.

"So tell me." Sylvia's tanned shoulder nudges Deirdre away from the wall of photos. "What's your secret?"

"To printing?"

Sylvia bumps Deirdre again. "To being so in luuurve."

Nelson doesn't say, *My girlfriend is incredibly hot.* Because that is not the only reason why he loves her.

He wants to have a child with her.

Through the windows the afternoon sky is a still, empty blue. Smiling, Dee and Sylvia land on either end of the pale green sofa.

Deirdre raises her drink. "'Live today, forget the cares of the past.' Epicurus."

"How very wise. But really, what about the, you know—" Sylvia glances at Nelson, then waves her free hand up and down her front.

Heat flushes up Nelson's neck. Is that meant to be a sexual gesture? He says to the budget, "I *am* in the room, you know."

Sylvia leans forward and whispers to Deirdre, loud enough that Nelson can hear, "The ties, girl. The shirts from Sears. I mean, come on," and Deirdre says, "Stop it," but she's smiling. Avoiding his eye.

"I should go next door," says Nelson. He stands, shuffles the pages of the budget together, picks up his drink. But Deirdre is already at his side.

"Don't go," she murmurs. She's really buzzed. One of her small hands is on his back, the other grazes up his front. He has a hard-on already.

Sylvia watches. She slips her feet out of her pointy sandals, lifts her long legs up to the sofa cushions and stretches out.

"I don't care what he wears," says Deirdre. "He has the most beautiful face."

Nelson mutters, "I should go next door."

Sylvia rolls the ice around in the bottom of her glass.

"Never judge a book," says Deirdre. Her mouth is close. If Sylvia wasn't here he'd pick her up and throw her on bed right now.

"Evidently," says Sylvia. She tips up her drink, and he can hear the ice hit her teeth.

Deirdre touches a button on his shirt. "It makes him more fun to unbutton."

"Haaaaa?" says Nelson. He steps backward.

Sylvia's lips twitch. "Go, girl."

"I'll leave you two to it," he says, and he gathers up the papers. It's important that Dee has a friend. He should give them some girl time.

"What about you?" says Dee, as she heads back to the sofa. "Is there an important man in your life?"

As Nelson's stepping out, Sylvia says, "Is there such a thing?"

He closes the door and stands at the top of the stairs. The sun is intense. He's forgotten his drink. He slides down the door till he's sitting on his heels over the hot metal grating. He's going to have to take a cold shower. The budget. He's forgotten the budget! No, it's here, in his hand.

Christ.

He looks at the phone camera prints. On every one of Reynolds's notes, the column of numbers adds up to five hundred thousand.

34: FETZER

A BIG PEACE RALLY happened the same day as our September show. The new phenomenon of regular protests was exciting in concept, but the rally itself turned out dull. A permitted march, long on rhetoric and short on drumming. We had raced downtown after the show and joined the edge of the crowd overflowing the bottom of the South Park blocks. Again thousands of people. Again, no black faces. Almost no people of color at all. Then we marched to the plaza in front of the Federal Building and stood and listened to too many speakers. And did they use our hard-won Saturday attention to focus on the imminent danger to Iraqis and our kids in uniform? No, it was Palestine this and striking dock workers that.

Soon I was itching to stop the talk and get on with the walk. Now I don't dance, but there was something about that loud and tight syncopated drum band during the August Bush protest that had got my feet moving and my hands clapping. Limbic, I know, but we spent so much time in the other parts of our brains, ferreting out details and building arguments—none of which seemed to be doing much to stem the tide of corruption and destruction—that a good loud yellfest made me hopeful. Like, *if you dumbasses won't listen to reason, you'll listen to this.*

Another damper on the rally that day, at least for me, was worrying about Nelson. He spent the whole time quiet and droopy-eyed, and probably tormented with conflict. Earlier we'd been sitting in the studio at the start of the show, our headphones on and our stack of readers in front of us, waiting for the opening music. I asked Nelson if Dee would join us later at the rally. She was taking time off work to make prints for her show, and I figured she might want a break.

"You kidding?" Jen interrupted through the studio speaker. "She's too busy getting shitfaced in her bathroom."

Nelson said, "Christ, Jen. That's unfair."

Silence. Two days of stubbly growth rasped under my hand.

"You don't understand the pressure she's under," said Nelson. He glared at me even though I wasn't the one saying anything. "It's nerve-racking to put your heart and soul out on display."

I spread my hands at the studio, at the mics that in a few minutes would send our small voices of embattled conviction out across the airwaves.

"This is different," said Nelson. "Art's more personal."

In the engineer's booth Jen was shaking her head.

"Anyway, she's Irish." Nelson made like he was checking to see if his notes were in the right order. "It's her culture." He adjusted his headphones, and in a few seconds we were on air.

Then it turned out to be a mistake to let Nelson drive us to the rally. He seemed fine during the show, but as we were heading over the Morrison Bridge and I was checking out a tugboat on the river, a long honk jolted me out of my reverie, and we were all tossed sideways.

"What the fuck?" yelled Jen. My heart was banging.

Nelson just blinked and gripped the wheel tight. "Oh god, oh god, I'm sorry."

"Pull over," I said, and at the bottom of the bridge Nelson pulled into a loading zone. He rested his head on the steering wheel. "I'm so sorry." He looked down at his shaking hands, then climbed out and walked a few paces from the car.

"You didn't see it?" said Jen.

"I was watching a tug. I thought he was just changing lanes."

Jen pressed her palms to her forehead. "Dude, you're a fucking back-seat driver when we don't need it, then you're out to lunch when Romeo takes a fucking nap at forty miles an hour."

My heart was slowing. "Redirect your anger, Jen."

I should have told Nelson and Dee to pack their bags and not come back till they'd figured out whatever the hell it was they needed to figure out. But you don't do that, do you? You go with the flow, even though part of you suspects that what you're doing isn't all that effective—like walking around downtown Portland on a Saturday chanting slogans at empty office buildings—but you keep doing it, because you can't think of an alternative, and it isn't till later that you see things as clearly as you should.

35: JEN

"QUIT STANDING UP FOR him," I say. "He's being an asshole and you know it."

Fetzer stares at the empty white square in the newsletter layout and sighs. The locks click in the door and we both look up as Ner*donk*ulus steps in.

"Where the fuck have you been?" I say.

"Sorry," he says. "I got waylaid. How's it going, anyway?"

Waylaid my ass. Give the guy a new bed and he can't find his way out of it. And he has the audacity to smile. *And* for crying out loud he smells like sex.

"Take a shower," I say. To think we used to call this guy Mr. Clean.

He tries to hand-comb his hair down. "Really? Um. Okay. Apologies." He spots the white rectangle in the layout. "You doing the newsletter?"

I fold my arms. "No. Needlework."

"Oh." He clears his throat. "It's Thursday already, huh."

Fetzer points at the empty square. "This space? It's waiting for your follow-up on Yucca Mountain."

"Ohhh," says Nelson and he nods like he has a clue. "Okay. Thanks."

Fetzer flicks a hand at the screen. "I wasn't offering you a gift, I'm saying it's not in your goddamn drafts folder."

Nelson rubs his jaw like he's thinking. "It must have slipped my mind."

"Well, I resent that," I say.

Nelson's don't-shoot hands go up. "Whoa. I'm sorry it's late but I'll do it. Please, calm down."

"Calm down?" My chair spins off behind me. "Calm fucking down?"

Nelson backs away. Fetzer's hand is making a print on my T-shirt.

"We can put in a 'best of,'" says Fetzer. "Let's just get it out on time, okay? Then focus on the elections."

"Look," says Nelson. "I'm really sorry." One paw reaches onto my arm. I want to slap his hand away, but nobody ever touches me and those big eyes have me caught.

"It was undeniably inconsiderate of me," Nelson says. "It won't happen again."

"You need to check this out, too," says Fetzer.

With his other hand Nelson takes the printout from Fetzer. It's the new memo I dug up from Reynolds to the president of Harry Lane U, showing a budget for the VIRAS project that doesn't match the proposal. Nelson's hand slips from my arm, leaves a cooling patch.

"Off by half a million," says Nelson.

"Yup," says Fetzer.

Nelson says, "That guy I heard at the die-in, he seemed sure it was four and a half. And he didn't sound like a student."

"And you never saw him?" I ask.

Nelson shakes his head. "No. I was intent on getting Dee out of that mob, so—" He looks at the printouts again. "Sorry. Christ, I'm fucking up all over the place."

Now that made me blink. He swears, like, once a year.

Fetzer says, "Yes, you are. Please stop."

"Dude," I say. "All we need is for you to focus."

Eyes down, Nelson nods.

I say, "Plus we've got that Science and Sustainability conference coming up next weekend."

Fetzer whacks his forehead. "Shit. Yeah. San Francisco." He looks at Nelson. "You're doing that talk you proposed, right?"

Nelson winces. "Yeah."

Fetzer rolls his eyes and pulls out the cell. "Hope Franky can stay," he says, and hits the Franky speed-dial.

I say, "It's barely more than a week. Are you ready?"

Nelson smooths his shirt against his chest.

"I've been working on it. And again, sorry," he says. Then he turns up the basement stairs.

Fuck, I'm tired. The chair rolls a little when I sit on it. Fetzer wraps up with Franky, and I check out the conference website.

"Did you know he's one of the highlighted speakers at the conference? They're putting him in the main hall."

Fetzer stares. "What?"

"Guess that would be a no. He didn't say anything to you about them arranging a hotel or anything?"

Fetzer snorts out a laugh and pinches the bridge of his nose. "Nelson, Nelson, Nelson."

36: FETZER

DEE PULLED A SMALL tantrum the night before we left for San Francisco. Why did we have to go away so often? Didn't we know she needed Nelson's support more than ever? Her show was approaching and she was freaking out, couldn't we tell? Plus she needed help getting the framing supplies: how was she going to get the framing supplies in time?

Drama number one.

Luckily Franky was there to put an arm around her in his brotherly way, and offer to help. She wiped her eyes. Her bitten nails were nail-polish red, courtesy of Sylvia's latest visit.

Then if that wasn't enough, the next morning when I got up in the dark I found Jen asleep on the kitchen sofa.

"What's going on?" I asked.

She groaned and turned her back to me. "Those two. All goddamn night long."

"You can hear them?"

"Ugh. Can't you?"

"No." Then I realized: Jen's room shared a wall with Deirdre's place. "Why don't you say something?"

Jen rolled on to her back and sighed. "After the first time, it seemed like too late."

Poor Jen. She made no effort to get close to people, but I knew she was lonely. I sat on the arm of the sofa. "Just ask them to move the bed."

"And admit I've been hearing them for weeks?"

Dee and Nelson's footsteps crunched outside on the gravel, and we watched them make their way past the front of the house in the dawn light. Jen whipped her blanket into a ball, grabbed her pillow, and trotted up the main stairs.

WE WERE HEADING SOUTH past Salem with Jen driving when Nelson pulled out a fat envelope.

"Found this this morning," he said, and held it up. It was rumpled and unopened, and bore the logo of the Science and Sustainability conference.

"I thought you got that weeks ago," I said.

"I lost it for a while. During my 'delinquency.'"

To his credit, during the days after the talking-to he'd pulled himself together, and Jen and I were glad to have the old Nelson back. He'd gotten caught up on site updates, finished his presentation on carbon sequestration, and even practiced it on us.

Nelson unfolded the contents of the envelope and scanned each insert before handing it to me. Glossy pamphlet. List of nearby hotels, which was irrelevant since they'd already reserved us rooms. Then he paused on the calendar of events.

"Oh, shit."

"What?" said Jen.

Nelson's eyes bulged at the calendar. "Oh my *god*."

"What?" I said and grabbed the damn thing.

And the presentation to be delivered by John Nelson of Omnia Mundi Media Group at 11:30 a.m. on Saturday? "Big Food: A Crisis of Democracy."

Drama number two.

"How the hell did this happen?" I said, then to Jen, "He prepped the wrong talk."

Nelson shoved his hands in his hair. "I submitted two ideas. I thought they liked the other one. I mean, I don't remember. If I got back to them. I have nothing."

Jen snorted.

"Turn around!" yelled Nelson.

Jen lifted a demonstrating hand. "Freeway, dude."

"Get off! Turn back! I need to get—" Nelson bounced like he was sitting on coals. "I need to prepare a different talk."

"Calm down," I said. "Just tell them you've changed the topic."

"Can't," said Nelson. He snatched back the glossy pamphlet and held it open. "The whole *conference* is about food."

And indeed, the theme that year was *Feeding the World: Food Security and Sustainability*. His in-depth survey of the latest innovations in CO2 capture, transportation, and storage wasn't going to cut it.

"Turn back," said Nelson, with enough force that Jen veered us off an exit.

"There's this other thing I've been working on. I started in the spring. It was going to be an essay. Maybe a book. It's good. Good material. Lots of data. I need that data."

Jen drove into an empty lot and stopped. Turned off the car. It had started to rain.

Nelson breathed in deep. "I can do it. If I get the material, I can pull it together."

Jen reached around for a laptop and the Ear. "Can't we just grab it remotely?"

"Some of it's hard copy," said Nelson. "Plus clips on CDs. Never made it onto a hard drive."

He turned to us with those hangdog eyes. "We'll miss the reception. Sorry."

And who can yell at something with eyes that big?

"No sweat," said Jen. "I hate those things, anyway."

"You need to network," I said to Nelson. "You should fly down. We'll join you later."

Nelson chewed his lip. "We've been hitting Franky up for a lot lately. A last-minute fare's going to be spendy."

"We'll make it up to him," I said. "Now let's get you home."

I should've remembered that dramas come in threes.

"IS THAT SYLVIA'S CAR?" said Jen as we passed a gray Audi TT on Thirteenth. "Why's it parked there?"

From the back seat came only the steady tap of Nelson typing. I got a vague sinking feeling, but all my conscious brain came up with was the question: why would she park two blocks away when it's raining?

Music thumped from the house. Acting deaf, Nelson made a beeline for a filing cabinet in the basement. Up in the kitchen Franky was hopping around playing air guitar. He saw me and Jen and scrambled his way to the boom box to turn it off.

"Heyyyyy," he said. "Back so soon, huh?"

"Yup."

"Everything okay?" He pulled his sweatshirt straight and combed his fingers through his hair.

"Nelson forgot something important."

Franky nodded. "Okay."

The door closed downstairs, and I could see Nelson walk past the front of the house on his way to Deirdre's.

"Is Sylvia around?" said Jen.

Franky's eyebrows went up. "No?" Like it was a strange notion.

Somewhere in the back of my mind I was relieved that it wasn't Sylvia's car after all, and my most pressing problem was how to ask Franky for more money. I started telling him what had happened, but Franky, ever gracious, made the offer before I even finished.

"You're the bomb, Frank," said Jen. "I'll book his ticket."

There was muffled shouting outside. Nelson's voice, and Deirdre's. I headed for the living room window in time to see Sylvia, her head down against the drizzle and pulling on a long shiny raincoat while she walked pretty much as fast as a person can without breaking into a run.

"How could you, how *could* you," Nelson yelled, and he and Dee came into sight. Deirdre crying, yelling something incomprehensible back. The two of them screaming, circling each other like moths. Deirdre in her robe, pulling it tight around her. Nelson yelling, "How long has this been going on? Huh? How *long*?" Deirdre shaking her head and crying.

Drama number three, and my heart was on the floor between my feet.

"Forget the ticket," I said. "He's coming with us."

JEN GATHERED THE FOLDERS and CDs Nelson had pulled from the filing cabinet. I had the happy task of getting the soap opera off the street and into the kitchen, where I gave it cups of tea and Franky brought down towels because it was pretty soaked.

"I tried to stop it," Dee wailed. Her rain-flattened hair made her look gaunt, reminding me of the night she arrived. "She won't take no."

"I can't believe this," Nelson kept saying in a voice that didn't sound like him: sharp and barking. He wouldn't look at Deirdre. "Can't *believe* it."

At some point Jen came up from the basement. "Um," she said from the top of the stairs. "I updated iDVD on the Mac laptop. In case you want to make something interactive."

Nelson closed his eyes and muttered, "Oh god."

"There were some, um, video clips. And good graphs. I'll help you put it together."

Nelson said, "Yeah, uh, the corn surplus one."

"Uh-huh." Jen stepped a foot closer, like she wasn't sure if it was safe. "And a gnarly sequence on Kraft Foods, and another one about Percy Schmeiser."

"Yeah. That's a good one." Nelson set aside the towel and stood up. "I need to change. Franky, did they mention me needing to fly down?'

"You're driving with us," I said.

"The reception," said Nelson.

"You're driving with us."

"The reception's fluff," said Jen. "We're going to help you make a kick-ass presentation."

NEW SHIRT, NEW TIE, and he'd traded his tan corduroy jacket for his only suit, but he still looked like a chemistry professor who'd stumbled out of an exploded lab. We bundled him into the back seat with his files and a laptop and a hunk of carrot cake the size of half a brick. Deirdre stayed inside and cried.

Jen leaned into the back. "We've got the Ear, okay? Any time you need to log on, just let me know. And I brought the printer." She plugged it in to the door panel. "Paper's low, so we might need to stop at an office supply store."

Nelson stared at the foil-wrapped lump of cake on his lap like it was somebody's ashes. "Okay."

"Here." Franky handed him a thermos through the window. "Earl Grey."

"You going to be able to handle things?" I asked Franky.

Franky nodded. "It'll be okay."

I gave his shoulder a squeeze. "Glad you're here."

Franky said, "Me too." Jen started up, Franky whacked the roof, and we were off.

Once we were on the freeway, Jen said, "Um. If you need to edit any of those clips? There's iMovie 2 on there too."

I turned around at the silence. Nelson was still holding the brick of cake on his knee.

"I don't think I can do this," he said.

"Yeah you can. You were all over it before."

"It's not developed. Big holes. We should call and cancel."

"No way," said Jen. "I saw what you had. It was like, a ton."

"I'll just make a fool of myself," said Nelson. "Of Omnia Mundi. It's better if we cancel. Say I'm sick or something."

"Lie?" I said. "Since when do you lie? The John Nelson I know isn't a coward."

His mouth bent into a wavy line and he gazed out the window. "Christ," he whispered. His irises flickered, catching the city as it rushed past. "This is all my fault."

"What the hell are you talking about?"

"I shouldn't leave her like this."

A worried glance from Jen.

"You can't—" said Nelson, and he gestured at the river. "You can't be in a relationship and just take off whenever you like."

"Yeah, you can," I said. "People do it all the time."

Nelson squeezed the cake. "But it's not. It's not good for us. She needs. She—we need to be together. Stability, you know?"

Jen merged onto I-5 for the second time that morning. Eleven hours to go. It was going to be a very long day.

"What if she leaves?" said Nelson. "God, she might just leave. Leave!"

Spray from a semi-trailer coated the windshield, and Jen flicked the wipers on high.

I said, "She's not going to leave."

"How do you know? She might be packing. Sylvia could be helping. Franky could be taking her enlarger out, *right now*."

I held the phone over the back of the seat. "Why don't you check?"

"Nelson?" said Jen. "You're giving this talk. There's nothing else to do. So get it together, will you?"

Nelson took the phone. He hit the speed dial. Hung up. Stared out the window. We were approaching Tigard and the specter of Nelson canceling, or worse, delivering a crappy lecture was beginning to take on a more solid form. I reached over and grabbed the phone.

It was seven rings before Franky answered.

"Hey," he said, out of breath. Like he'd been carrying an enlarger down the stairs.

"Hey. So. How are things?"

"Oh. You know. Pretty upset."

"Yeah. What's she doing?"

"Well, she stopped crying."

"Okay. Any evidence of her packing up and leaving?"

"Huh? No way. She's lying on the sofa and holding a photo of Nelson. I was just upstairs getting her a blanket. She was really hoping Nelson would call."

"Hold on a minute."

Nelson's eyes were swimmy. He reached for the phone and I turned on the radio to cover the next five minutes of mumbling and sniffing. When the phone reappeared at my shoulder, I took it and turned the radio down.

"So?" I said.

Nelson had his hands on his knees and a spelling-bee stare. "Franky offered to fly her down."

A "no fucking way" glance from Jen.

Nelson said, "Which would be really great."

The specter of Nelson giving an *exceedingly* crappy talk loomed large.

"Actually," I said, "That wouldn't be—"

"But I said no. I need to concentrate. And she was okay with that. I mean, I think she was. It's hard to tell, I guess. I thought she was okay about everything before, but I wasn't seeing the signs. I have to be more attentive. Relationships take work. Neglect can—"

I said, "Big Food: A Crisis of Democracy."

Nelson drummed his fingers on his knees. "Yeah. Subsidized overproduction. Ten billion bushels of industrial corn a year. Food corporations hijacking the political agenda. It's good stuff."

"It's excellent," I said, and the specter of a crappy talk faded.

"Do you think it's okay that I told her no?"

"It's fucking perfect. Now here's Woodburn already, so will you open the goddamn laptop and get to work?"

37: JEN

THE DRIVER'S DOOR OPENS and Fetzer drops his ass into the seat beside me. "Is this blowing your mind or what?" He slams the door and the Ear wobbles.

"Careful!" I say, but the reception only dips for a second.

The parking lot is distorted through the rainy windshield. We're in some lame small-town "center" with a print place and a café. Fetzer wipes his hands over his wet head, the sound raspy against the backdrop gurgle of drains and gutters and the rain on the roof of the car.

"I found this picture of the earth," I say, and shift the laptop so he can see.

"Nice," says Fetzer. He turns on the radio. Spins through crap. Turns it off. Sits back. "I mean. Ho-leee."

"Yeah. Huh."

Fetzer lifts his hands. "I never saw it coming."

"Hell no. Me neither."

"I mean, I saw *something* coming, but not this. Not"—he lifts his hands again—"*Sylvia*."

"Nope. Not Sylvia." So I've got the earth, a feedlot, a seedling, some obese people. I need a better seedling.

Fetzer says, "I mean, what the hell got into her?"

"She belongs to the predator class," I say. "What do you expect?"

"I meant Deirdre."

"Oh. Yeah. Like how much sex can one not particularly robust person need?"

Okay, Google, how about "new seedling"?

"Any help Sylvia might have given us on Harry Lane is blown," says Fetzer.

I shrug. "She tells us shit we'd find out anyway. Saves us some time is all."

"And prepping the wrong fucking talk."

"Jeez, yeah."

Fetzer tips his head back and groans at the vinyl ceiling. "Holy. Freaking. Shit."

"That's the exact phrase I was reaching for." I turn the laptop and Fetzer looks at the bean seedling image out of the corner of his eye. "Uh-huh. Nice."

A peach-colored shape bobs in front of the car, that dumb umbrella. Why we have a peach-colored umbrella just hanging out in the car is anybody's guess, but it comes in handy when the guy in the tie needs to stay dry.

My door opens, and I scoot forward so Nelson can get in the back.

Rain hammers the roof of the car. Slides down the windows. "It was four bucks and ten cents," says Nelson. Calm. Like Deirdre never showed up and we'd gone through the last few months without her. Like he'd opened that envelope weeks ago and he's just putting the final touches on the right talk.

"I'M SWEATING ALREADY," SAYS Nelson. Fetzer and I pan the auditorium. There's the murmur of small-talk and people are shuffling sideways past the folks who've already taken the aisle seats.

As usual, everyone looks more grown up than me.

"This place is huge," I say.

"John Nelson?" says a voice, and a tall East Indian guy in a gray suit a lot like Nelson's steps up, shakes Nelson's hand. "Peter Choudhury, conference coordinator. Good to meet you."

"Pleasure to be here," says Nelson. Caffeine grin.

Introductions all around, and polite talk about how I look taller than my bio photo. Implied: Fetzer looks shorter, ha ha.

"Sorry we couldn't make it to the reception last night," says Nelson.

"Last-minute schedule conflict," says Fetzer.

"Yes, it was a pity, but I hope you can make tonight's," says Peter. "There's an environmental ethics professor from Spain who wants to meet you, and several other people you should connect with. You have any AV requirements?"

I hold up the laptop bag. "This has to project. I've got a 13-pin and a 15-pin VGA cable and a line amplifier. Hope your projector's native rez is at least ten-twenty-four by—"

"You need to talk to Spike, down there in the black shirt?"

Spike is way down there on the stage, crouching at the base of the podium and dealing with something that's probably wiring. On the other side of the stage is a video camera on a tripod. Good, because I forgot ours. "'Kay."

"Where should we sit?" says Nelson, and Peter walks us down the aisle. Front row seats all have perky little tented *RESERVED* signs. Four of them in green. "These are the speaker seats," says Peter. "For the three of you and I'll take one when I'm done with the introductions."

It's a big stage, with those super-long black curtains in the back.

Fuck. He's going to be up there.

Nelson's staring at the podium, and his smile goes limp through what's probably another urge to run to the bathroom. Guy's been three times this morning. When Peter's gone I say, "Dude, it's going to be awesome," then I hop up onto the oak slats of the stage and head over to Spike.

PETER STEPS DOWN, AND Nelson steps up through the small applause. His shoes are at eye level. Damn, he keeps those things shiny. Rustles and shuffling all through the hall. Nelson glows bright and warm on the black stage. His eyes stand out and his hands seem big and sharp. He looks so *calm*. I'd be trying not to puke—there must be eight hundred people in here. He looks out into the distance, but I know the light's so strong on him he can't see past the edge of the stage. Makes it easier, I guess.

Someone coughs.

"Thank you," says Nelson. His voice is large over the PA. He blinks, slowly. No white knuckles on his hands holding the sides of the podium. "It's an honor to be here. Today I'm going to share with you some thoughts on the food industrial complex."

He glances down, moves his hand, and behind him two stories high on the screen, the collage I made fades in, slow and silent.

Awesome.

"Our species," says Nelson, then he pauses. Floating behind him in the dark are cornfields and obese bodies and dustbowls and buckets of grease. "Is the first . . ." He scans the audience. "To turn its food supply into a profound threat to its health."

You'd think there was no one else in here for how quiet it's got.

"THIS CORN SURPLUS HAS to go somewhere, and so the marketers have convinced each of us to consume about a ton of it a year, either directly or indirectly."

Cool, here comes the long montage.

"Fast food is simply corn in disguise. Most meat is really corn consumed in the feedlot. Soda is corn syrup and water."

Those transitions look so fucking cool.

"We're not only eating this overproduction, we're subsidizing it through taxes. And with each bushel of corn requiring a quart of oil to produce, from an ecological standpoint it's an absurdly wasteful way to produce food."

Fetzer nudges my knee. With his hand close to his chest he points down the row. Upturned faces all the way down the line, faint masks in the screen's light. Even though she fucked up, I kinda wish Dee was here. She'd be so proud. Hell, I'm proud.

". . . eating the culinary aftermath of Reagan-Thatcher fundamentalism . . ."

This is turning out so goddamn well. Need to make sure we get that video. Could make a new section on the site. Get him speaking more and build up a library. Right now there's only that one other video, the lecture he did in Chicago in 2000, and the audio is crappy. Oh yeah, and that interview on Talking State. But they never gave us the footage in 3/4 inch, we just have the shitty VHS copy off the TV.

". . . the food arrives on our plates seemingly stripped of consequences, but the consequences exist . . ."

Couple more like this and we could make a DVD. Even this by itself. Could intercut him speaking with other footage. Yeah. And next time he talks, gotta make sure there's two cameras, one for close-ups.

". . . crisis isn't just about food, it's a crisis of democracy, which has failed to prevent food corporations from hijacking the political agenda . . ."

Okay, final montage.

". . . but these food and farming trends have occurred in the blink of history's eye, and there's nothing inevitable about them. They can be reversed . . ."

Pause at the earth from space, then rice paddies, yep.

". . . but fundamental changes will happen only when the food system disengages from the logic of neoliberalism—"

The screen behind him fills with the small bean plant pushing out of the soil. Corny as hell, but you can see every grain of humus and it's so fucking beautiful. Nelson's eyes, big and round, connecting with the audience he can't even see.

"—and engages with the logic of ecology. The next big social revolution will see the separation of business and governance. We can, and must, take responsibility to pressure that change at *every* opportunity. Thank you."

Nelson shuffles his papers, and the applause cracks, hard and loud. He glances up, nods, keeps shuffling the papers. Why act shy now, dude? It's over!

The applause keeps going. "Thank you," Nelson says into the microphone. "I'll take questions now."

Fetzer's eyes are buggy. He's happy. Relieved. Me too.

Nelson's smiling, making "quiet down" motions with his hands. "Thank you," he says again.

The house lights fade on and it's like waking up from a dream. Here we are, sitting on theater seats, everybody pretty ordinary. Academics, scientists, government types. A guy with black-rimmed glasses and hair to his shoulders, probably an architect. Everyone looks dazed and eager at the same time.

Finally the applause is dying down. A couple of hands go up, and Spike scuttles past with a wireless mic. A few seconds later a woman in the back says, "Thank you for such a comprehensive and wide-ranging analysis of the subject. I'm from Wilson University and our recent study found the largest major food multinationals have revenues that rival the GDPs of many countries. So my question is, how do you see the . . ."

Fetzer mutters in my ear, "I gotta clear out of here."

"We can't leave Nelson."

Nelson is into his answer, gesturing; his eyes sincere on the lady in the back. He sure doesn't look like a man who's been screwed over and driven eleven hours and stayed up all night writing a lecture and delivered it nonstop for an hour.

"Come on," I say. "He was awesome."

"He was. But I am crashing here."

Nelson finishes the answer and hands spring up through the auditorium like blades of grass.

"I saw them setting up coffee and cookies in the lobby," says Fetzer. "Want some?"

"Cookies? *Cookies?* Did you hear *anything* he said?"

Fetzer flaps a hand at me and leaves.

38: NELSON

NELSON SITS ON THE edge of the hard plastic seat, one knee bouncing. Franky picks up, answers with, "Omnia Mundi Media Group."

"Franky, hi, it's me."

"Oh, hey, Nelson. How did it go?"

"Great. Listen, is Dee there?"

"Absolutely," says Franky, and there's the clunk of the receiver being put down.

Nelson's stomach growls for breakfast. He's in a phone booth in the hotel lobby, trying to get some privacy. All around him is an expanse of patterned carpet and the undulating chatter of conference-goers. He considered calling Dee on her cell, but the thought of her picking up Sylvia's gift gives him the creeps. It's bad enough she's still sleeping on the bed Sylvia gave them. But he doesn't want to think about it. Doesn't want to talk about it, either.

It's just a tiny little hole, the phone mouthpiece. Amazing that a voice can get through.

Faint sound of footsteps in the phone. The tiny hole is the open end of a thready tube that winds up into space and back down to Portland.

"Hello?"

He exhales. "Sweetheart."

"I miss you so much," she says. And there's so much longing in her voice.

"Hah. Oh yeah, me too. Wait, I didn't mean 'hah' like I didn't believe you. I'm just keyed up. Gosh, sorry I didn't call earlier."

"How was it?"

He says, "Fantastic. The whole thing went without a hitch, and Jen's slideshow was incredible. Sorry I didn't call yesterday, but the questions went on forever, then we had to leave the auditorium to make room for another session, and so a group of us convened in this other room that wasn't being used, then after a while about fifteen of us went out to a restaurant, which overwhelmed the poor restaurant, but they put us at these two round tables, and halfway through the meal I switched so I could spend some time with the other table. Then we were late for the reception, so we rushed back here and got to meet all these other people, like this amazing woman from Nigeria who is working on the oil exporting companies, and Spanish environmental ethics guy, aaaand, then what, then a few of us went out again to a bar after that, and I fell asleep in the cab on the way back, and I guess somehow I got into bed because that's where I woke up."

"I'm so proud of you." She sighs. "Wish I could have been there."

"Oh, me too. And today there's a bunch of talks we're really excited about. Actually, babe, I need to run. Jen is—" He laughs again. "Literally pulling me—pulling me out of this booth. Love you sweetheart."

"I love you, John."

"See you tomorrow night," he says.

"I'm counting the hours."

Then the tiny hole clicks shut and the thready tube is broken. For a second he imagines the end of it flailing somewhere in space.

Jen grabs his wrist. "Come *on*."

And he sees himself tearing down the middle, as if a zipper was being pulled. One half follows Jen and carries on with the conference; the other half stays in the anonymous booth in the anonymous hotel lobby, and dials Deirdre again.

Jen says, "'Decoupling Environmental Degradation and Economic Growth.' We're late."

"I haven't eaten." Not that he cares. He's running on adrenaline.

Jen hands him a banana. "Let's *go*."

DEIRDRE'S METAL STAIRS WOBBLE under his bounding feet. His hands are cold and wet from the railing and slip on the doorknob, but it pulls open of its own accord and there she is in the dark foyer. His wet hands catch in her hair. Drag over her skin. Slippery mouths. She breathes like a diver. "Forgive me?" she says—he thinks she says, but it's more like an echo off his flesh. Her gray sweater tangles, then is over her head. "Forgive *me*," he says. Slippery mouths. They're both breathing like divers. She grunts, her head knocks against the wall, her hands pull on the small of his back. He shoves the door closed with his foot, and the rainy October night is gone.

39: FETZER

AFTER THE "BLOWUP," AS it became known, Deirdre and Nelson were even more into each other. And he was also pulling his weight at work. Impossible, but true. He'd become a tornado of activity.

"Maybe he's taking uppers," I said to Jen.

"If you count Deirdre as an upper," she said.

But Sylvia? It was like we'd never known her. The only evidence was Dee's cell phone, which she offered to give away, but I thought she should keep it for emergencies. Nevertheless, she stopped taking pictures with it. Personally, I was just happy for the calm.

We met Kate Simms again at Nguyen's diner, and again she brought the baby. He had a blob of blond hair, and shiny dribble on his chin.

I dove right in with, "Harry Lane U won't let us rest."

Kate laughed. "No rest till we die, right?" then she hitched the baby higher in her lap and grimaced. "You hear the news?"

Indeed we had. Paul Wellstone's death was fresh news that morning. The reelection battle Wellstone was locked in was key to controlling the Senate, and the midterm elections were only days away. Things looked grim.

"I bet it was assassination," I said.

Kate's eyes widened. "Where'd you get that idea?"

"He was getting death threats. And you look at the statistics. Democratic politicians are way more vulnerable to air 'accidents' than Republican politicians."

Kate put on a humor-the-crazies voice to say, "I don't think statistics are enough evidence for foul play, Mr. Fetzer."

"Let's not get into that one," said Nelson. He smiled and handed Kate a napkin in time for her to catch a thread of baby drool before it reached the table.

We didn't tell her about the VIRAS budget discrepancy we'd found; instead we asked what she knew about the university's finances. She filled us in on their endowment and major donors, but she didn't have any info about unusual practices.

Then Deirdre joined us on her break, and within a minute she was holding the baby.

Her eyes closed and her nose sank into the baby's hair. "He's brilliant," she whispered into the downy scalp.

"Not yet," said Kate. "The neighbor's cat is still smarter."

Nelson stared at Deirdre.

Oh, here we go, I thought. *Here. We. Go.*

Kate saw it too, and she smiled and arched her eyebrows at me like the town gossip.

Nelson put an arm across Dee's shoulders and let the baby grip his finger in a tiny fist. They were so absorbed it was like the rest of us had gotten up and left.

Nelson told me once, in private, that he and Lise had been trying to start a family. He hadn't forgiven himself for breaking her heart. Or his own.

Jen folded her arms. "You hear Rumsfeld says Saddam's got anthrax?"

Jen, on the other hand, told anyone who asked, and some who didn't, that she was never having kids. "Shitty world to bring a kid into," she'd say. "Starting with me being a shitty parent."

"And mustard gas, sarin, and VX," said Kate. "You surprised? He tortures children."

Nelson muttered, "Oh god," and Adrian let out a shriek and hit Deirdre's chin.

"To force confessions from their fathers," said Kate. "Journalist friend of mine was there in the spring. No one would talk to him, they were so terrified. He had to go far north before he found anyone who'd speak out."

Our bagels were chewy, the coffee hot. Outside a young man walked by with two fluffy white dogs. Not for the first time I wondered how it was I got to live in a peaceful part of the world, considering how many people didn't.

I said, "We can't go in, though."

Kate held up a hand. "I shouldn't be discussing foreign policy."

Nelson looked up. "It's the U.N.'s call. Bush would be insane to go in without international backing."

"He's already insane," said Jen. "And it would be a total disaster."

"Listen," said Kate. "I'm interested in your local investigative work, but I can*not* be talking politics with you."

"It's that bad at the *Herald*, huh?" I said.

She frowned. "It's not *bad* at all. It's professionalism."

The baby started crying, and Dee lifted him by his armpits to pat his feet against her knees.

Kate said, "Look, guys, thanks again for the information you've been sharing." She took the baby and tucked his blanket around him against her soft bosom. "Let's just stick to that topic."

"Sure," I said, but I was thinking, *These journalists, they're all the same. Even the so-called progressive ones.* But I didn't want to scare off our only, if partial, ally in the local mainstream media. "We're going to visit one of Nelson's old professors," I said. "We'll let you know if anything turns up."

The crying got louder, and the kid seemed to be settling in for the duration. "And I'll try to get hold of Reynolds again," Kate said over the noise. "He wouldn't comment last time."

"Why bother?" said Jen. "It'll just be the party line."

Kate squished her mouth. "Because it's my job. You advocacy folks, sheesh."

"Advocacy?" said Jen, "Oh, and you're not?"

Kate bounced the baby, but the wailing didn't let up.

"Okay. I'll admit the *Herald* and I rub each other the wrong way from time to time, but I do try to adhere to its stated creed of unbiased reporting."

Jen put down her coffee and her smile was half a sneer. "No such thing. And at least we admit our biases."

Kate said, "Hah! I see." The baby thrust out his tiny arms and screeched, his open mouth purple and toothless.

40: NELSON

NELSON'S EYES ARE SCRATCHY from staring at the TV. His stomach growls, but he can't be bothered fixing food. On the other sofa Fetzer groans and covers his face. "This isn't happening."

"Dude. It's happening," says Jen.

Fetzer spreads his fingers to peek at the preliminary election results. "I'm moving to Canada."

"Move to Canada, see what fucking good it does."

Nelson presses his lids closed, but his eyes only burn more. A small earthquake bumps through the cushions from a sudden movement by Jen, then there's the crash of a bottle landing in the recycle bin. Jen pops the top off another bottle and tilts back her head. Her hair across the back of the black sofa is like bundled copper wire, and Nelson is pricked with sadness that there isn't someone in her life who loves that hair.

Franky clumps up the basement stairs. "How's it going?"

"Not good," Nelson says. "Mannix is gaining ground for the governorship."

"Bummer," says Franky. He sits down next to Fetzer.

Fetzer's boot heels are way out on the floor, and his head is jammed against the back of the sofa. "Nationally, we are mega-screwed. Someone get me a beer?"

"Sure," says Nelson, but when he gets up, his body is so leaden he wishes he hadn't offered.

• • •

His neck hurts. He pulls his hand out from under him and it's numb. He opens a sticky eye, the one that isn't pressed into the black sofa fabric. The light is bluish, and the sound of soft rain outside is comforting, and then he remembers.

The mid-term elections are over.

It's her feet on the basement stairs. He must have woken with the sound. He shivers when the morning air touches the parts of his body that had been insulated against the sofa. Something hard is between his ankles. It's Jen's foot. Jen is curled, fetal, at the other end. He's never seen Jen like that—she's more of a sprawler. Fetzer's on his back on the other sofa, a soft snore coming from his mouth with each breath.

"Hi," whispers Deirdre from the top of the stairs. "I missed you."

Nelson shifts over and she sits between him and Jen's folded legs. Dee's gray sweater is beaded with dots of water, and she smells like wet wool and fall.

"It's raining again," she says.

He wraps his arms around her and is so very glad that she's in his life, because out there winter is coming, and his country is going to hell in a handbasket.

At the diner the other day, watching Deirdre hold Adrian, he longed so hard for a quiet life and a child with her that he had to breathe against the sore place his chest.

What a baby would do for them all. When Adrian curled his little fist around Fetzer's stubby finger, Fetzer's face changed like water, his big mouth going soft. Then when Adrian was wrapped in Deirdre's arms, Nelson could have cried for how perfect it was.

He drops his face into Deirdre's sweater and inhales. At least he has her.

If Jen and Fetz weren't sleeping right here, he'd peel that sweater off, and everything else. Since the blowup, he's made love with her everywhere but on that bed.

"Does it always rain this much?" Deirdre whispers. "Feels like you could drown."

Light from the television flickers over Nelson's tea. The scrambled tofu Dee made for them before she went to work sits in cold clumps on plates. The air is damp. Newspapers are spread all over the coffee table and the floor. Fetzer hands him one. "A commanding performance by the Commander in Chief," it says. "'Call it affirmation or reaffirmation, the midterm election has given a powerful boost to President Bush, the conservative agenda, and the long-term prospects of the Republican Party . . .'"

Fetzer stands, looks around the living room like he's mislaid something. "Why are we Americans so in love with sending our kids to war?"

41: JEN

<TheJenerator> A new day, people. A new era.

<schrodingers_cat> Now the fuckers can *really* get away with whatever the hell they want.

<TheJenerator> Never could figure out how populations let fascism happen, but we're witnessing the process as we speak.

<VioletFire> Fascism creeps in, and people swallow teh doublespeak and think it's great they're safe.

<TheJenerator> totally

<TheJenerator> A generation from now they'll look back and whine, "But we didn't realize."

<ignite> idiots.

"This rain changes the light," says Deirdre. She sets the soy spread in front of me. She's been extra nice since the blowup. Just as well, 'cause there's only so many crises I will tolerate.

"Thanks," I say.

Nelson's hair is messed up, and there's a shadow on his jaw. He never used to come to breakfast without shaving.

She drives me crazy. So does he. They all do, but shit, I'd way way *way* rather be in here than out there.

<schrodingers_cat> i think hate my country

<VioletFire> ive been trying not to say that, but, yeah.

<TheJenerator> I think I hate this whole fucking country too

<TheJenerator> I just haven't had the girl-cojones to admit it.

<TheJenerator> Always thought it was worth it trying to make it better, but now? Every morning I check the Web, check the blogs, and open the same papers to the same crap.

<TheJenerator> And what do I get for it besides more dead trees and newsprint all over my hands?

<TheJenerator> More shit to be paranoid about

<TheJenerator> and less and less ways to fix it.

<ignite> girl-cojones?

<TheJenerator> All hail the Project for the New American Century.

<TheJenerator> yeah, what, you don't know about those?

"Well, this eases my mind," says Fetzer, and he nudges the nearest paper around with his foot. "Bush's top priority is to get that damned department of Homeland Security going."

"Unaccountable to the public," murmurs Nelson.

"Got to have a big building for Total Information Awareness," I say. "Total takes up a lot of space."

<VioletFire> You know they're logging this

<TheJenerator> I KNOW fuck they can frog march me off to some undisclosed internment center I am NOT going to shut up

<schrodingers_cat> go, jenerator. By the way, if I never see you again, it's been real

<TheJenerator> stick this up your total information awareness, fuckers.

<TheJenerator>........................../´¯/)

<TheJenerator>.......................,/¯../

<TheJenerator>......................./..../

<TheJenerator>................./´¯/’...’/´¯¯`·,

<TheJenerator>............../’/.../..../......./¨¯\

<TheJenerator>............(‘(...´...´.... ¯~/’...’)

<TheJenerator>.............\.................’...../

<TheJenerator>..............’’...\.......... _.·´

<TheJenerator>................\..............(

<TheJenerator>..................\.............\...

<ignite> beautiful

<VioletFire> LOL!

<zoozer> omg that's awesome

Deirdre helps herself to toast. "Let's put this into some perspective, okay? At least you can still get on a bus and not be wondering if you'll be bombed to bits on your way to work."

Nelson looks up from his paper. "It's not so much our personal safety we're worried about."

"Well, I kinda am," I say.

"We all should be." Fetzer holds a stumpy finger on the paper and reads out loud. "By winning control of the Senate and expanding their House majority, congressional Republicans are positioned to push their agenda of new tax cuts, an aggressive response to Iraq, and appointments of conservative judges."

"They're gonna rip ANWR to pieces," I say.

Deirdre spreads peanut butter. "What's ANWR?"

"Arctic National Wildlife Refuge. Most amazing fucking place on the planet. Happens to be sitting on oil."

<ignite> anytihng happening in yr town, jen?

<TheJenerator> Like what?

<ignite> dissent

<TheJenerator> plenty, ig. Vigils every night outside this theater that happens to be called the Bagdad.

Deirdre groans and says, "Can't believe me photos are due in *three weeks*."

<TheJenerator> And this one university has a *lot* of protests going on right now. And there's weekly marches from the square. Plus the big monthly protests.

<ignite> my town's so small it's lame. There was a peace protest last month, and two hundred people showed up. Plus two hundred pro-war sheeple.

<TheJenerator> Disheartening

<zoozer> *Baghdad

<TheJenerator> I know, they spelled it wrong on the sign back in the 20s.

"Christ," says Nelson. "Did you read this about that new Ashcroft policy? He's ordering all males from Muslim nations to special-register in person at the INS."

"Mega-creepy," I say.

"What's next," says Fetzer. "Detention camps?"

Deirdre pulls her hands under the table. "I hope the curator doesn't reject too many."

Nelson says, "It'll be *fine,*" to Deirdre, and do I detect a note of frustration?

"But what if it's *not*?" she whines. "What if no one comes to the opening?"

"Oh, they'll come," I say. "I'll send an announcement to our mailing list. Reynolds will be there, right?"

Deirdre shrugs. "Nancy hasn't said otherwise."

`<TheJenerator> Iggy, that university with the protests I mentioned, it's Harry Lane. I'm helping organize a guerilla performance there.`

`<VioletFire> Cool`

`<TheJenerator> Yeah. That girl who moved in is having an art show there. We got banned from the campus for pissing off this deptarment head who's in the pocket of the Pentagon, and she's putting up all these pictures of us in the university gallery. The guy who banned us, he's going to be at the opening reception.`

`<ignite> Hilarious. The subject matter will be a surprise?`

`<schrodingers_cat> SQTM`

`<VioletFire> I love it already`

`<TheJenerator> this activist group is planning something theatrical for the reception.`

`<schrodingers_cat> So your new house mate is turning out to be pretty cool`

`<TheJenerator> She's alright I guess. Kinda unpredictable and high-maintenance.`

`<schrodingers_cat> She's letting you do subversive shit at her reception.`

`<TheJenerator> hell, no, she doesn't know about it. She's so fucking freaked out about getting ready in time, no point adding to her worries.`

`<VioletFire> Jen, your thoughtfulness makes my heart ache.`

Deirdre stands up. "I have to get to work." That red polish is flaking off her nails. Weird how it suits her better that way. She takes a mint out of her pocket and puts it in her mouth. She's always eating those mints.

42: NELSON

HE HOLDS HER HAND. Squeezes it with pride. Her framed photos are only leaning against the gallery walls, waiting to be chosen, but he can't stop looking at them. Away from her wall at home, separated by mats and frames, each one is a moment from their lives. Fetzer gesturing with a screwdriver, the tool a blurry arc in the air beside him, his eyes catching the camera the moment before self-consciousness sets in. Franky and Jen next to each other at the table the second after a joke, a twin smile starting between them. The eye misses but the shutter snaps and keeps forever.

"Good," says the curator, Toshiko. She's as humorless and efficient as Deirdre described. She picks up the one of Sylvia in the diner. Deirdre had asked him what he thought about including it. His first reaction was a knee-jerk "No."

But in the photo, sitting alone at a table for two, Sylvia is fiddling with her rings, and her eyes are aimed sideways like she expects to be ambushed. He's never seen her nervous, but the camera caught the moment.

"This one," says Toshiko. Her mouth pinches. "I don't know." Sylvia goes back against the wall and Toshiko points with her toe. "Maybe. I'll come back to it. She seems out of place. The others are a set, you know? But she's different."

Nelson's scalp itches under his stringy blond wig. Toshiko had barely glanced at him in his hoodie and his ripped jeans, and now she's ignoring him altogether.

Deirdre says, "She doesn't live with us."

"No," says Toshiko, as if she knew this already. "But then neither does he, right?" and she points to Mr. Nguyen reaching up for a bulk can of paprika. "But he seems to be part of the same world." Toshiko sighs and moves along the line. Franky at the sink. The one he hated. He'd relented and let Dee put it in. The homeless guys with their shopping carts. Chuck in this camo jacket. Eb's shaking face turned away. Sinclair's ducking-down smile. The moment self-consciousness sets in.

"I'll take them all for now," says Toshiko, "and see how they shake out when they're hung. Maybe I'll put that woman in the lobby. I usually put a piece or two in the lobby." Toshiko's hair is black and straight like Deirdre's, but not as long. "Good," she says again, and looks up. Whether she means the work is good, or it's good Dee made the deadline, or it's good that there's more than she can use, Nelson can't tell. And it doesn't matter. Dee's made it. Her show will open next week.

"Did you see the announcement cards?" says Toshiko.

Deirdre's hand twitches in his. "Announcement cards?"

"Yes," says Toshiko, like Dee should have known. She opens her folder and pulls out a handful of slippery postcards. 'DEIRDRE O'CARROLL.' it says in gray on white. 'PHOTOGRAPHS.'

"I am so proud of you," Nelson murmurs in Deirdre's ear.

"We send out nine hundred, give a hundred to the artist."

Dee stares and stares at the card in her hands. *Deirdre O'Carroll. Photographs. The Center for Photography, Harry Lane University. Reception: Thursday, December 5, 2002, 6–8 p.m.*

"This is who I am," whispers Deirdre. "This is what I do. This is where I'll be. And this is the time I'll be there."

Nelson isn't sure what to say. He squats down to look closer at the photo of Jen ripping up Bush's picture in the newspaper. Such determination on her face.

"Everything okay?" asks Toshiko. "That is the correct spelling?"

Deirdre says, "Yes. Yes. It's brilliant. Thanks."

The gallery door creaks and an apple-green shape moves into the room. It's Nancy. "Well, hello there, Miss O'Carroll," she says. Her teeth are bright.

Toshiko says, "See you at the opening," and leaves.

"So here are my guys," Nancy whispers to Deirdre. Her voice squeaks up with "guys" and her hands tighten into excited fists like she's about to take off sprinting. "Oh, oh, oh, here they are." She looks over her shoulder to check Toshiko's gone. "She has no idea. I can't wait for opening night."

Her shoulders do a happy hunch and she turns back to the photos. "Jen Owens with the heavy curly hair. Mmm-hmm. And John Nelson—is that really him? Girl, you make him look *sexy.* And dear old Mr. Fetzer. Heee. He's so cute and bald now. He is something else."

Nelson stays crouching on the floor and hides his smile.

Nancy stands in front of the one of Franky lounged along a sofa watching TV. "Oh, and who is *that*?" Franky's hair is perfectly imperfect, his muscles visible under his T-shirt. Nancy turns her wide eyes Deirdre's way. "You been keeping a secret all this time? Now that's not fair."

"I'll be introducing you at the opening," says Deirdre, and Nancy says, "You better, girl," and laughs.

Then she's looking at the one of the die-in from the eighth floor of Hewell. "You vote?"

"No. I couldn't."

Nancy's fists bang onto her ample green hips. "You telling me you didn't register?"

"I'm not a citizen."

"Oh, I forgot." Nancy then wags a finger. "Well, you make sure you're a citizen next time around. We need the numbers, you hear?" She points at the one of Nelson sleeping. "If it means marrying sexy nerd boy, do it."

Nelson stands up. Clears his throat. Deirdre's silent laughter is turning audible.

"I'm not joking." Nancy shakes her head. "Desperate times, girl. Desperate times."

"Uh, hello, Nancy?" says Nelson. The green form whirls around, and he's caught in her staring frown. She steps closer, and her manicured hand presses above her bosom.

"Holy shit! John Nelson! I took you for a work-study student."

She points at him and says to Deirdre, "He's good. He is good. Hah!"

After Nancy's gone, Deirdre says, "Hey, sexy nerd boy," and kisses him hard. He shuffles her backward until she's against the wall. "The windows," she whispers, and they shuffle around the corner and into a storage closet Toshiko had left open.

Afterward they pick up the tubes of plastic cups and packets of napkins that had tumbled down around them.

Professor Krakowski has aged. His hands are bent with arthritis, and there are brown blotches on his face. But there's still that faint Polish accent and boyish smile, and he was so pleased to see Nelson after all these years. And so pleased to meet Deirdre. He took her hand in both of his. "John is a fine, fine person. I am glad to see he has found someone so lovely."

And when they told him why they're in disguise, and Fetzer popped off his wig, he laughed and laughed.

"Honestly, Professor K.," Nelson said as he fingered the fabric of his hoodie. "I don't usually look this scruffy."

"Yes. I remember you always wore that jacket," said the professor, and he gestured near his elbow. "With the patches."

"You're kidding," said Jen.

"They're very sturdy," Nelson countered.

The professor nodded. "I had one like that for years, yes."

Now, with their cups of tea refilled and the plate of cookies almost empty (thanks to Fetzer) Professor K. says, "Reynolds has been trying to make me retire. But this is my life. I will not go." He surveys his cramped office. Piles of books on the floor. Stacks of folders. Rare plants on the windowsill. "But there is pressure, yes. And the young teachers, they are scared of him. If you have spoken out, and you are on a renewable contract, it will not be renewed."

Jen asks, "Is he acting particularly weird or anything lately?"

Professor K. lifts a hand with his shrug. "Reynolds is always paranoid about one thing or another. Now it is hackers."

Jen shifts her weight in her chair. "Any particular reason?"

The professor gazes at his monitor bristling with sticky notes. "Perhaps someone would steal the students' personal information? The social security numbers?" He turns back to Jen. "But I don't think student safety is Reynolds's true motivation."

"What's he worried about?"

"Well, with this defense contract, I suppose he has legitimate reasons to keep secret the work. But it should not be such a big deal. The university upgrades security often. But these memos coming out—" The professor shakes his head. "He has become strident. Ah, but we do agree on one thing. Harry Lane University should contribute to the defense of freedom."

"Excuse me?" says Nelson.

"Saddam Hussein is an evil man. He destroys minorities in his own country. He must be stopped."

Nelson reaches for his tie but ends up fiddling with the zipper on his hoodie. Until now he's never heard Professor K. express anything but the most peaceful opinions.

Jen leans forward. "You know when the next security overhaul's scheduled?"

The professor scratches behind his ear, and keeps absently rubbing the spot. "I think my computer is scheduled this week."

"What kind of upgrades?" says Jen.

Professor K. laughs and waves a hand. "You young people, you are so interested in the computers. I have no idea."

"What about President Wellesley?" says Fetzer. "How's he doing?"

"Oh!" says Professor K. "It has become absurd. Reynolds is the indulged child. And now people are whispering strange rumors. It is sad. Sad for the university. This is a fine university."

"What sort of rumors?"

Professor K. waves the rumors away. "Ach, stupid things. That they are homosexual lovers."

"Could it be true?" says Fetzer.

"It is untrue. When you get as old as me, you know these things. They both have wives, families, grandchildren. I know sometimes a man can have a secret life, but no. These men, they are not homosexual."

"What's going on, then?" says Fetzer.

"Could it be blackmail?" says Nelson.

Professor K's swollen knuckles rest in his lap. "That is my guess, yes."

Jen leans forward again, urgency in her voice. "What about?"

Professor K. looks up at her. "I'm sorry, my dear, but I have no idea."

"OKAY," SAYS NELSON. "NEXT stop, Students for Peace."

"That dude's kinda cool," says Jen. "Apart from being a hawk."

"My favorite professor of all time," says Nelson. "We used to call him Special K." Nelson takes Deirdre's hand. "This way, troops."

The large basement room is crowded with people busy with sticks and cloth and glue guns. Everyone's white. Nelson's been noticing this more now since Fetzer brought it up after that big rally.

"We're making puppets," says a plump girl with ringlet hair, even though they haven't asked. Tibetan prayer flags string the ceiling.

"Beatrice?" says Jen, and another woman steps forward.

"Finally get to meet you," the woman says. She's tall and slender, and shaved bald like Fetzer. Hugs all around. "You must be Deirdre the photographer," she says, and she gives Dee a quick hug. The woman is built like Sylvia, and Nelson feels a twinge of jealousy. "Thank you so much, you know?" says Beatrice.

"What for?" says Deirdre.

Jen goes, "Ohhh," kind of loud, and grabs Beatrice's arm. "Is that Brian?"

At the sound of the name a guy looks up.

"It's Jen," says Jen, "from Omnia Mundi."

The guy grins and wipes his hands on his pants. If it's Brian, the dreadlocks are gone. Just brown curly hair.

"Brian we met at Maryville?" Nelson says, and the guy is pumping his hand.

"That would be me. Oh man, I've been meaning to get in touch with you folks."

Nelson points at the floor. "You're—a student here?"

"Yeah!" says Brian, as if he can hardly believe it himself. "Political Science."

"Brian joined us this semester," says Beatrice. "Hey, look, I have a class. Will you guys be around long?"

Fetzer checks his watch. "We need to leave by eleven."

"Okay. Let's figure something else out. Maybe after your show opens," she says to Deirdre, and Deirdre smiles.

Nelson didn't expect students to be anticipating the exhibition, but Jen must have told them.

"Hey, can we, like, step outside a minute?" says Brian.

Great. He's going to give them more EFB instructions. Right when they're busy with so much else. And Nelson really can*not* take a trip so close to Dee's opening.

"Dudes," says Brian when they're outside. "I heard you were at the Bush protest."

"Wouldn't have missed it for the world," says Fetzer.

"Like, I heard you saw what happened." Brian puts his hands in his jacket pockets and looks aside. Looks back. "Emma told me you guys tried to help. But the cops pushed you back."

Nelson can't recall seeing Emma, the girl who was apparently eyeing him at the Maryville firebombing, but he probably wouldn't recognize her in daylight.

"Ah. Yeah," says Fetzer. "It looked really rough."

"I'm, like, so grateful, you know?" says Brian. "Feels like family, you know, when you hear that folks are looking out for you even when you don't know they're there."

Jen lifts her hands, lets them drop. "We felt bad we couldn't reach you."

"How are your eyes?" says Nelson. He wishes they'd checked up on Brian afterward. All it would've taken was a phone call.

Brian rubs a finger in one. "They're still messed up. I can see fine, but they're really sensitive. Like anything makes them sting, you know? Hey, and another thing—" He pulls his hand away from his eye, makes a disciplined fist, smiles through gritted teeth. "Gotta stop doing that. Anyhow, I want to apologize for the Maryville action. The way it worked out."

Fetzer folds his arms. "You mean making the horses run past the fire?" he murmurs.

Deirdre inhales. "You! You did that?"

"Shhh!" says Jen.

Brian's forehead crinkles like a potato chip. "Yeah. And it was stupid. I took this oppression awareness workshop, see? Made me confront the things I was doing to preserve my own power, you know? First thing I thought of was those poor fucking horses."

"I should bloody well think so," says Deirdre.

Jen hisses at her, "Shut up. You don't know anything, remember?"

"But she's right," says Brian. "We wanted this really awesome video. And we got it." He puts a hand on Jen's shoulder, then the other hand on Nelson's and says, "Jen. And John," and for a moment it's like they're about to be knighted or something. "Great work. It looks really good."

Nelson says, "Thanks," and almost adds, *for finally remembering my name.*

"But it came at a cost. It was perpetrating even more trauma on those animals."

Before he knows it, Nelson pulls Brian into a hug.

43: JEN

"WHY'S THE LAMINATOR UNPLUGGED?" I say.

Nelson comes over. "We hardly need to do any laminating right now." He bends down and plugs in another cord, and the stupid Christmas lights come on. Colored lights wrap around the basement stair banister, and go all the way down to the tool room door. Little white lights festoon the top of the map wall. Nelson's got a silly grin.

"Anyhow," I say, "maybe the president has nothing to do with it. Maybe Reynolds is embezzling on his own."

Fetzer lowers his butt onto the vinyl sofa with a grunt. "How could he be that stupid? An audit would catch it in five minutes."

Nelson holds up one of the handwritten notes. "He's obsessed with five hundred thousand of something, and the VIRAS budget he's handling is a half a million less than we thought. Where did it go?"

I say, "You realize the window for me getting back in might be rapidly closing, right? That admin workstation I used before has already been patched."

Fetzer examines the backs of his hands. "You think you can try one more time? Maybe get into accounting? Or payroll?"

"Thought you'd never ask." I sit down, crack my fingers, and launch Mole.

"You want coffee?" says Nelson. He used to flip out when I hacked, now it's like, doo-tee-doo, whatever. I am also pleased to note that he smells clean.

Preparing for the port scan. The rush of a fresh hack is on me, but what the hell, coffee never hurts. "Sure."

Nelson goes upstairs. Fetzer watches.

"Come on, come on. One little vulnerability is all I need."

Nelson brings some papers down with my coffee. He and Fetz hang out on the vinyl sofa and I hang out in #rezist until Mole prints *Common Exploit Discovered!* Music to my ears. Or eyes. Whatevs. I type *exit stage left* and quit chat before Vi can say good-bye. That'll teach her for dumping me so fast last night.

NICE. DEE'S MADE SANDWICHES. Fetzer takes one, shoves half of its approximately sixteen square inches into his mouth.

"Time to gather around the electronic fire," I say, and Nelse and Fetz pull up chairs on either side of me.

"Tahini and cucumber?" Dee says to me.

"Yeah, when I'm done. Okay, so this is what I found. Reynolds got a President's Advancement Grant last month. A hundred grand."

Fetzer's coffee breath near my ear. "Shit."

"Also got them in October, September, August, and July."

"Quintuple shit," says Nelson. "What the hell is this mother of all grants?"

Right when I look up Dee's camera goes click. And for some dumb reason a smile pops out of me, and she clicks again.

"Perfect," she says, then, "You have fantastic hands."

"These?" My big white freckled hands. How many keystrokes have these fingers typed? Millions, probably. At home on a keyboard.

Fetzer says, "Jen?"

"Right. Yeah. It comes out of the President's Advancement Fund."

The print emerges and I snatch it up. "Found this in a handbook: 'The President's Advancement Grant shall be awarded by the President to applicants whose proposals show potential for significant advancement of the university. The President may award multiple grants per fiscal year from the President's Advancement Fund and other nondesignated or unassigned gifted funds, at the President's discretion, and to the extent such funds are available'—blah blah blah."

Nelson takes the printout. "Is there an application process?"

"Way ahead of you, tie guy. Got Reynolds's applications right here. They're all about testing software, and they are total BS."

Nelse and Fetz get to reading a couple of the applications. After a minute Fetz says, "I can't understand a goddamn thing."

"Exactly. Assuming you're an auditor, you're supposed to be so blinded by the science that you don't inquire further."

Nelson snaps a carrot stick between his teeth. "They do seem to be padded with a lot of jargon. I don't even understand the outcomes."

Fetzer rubs a hand over his mouth. "If the prez thinks they're real, then maybe it's not blackmail."

Nelson's shaking his head. "If this is out of the Pentagon funds, they're not gifted or unassigned."

"Right," says Fetzer. "No way the prez isn't in on this."

There's another click and I look up. With her free hand Deirdre sips on something cloudy with ice. Something about that sip makes me ask, "What's in the glass?"

She winks. "Lemonade."

Fetzer grabs the glass, sniffs. "Lemonade with some *help*. It's barely lunch time."

"It's just a wee bit of gin, Jaysus."

Again with the explanations of how stressed out she is. Again with Nelson's acquiescence. Again with Fetzer starting out critical then rolling over like a dog getting its stomach rubbed.

She offers gin and lemonade all around, then, "Let's sit out the back. It's all yellow with fallen leaves." She picks up the plate of sandwiches and hands it to Nelson. "A picnic!"

Charmed, Nelson says, "Maybe it's a good time for a break?"

"When was the last time we ate lunch in the sun?" says Fetzer. He pokes my shoulder. "You could use the vitamin D."

"You know I was born with a tag that said, 'Store in a cool dark place.'"

Fetzer just shrugs and follows Nelson and the sandwiches out the door.

"Subject to change without notice," I mutter, and I start backing out of Harry Lane U.

44: FETZER

A SURPRISING NUMBER OF people turned up to Dee's opening: radio folks, infoshop folks, plus the students were drawn like moths to the free wine and snacks, and faculty and staff followed the whiff of rumor that this wasn't going to be an ordinary Center for Photography reception. Within half an hour the place was packed and the air was full of chatty hubbub, as people mostly ignored Dee's work and took the opportunity to catch up with each other.

The photos looked great. And the framing—the result of several nights' work by Dee and Nelson, with Franky's help—was classy. However, Dee's feet seemed to be nailed to that shiny wooden floor. Nelson stood close, greeting people who came by, while she maintained a fragile smile.

Jen said, "Check it out," and pointed at one of her doing the weekly filing, papers spread all around. I was caught in the top corner, small in the distance, emerging from the basement bathroom zipping up my fly. Made me laugh.

Right then Students for Peace Beatrice and Brian came in. The atmosphere shifted. People made wary eye contact. Maybe it's just rival student groups, I told myself. I waved at Beatrice when her scanning gaze swung into my quadrant, but she didn't recognize me. I felt naked without my disguise.

Then a guy with a backpack tapped Jen on the shoulder. Jen nodded and made a half-hidden gesture with her hand, and the guy moved on.

"Who was that?" I asked.

"Jordan. Students for Peace rep."

I didn't recall him being there the day we visited those folks in their puppet-filled room on campus. He moved around the gallery, tapping people but saying nothing.

"How come you know him?" I asked.

Jen shrugged. "Been in touch."

I should have known right then that it wasn't going to be an ordinary reception at all.

The curator lady, an Asian woman, interrupted us with a glass of pee-colored wine in each hand.

"Excellent turnout," she said. Slight accent. "Do you want some wine?"

Dee practically grabbed and gulped. Jen wandered off. The curator held the other glass toward Nelson and me, but we shook our heads so she ended up sipping it herself.

"A different mix than usual," she said. "Younger."

By then I figured about half of them were Students for Peace. A young guy with a long beard rummaged in his backpack. Two girls dressed from a dumpster that had gone through a black dyebath were watching the room like scouts. Something was up.

Deirdre's smile had relaxed. "I like the way it's hung."

The curator dipped her head in what might have been a residual bow. "Thank you."

"Are art receptions generally like this?" I said. Meaning, such an ADD-infused waste of everybody's time. Pity Sylvia wasn't there. She would have livened things up with at least a stream of gossip. I sure missed her.

"Like what?" asked the curator.

"Excuse me, but are you John Nelson?" said a woman.

Nelson's hand left Deirdre's, went out to the woman in a dark blue blouse. He smiled like a welcoming chaplain. "Yes, I am."

"Laurie Gefter," she said, "County Commissioner."

The curator lady wiggled her fingers in good-bye and made a beeline for some richer-looking people in suits and jewelry.

"I thought you looked familiar," said Nelson. "Good to meet you in person." Then he introduced Dee and me.

The commissioner had a pointy greyhound profile. "Your investigation of those Pentagon contracts was quite eye opening." She gestured with her wineglass. "And now you're in this ironic exhibit—you're becoming one to watch for surprises."

Nelson puffed out a self-conscious sound, put his hands in his pockets. "It wasn't just me; we're a team, Omnia Mundi." He nodded at me. "Irving Fetzer and Jen Owens are my colleagues. And the exhibit is thanks to Deirdre, of course." His smiling eyes, loving on her.

You lucky girl, I thought. *You better treat him right from now on. Hold on to what you've landed by some miracle of fate.*

The commissioner waved her glass so close to Nelson I thought her wine would splash. "I'm amazed the university approved. Was the exhibit planned before or after your investigation?"

Nancy was by the snacks, her orange skirt and jacket flashing between other bodies dressed in wintery black and gray. I wished she'd come our way. I wanted to check up on Jen, too, but Dee was looking so vulnerable I felt obliged to stick close.

"They happened independently," said Nelson.

The commissioner dragged her eyes around the room. "Fascinating," she said, then the orbit of her wineglass swung again past Nelson's lapel. "Your website is the first place my staff look when they need anything environmental. And your archive of city and county environmental policies is a goldmine."

I said, "Good feedback, thanks."

"And the site works so well thanks to Jen," said Nelson. "Over there, long red hair?"

The commissioner turned, her eyebrows up, searching. Jen had a circle of scruffy young people around her. Two guys were balancing skateboards on their ends. It was dark outside the plate glass windows, and the sidewalk was full of people coming, going, staring in. Franky came through the door and I waved, but he saw Jen instead, and headed in her direction.

Across the room Nancy was talking to an elderly man. She sent me a wink.

Dee whispered in my ear, "Can you get me another glass of wine?" But there was such a long line at the wine table I said, "In a minute."

With a commissioner as an audience, Nelson was in his element. He said, "Ms. Gefter, I wanted to ask you what you thought about the Bull Run watershed. Whether anyone's proposed building a second reservoir."

"Oh, call me Laurie, please," said the commissioner.

Right then the air in the room changed. Faces swiveled toward the door. Two men in dark suits had come in from the night. Both broad-shouldered, both white. One was Engineering chair William Reynolds. I guessed the other was the university's president, Gary Wellesley. They walked the floor like it was their own.

"Here come the big guns," murmured Nelson.

The men greeted people, shook hands, moved under halos of magnanimity.

The curator nodded at them, her hands folded precisely. Right behind Reynolds was a photo of Jen stretched out on a sofa with a laptop on her knees.

The commissioner shook her head and whispered, "I have to say I'm surprised they're being so gracious about it."

Nelson turned his back to the two Big Men and bit down on a smile. Jen had seen them, and was ducking behind people. She pointed us out to Franky, and Franky pulled his hands out of his pockets and headed over.

"Hey, Deeeee," he said, and he engulfed her in a hug. "This looks awesome. Hey pardners," he added to me and Nelse. "Labels go up okay?"

"Sure did," I said.

"Thanks for all your hard work," said Deirdre.

"Nahhh." Franky flapped a hand. "It was nothing. You're the artist." He looked around at the crowd. "Wow, look at all this, huh? You rock."

"She certainly does," said a familiar voice.

"Kate Simms!" I said. Finally, someone I could talk to. Then it was introductions time. Turns out the commissioner and Kate knew each other: no surprise, considering their lines of work. The talk got small, and soon the commissioner was staring into her glass like she just realized the wine wasn't all that good. Deirdre stared at the commissioner's glass like she wanted to take it off her. Kate wandered away to look at the work.

I watched President Wellesley peer at the photo of Sylvia in the diner. I was surprised that one had made it past Nelson, but after checking it out, I could see why. Sylvia looked so out of character, it was almost a vengeance piece for him.

"Can you get me another wine?" Deirdre asked again.

"It's not particularly good," said the commissioner.

"How about orange juice?" I asked. The juice end of the table was almost free of people. I ignored Dee's desperate stare and watched Jen watch Reynolds from behind a group of West Hills matrons. Nelson took quick glances over his shoulder. I myself was shifting from side to side to keep at least one body between me and the Big Men's line of sight.

Nelson said, "Anyhow, Laurie, about Bull Run. From an environmental perspective, ironically, another reservoir might turn out to be better than augmenting the supply with well water like we do."

Across the room Reynolds said something jokey to the curator, then turned to look at a photo. The bottom of his suit jacket rucked up around his hands in his pants pockets. He leaned in closer. His hands exited their pockets. Glasses came out of a case. Glasses went on. Head zoomed in close. He checked the label. It said, "John Nelson, consulting wall map." I knew, because I had typed it out.

What he then said to the curator was inaudible from where I stood, but her face went from attentive to blank. Next photo. Me standing, legs apart, arms folded, two gallon jugs of biofuel between my boots, and glaring into the lens. Right after Dee took it I'd said, "Will you quit catching me before I've shaved?"

Reynolds's hands became fists by his sides. He turned to the room. Forty, fifty people. More coming and going through the door. The president noticed Reynolds's change of mood and was looking with puzzled urgency at the work. Reynolds spotted Nelson, deep in conversation with the commissioner. I had a paper clip in my pocket and I flicked it at him, but he was on a roll. Reynolds advanced, but before he reached Nelson, a cell phone rang. Then another. Then another, and another. The air was full of jingles and chirps and bells. Reynolds stopped, patted his pocket. Nervous laughter from around the quieting room.

Except Nelson, whose voice sailed like an arrow through the lull: "—because of the radon in the well water—" He looked up. The commissioner looked up.

"I heard HLU builds war technologies," said a man into his cell phone.

The curator, white-lipped, called out, "Please take your phone conversation outside."

"Harry Lane U expels dissenters for noncriminal activities," said Beatrice into hers. Reynolds's face was a tomato.

An elderly woman who I wouldn't have placed as a member of Students for Peace, said, "Did you know that the militarized civilian university is tied to the emergence of the national security state?"

Reynolds's fists opened and closed.

Brian jammed his phone to his ear and cried, "Harry Lane U is undermining its own commitment to peace and justice."

The president stared at Reynolds. The curator moved around, waving her arms. "This is private property. You cannot disturb the customers."

"They're trying to shut us up as we speak," said a boy into his phone.

There were titters around the room. Through the plate glass windows people watched. Others stood in the doorway.

"There's a song about it," said a woman with a long braid, and she started singing, "*Tell* the poli*tic*ians we don't *want* their *war*," and others joined in, chanting into their phones, "*Save* the people *of* Iraq, *push* the US *war* machine back."

"Stop," shouted the curator. "I'm calling security." But a drum started up, and the cell phone people began dancing to the beat. "*Tell* Bush we won't *let* him kill—"

The lights went out. The singing got louder; the phosphorescent green dots on the cell phones jiggled. Nelson tugged my jacket.

"We should go."

"I want to see how this turns out," I said.

Men in uniform appeared from nowhere. The dancing was getting bouncy. Reynolds and President Wellesley had disappeared. Franky said, "Let's go," and between him and Nelson, Deirdre and I were apparently leaving. We waved at Jen and she followed.

It was misty outside, making halos around the campus lights. We walked, heads down, through excited chatter.

"That was awesome," said Jen. "Your art's actually doing something."

"It's always done something," Nelson snapped.

Franky stopped. "Are you kidding?" he said. "It totally *sucked*. Poor Deirdre!" And that's when I realized she was crying.

"It was obnoxious as hell," said Nelson. He pulled her close. "I'm behind the message, but it was terrible timing. It upstaged her work."

Jen spread her hands. "It's not like hardly anyone was looking at it, anyway."

Brian ran up. "Jen," he yelled, and they high-fived. "Awesome!"

Deirdre pulled away from Nelson and shrieked, "You *knew*, didn't you?" She shoved both hands against Jen's chest.

Jen stumbled off the path. "Whoa. Sensitive parts there, okay?"

"You helped them plan this?" I said.

Brian's smile fell off his face. "You didn't know?"

Jen held her arms across her front. "I was going to tell you all. Just, Dee seemed so freaked out I thought she'd put the kibosh on the whole thing."

"Are you *insane*?" yelled Nelson.

Brian got down on one knee, took Dee's hands in his and said in a mournful voice, "Deirdre the fantastic photographer, we thought you were down with it."

Jen reared up and pointed at the ground between our feet. "You want insane? How about *this* place is insane. You think it's sane to aid and abet war? Huh? You think it's sane to sit back and watch imperial expansion unfold?"

Dee wrenched her hands from Brian's grip and lunged at Jen. I grabbed her, held her tight until she stopped struggling, then turned her down the path. In the gallery behind us, the lights were back on. On the bright white walls we were stuck inside her black-and-white rectangles. The crowd outside was growing. Campus cops were escorting people out. There was shouting, laughing, singing. The song stayed with us until we turned the corner.

45: JEN

"CAN I SEE THE stapler?" I say.

Nelson picks it up, holds it out. A staple falls into my coffee.

"The silent treatment's getting tiresome," I say.

Dee's laundry basket bumps my desk as she navigates around the fax machine. My coffee sloshes. She keeps on going. Fetzer glances over at the spill then goes back to typing.

Guess it's gonna be me going upstairs to get the sponge.

When I get back, Nelson's saying to Dee, "Hey, we missed this this morning. You got two whole columns." He folds the paper over, and he and Dee stand shoulder to shoulder to read.

"Is it good?" says Fetzer.

"'Deirdre O'Carroll,'" says Nelson,"'revives the tired hybrid of art photojournalism long enough to get me interested in a group of Portland's more obscure yet dedicated citizens.'"

Fetzer pulls in his chin. "Obscure?"

Nelson's eyebrows pop up. "'Ironically, the very citizens who exposed Harry Lane University's out-of-character relationship with the Pentagon, which makes this show a transparent and clumsy attempt at greenwash.'"

Fetzer rolls his eyes.

"Someone didn't to do their homework," I say.

Nelson scans down the paper. "'. . . work bucks the current Northwest trends of nature and narrative photography . . .'"

Fetzer says, "So he likes it but he doesn't have the balls to come out and say so."

"Rest of the column's about Toshiko, how she was in charge of a corporate collection before she took the job . . . 'finding her feet in an educational setting' . . . huh. And it looks like the entire second column is about the protest."

My desk now clean of coffee, I drop the sponge at the bottom of the stairs.

"Great," says Nelson with disgust. "The protest is contextualized within a bunch of uninformed nonsense about impromptu theater. He likens it to those groups that stand still in train stations."

Deirdre hides her face in her hands and bursts into tears. Again. There are murmurs and hugs from Nelson, and Fetzer passes her a tissue.

"Hey," I say, and shrug. "It's publicity."

"Shut up," says Deirdre into her hands. Nelson rubs her back.

"It's all wrong," she wails. "Everything's all wrong."

"It's fine, sweetheart," says Nelson. "The show looks fantastic. Everyone says so. And this means more people will go see it. Sure, the protest and Toshiko got the lion's share, but without the controversy you'd probably get a shorter review."

The phone rings and I reach over. "Omnia Mundi Media Group." *How may I neglect your call?*

"Is that Jen?" says a deep voice. Nancy.

"Yeah. Hi."

"Not good news. I saw today the gallery's closed."

"Closed?"

"Uh-huh. People were taking the work down. I feel so bad for little Deirdre."

Little Deirdre is sniffling. Now how am I going to avoid getting my eyes clawed out?

"Crap."

Nelson's cutting the review out with scissors. There's a picture of one of her photos, I can't tell which from here. Deirdre watches him like it's all pointless.

Nancy says, "Uh-huh. I heard Toshiko's been canned, too."

"How's Reynolds?"

At the sound of the name, all three of them look up.

"Not a happy man," says Nancy. "Not a happy man. Listen, I gotta go, but I'll be in touch."

"Okay. Thanks," I say, and there's a click.

The phone goes crooked into its cradle. I straighten it. Pick a piece of hole-punch confetti out of the little groove along the bottom.

"So?" says Fetzer.

Nelson's mouth is a bad-tempered line.

I say, "Let me preface this by saying, 'not responsible for direct, indirect, incidental, or consequential damages.'"

Their irritated frowns.

"Unfortunately, the show has been, ah, closed."

Nelson's hand slams down on his desk. "*Look* at what you've done." He's up and weaving around chairs, and I'm backing up against a shelf and the shelf's rocking behind me. Something hollow rolls over, smashes, shards flying out along the floor.

"I didn't know, man, I didn't know it was going to turn out like this."

"She worked *months* on that show."

"It wasn't meant to make it close, jeez."

Fetzer's between us, his boots crunching on glass. It was a light bulb. His hands, his voice, guiding Nelson into a chair.

"Okay," says Fetzer. Hands on his hips. He looks at me. "You helped them plan it?"

"No! I just told them when it was going up."

"You seemed pretty close with them for someone who just passed along a date and time. Did you *ask* them to do something?"

The inside of my mouth is coffee-sour. "Look. How many times do you get to put up photos of yourself in a place you've been banned, huh? I was just trying to get more mileage out of the opportunity."

"Mileage?" Deirdre squeaks. Her arms are bolt-straight by her sides. "That's all my work is to you, something to get *mileage* out of?"

"Dee. You have to believe me. No way did I think your show would close. I wouldn't have even thought of doing it if I knew that."

"Oh come on," says Nelson. "You know Reynolds has zero tolerance. You seriously thought he'd just sit back and take something like that?"

"All of you!" yells Deirdre. "All of you just used me like a rag. Reynolds would've had the show closed anyway. Soon as he recognized you."

"Yeah." I point at Nelson. "Yeah. So don't accuse me of not thinking it through."

Fetzer rasps both hands over his dome. "Didn't even think of that. He might have closed it anyway."

"We don't know that," snaps Nelson.

Dee shrieks, "He bloody would've. All you wanted was to get back at him. And my work was an oh-so-convenient way—"

Nelson's in her face and pointing. "That's not true."

"It *is* true."

"You have *no* right to be angry with me. I have supported you every step of the way. I have sac—"

Dee screams, "Shut up!" and flings herself away from Nelson. Nelson thumps his ass down on the vinyl sofa with his back to us and folds his arms. I'm storming upstairs like a kid but I fucking don't care.

"Stupid *protest* had nothing to do with it," I yell.

46: FETZER

UP IN THE LIVING room Jen had turned on the TV. She muttered, "Didn't make a *single* bit of difference."

"Okay already," I said. I was itching to get out, but the basement was off limits while Dee and Nelson sorted themselves out. And the front door was nailed tight. There's a window onto the porch, but it was glued with years of paint. I started in on it with my Leatherman, and Jen watched, but she didn't say a word about security. Chips of ancient oil paint and floppy strips of latex collected on the floor. Our dirty white trim had apparently been turquoise in the past, and dark green some time earlier. Finally I was able to jiggle the window open, and I could just get my leg over it and myself out onto the porch. That porch was in sorry shape. The broken bottom stair had collapsed, and half the railing on Deirdre's side had fallen into the bushes. But the top step held my weight, and I sat down. The air was fresh and cold. A band of sunlight flushed sunset-orange along the roof of the warehouse across the street. The front yard was all weeds and skinny bushes, and it struck me that I neglected the garden in inverse proportion to the sense of responsibility I felt about the people I lived with and the world we live in.

Behind me the TV came muffled through the window. The cadence of the dialogue, the laugh track. I had a picture in my head about Nelse and Dee downstairs. She'd be crying. He'd be contrite. They'd say sorry. Lovey dovey.

At least being a pair, they had built-in checks and balances. Jen, on the other hand, was emotionally alone and she liked to act alone, and it was getting harder to deal with.

I twisted around and looked back at the window, but I wasn't in Jen's line of sight. So I got the pack out and lit one. Good and hot in my throat and I fumbled the lighter back into my pocket, nearly dropping it through the gap in the steps. Look, I don't really smoke, okay? If they knew, I'd never hear the end of it about financing big tobacco. Even if it's only a pack or two a year.

Down the end of the street by the train tracks was a rattling sound. The homeless guys came around the corner, one of them pushing a shopping cart. They looked like circus bears, lumbering and swaddled with coats. When they were alongside the house the skinny black guy glanced over at the porch. I nodded hello. He ducked his head and they all stopped and the cart stopped its rattling.

"Spare a cigarette?" said the guy. His smile was graceful under his sweeping high cheekbones, but the missing tooth negated any chance of elegance.

I tossed him the pack, then the cheap plastic lighter.

His gappy smile widened. "Hey, man, thanks."

The tall vet in fatigues said, "She live here? Deirdre the donut lady?" His gray beard was stained yellow around his mouth. Guys like that bring a tear to my fucking eye, I tell you.

"Yeah. She lives here."

"She's nice."

I nodded and blew out smoke. "Heart of gold."

The guys shuffled off. Overhead crows were flying home across the river for the evening, the stragglers looking like big slow bats. I stubbed out the cigarette on the peeling paint of the porch.

That's so cowardly I hate it even more

PART FOUR

47: NELSON

FOR SOME ABSURD REASON the kitchen sponge is sitting on the bottom step. Nelson picks it up on his way up the stairs.

It definitely was a *lot* worse because of the protest. At least Dee would've had a good time last night. But no, she had a horrible opening reception, and now on top of that her show's closed.

And there's Jen, sunk into one of the black living room sofas, watching TV. She hates TV. What the hell is going on? And why is Fetzer climbing in through the window?

On the TV someone says something and Jen's stomach bobs with a soundless, smileless laugh.

Fetzer closes the window and dusts off the seat of his pants. "Everything okay?"

"Okay?" says Nelson. "No. Everything is not okay."

Fetzer says, "Sorry to hear that. You want some carrot cake? What happened?"

Nelson rinses the sponge in the sink. "No, I do not want some carrot cake, and you know what happened. You were there."

Fetzer stands stupidly in the way of the kettle. He smells like smoke. "I mean, after that."

The TV burbles.

"I want to make tea," says Nelson.

Fetzer moves out of the way. Nelson holds the kettle under the tap.

"What do you mean, 'after that'? I sat there like an idiot for half an hour then came up here. Any other details you'd like me to elaborate on?"

Fetzer's still frowning. "Where's Deirdre?"

Nelson resists the urge to bang the kettle hard on the side of the sink. "She came up here with you guys. God, have you been smoking?"

Fetzer's puzzlement mixes with something dawning. "I thought she was with you."

The kettle overflows.

Fetzer puts a hand on Nelson's shoulder and says, "She's probably next door." But it's clear he knows she probably isn't. The fear that's been stitching Nelson's dreams has come true. Deirdre has left.

Fetzer reaches across the sink and turns off the tap. "Try her cell."

Nelson mumbles, "She put it in a drawer."

Fetzer calls over his shoulder, "Jen, call Nguyen and see if Dee's there, okay?"

Jen pulls forward to the edge of the sofa. "What?"

"Just call, okay?" Then Fetzer says to Nelson, "We'll go next door and check. She'll be there, okay? But we'll check."

Nelson whispers, "She won't be," but he follows Fetzer past Jen on the sofa.

Jen watches like it's a suspicious parade. "I, uh, thought she was down there with you," she says. As if that's any help. Then there's the sound of her dialing. The laugh track erupts from the stupid TV. By the time Nelson and Fetz reach the bottom of the basement stairs Jen's saying, "Okay. Well, thanks anyway, Mr. Nguyen."

Fetzer yells up the stairs, "Get Franky," and Jen calls down, "I'm on it."

Nelson closes his eyes. Deirdre has left, and they all know it.

"FRANKY, TAKE YOUR CAR. You look south of Division, we'll look north. Nelse, come with me. Jen, stay here in case she comes back."

Franky wraps a thick gray scarf around his neck. Thank god he could come. Jen lifts the home phone and waggles it. "I'll call you the minute."

The TV's off. It's now dark outside and there's a wind up. The loosened window rattles with each gust. Nobody's made dinner, but the thought of food makes Nelson nauseated, anyway. He shelters his hands in his coat pockets.

As soon as he'd walked in on her and Sylvia, he'd known. From the bed, their two pairs of eyes, frozen, staring. He couldn't keep her. She was already on her way.

"Ready?" says Fetzer, and Nelson nods.

THEY GO UP AND down Division. Into Ladd's Addition a ways, since she likes going there for walks. Then they do the bars. In every one of them it's hard to see in the smoky light, and impossible to call out over the music and the chatter. They lean in close to bartenders and ask, "About five-two. Straight black hair. Irish accent." Fetzer keeps adding, "String-beany, long face." Nelson wants to qualify that with, *Beautiful skin, and topaz eyes, and the most delicate mouth that bends into a V when she smiles,* but by then the bartenders are already shaking their heads.

"Haven't seen her tonight," said one of them, and Nelson had to swallow against the sore place in his chest. It's his fault. If he didn't work so damn hard he'd spend more time with her.

"Where are you now?" says Fetzer into the phone. Rain sparkles on his bald head. Nelson's hair is wet and the wind bites at his ears. Fetzer tells Franky, "Keep going farther. If she kept walking she could be miles out by now." Traffic streams by in a river of red and white lights.

"If she got on a bus," says Nelson, "she could be approaching Olympia by now."

Fetzer closes the phone. "Let's not think like that, okay?"

THEY'RE STEPPING OUT OF a pool hall on MLK when Jen calls. After a second, a grin bursts out on Fetzer's face, and Nelson is rinsed with sweat and relief. Then Fetzer's grin fades. "Well," he says, "at least she's back."

Nausea churns with the relief. "Is she all right?"

Fetzer drops the phone in his pocket. "She'll be fine. A taxi took her home. She apparently had a business card on her—when the hell did she get business cards, anyway?"

"Jen made her some, remember, for her housewarming. Is she okay?"

"Huh. She should've handed them out at her opening. Well, thanks to the card, the driver knew where to drop her off."

"Is she *okay*? God, Fetz, did Jen say if she looked *okay*?"

"Sounds like she's fine, except perhaps"—Fetzer pinches his mouth—"her liver."

48: FETZER

THE POOR GUY NURSED her through the night. She was passed out, but her pupils and her pulse left me pretty sure it was alcohol and not anything else. Besides, she stank of it. Keeping her upright and shuffling around was a challenge, but it got even more challenging when she came to enough to barf all over the kitchen floor. Me and Jen went to bed. Saint John tended the sick, and Saint Francis tended the desperate of spirit and cleaned up after the sick.

Next morning we came downstairs to Nelson and Dee spooning on the brown velvet sofa. The smell of booze and vomit hung around till we opened the liberated window and stuck an extractor fan in it. It was sleeting outside. We wore extra sweaters, and the conversation around the table was all contrition and vows. Deirdre was the color of putty except for around her raccoon-eyes. She couldn't remember most of her evening.

She said, "Some fellas bought me a drink in a place with a neon sign, round with something in it like a crab or a spider—"

"That crab house?" said Jen. "They have a bar in there?"

"—then we went to this other place, but I wasn't paying attention to how we got there."

I let out a "Jesus fucking Christ."

Nelson covered his face with his hands. "Don't tell me you got in their car."

"Bloody stupid, I know."

Nelson groaned and stretched back in his chair. "God, you could have been raped, killed."

There were more admonitions from us, apologies from her. I mentally thanked the guys she hung out with for not being animals. Then Jen changed the subject.

"So, ah, Students for Peace sent this email for you." She handed Deirdre a printout. "They're really bummed your show closed. And I shoulda asked you about the protest. I'm sorry."

An apology. This was significant.

Deirdre read the note, but her expression didn't change.

"Tell you what," said Jen. "I'll put your whole exhibition on the web. I'll set up a domain name and everything."

"Good idea," I said, pleased to see Jen making amends.

Dee handed back the printout. "Don't bother."

But Franky was into it, and Jen said people were emailing trying to find out what had happened to the show. Nelson, who had barely spoken to Jen since the reception, said, "It's a good idea, Dee."

She rolled her eyes. "Fine. Anything for a quiet life." And that was the signal we could go back to work. Jen and I nearly knocked heads reaching for the papers on the floor. And since we'd all been too preoccupied to check the independent sites for a day, that morning's news was a surprise. Hundreds of Middle Eastern men and boys had been arrested around the country. Not exactly rounded up—they'd gone in voluntarily for Ashcroft's new fingerprinting and registration scheme, but they never made it home.

Jen brought a laptop to the table, and her searches found stories from distraught wives and mothers who had no idea when they'd see their men again. And blogs were talking of evidence of abandoned Japanese wartime detention camps being refurbished.

Nelson said, "It puts our own small lives into perspective."

Franky said, "Yeah. We've got it good."

"I dunno," said Jen. She gestured at the laptop. "We're in no less danger than these dudes. Feds just haven't figured out how to round up white dissenters yet. They can't use the brown paper bag test, but you know they're working on something."

"I just meant we gotta be grateful," said Franky. "Look what we have, guys. It's way more than lots of folks."

Just then the phone buzzed in my pocket. I pulled it out. It was a text.

I kept trying to make sense of the text but it just said *Intrusion Detected*.

Jen frowned at the interruption. "What?" she demanded. "Who is it?"

I held out the phone for her to see, and she was out of her chair and scrambling down the stairs before I could blink. "Intrusion!" she yelled.

We followed Jen down. She was typing faster than I'd ever seen. "That firewall was just fucking *updated*." She threw up her hands. "I don't know what they're using." She was up and over at the server rack and a second later the computer went dark. The lights went off on the servers. The fans stopped. The basement was quiet in that way where you realize you'd gotten used to a noise.

Jen sat down in the nearest chair and pushed her hair off her forehead. Breathed in. Breathed out. "Hopefully the mirror site is fine. Should be."

"What happened?" said Franky.

Jen swung the chair to face us. "We've been hacked."

"Who by?" said Nelson.

"Maybe I can tell when I check the logs. But shit, no prizes for guessing, right?"

Nelson dropped his butt on the vinyl sofa and frowned, incredulous. "You think *Reynolds* would do this?"

"Probably not personally," said Jen. "But he'll have contacts."

"Did they do any damage?" I asked.

"Fucking hope not," said Jen. "It was what, fifteen, twenty, seconds?" She rested a hand on the nearest tower like she was calming a frightened pet. "The intrusion detection picked up as soon as they got past the firewall, so unless they lobbed a bomb into the system, I doubt they got very far."

"A bomb?" I said.

Jen closed her eyes. "Fuck. I'm going to have to go through and clean out." Then she pointed at Franky. "See? Don't give me that Hallmark positive-thinking BS, okay?"

Franky said, "Huh?"

Jen jabbed her finger. "This is *war*, man. Just 'cause we're not in matching outfits with little ribbons and medals doesn't mean it's not happening. Class war. Resources war." Her hands scythed the air. "War against the *whole* fucking planet and *everyone* who lives on it who isn't in the elite."

She was pink in the face. Franky, like he was speaking to a simpleton, said, "I know about that. I'm just saying, like for instance they didn't get very far, right? So that's cool, see? On the day to day, gratitude is the best attitude."

"You don't get it, do you?" Jen picked up a nearby laptop. "We're on the front lines, Frank. And it would *really* help morale if you *quit* talking like a fortune cookie and started getting even *semi*-realistic about shit."

49: JEN

I'M NOT DEPRESSED ENOUGH. Must be time for a news fix.

WAR IS UP TO SADDAM. Well fancy that. "President Bush flatly rejected arguments from antiwar protesters, saying the choice for war is Saddam Hussein's. 'They've got all the right in the world to express their opinions. If they tried to do that in Iraq, they'd have their tongues cut out,' Bush said."

Tongues cut out. *Tongues* cut out.

As Franky would say, look on the bright side: nobody's actually torturing us. Yet.

But fuck, what if it came to that? Do we even really know what's happening to all those Muslim guys they rounded up?

And here am I, sitting in our quiet kitchen. The newspapers on the floor like every other day. The Crusher taking up space in the living room, temporarily up here for its recovery. And Dee's collecting bottles by the stove.

"Yo, Deirdre," I say. "Recycling?"

She pauses with two full paper bags in her arms. "Yeah," she says. No smile.

"Cool," I say. She's been cleaning a lot the last couple of weeks. And she and Nelse have cooled down—not so much activity through the wall, thank you, Jesus. He's working hard, she's pulling her weight. Finally. And she's not as ditzy. In fact, she sort of plods around. Doesn't laugh as much. Weird thing is, I sort of miss the old ditzy Dee. Why can't she combine Righteous Dee with Ditzy Dee for something more balanced?

She glances up from the bags. "These are getting heavy."

"Right. Listen, it's pouring outside. Put those down and come have a look at this." I pull out a chair and she sits. Then I turn the laptop so it's facing her. "Ta-da!"

Her eyes latch onto the screen, and her fingers touch her collarbone. "Me website?"

"For all the world to see."

She stares. The first photo is the one of the vigil outside the Science building at Harry Lane.

I say, "I figured it shouldn't start with a picture of one of us, you know? 'cause that would be, like, privileging whoever it was."

Her name is across the top in simple white caps. My hand leaps for the touchpad, but I pull back and say, "Click the arrow? Yeah. The photos look cool against the dark gray, huh? And the captions come up when you roll over—yeah. And the arrows take you to the next one or back. And click there to get home."

Her other hand is over her mouth. "You did this for all of them?"

"Sure. Piece of cake."

"Oh," she says, and there's a tiny break in her voice that shoots right into me.

She clicks. It's the one of me and Fetz pouring fuel. "You've kept the contrast," she murmurs. "And the detail."

"Yup. I didn't have to manipulate them at all."

Another click, and it's the one of Frank and Nelse walking to the car. A symmetry in their arms and feet. Something I noticed as I was scanning them. They're actually pretty interesting pictures if you look at them for a while.

She clicks. There's me at the Crusher, my hands like starfish on the keyboard.

"I set up an email address, too, so you can answer questions."

"An email address?" she says. "That's scary."

I'd Googled her, didn't find a thing that matched. There's a Deirdre O'Carroll in Florida who's a swim instructor, and another one in Ireland, but she's studying to be a nurse.

"What's so scary about an email address?"

She clicks again. Broken floral carving along the top of the porch. And again. Nelson looking out a window, evening light texturing the cloth of his shirt.

"I am no longer a passenger," she says to the screen. "I have come ashore."

"Huh?"

Her head lifts and her pale eyes are on me. "I love it."

I want to hug her and I hope she wants to hug me, but her elbows pull in a tiny bit closer to her sides.

I say, "Click on the envelope icon to access your email."

"Jaysus," she whispers. The cursor hovers over the envelope. "What if there's a message?"

I shrug, smile. "Check and see."

She clicks. Webmail comes up. Two messages: One, 'test-ignore' from me. The other's subject is, 'your photos'.

She sits there.

"Click on the subject," I say. "Haven't you ever used email before?"

She clicks. It's a message from Beatrice. Cool. Saying how glad she is to see the photos again. With yet another apology for the closed show. And yet another reassurance they thought she knew. Yeah, yeah, everybody's got to rub it in.

"I wish I didn't have an email address," says Dee.

"O-kaaay," I say.

She turns and her eyes are full or warning or fear, I can't tell. "Because every day now I'm going to check it."

"That's the general idea."

Her eyes skitter back and forth on mine. "In hopes that Sylvia will write."

"Ah." I stand up. "Look, there's diagnostics I need to check on, so—"

She grips my sleeve. "Don't you ever—?"

"Can I have my arm back?"

She lets go. Barely audible over the hum of the fridge, she says, "You're so bloody self-contained."

I shrug again. Pull a face. "Sorry. I guess." My new strategy: when in doubt, apologize.

"No. I envy you."

Her eyes have stopped skittering. Now I can't look away.

"You know that part in Peter Pan," she says, "where Peter is marooned on a rock, and the tide is rising and he knows he's going to drown?"

My hands up, a barrier. "Okay. This is getting weird."

But she grabs one of my hands, holds it in her small hot paws. "He's sitting there and his heart is pounding and the water is lapping at his toes. And it suddenly occurs to him, 'To die would be an awfully big adventure.'"

Her lips move and twist. Her hands feel feverish.

Don't know what to say.

She leans forward and I jerk back, step away, hands in pockets, hands out of pockets, wake the Crusher up. Progress bar's only halfway though. The laugh out of me is shaky, grating. "What the fuck was that about?"

"Thanks for making the website," she says in a voice gone flat. "I'll be saying a prayer of thanks to the blessed Virgin, too."

The progress bar seems to have stopped. "That was a joke, right?"

So close I catch the mint on her breath, she says, "Will you check me emails?" She probably eats the damn things to cover up the alcohol.

"Uh. Okay."

Then she's walking away. Heading for the basement. Not looking back.

Now what the *fuck* was that all about?

50: NELSON

NELSON REACHES ACROSS DEIRDRE for the clock. 4:17 a.m. He flops back against his pillow and sighs.

She's lying facedown, and her breath scrapes in, then falls out. There's the data about depleted uranium he has to look at before the end of the week, and that Wetlands Defenders interview to transcribe. But it's too early to get up.

Even the highway is quiet. The lamp on the floor at the far end of the room makes a cave of the space and casts shadows across the ceiling. More rain coming this week. A lot more rain. Biblical rain. When Greenland melts, that'll be biblical. The Atlantic will fill the Amazon basin. The Willamette will flood this house. No wait, it's supposed to be fire. "God said fire not a flood next time." Pete Seeger. No, Peter, Paul and Mary.

They thought they had problems, but from here the sixties looks like a hopeful, breakthrough time. Turmoil mixed with a big fat promise of a better world. Now there's just the turmoil and something unimaginable coming up ahead. No world as anyone knows it.

Nelson pulls the cover off Deirdre and rests his palm on her hot back. She's damp. She got so drunk again. It was Sylvia's letter that did it. Handwritten on heavy paper, it was addressed to them both, and it sounded so unlike Sylvia that he thought it was a hoax. Deirdre assured him it was Sylvia's handwriting.

The letter was full of regrets about the hurt she'd caused. And her desire to change. "I want to be less selfish," she'd written. "I want to do more for the world. And even if I never see you again, John, I'll always remember your inspiring spirit."

"Are you *sure* this is from her?" he'd repeated.

But after a while the letter had a calming effect, and an argument he'd been carrying in the back of his mind went quiet. He was able to finish his piece about a raid against an English GM research facility before heading for bed. But he found Dee sitting on her bathroom floor, empty gin bottle beside her, moaning, "I have strayed, I have strayed, far from the path."

The Catholic stuff again. Her arms fell loose around him as he pulled her up. Her mouth left a wet smudge on his shirt. He sat her on the couch, wiped her face with a washcloth, made her drink a glass of water. He wished there was more he could do.

"I am a sinner," she moaned.

"You seeing Sylvia again?" he'd snapped, but she just murmured "No" and clung to his neck.

The night they came back from the station retreat and found her dancing, she was so happy. He wanted her so much back in July he thought he was going to short-circuit. Now he needs her just as much, but it's different. He needs the frequent familiar of her. He needs her ribs under his hand, like this. He needs her skin under his lips, like this. And he feels so helpless when she gets so drunk. Too drunk to make love.

He nuzzles her sleeping neck. Her breath struggles in, falls out.

Not that it didn't cross his mind last night.

He was so eager to get to bed. Felt good about getting the GM raid story done. Looked forward to the reward waiting for him. Instead it was half an hour of getting her up, getting her warm, stopping her crying. And later as he pressed up against her still body he suspected he could fuck her and she wouldn't notice. Or wouldn't care.

He hates it that he's even thinking like that.

He tugs her T-shirt straight. Smooths her hair around her ear. Whispers, "What's wrong, Deirdre, what is wrong? What can I do?"

The shadow of a chair looms across the ceiling.

Yesterday Rumsfeld "did not rule out" the possibility of using nuclear weapons in Iraq.

The shadow seems to shift. Fear flickers under Nelson's skin.

And North Korea's saying its missiles could reach the west coast of the U.S.

The West Coast. The roadtrip unfolds in him: San Diego. Los Angeles.

San Francisco. The long stretch to Portland with only small towns in between. Who would the North Koreans bomb first? Portland? LA? Vancouver?

Her shocked face when he'd brought it up. What if he volunteered to go to Iraq, he'd asked, his voice halting around the size of the idea. "It seems so pointless trying to have an effect from this distance."

"Join the *army?*" she'd said.

"No, no," he'd said. "To be a human shield."

Her mouth hung open.

"Bombs," he'd said, "made by my country, will be killing civilians in a country that never did a damn thing to me. And simply protesting against it is having no effect. I need to do more."

But Deirdre put another mint in her mouth and shook her head. "Are ye *mental*?"

And he hasn't brought it up again. And, to be honest, it's a relief. The most scared he's ever been was the time the loggers caught them building tree-sit platforms in the forest and had raised their rifles. He'd probably shit himself within five minutes over in Iraq.

In the distance an ambulance wails. Someone else's emergency. He tucks a strand of hair away from Deirdre's face. In war movies bombs scream when they fall. In slow motion, a bomb blast: the shock wave bursts the windows and punches through the walls. Glass and splintered wood fill the air. She wouldn't even have time to lift her head and they'd both be gone.

The clock now says 4:32. Another big peace rally today. If he can get started now on the Health Effects of War essay, that'll mean more time later to research the growing number of city- and county-initiated antiwar resolutions for next week's show.

He pulls himself to sitting. The floor is achingly cold under his feet. He arranges the covers around Deirdre, then goes over to the desk, where his slippers and his files sit waiting.

"YOU'RE LOOKING BETTER," SAYS Fetzer. "You looked like crap this morning."

Nelson nods. Deirdre rests a hand on his back. He says, "A little better."

The drumming is loud. It's a big happy crowd today but he has a headache. It's the first time Dee's joined them for the monthly rally, and he wishes he was more into it. He should have taken some aspirin when she offered. He watched her crunch five of them this morning before breakfast.

"Check it out," says Jen, and she points down a side street to the mass of people several blocks away, moving in the opposite direction. The march is so long it's almost joining up with itself. Jen turns the video camera toward the sight. Nelson writes, "Nearing end of route. View down Madison shows start of rally still packed. Energy remains high."

"This is even larger than the last one," Fetzer says to Dee. He's grinning. Nelson feels like grinning about as much as he feels like poking his pen in his eye.

They pass people burning a flag. They pass belly dancers with their hips swinging and their arms in the air, and Nelson hopes their bare bellies aren't too cold. There's a weak sun but it's chilly. He forgot his scarf. They pass a parked SUV with *I LOVE FOREIGN OIL* scrawled on its windows in grease pencil. A noisy group advances from a side street. Nelson writes, "Radical feeder march? Est. 150–200." Then he adds, "black bloc."

They pass a large folding table set up on the sidewalk, covered in a purple cloth and fronted by a banner saying *WHO WOULD JESUS BOMB?* Behind the table long-robed priests hand pamphlets to passersby. After a minute Nelson has to run back and grab Deirdre, who has stopped to gape at the priests.

"Try to keep *up*," he says, and he bundles her along.

The radical feeder march gets closer, and a lithe kid in shabby black breaks away and bounds up to them.

"Dudes!"

"Brian, hi," says Nelson. He feels like dealing with Brian's energy about as much as he feels like poking his pen in his other eye. Brian walks with them, chatting a mile a minute. He takes Dee's hand and kisses the back of it. "And how is Deirdre the fantastic photographer?"

For crying out loud, Dee's batting her eyes. "Enchanté," she says, and giggles.

Nelson resists the urge to step in between them.

In front of them walks a couple in their sixties with identical *THROW BUSH OUT* signs. Brian skips ahead until he's face to face with them, walking backward. "Hey, great to see you here," he says. He points at the signs. "Think that'll solve the problem?"

"Oh, he must be stopped," says the woman in an earnest schoolteacher voice. Jen snorts. Nelson rolls his eyes. Poor woman's underestimating who she's talking to.

Brian bounces on his toes. "Nope. That won't do it. This war isn't the result of a bad president. It's the result of a socio-economic system that is racist and exploitive of the vast majority of the world's population."

"Right on," says Jen. The couple glances back at her, their eyes uncertain. Nelson makes a quiet-down motion at Jen.

Brian keeps walking backward. His smirk is quick to come and go. "What kind of car do you drive?"

The man and woman look at each other. "Uh, a Subaru," says the man. "And a Civic," says the woman, nodding with approval at their vehicular modesty.

"You rich?" says Brian.

"Oh no," says the woman, and she smiles at the idea. "We're just ordinary folks."

Brian points. "You're rich, lady! Rich by global standards! And this war's going to benefit you and the rest of the economic elite at the expense of everyone else."

Before the couple can reply, Brian says, "Later, dudes," and springs away. He disappears among the marchers.

Nelson envies Brian's energy. His single-minded passion. But not his tactlessness.

"That was interesting," says Jen.

"Rude," mutters Deirdre.

"We are *not* part of the economic elite," huffs the woman. Her knuckles tighten around her sign.

"Well, he has a point," says Jen. "This isn't just Bush's war. The invasion of Afghanistan and Iraq were planned years ago, before Bush."

The man stops and turns, and Fetzer almost bumps into him. "That's ridiculous," he says. The march flows around them. The man points a rigid finger. "If Gore got in, there wouldn't be this war. It's Bush's revenge for Bush Senior. Plain and simple."

"Maybe not during Gore," says Nelson, "But eventually. The invasions have been planned for some time."

"Says who?" says the man.

"The Project for the New American Century," says Fetzer. "They drew up a report a year before 9/11."

"Rove was part of it," says Jen. "And Rummy and Wolfowitz. Perle, Cheney, Jeb Bush. They're all in on it."

The march keeps flowing around them. The man narrows his eyes. "Then how come it's not on the news?"

"Media blackout," says Jen. "But you can find it on the internet."

The man pulls in his chin and says to his wife, "A conspiracy theory. On the internet." His wife rolls her eyes.

"No, seriously," says Nelson, but the man grabs his wife's elbow and yanks her along. Nelson resists the urge to tell him to be more gentle.

They let a few people get between them and the couple, then they start walking again.

Three pro-war protesters pass in the opposite direction, chanting "Go USA, go USA." Their signs say, *SADDAM HAS THREE THOUSAND INNOCENT LIVES ON HIS HANDS*, and *Except for ending NAZISM and FASCISM, war has never solved anything*. Bringing up the rear is a man with long hair under his backward baseball cap. His sign says, *Get a brain! MORANS!* in wobbly letters.

Jen snorks out a laugh. "Morans?"

"Fuck you, hippie," says the man, and he moves on.

"May contain traces of nuts," says Jen.

Nelson resists the urge to sit down and put his head in his hands. They turn the corner and approach Pioneer Square. And the square is *still* full of people waiting to start the march. Nelson smiles for the first time that day. "Wow," he says. In the notebook he writes, "25 blocks full. Largest so far?" The crowd thickens as they near the square.

"Hey," says Jen, and she jumps to see over the mass of heads. "I think that's Isobel from the station. To the left of the stage."

Nelson jumps too, and he spots Isobel's long gray cornrows.

Isobel waves her clipboard as they approach. "Jen! Irving! John! Isn't this fantastic?" Her big mouth stretches open in theatrical surprise.

"Biggest antiwar gathering I've seen in decades," says Fetzer.

Isobel nods so hard her braids dance. "And this war hasn't even started."

"Yup," says Fetzer. He puts his hands in his pockets, rocks back on his heels. "We're ahead of the game, for once."

"I *know*!" she cries, then she touches Nelson's arm. "Oooh, I just thought of something. Zenia Rafeedie can't make it. Could you say a few words in her place?"

Nelson is instantly sweaty, despite the cold.

"About Palestine?" he says. "Um, not really. I'm not qualified to talk about—"

"No, no, no," says Isobel, and she laughs and flaps her hand. "Just say *some*thing. War and the environment or something. I've got a ten-minute gap and it would really help me out if you could fill it."

The sweat doesn't stop coming. "Uhh." He runs a hand through his hair but it makes his scalp cold. "I didn't exactly come prepared for—"

Fetzer whacks him on the back. "Sure you can."

"Look, I didn't get much sl—"

"You can do it," says Jen, and she points to Nelson's head. "Fuck, you've got whole books stored in there."

Isobel's shoulders slump and she does a mock-sad face. "Pleeeeease?" she says.

Deirdre looks at him with adoration. He says, "Uh. I guess."

"Fan*tas*tic," says Isobel. She snags the sleeve of a man wearing a headset. "John Nelson is taking Zenia's place."

The man cocks his head. "John Nelson? Awesome. Right." He checks his watch, looks at Nelson, and says, "You're fifth up. Hopefully everyone'll be back by then."

THEY'RE ALLOWED TO HANG out on the steps up to the stage so they can see over the crowd a little bit. But the crowd is too big. There are no stage lights to blind him into pretending there's no one out there. Deirdre keeps up a steady stream of encouragement in his ear. Isobel pats his arm each time she goes up to introduce another speaker. Each speaker climbs up the steps. Says articulate and eloquent things. Comes back down. Nelson knows, or knows of, all of them. He offers congratulations. Handshakes. Forces himself to smile. Everyone agrees the march is the biggest ever. Everyone is hopeful that this means something. Every time Nelson tries to formulate his talk, his mind goes blank.

The crowd is cheering. The fourth speaker comes down the steps. Isobel's voice over the PA says, "Our next scheduled speaker, Zenia Rafeedie of Free Palestine Now, is unable to make it due to transportation problems. Instead we have John Nelson from Omnia Mundi, who will say a few words about war and—" Isobel turns and looks sideways down at Nelson. She smiles. "War and the environment." She raises her hands clapping and steps away from the microphone. The crowd claps thinly.

They are disappointed Zenia isn't here. En masse they will walk away. Nelson will be responsible for the critical depletion of numbers that will occur before Isobel can wrap up the event. Omnia Mundi will lose respect. Their show will go off the air. Fetzer and Jen will hate him. They'll split up.

He swallows. Climbs the stairs. Someone grasps his hand, squeezes. It's Jen.

From the stage the crowd swells out of the square, fills the streets as far as he can see. Open faces looking up at him, smiling, waiting. Signs bob.

An ocean of goodwill. A sea of hope.

Love surges up so fast in Nelson his knees feel like they're made of string.

"Oh my god," he says, but he's not near enough to the microphone so he takes a wobbly step closer. One of the signs says, *No Blood for OIL.*

"Oil," he says. He clears his throat. "Oil. Our lives are bound up in it. And we're about to go to war over it. Again. We have this way of thinking about oil that seems completely normal, but is actually—insane."

The crowd claps.

"We suck vast amounts of it out of the ground—a dangerous process in itself. Then we set fire to it!" Nelson spreads his arms. "We send the smoke into the air! That smoke—and I'm simplifying the science here—is going to destroy life on earth as we know it. How *insane* can you get?"

More clapping.

"We're living with old, leftover ideas about oil. It was once important to our sense of power. Sense of progress. But these old ideas will be our downfall. And we're taking the whole planet with us."

The crowd is quiet. Helicopters thrum overhead.

"The story we tell ourselves, about oil, may look like it's changing, but only at the edges. Sure, we like our bicycles and our canvas grocery bags, but we're a minority. The sacred story of oil still has primary currency. Those of us who think differently are considered odd curiosities. We don't fit."

Laughter from the crowd.

"And maybe we don't want to fit. Maybe we make a lifestyle out of not fitting. We feel proud we don't blindly follow the status quo."

Laughter and cheering from the crowd. Signs bob like buoys on a sea.

Nelson holds up a finger. "But let's not be too proud." The crowd goes quiet. "Let's not be too proud. Because the earth is in deep trouble.

"Everyone here"—Nelson lifts his arms to the beautiful crowd—"imagines a different story of oil. Some of you are diehard cyclists." A few whoops and cheers fly up from the mass of faces. "Some of you work with renewable energy and peak oil. All of you know that killing people over this oil is crazy, and at least that part has to change." The cheering swells and Nelson pauses. "We're beginning to transcend the sacred story of oil. But it's a tiny beginning. Let's not get smug. Let's never feel like it's enough."

Clapping again, louder this time.

"Marching like this is good. It reminds us we're not alone. But we have to do more than walk through the streets, then go home to our oil-heated houses to watch the news. We *have* to transcend, we *have* to tell a new story. One that says it's not eccentric to get rid of the car, it's not crankish to install solar panels, it's not weird to avoid plastics. It's *normal*. These things need to stop being charming and self-righteous; they need to become *normal*. Small gestures are a start, but we need to ratchet up our efforts. And we need to make it easy for others to make these choices, too. Others who have fewer choices than we privileged folks. We must transcend."

Their beautiful faces, receiving, giving.

"We *will* transcend the story of oil."

The cheer mushrooms up, echoes off the buildings. Signs dance like wave caps stretched as far as he can see. Nelson's knees are titanium. His head is crystal, clear and solid. His heart is a ruby, dense with love. He lowers his arms and walks away from the microphone. Hands pat his back, squeeze his arms, rest on his shoulders as he makes his way down the stairs. Fetzer's eyes, Jen's eyes, bright, alive, loving. Isobel yelling in his ear, "Good job!"

And Deirdre. He holds her tight. "Let's get married," he says into her neck, and he's not sure if she heard over the noise of the crowd, but she pulls back, grips his shoulders.

"Yes!"

51: JEN

FRANKY'S STUPID BOUNCING ROCKS the whole sofa. "It's you!" he shouts at the TV. As if it's not blindingly obvious to the rest of us who were actually there. It's a semi-distant shot, but it's Nelson on that stage all right. His moment of glory. Good thing I also caught it on camera. Add it to the DVD I'm planning.

"Quit bouncing," I say.

Fetzer says, "You shoulda seen it, Franky." He gestures at the TV. "He just stepped up there and had the crowd eating out of his hand in half a minute."

Deirdre whines, "But you can't hear what you're saying."

Nelson sits with an arm across her shoulders, relaxed, unblinking. Like it's anyone but him on the news.

"Course not," I say. "Broadcasting a dissenting opinion would be collaborating with the enemy."

The reporter on TV says, "No violence marred today's event like it has in some of the earlier rallies," then the screen switches to a helicopter shot. The square, the streets, the waterfront, like someone spilled colored confetti over the city.

"Notice how he managed to get the word 'violence' into the first sentence?" I say.

"About eleven thousand people turned out to voice their opposition to a possible war—"

"Twenty-five to thirty!" shouts Fetzer, and he's half out of his seat and jabbing his finger. "Twenty-fucking-five to fucking thirty!"

Man, he is not often this pissed.

"—but when I listened to their arguments no one seemed to be able to address the complexity of the situation."

Fetzer slams back into the sofa and yells, "Shit on you." The screen switches to a young protester. "It's just wrong to invade a country that hasn't done anything to you," she says.

The reporter says, "Others turned up today to voice their support of President Bush's policies, and to support the efforts of any soldiers who may be called to serve if such action becomes necessary."

"Fucking cowards," Fetzer yells. "Couldn't report a story if it crawled up your fucking assholes."

"Dude," I say, "What do you expect?"

Fetzer palms his face. "I dunno. I thought maybe this time it'd be different. There were so goddamn many people!"

Onscreen it's one of the couple dozen *morans* we saw, a fifty-ish woman with dyed blond hair. "The president needs to be strong," she says. She blinks into the sun. "He needs to be resolute in standing up to this bully. And we need to stand behind him as a nation."

Fetzer mutters, "You ever get the urge to just bomb something, Jen? TV station for instance?"

"All the time, dude, all the time."

"Not funny," says Nelson. Him and his middle-class caution. Man, the things I'd do if he wasn't around.

There's an edge in Dee's voice. "If you'd been anywhere near real bombing you'd know it's really not funny."

Fetz says, "I know, Dee. Just letting off steam."

"Hey." I kick her toe so she looks at me. "Show some respect. Dude was in Vietnam, okay?"

Dee puts a hand over her mouth and looks at Fetz. "Sorry."

Fetz reaches to pat her knee. "S'okay."

Girl gets away with anything.

Behind the *moran* woman on TV a mass of protesters are marching past, and they're way more interesting. A woman waves her sign, *The Corporate Media is Complicit!*, and grins. A fat guy in a circle-A jacket flips his finger in the direction of the camera. Makes me smile that the editor never saw them. Bottom-feeder production values.

Franky says, "They sure gave the pro-war lady a lot more airtime."

I raise my beer to him. "The corporate media, Frank, of which you are a willing, if peripheral participant, has a primary goal of what?"

"Huh?" says Franky. "No, I'm not."

"Controlling public discourse, Franky. To the point where people think of themselves as consumers rather than citizens. Got that? Consumers. Of Coke and American Idol and Nike and Disney and Nintendo and infotainment." I nod in the direction of his feet. "And designer boots."

Franky looks at his boots then frowns at me. "I got to keep these after that magazine shoot. What's that got to do with Nelson's speech not being on the news?"

"Consumers are focused on consuming, right? And that distracts them from participating as citizens. And that leaves governments and corporations free to do what they want, because no one's paying attention. And *that's* how they get away with murder."

"Despite operating in a so-called democracy," adds Fetzer.

Franky goes back to watching TV. "You're just jealous."

"Intelligent critique would get people thinking, and thinking would disrupt the distraction—wait, what?"

Franky crosses his legs and more boot shows. "Admit it, Jen, these boots are awesome."

"Excuse me?"

Dee says, *"Mundus vult decipi, ergo decipiatur."*

"You people are weird," I say. Time for another beer.

"The world wants to be deceived, so let it be deceived," she says as I go past.

"Thanks for the downer," I say, and grab the last Cold Creek Porter.

An ad for a Toyota Landbruiser comes on. The car bucks its way in slo-mo across a pristine southwest landscape.

"You're right, though," I say. "The whole fucking world wants to be deceived. Except for the point zero zero zero zero zero one percent that won't settle."

52: NELSON

NELSON DRIZZLES MORE SHERRY on the mushrooms and stirs with a wooden spoon. Excitement buzzes in his chest.

"Hi," says Franky. He puts a bag of apples on the counter. "So, what's the occasion?"

Nelson smiles at the mushrooms. Deirdre says, "It's a secret. Till we tell." She's wearing his favorite sea-green blouse with the ruffles. She looks fantastic.

Franky tosses his keys and catches them. "Can't wait." The mushrooms sizzle. They're such a rich, dark umber.

"You guys need anything?" says Franky. He tosses the keys again, and this time Dee catches them with a squeal.

Like the sound he heard that day behind her door. He had rushed in thinking she was hurt. From her bed, her and Sylvia, their two pairs of eyes, frozen, staring.

Nelson rests the wooden spoon across the pan. It's over now. He shouldn't even think about it.

"Know what?" he says. "Let's splurge." He pulls a twenty out of his wallet. He almost never spends twenty all at once. "Get some dessert. Something creamy. Tiramisu."

Franky waves away the money. "Nah, I can get it. But Jen won't eat that, right?"

"Take it, okay. Get something vegan for her, too." Franky makes a reluctant face but takes the twenty, and Nelson goes back to stirring.

It's time to celebrate. He's applied for the license. They have a date. They're going to announce it at dinner. And once they're married, they'll figure out how to get her on medical insurance. Maybe something through Mr. Nguyen, if she can get enough hours.

"And we'll have a child," she had murmured into his chest last night. "An American child."

No time like the present to start trying, he'd said, and they didn't use a condom, and just knowing that there could be a spark of new life—

Nelson pauses the wooden spoon. The moment feels huge and wonderful, like all the stars in the sky.

But he should mention to her about cutting back on the drinking.

"So, tiramisu," says Franky, "and what about a marionberry pie? I know Jen will eat that."

"Yeah," says Nelson. "Get a pie."

"And how about"—Franky does a dance move that ends in a flourish—"ice cream?"

"Brilliant," says Deirdre, and she giggles. It's good to hear her giggle. She's been kind of low lately. But things are getting better. It'll be so good when they're married.

Even though it's happening a little sooner than he expected—when he asked her the day of the big rally, in his mind's eye their wedding would take place in the spring or even summer. But, like she pointed out, since they know it's going to happen, why put it off? And after her ambivalence a few months ago, it's feels good to simply go with the flow.

And once they're married she can apply for citizenship. Not that he'd expect anyone to want to be a citizen of this insane nation right now, but from a practical point of view, they'll feel more secure when she's legal. They need the stability. It will help her, and help him, too. He can be more effective.

The mushrooms are done and he takes the pan off the burner. Deirdre hugs him from behind. "Those look yummy," she says.

To think he considered leaving all this to be a human shield in Iraq.

53: JEN

FETZER OFFERS NANCY COFFEE.

Her blue heels clop across the living room floor. "Sounds good," she says.

Nelson nudges the coffee table so Nancy can get her large self in there without having to squeeze. He's such a Nelson, but those social graces come in handy sometimes.

"Cream?" says Fetzer from the kitchen.

The sofa sags under Nancy. "No thank you. But three sugars, if you don't mind."

Nelson sits down next to me on the opposite sofa, elbows on his knees. Nancy's blue pumps glow like they're radioactive under the coffee table. She never seems as radical as Fetzer says she used to be. Sure hope I don't get all conventional when I get older.

She says, "My doc tells me I need to give it up—sugar, that is. I don't even tell him about the five coffees a day."

Nelson politely smiles. Fetzer sets the tray on the table. Nelson stares at the four coffees and I know he's mentally going, Where's my tea? But Fetzer's forgotten.

Nancy leans toward the tray. "If you don't mind my asking, what the hell is that?"

"That?" says Fetzer. He sits next to her. "Sugar."

Nancy sits back and shakes her head. "No it's not."

"It's Sucanat," says Nelson. "Unrefined dried cane juice."

"No offense," says Nancy, "but it looks like they didn't sift out the dirt."

"It's got less sucrose than white sugar," I say. "Metabolizes slower. And it isn't filtered through beef bones."

Nancy's wide eyes clamp onto me. "Beef bones?"

"Let's focus on what we asked Nancy here for," says Fetzer.

Her fingers curl back and those nails dig in to her pink palms. "You telling me sugar goes through *beef* bones?"

"Well," says Nelson, "Strictly speaking, the charcoalized byproducts of animal slaughter."

Nancy's fingers splay. "Stop." Her eyes close and her eyebrows stretch way up on her forehead. "You just did in five seconds what my doc's been trying to do for five years."

"Truth," I say, "may cause side effects in certain individuals."

Her eyes open and she snorts. "Much obliged, I'm sure."

"Aaaanyhow," says Fetzer. "We didn't ask you over to talk about sugar. We've come to a dead end on HLU and Reynolds, and we wanted to run some things by you to get your input."

Nancy's eyebrows go up again. "My input."

"Maybe bounce some ideas off you," I say.

"Hunh," says Nancy. "You already bounced me out of the old age I was looking forward to, baking cookies for my grandkids. If you got any more life-changing revelations in that stack of paper of yours, maybe I should come back in a few years' time. Like when I'm about to die."

Fetzer rubs his hand over his shiny skull. "You can bake with Sucanat."

Nancy wrinkles up her nose. "Looks gritty to me."

"It melts," he says.

Her mouth curves down. "I'll take your word for it. So what's going on?"

Fetzer says, "Well. We're wondering how things are going with your boss."

"Still weird."

"I'm going to cut right to it," says Nelson. "We suspect Reynolds is blackmailing President Wellesley."

Nancy digs the spoon into the Sucanat, pauses a second, then drops a heap of it into her coffee. "Holy shit." She digs the spoon in again. "No denying it, the guy gets whatever he damn well wants from Wellesley, and he gets it on a gold platter."

"Do you know why?" I say.

She goes in for a third spoonful. "No. But everything he gets comes from Wellesley. No one else gives him the time of day, unless Wellesley says to." She sits back, cradles the mug. "And now that you mention it, I've been hearing things."

She sips her coffee. Nelson fiddles with a pen.

"Not bad," says Nancy to her coffee, and I'm thinking, *For fuck's sake, what kind of things?*

"Kinda molassesy," she adds, "but not too strong."

"What sort of things?" says Fetzer.

Nancy sips again. "Through the wall. He raises his voice but I can't hear the words. And sometimes when I barge in on him he shuts up real fast."

Fetzer says, "Can you barge in on him some more?"

Nancy smiles at her coffee. "I do seem to be letting my manners go these days."

"Maybe it would help if we go over what we've got," says Nelson, and he tells her about the discrepancy between the Pentagon contract for five million, and the four and a half mil assigned to it in the department budget. Nancy's mighty curious how we got hold of the budget, and I just say, "I plead the fifth."

Then Nelse tells her about the five President's Advancement Grants that Reynolds got this year, adding up to five hundred K.

Nelson fans Reynolds's grant applications across the table. "And we're pretty sure these are bogus. The awards are a fraud."

Nancy picks up one of the applications, looks it over. "I did not see these."

"So, if you hear anything that might be even slightly related," says Fetzer.

"It's your patriotic duty," I say, and make my voice deep. "If you see something, say something."

Hilarity fails to ensue.

Nancy now looks dazed. She slides the application back onto the coffee table. She takes a sip of her coffee. "I kinda wish you hadn't told me this."

Fetzer looks at the floor. "Yeah."

"I need to keep my job," she says.

"Your name never came up on anything we looked at," I say.

"I *know* that." She slams the words between us. "'Cause this is all new to me. But now I gotta go back to work knowing. And that's not gonna be easy."

"Sorry," says Fetz. "You have our word that no matter what, you won't get associated with any of this."

She bangs her coffee mug on the table and bears down on Fetzer. "How do you even know this shit?"

He smiles, leans back and crosses his legs. "'Fraid I can't tell you that, Nancypants."

Nelse and I share a WTF glance.

Nancy stares at Fetz for a few tight seconds, then whacks him on the knee and laughs. "No one's called me that in *years*."

"Do you miss it?" says Fetz. "Activism?"

"Oh, I'm still active. Just 'cause I dress for the office doesn't mean I'm not working for a better world, nuh-uh."

"Cool," I say. "What are you working on?"

She gets a satisfied look. "I coordinate campaigns for NorthEast Portland Health Concern. Right now we're pushing to get a soymilk option on school lunches."

"Because many African Americans are lactose intolerant," says Nelson.

"Exactly."

"We should do a story on that," I say. "Milk and cheese being carbon-intensive foods that not everyone can even digest—"

Asshole Fetzer interrupts with, "Speaking of activism, what about yesterday's rally, huh?" Then he asks Nancy why aren't more people of color at the rallies, and I'm thinking, *Dude, we've thrown her one curveball already. Maybe now's not the time.*

And Nancy's eyebrows are up yet again. "Those rallies of yours are all organized by white people, that's why." She crosses her legs and her hands get going, those manicured nails slicing the air. "They tell their white friends. They advertise in white places. They don't come into the black communities and let us in on what's going on, or ask us to get involved."

"Well, okay," says Fetz. "But they're no secret. There's been a lot of flyers, it's been on the radio. On Indymedia—"

"Indymedia here is pretty white," I say.

He says, "It just seems tragic when the kids most likely to be sent to die in Iraq are going to be of color."

Nancy leans forward. "Hell yeah, it's tragic. But look at your alliances. It's still mostly white groups, like unions, right? Or if it's people of color, they're far away, like in Iraq or Palestine." She sits back, her nylons rasping. "We got our own Palestine right here. People shoved to the bottom and held there and the police on the border so they don't get out. And nobody on the other side of that border says hey, something's wrong here. You're protesting all those billions that go to the war machine, why aren't you taking it a step further and demanding those billions go to our own communities? Our own people? Our own schools?"

I shake my head. "Damn straight."

Nelson, ever logical, frowns. "But that's exactly what most progressives *do* demand."

Nancy shakes her head. "Nuh-uh. Not in the same way. Not to where you get thousands taking to the streets. You think this is some new war about to start? It's not new. It's been going for*ever*. For the folks in Iraq, folks everywhere, lot of them right here in the US. You think it's going to stop because a bunch of white kids get their panties in a twist?"

Nelson lamely says, "If people of color joined in, it would send a stronger message."

Nancy hurls out a beefy arm. "You think we wanna go marching somewhere we aren't supposed to and get arrested for it? Hell, no! Jail isn't some romantic destination, let me tell you. You think black folks are saying hey, bro, let's go bust some shit up to protest the white war machine and then go to jail for it? How 'bout Latino folks, huh? All those undocumented ones? How 'bout Indians? You think that when a person of color gets arrested for protesting they get out of jail the next day suffering nothing more than lost sleep and needing a shower?" She sits back with a huff of air. "Think again."

"Amen," I say, and Nancy nods.

Fetzer takes a soft slurp from his coffee. You started this, dude, get back in.

"Wow," says Nelson. He rubs his chin. "Then we've got one giant communication failure happening here. See, the big rallies are legal. That's the point. You agree to walk between *A* and *B* and the police agree not to crack your skull for it. And the whole raison d'etre of the antiwar coalitions is that all oppression is connected. It's part of the message. It *is* all connected. We're not ignorant of that."

Nancy sniffs. "Well, the message is not getting across. You call for peace around the world, but when it comes to peace at home most white folks just want peace on the plantation. Why should we join your marches when we don't see you defending us in our own struggles? You can get eleven thousand people—"

Fetzer lifts his hand like he's in a classroom. "Twenty-five to thirty."

"Twenty-five to thirty thousand, then, see? You march through downtown because you feel bad that folks you don't even know in Iraq are gonna get slammed."

"They've been slammed for decades," I say.

Fetzer stares at his hands and nods.

Nancy smooths her skirt over her knee. "Exactly."

I say, "Class war. Resources war."

"War in slow motion," says Nelson.

Nancy dips her head into a deep nod. "Exactly." She sits queen-straight, picks up her coffee, and sips.

54: FETZER

WHAT NANCY SAID GOT under our skin. We started this thing where whenever we were discussing something, for the show, for the newsletter, whatever, one of us would ask, "What's this look like through a race lens?" And sure enough, shit we hadn't even thought of would bubble up.

Meanwhile, the world around us grew more bizarre. As the weather grew colder, the propaganda drumbeat intensified. The majority of Americans believed "Al Qaeda" and Saddam Hussein were the same guy, because Bush said it enough times to make it "true." The weapons inspectors in Iraq kept coming up with nothing, but Bush declared Iraq in material breach and threatened to dismiss further weapons reports sight unseen. And it was like we had state-sponsored media for the level of critique that was presented. The tiny independent media was doing its best to balance things out, but who was listening? The population was fearful, and fear clings to the status quo. Every month saw coordinated protests nationwide. But unless you happened to be downtown during a rally, or caught the two minutes at the end of the nightly news, the two minutes that included equal time to some "we gotta nuke those ay-rab fuckers to keep our children safe" man-on-the-street, you wouldn't know there was a peep of protest at all.

I felt like I'd died and woken up in some parallel universe. Everyday details remained strangely familiar, but the big picture was very, very wrong.

One point of relief was that, after announcing their wedding plans, Nelson and Deirdre seemed to be doing better. Emphasis on "seemed."

Work-wise Nelson was on track, throwing himself into upcoming radio shows and writing new essays. He and Jen were planning more talks, and a couple of invitations had come in already on the strength of the San Francisco conference.

Another point of relief was that Dee had stopped taking photos. This bothered Nelson, but I was happy to go about my business without every dumb Kodak moment being captured for posterity. Instead she surprised us by focusing on cleaning, which led her to find my old socket set, the one I'd replaced, but I was pleased to get the old set back because it's better quality.

On a darker note, we also passed the third anniversary of the WTO protests, and it was an occasion for reflecting on how much things had changed. Back in '99 the global justice movement was fresh, focused, and energized. There had been a sense that the possibilities, not just for us in the privileged North but for millions across the planet, were being transformed. But 9/11 changed everything. Radicals of all stripes, us included, had lost our bearings, our confidence. The PATRIOT Act, Operation TIPS, Total Information Awareness, "Enemy Combatant" being redefined and stripped of habeus corpus, and the new Department of Homeland Security overseeing it all—it gave us pause like we hadn't felt before, at least not in my living memory.

Then the new year rolled around, and although we drank a toast to the minute hand on the clock, there was a lead blanket around my heart that said this wasn't a time of renewal, and things were going to get worse before they got better. We opened the papers that week to the news that for the first time in Harry Lane U's eighty-year history, military recruiters had set up offices on campus. When the term started, students picketed the office daily, but the military presence marked another shift toward what was becoming the strange new normal.

ONE CHILLY JANUARY DAY, Franky came by for breakfast. It was my fiftieth birthday, and everyone had forgotten. We didn't do birthdays much, but I was sort of hoping my big five-o would not pass unnoticed. However, my only present that morning was the good news that our own Senator Wyden had stalled the funding for Total Information Awareness. But it was a hollow victory. We knew they'd figure out a way to appropriate funds from somewhere else. Give it another name, whatever. I sat there thinking a cake would have been a more tangible pleasure.

"How was Seattle?" said Nelson. Franky was going up there for a regular magazine gig, plus he'd met a girl who was "really nice and laughs a lot." It seemed like a good time, I thought, for Franky to build some relationships away from us. Despite his loyalty and his good intentions, he needed to be around younger people. The laugh-a-lot kind.

"Seattle was excellent," said Franky, enthusiastic like he was digging into a steak instead of oatmeal. "We had a really nice dinner at the Olive Garden, then we met up with a bunch of her friends and played mini-golf. We had so much fun it was unbelievable."

The kettle started to scream. "Unbelievable," Jen deadpanned, and she got up to turn it off.

"Leave him alone," snapped out of me so fast I didn't see it coming. Something about that simple young affection I didn't want messed with, mired as we were in local conspiracy, the nation heading for war, and the papers full of lies—and the not-so-simple relationship between Nelson and Deirdre. They'd sprung a February wedding date on us. Now, I'd always known Nelson was the settling-down type, but I didn't think the same about Deirdre.

The night they announced their wedding plans, they'd cooked us a fancy dinner. I'd offered my congratulations, and opened the last of Mrs. Krepelter's Pinot Noir. Franky had hooted and slapped everyone on the back. Jen said, "You're what?" like she didn't understand the concept.

City hall, it was going to be. Just us as witnesses. "When the first crocus buds appear," said Nelson. He pulled Deirdre close. "You'll love the long, slow springs we have here. From February through June, there's a new flower out every week."

She smiled. Said nothing.

The next day he and I were picking up containers of fryer grease from behind the diner. I probed, but Deirdre was apparently not pregnant. I asked, "So why now?" and got Nelson's giddy response: "Why not?"

We grunted as we picked up the buckets. "Because you've only known each other for eight months," I said. I didn't mention the other reasons.

"We've been through a lot in those eight months," said Nelson. He wiped his hands on his jeans. This was one of the few tasks he didn't wear chinos and a tie for. "I think we can get through whatever comes our way."

55: JEN

"HERE'S YOUR MAIL," SAYS Franky. He's panting, and there is actual steam coming off him.

The bundle is an inch thick. It's been like this every day for the past month. We're going to have to hire someone to handle it. "Cold out?" I say. Stupid small talk. Of course it's cold out, you can see icy puddles from the living room window.

Like we can hire someone.

"Freezing," pants Franky. He puts his hands on his sweatpants hips and bends at the waist. "S'good, though." He unbends, breathes out like he's exhaling a toke. "Makes me run faster."

"Uh-huh." Among the mail is the New Western Light catalog. Oh shit, that reminds me.

"Hey, Deirdre?" I call up the stairs. Then to Franky, "No hate mail today."

"Cool," says Franky. He leans in close. "Everything ready for later?"

"Almost. Fetz is running errands right now. Nelson's picking up the cake, and he'll keep it at Deirdre's. They'll set the room up later. Kate's coming, and Isobel and a few others."

Franky nods. "Awesome. What kind of cake?"

"Some fancy shit with chocolate and raspberries."

"Oh, awesome," says Franky.

Do I mention that it's probably not fair-trade chocolate? Do I mention that ninety percent of Ivory Coast chocolate plantations use slave labor?

Do I point out that countries where cocoa is grown aren't allowed to make the finished product? That the North monopolizes that industry? And do I even begin to delve into the real cost of those out-of-season raspberries in plane fuel and trucking and refrigeration? No. Everyone's in denial. And I am tired.

I call up the basement stairs, "Deirdre?"

A small thump overhead, like she's getting up off the kitchen sofa.

"I'm kinda worried about her," Franky whispers. "Even though they're getting married and everything."

"Huh," I say. "I kind of am too." More *because* they're getting married and everything.

She comes down the stairs with a sigh. "Franky, lad, did you have a good run?" She's smiling but I suspect she's just going through the motions.

I hold up the New Western Light catalog. "You got an email from these people. They maybe want to use your pictures in something."

She takes the catalog. Thumbs through it, barely looking.

"Like a book or something?" says Franky. "That's a cool opportunity."

I'm not jealous. Not in the least. "They saw your pics on the website."

She hands back the catalog. "That'll be the phone," she says, and because the basement extension is spread all over a table due to Fetzer fixing a connection, I have to run up the stairs.

"Omnia Mundi." Dee's cup is on the floor by the velvet sofa. She's supposed to be making cookies while Fetz is out getting new hoses and filters, but she hasn't even started.

The phone says, "Hi Jen. This is Nancy."

FETZ PICKS UP AFTER three rings.

"Dude. Nancy's coming over. Something's up. Get your ass home."

"Already on my way," he growls.

Guy's been grumpy all morning. It's going to be a trip watching his face when we take him next door tonight.

THANK GOD NELSE TURNS up from stashing the cake next door and he's getting Nancy established with coffee. Dee's gone to work, and Franky's keeping Nancy occupied with chitchat while she stirs about a quart of Sucanat into her cup and beams out smiles at him. She's all in red today, and on the black living room sofas with those shiny red heels and the red hoops in her ears she looks like something off a Chinese lacquer box. Good thing about having a laptop is you get to sit at the kitchen table and look busy and nobody bugs you. Time to check in with my peeps.

`*** TheJenerator has joined #rezist`

`<VioletFire> iggy, that was probably just some infected machine scanning you`

`<TheJenerator> Hello, all`

`<ignite> Hi jen`

`<VioletFire> JenJen!`

`<ignite> Jen, You ever figure out who hacked you?`

`<TheJenerator> Not yet. Did a close-up manual inspection against a backup. The malware looks custom built.`

`<TheJenerator> Transmitting to a little Linux server on a small Belgian ISP, but, you know. So what.`

`<VioletFire> they gain root?`

`<TheJenerator> Nope. My antivirus alerted me before they got too far. Thank god.`

`<VioletFire> Hell yeah. But still.`

`<TheJenerator> Yeah. It sucked donkey wang`

Anyone could try us for vulnerabilities. Doesn't have to be ideological. But that attack was pretty sophisticated. Someone knew we'd be well-protected but tried anyway. Can't help but think of Reynolds. If not him, then some lackey of his.

And that's the white nose of the Toro pulling up behind Nancy's car. Thank you, Jesus.

"I brought you these," says Nancy, and she reaches into her big red tote bag to pull out a golden cookie tin. Nelse and Franky crane their necks to see what's inside. "We parted ways last time a little hot and bothered," she says. "But you guys oughta know," and she turns to include me, "I respect what you do. I wouldn't be here if I didn't."

Fetz comes in, walks straight over to the coffee pot.

"And you," Nancy calls out to Fetzer as he's clattering around the kitchen. "I'm glad you asked. It's more than what most would do."

Grumpy Fetzer turns to face us. "Huh?"

Nelson tells her we're grateful for the feedback, we want her input to improve the way we work with diverse communities, yadda yadda. All of which is true but he frames it so slick, if I didn't know the guy I'd think he was a politician.

Fetzer comes over with his coffee. Jerks his head at me, like, *join us.*

`<TheJenerator> being summoned. gotta go.`

`*** TheJenerator has left #rezist`

Nelson adds, "And we recognize that the ability to be angry in public without coming across as the wrong kind of person is a privilege. One that we enjoy, and you do not."

Nancy nods once. "That is a useful recognition to come to."

Fetzer says, "Yeah. And we want to build alliances. Real ones. And we want to learn. Hope you can help us."

"It would be my pleasure," says Nancy, and she holds out her hand. They shake. Everyone's hands go out. Hers is strong and dry in mine, her brown skin against the pink-white of my fingers. Her hand that's raised a daughter we haven't met but she's trying damn hard to make sure the kid grows up whole and healthy, and fuck, every day that must be one helluva scary challenge, raising a daughter by yourself—holy cow.

Nancy's smile is bright. She gestures at the golden cookie tin. Inside are chocolate chip cookies. "Sucanat melts okay," she says, and winks at Fetzer.

"Oooh," says Fetzer, and helps himself.

Do I mention it's probably not free trade chocolate?

Franky takes one and says, "Thanks, Nancy."

That the people who picked the very beans are in the same indentured situation as Nancy's ancestors? That we could stop it if we wanted to? Trade embargoes? Boycotts? But who's going to boycott chocolate? It's a cultural addiction. Like slavery.

Nancy chuckles and pushes the cookie tin closer to me. "You don't like my cookies?"

The following actions do not represent the views of Jen Owens.

Except, damn. This cookie is mighty tasty. Probably has butter in it. I'm going to want more than one.

"So," says Nelson. "Something urgent's come up?"

Nancy looks at her watch. "Yeah. Reynolds is heading for some kind of crisis. He was on the phone all yesterday. There was yelling. Then around the office he'd blow up over stupid little things. Then this morning walked in on him just as he was saying, 'You'll never get away with this.'"

"The blackmail?" says Nelson.

Nancy lifts both hands. "I don't know."

Fetzer glides a hand over his freshly shaved dome. "Which phone does he use the most?"

"The one in his office," says Nancy.

"How about his cell?"

Nancy shrugs. "I don't see him use it much at work."

"Good," says Fetz, "that'll be easy." And I think I know where this is going.

Nancy's eyes on us, back and forth. Is this a sugar rush or am I just excited?

"Wow," says Franky through crumbs. "You gonna bug his phone? That's so like in the movies."

"Ohhh," says Nancy, and she rolls her eyes. "Oh ho. Ho."

I say, "I could go in there as an HVAC tech."

"What if you got someone in to polish the woodwork?" Fetzer asks Nancy.

Nelson rubs his chin. "I could wear a fake beard."

"Forget it," says Nancy. "He's so allergic to any of you his throat would swell up if you came near him."

"But you could let us know when he's out."

Nancy shakes her head. "He's been unpredictable. Canceling meetings."

"I could do it," says Franky.

"Seriously?" I say. Prettyboy never volunteers for the front lines.

"No," says Fetz, his hand out flat.

Nancy says, "Is it hard? What if I did it?"

Fetz smiles. Rubs his hands together like a crazy lab scientist. "Merely a minor learning curve. Come downstairs. When you see what we've got, you'll be all over it."

"IT'S STRAIGHTFORWARD," SAYS FETZ, "but you have to do two things. Install the bug in the phone line where it goes into the wall, and put a receiver somewhere close by. Like in a broom closet."

"And this is the bug," says Nancy. The black cylinder is dwarfed by her long nail. "And this is the receiver?"

"Yup. The bug is too weak to transmit more than a hundred feet. It transmits to the receiver." Fetzer connects the receiver and the tiny VOX circuit board to the tape recorder. "The receiver is too big to hide in a phone, but it'll put the signal onto tape."

Nancy snorts. "And you'll be outside in a white panel van?"

Fetzer says, "We'll pick up the tapes from you once a day, or more if you think there's something good."

"You mean I gotta change the tape?"

"'Fraid so," I say. "But you could keep it in your desk drawer."

Then Fetz rummages around in a box and pulls out a wall socket and some phone cord. "You'll need to attach the bug to the screw terminals at the back of the phone jack. I'll demonstrate on this one."

Fetz strips the end of the wires and says to me, "Show her how to tape this in." I grab some electrical tape and stick the bug belly-down inside the socket box. The copper coil on top makes it look like a tiny cupcake. Nancy cranes to look at the bug and I get a whiff of her perfume. She says, "It's going to record everything?"

"Only phone conversations," says Fetz. "It's not a microphone, it's just tapping his phone circuit."

"Will the tape come on automatically?"

"Yup. But you have to have it set on Record."

I add, "Hold down the Play and Record buttons till they lock, then let go. The voice activation will make it start and stop."

Nancy nods. Fetzer grins. "He can make a call at midnight and it'll pick it up."

Nancy looks at the receiver like it's a snake. "I dunno. Sometimes he goes into my desk looking for pens and shit."

Nelson clears his throat. "Do you, ah, if you don't mind me asking, keep tampons or pads in your desk?"

Nancy's finger-splayed hand pushes flat above her bosom. "Well. Uh-huh."

"Will this fit in the package?"

"I believe it will."

"Great," says Nelson. "Just keep an eye on when the tapes run out."

Fetzer bundles up the VOX and the receiver and the recorder and puts them in a paper bag. He looks up. "Your desk's wood, right, not metal?"

Nancy nods.

"Good." Then he drops two latex gloves in the bag and Nancy's eyebrows bounce.

"May as well take every precaution," he says.

Her hand goes up. "Now you're making me scared."

"Don't be. It's got my prints all over it, and if I was worried I'd take the time to wipe the whole thing clean."

Nancy stares at the paper bag. She shakes her head. "No."

"Dude," I say. "Come *on*."

Nancy folds her arms. "Sorry. I changed my mind."

"I thought you wanted to build alliances," I say.

Her black-brown eyes. "I *thought* you gave me your word you weren't going to involve me in this."

Fetzer says to the bag, "Yeah. We did."

"Sorry, Irv," she says. "But I can't put my ass on the line for this."

"We'll figure out something else," says Nelson. "You're right, we shouldn't have even put you in this position."

Great. *Just* fucking great.

THE DOOR CLICKS CLOSED. "That was embarrassing," murmurs Nelson.

"She's certainly changed," says Fetzer. "Guess it was stupid of me to expect otherwise."

"It would've been so *easy* for her," I say.

Fetzer says, "She's got a job, she's supporting a kid. Too much to lose."

"Lose to what? How the hell would she even get caught?"

"But what if she was?"

"That's practically impossible. Besides, she said she'd do it. Backs out soon as it gets a tiny bit risky."

"Hey," says Fetzer. "It was stupid to ask her. Period."

"It needs to be done, dude. I'm locked out, okay? Fucking vulnerabilities got patched. We going to just let this slip through our fingers?"

Fetzer sighs, swipes his hands over his baldness. "Let it go, Jen. We'll think of something."

Right. Like I'm going to wait around for *that* to happen.

56: FETZER

HONESTLY, I DIDN'T HAVE a clue. Dee complained about a "fizzy light switch" and I went over there to check on it, hoping the problem was on the room side of the wall and not deeper in. She opens her door and next thing I know there's a thousand people yelling "Surprise!" But when my eyes got used to the dark it turned out to be a more manageable number.

Kate, who I was surprised was even there, brought two bottles of Gevrey-Chambertin that I'll never forget. Isobel and a few other folks from the station came. A couple of guys from Veterans for Peace. Three kids from the infoshop—invited by Jen, but they were mellow and funny and put Jen in a better mood. She'd been pissy ever since Nancy left that morning.

Mr. Nguyen turned up with a tray of pastries. Dee's place was decorated all over with strings of colored lights. There was a little bit of dancing, but mostly we drank wine and talked, and nobody was in a hurry to leave. I forgot about Colin Powell's address to the UN, and the computer-generated diagrams of mobile WMD production facilities that were offered up as "proof" of Saddam's failure to comply. Instead, my mind drifted in and out of the conversations, and the colored lights winked on and off all around us. A strand came loose and dangled close to Deirdre's head. She was laughing at Isobel's jokes and the reflections off her hair turned red, then green, then gold, then blue, then white. She looked pretty in the soft light. More feminine, less angles. Funny that Nelson was so into her from the get-go. Never thought scrawny would be his type, but then Nelson didn't seem to have a type, unless you counted damsels in distress.

When Deirdre leaned forward to take a handful of corn chips from the bowl, a necklace fell out of the V-neck of her sweater. It was a tiny crucifix. She tucked it back in. I was going to ask her about it, but the conversation flowed on, and I soon forgot.

At one point Franky bent down close to me and said, "You having a good time?"

I raised my glass to him. "Doesn't get better than this."

"Yeah," he said, and he looked around the room like he was committing the scene to memory. "Wish Sylvia was here, though."

But that was the only time she came up.

Before midnight Dee and Nelson slipped out to the bathroom and came back with a big-ass chocolate cake. Fifty candles poking out of its dark shiny frosting. And the singing, everyone singing. Dee and Nelson's hands under the heavy cake, their eyes locked on it, their feet shuffling forward into the dark room, their candlelit smiles. Shoulder to shoulder, holding the cake steady like a sacred thing of joy they were bringing to an altar. It was one of those moments you don't forget. The sweetness of it.

THE PHONE VIBRATING IN my pocket woke me up. I was lying on Deirdre's sofa. The room was filled with gray light, and it was hard to tell what time it was. My bones were cold and a hammer banged randomly inside my skull when I sat up. Deirdre's green sofa looked dirty in the daylight. I turned around and Mother of God Deirdre's bed had Deirdre in it, and Nelson, and Franky. But in the next beat I took in enough fully clothed limbs poking out from under the covers that my heart slowed and I was able to pull out the phone and see it was quarter past ten.

"Omnia Mundi," I whispered. No one stirred in Dee's bed.

"Dude!" Jen yelled into my ear.

"Where are you?"

"On my way home. Ohmygod, you are *so* not going to believe this!"

"What—what are you calling from? I've got the cell."

"I took Dee's. Listen, I'll be there in fifteen. Be in the kitchen, okay?

JEN CAME INTO THE kitchen grinning. "Oh, *fuuuuck*!"

"Where on earth did you go?"

"Harry Lane," said Jen. She slammed the tape deck on the kitchen table. "This. Is. Incredible."

She had the tape cued up, and before I could say anything a voice came out of it.

"Six copies, Will." The voice was slow and flat, maybe drunk. Maybe just stressed. "Six copies. The whole goddamn timeline. Recorded conversations."

"Fuck," said Jen. She paced up and down. "Can you believe this?"

"No, you won't," said a second voice. It was Reynolds, I recognized his patronizing tone.

"Stamped and addressed," said the stressed voice. "They're going out today. Three papers, three networks."

Jen grinned. "That's *Gary Wellesley*. The *president*."

The tape player sat small and black on the green Formica table. "Jen—" I said.

"They'll ignore you," said Reynolds.

"You think I'm stupid? Three papers. Three networks—"

Reynolds said, "I heard you the first time, Gary." There was a beat or two of silence, then, "Yeah, you're stupid. I still have your hard drive."

"I know you do," said Wellesley, "and I don't care. I've got nothing left to lose."

"For Christ's sake, you've got everything to lose."

"I'm in *hell*, Will. When it's all public, at least I won't have to pretend I'm not."

"Jen—" I said again. That hammer was banging away, and one half of me wanted to rip her a new one, and the other half couldn't tear my ears away from the recording.

Reynolds sounded baffled. "You really want the public to know?"

"I want those recruiters off my campus."

"You know I can't change that."

"Figure out a way." There was another few seconds of quiet, then Wellesley added, "And I want the grant monies returned. I want the Pentagon contract canceled. And I want your resignation."

"That's not going to happen, Gary, not while I have your nasty little drive."

"This institution has turned into a fucking train wreck, Will. And I let it happen. Three papers. Three networks. You and me, going up in flames, and by god it'll be sweet watching you burn."

"That's career suicide."

"Better than living like this."

"Think of the shame, Gary. Your wife. Your kids. Your colleagues."

"I am *going* to expose *both* of us. Do not doubt that I will do this."

"Listen," said Reynolds. "Let's talk about this some more, huh? Over a beer? We can work something out."

"Six packets. Going out today. Unless you give me my hard drive. And a letter to the Pentagon. And a letter turning down the grants. And your resignation."

"Jesus, Gary. Let me work on the Pentagon, okay? I don't know how but I'll see what I can do, okay?"

"Those letters and my hard drive, Will. Nothing less."

There were a few seconds of silence.

"Fuck you, Gary. After all I've done for you."

"On my desk before the afternoon mail pickup."

"I should've given up that drive months ago, Gary, but I didn't. I protected you."

"On my desk."

More silence.

Reynolds said, "You're one ungrateful motherfucker."

"And you're a lying, manipulative, opportunistic bastard."

"I brought in a five-million-dollar contract, asshole."

"And I let you skim ten percent of it. And gave you every perk. Because I'm a coward."

"Well, fuck you, you sleazy coward," said Reynolds.

Another stretch of quiet.

"Do I get all the packets?" said Reynolds.

"Yep."

"You know I can still get you. None of your information is safe from me."

"I don't care. After I clean this place up, I'm resigning, too."

Then there was a click.

The look on Jen's face. Like she'd caught the biggest fish in the sea.

"What the *hell* did you go and do that for?" I yelled.

Jen's face dropped. "For? What did I do it *for*? The investigation. What the hell else would I do it for?"

"You *don't* go and do shit on your own."

"Well, who the fuck else is going to do it? Nancy bails, and you and Nelson get wasted. Fucking crisis was going down, dude. It's not like we could try next week and get the same results."

I was pacing. I couldn't help it. "You *still* don't go and *do* shit on you *own*. We're a *team*, damn it. But no, you sneak out to go *stenciling*. You organize a secret protest right in the middle of Deirdre's *reception*—"

Jen approached, pointing. "*Don't* you tell me what to do, you paternalistic asshole."

I grabbed her wrist. "For Christ's sake, we need to stick together."

She wrenched away. "You're always on my back about something."

"God*dammit*," I yelled. Despite myself I was following her up and down the kitchen. "Your impulsive *shit* is going to be the end of us."

She wheeled around. "You think I can't do an op on my *own*?"

"You have *got* to work with us, Jen, it doesn't *work* if one person's got their own agenda."

"I'm *sick* of waiting around for you two to creak into action."

"It isn't *about* what you want, Jen, it's about the goddamn *bigger picture*."

"No! *You* need to focus on the *real* problem, dude—"

"What, you being such an extreme *butt*head?"

"Picking on me when *Deirdre's* the one you should be worrying about."

"It's taken us *six years* to build up what we've—"

"Dude, you *just* don't want to see what's going on, do you?"

"You're blaming *Deirdre* for your impulsive shit now?"

Jen stopped pacing. We were both breathing hard. She draped her hands on her hips. "How'd you know about the stenciling?"

"In the trash. Found it wrapped up. Pretty sure it wasn't Nelson's."

She rolled her eyes. "You're stalking me through the *trash* now?"

"When it smells like spray paint, I dig around. You'd do the same."

Jen dropped her arms, whispered a resigned, "Fuck," and walked to the counter.

"What the hell's going on?" said Nelson from the top of the basement stairs.

Jen poured water into the coffee maker.

"What happened?" Nelson sat at the table and nudged the tape deck. "Why were you yelling? Is this something?"

"Jen went to HLU this morning," I said. "Caught Reynolds and the prez in a compromising position."

Nelson gave me a slow, disbelieving look.

"Figuratively speaking," I added, and I sat down across from him. Rewound the tape. Pushed Play.

Reynolds's and Wellesley's voices started over, and the enormity of what Jen had uncovered sunk in.

Jen set coffees in front of us. A peace offering. "Where the hell was he hiding those recorded conversations is what I want to know."

Nelson looked at his watch. "When's the afternoon mail pickup is what I want to know."

I wanted to know those things, too, but more than that, I wanted to know where the hell we were all heading—as a family, as a team.

57: NELSON

FETZER DRIVES THEM ONTO the bridge. The river is gray and opaque, the city translucent with mist. Nelson pulls on the blond wig. He's sick of the smell of it.

"Silly, huh?"

Deirdre smooths the bangs away from his eyes. Her gaze is soft, appraising. It's calm between them now. Nelson is grateful for the calm.

Those sounds behind Deirdre's door. He had rushed in thinking she was hurt. From the bed, their eyes, frozen, staring. Then it was limbs, the naked women's limbs of them scrabbling to cover up. And the space around him like lightning bolts, striking and striking.

Deirdre smooths the bangs again. "You look like a kid."

He breathes in. Breathes out. Calm.

"Slow *down*," says Jen. "Find a *park*."

Fetzer says, "Going to the parking building."

"Park *off* campus."

"No," Fetzer snaps. "We could be hours."

They've been bickering all morning. Fetzer's right, of course: Jen shouldn't have acted alone. But it's not as bad as the protest at Dee's reception. And if she hadn't tapped Wellesley's phone, they wouldn't be intercepting this smoking gun. And he had to smile when Jen gave them the play-by-play. How she'd borrowed a shirt of his and a tie, put her hair under a hat, and showed up with a briefcase at eight a.m. outside Reynolds's office. But Nancy recognized her and shooed her away because Reynolds was in there. So Jen found her way to the president's office. From IT, she'd said. Need to run diagnostics, she'd said. "Finally!" said Wellesley's assistant. Luckily Wellesley wasn't there.

Jen had the phone line tapped in two minutes. On her way out she passed Wellesley in the hall. Then she changed into regular clothes. She hung out in a waiting area nearby, with a book in her lap, earphones on, and the receiver in her backpack. She had food and coffee and was prepared to wait all day, but the conversation was over by ten. Then a quick change back into shirt and tie, an explanation to the assistant about leaving something behind, and she removed the bug, right under Wellesley's nose. He was flushed and distracted and barely glanced at her fiddling with the phone socket in the corner.

THE STONE BENCH IS cold and slightly damp. But the tacos are hot and tasty—the campus food carts reliable as ever. In the quad a young woman is playing a Bach piece for solo violin, a sonata, but Nelson can't remember which. "She's very good," he says to Dee and Fetz. A longing wafts through him, a kind he hasn't felt for a while. The burl on the violin shines in the weak winter sun.

The violinist finishes, and they clap as best they can while holding tacos. Since the lunch period ended the quad has emptied out. Even the vigil outside of Sci and Eng is gone. Hardly anyone else in the quad except Jen, on an identical stone bench on the opposite side.

Fetzer says, "He used to play, you know."

Deirdre lowers her taco. "You did?"

"Yeah," says Nelson. The woman packs away her beautiful violin.

"Why'd you stop?"

"Money got tight," he says through a mouthful of spicy beans. "Had to sell it."

"That's terrible," says Deirdre. "Why didn't you tell me?"

Fetzer goes, "Aww, crap. Crap!" and flings out an exasperated hand. "By the bike racks."

Reynolds. Dark suit, sandy hair, quick stride. Coming not out of the administration building, where they've been waiting for two hours, but out of Humanities.

"He's put on weight," says Nelson.

Fetzer pulls his headset forward, and Nelson does too. "Jen, for Christ's sake, can't you see? He's crossing the quad heading west."

"I see him now. Shit. I was watching the wrong door this whole time."

Reynolds is halfway across the quad. "Let's go," says Nelson.

Fetzer mutters, "Split," and Nelson pulls Deirdre up. The food lies abandoned on the stone bench.

"Pretend we're lost," he says to her.

She mutters, "Pretend?"

He pulls off the headset and stuffs it in his pocket. Reynolds is nearly across the quad. Nelson bounds into his path and says, "Excuse me?" Reynolds halts, frowning. In the briefcase in his hands is the goldmine they need.

"Mu-sic house?" says Nelson, and he draws a building in the air with his fingers. "Please tell where is the music house?"

"Concert hall?" says Reynolds, not even looking at them.

Nelson glances at Deirdre. She glances back. He grins at Reynolds. "Yes."

"That way." Reynolds gestures impatiently. "Four blocks."

Nelson keeps up his continuous nodding. "This way?" he points. "The name of road?"

"Just stay on this path." Reynolds points again, but his eyes are on the door he was aiming for, and he won't put down the damn briefcase.

Jen is approaching from behind. Nelson keeps nodding. "Thank you. Thank you." He gestures at Deirdre and himself. "We are on exchange."

"Good," snaps Reynolds, and makes to go around them.

Nelson blocks him again and suppresses a laugh. "From the Leiden University."

Reynolds pulls in a breath and his face relaxes. "Oh."

Jen drifts closer. She's wearing latex gloves. It's hard not to be distracted by her.

Reynolds cocks his head. "Ik deed een semester in Den Haag. Waar in Nederland kom je vandaan?"

Nelson nods and goes, "Ahhhh," long enough for Jen to bounce in close and grab the briefcase from Reynolds's relaxing hand. Reynolds swings, lunges, and trips. He lands on his side with a grunt. Obviously not as athletic as he looks.

Nelson yells, "Thief!" and Fetzer's suddenly beside them, saying, "Let me help you up. I saw that, you got an eyewitness," in what might be a Canadian accent underneath the wig and the handlebar moustache. Reynolds struggles up and Nelson grabs his other arm. "We must catch the thief," he says. "We go. Anika to stay with you." Deirdre gives him a furious look, but what can he do? Reynolds never met her at the reception, and they need collateral.

Fetzer says, "Stay right here, sir, we'll get that back for you."

Reynolds winces and lifts one foot off the ground.

"By the way, I'm not Dutch," Deirdre is saying as Nelson turns the corner. In sort of an American accent.

Jen is waiting inside the doors of the library.

"Elevators?" says Fetzer, and Nelson steers them left.

Inside the elevator Fetzer's breathing hard. Nelson's heart is thumping and he leans against the wall. He drags on latex gloves, and so does Fetzer.

The door opens on the third floor. Hands in pockets, they march past stacks and stacks of books. If he remembers right, way down at the end, tucked behind the last stacks, is a bank of photocopiers. Please please please let them still be there.

And they are. Even more than there used to be.

Jen squats and lays the briefcase on the floor. A coil of hair bulges from under her hat. "This better not be locked."

The carpet is an absurd shock of green and pink flowers. The locks click open and Nelson exhales with relief. The lid flips up. Six large tan envelopes. "To the *Seattle Times*," says Jen, and she takes the mini garment steamer out of her backpack and aims. The envelope flap wilts and curls.

She hands the papers to Nelson. "Copy."

Nelson pulls the jar of dimes out of his backpack. A dime slips into the metal box and the copier lights up.

Jen pulls a CD out of the envelope and swaps it for a blank one from her pocket. "Looks like he forgot to burn that one." Then she pulls a cassette tape from the envelope. "Crap. I wasn't expecting obsolete technology."

"There's some tapes in the car we could swap it out with," says Fetzer.

"No time," says Nelson. "We've been three minutes already. He might leave. Besides, our prints'll be all over them. Fetzer, can you do some copying?"

"Sure," says Fetzer, and he scoops up a handful of dimes.

The copiers are slow, but between the three of them they get a duplicate set in two minutes, and Nelson and Fetzer are handing the briefcase back to Reynolds within another three. Jen and the evidence are waiting for them at the car.

They laugh on the way home at Deirdre's description of Reynolds, almost in tears over his precious stolen briefcase and his sprained ankle.

He'd thanked them repeatedly. They'd said "you're welcome" in their various fake accents, and he'd limped away.

A successful op. A successful return to campus, and with Deirdre, too. Life is good.

FETZER STRIDES AHEAD OF them into the basement and drops the copies on a desk. "We can't break this. We're too fucking small."

Jen rolls her eyes. "Here we go again."

As soon as Fetzer says it, though, Nelson realizes it's sadly true. "Too small to be listened to, or too small to be safe?"

"Both," says Fetzer, "We should give it to Kate Simms."

Jen's palm hits her forehead so hard it's got to hurt. "Give it? *Give* it?"

Nelson holds up his hands. "Let's not overreact."

"I busted my *ass* getting us to here," says Jen.

Fetzer wags a finger. "And I'm not gonna watch your ass getting truly busted over this story."

"How could they even link it to us? There's no prints! Nothing's missing!"

Nelson says, "We've been a thorn in Reynolds's side. And he knows you're capable of hacking, right?"

Jen looks up at the basement ceiling. "Yeah. He'll assume."

Something's been bothering Nelson since they listened to the tapped phone conversation. "How would Reynolds even have the president's hard drive? It's not something you can just walk in and help yourself to."

Jen shrugs. "A tech probably saw whatever's on it during a routine upgrade. And Reynolds got wind of it. He's got contacts among the SysAdmins for sure."

"I wonder what's on it. Like, how bad it is."

Jen says, "Unless he reinstalls the drive on a computer that's on a network I can crack, we'll never know."

Nelson thumbs through the copies they made. It's all there, confirming everything. And it's solid. Fraud and blackmail. Harry Lane University, one of the finest in the region, come to this. And the biggest story they've ever had, come to this. "Fetzer's right," he says. "We're too close. Kate's a step removed. And she's got the *Herald* behind her."

Jen folds her arms. "So we hand it over. To the corporate news media." She shakes her hand wildly near her ear. "Are you even hearing what that sounds like?"

Nelson keeps his voice calm. "You know Kate will honor it."

"No, actually, I *don't* know Kate will honor it. And it's not just Kate, it's her editor. It's her managing editor. It's all the crap she's internalized from working there for so long." She points as she paces away. "You know I'm right."

"Under most circumstances," says Nelson, "I'd agree, but this feels exponentially risky."

Fetzer says, "Especially since the Pentagon is involved."

"Only tangentially," says Jen and she strides back. "Come on. Like they care about some stupid college power play?"

"No," says Nelson, "especially with hacking redefined as terrorism."

"Would it feel worth it?" says Fetzer. He picks up the CD and tosses it down. "Going to federal prison? For this?" Fetzer then mutters, "On second thought, go ahead, get busted. Save me the trouble of worrying about what you'll do next."

"Fuck you," says Jen.

"Hey!" says Nelson. "Come on, you two. This is getting ridiculous."

"Who's getting busted?" says Deirdre. Nelson didn't even hear the door open. He touches her face. Soon they'll be married.

"Jen is," says Fetzer.

Jen lifts her arms in helpless annoyance. "He wants to get rid of me."

Dee's eyes stretch wide, "What?"

Fetzer sighs. "I was kidding."

Jen puts on a sarcastic smile. "No, you weren't."

Nelson spreads his hands. "Jeez, you two. Please."

Deirdre holds up a brown paper bag. "How about stuffed peppers for dinner?"

"Great," says Nelson. "Um, there's those leftover chickpeas, too."

At the bottom of the stairs she turns. "Shall I open a bottle of red to breathe?"

Fetzer shakes his head, distracted. "Sure," he says, and Deirdre heads up to the kitchen.

"So, Jen?" says Nelson. "We call her?"

Jen throws up her arms again. "I hate this. Don't you hate this? We're just giving up."

Nelson bounces a pen against the tip of his finger. Jen seems to be getting more agitated by the day.

Fetzer rubs the stubble on his head. "If we don't give this to Kate now, I say we lock it away. Least till we're in a different political climate. Right now, anything perceived as anti-military risks being misconstrued as treasonous."

"That's so cowardly I hate it even more," says Jen. She folds her arms, paces over to the map wall, paces back. "Okay. But she *so* fucking owes us."

Fetzer stares at nothing and nods for a while. "We are handing her a scoop, that's for sure."

"I won't deny it hurts," says Nelson. "But we're not in it for the glory. Getting this out in front of the public is more important. And besides, blackmail and college politics aren't even our beat."

"True," says Fetzer. "Kinda lost sight of that detail." He dials. Presses speakerphone. Kate picks up on the second ring. But it turns out she's leaving tonight for vacation, won't get to see the package till next week. And no, they don't want to discuss details until after she's seen it.

Fetzer winces at the speaker. "We'll have to wait till you get back, then."

Kate says, "Now you've got me looking forward to coming back to work." She laughs, and Nelson can picture her smile.

58: JEN

DEIRDRE HANDS ME A bowl of soup. She has a bizarre smile on her face. "It's split-pea tonight." She ladles another bowl for Nelson, who merely says, "Yum."

Does he have any idea how weird she's getting?

Like, the day after they got married, I found her in the church. I felt like a tourist looking around, and whispered, "I've never been in here before." The red and blue and green light from the windows was all over her.

"Mass is finished," she said, "but I had a feeling I should stay, so I waited and prayed, and here you are."

There were those padded kneeler things they have along the floor. She got down and clasped her hands. It looked stupid.

"Listen," I said. "I'm not, like, stalking or anything, but I saw you go in here the other day when I was riding by. And then you weren't around this morning so I figured. Well. Anyhow, I just came to say sorry. About your show. You keep saying it's okay but it's not. You're, like, still pissed. I can tell."

She squeezed her hands together and closed her eyes. "If we pray, we will be forgiven."

"What?"

"God is the only one who can forgive."

"Look, does Nelson know about this? You just got married. Shouldn't you, like, be hanging out with him?"

"May the judgment not be too heavy upon us," she murmured.

There was the requisite statue of Mary looking all sad and submissive. "I don't care about this crap," I said. "I want things to be normal at home. I'm sick of feeling like shit."

Two old women kneeling near the front turned like twins and sent me death rays.

"Pray with me." Dee's hand grabbed mine. Hers was hot. The wind gusted outside, and colored light splashed through the windows then dried up again. I yanked my hand back.

"You'll feel better," she said.

But it was drafty and I was shivering. "This is insane," I said, and walked back up the aisle, through the gusts of color from the windows.

Deirdre ladles some extra soup into Nelson's bowl. He says, "Thanks, babe," like she isn't turning into a religious nut.

And Fetzer slurps his soup like he isn't turning into a pedantic control-freak.

If rash, irritation, or swelling develops, discontinue thinking.

"So Deirdre, you got another email," I say.

Nelson says, "How come you read her emails?"

I shrug. "Good question."

Deirdre ladles soup for herself. "I can't be bothered with it."

Does she really miss Sylvia that much?

"Who from?" says Nelson, since Dee seems uninterested. He sips soup off his spoon.

I say, "Would you believe it: New Western Light."

Nelson looks up. "The publisher?"

"Yup. They're interested in her photos."

He gazes at her with those doe eyes like when he was in front of the judge, in front of us, when he said "I do."

I'll admit it, I was moved. I had a tear. But how come he doesn't see what's happening? How come no one does?

"For a book?" says Nelson.

"Yeah," I say. "They want to discuss it, anyway."

Nelson nods, looking satisfied.

Fetzer wipes a napkin across his smile and he sits back in his chair. "A book? Who woulda thunk, huh? Good job."

And for the first time since December, Deirdre's eyes seem to focus right. "I could do that."

"It's kinda messed up, though," I say. "We work our asses off for years, and who gets the attention from the radical book publishers? The girlfriend."

Soon as it's out I wish it was back in. Hands up. "Sorry!"

Nelson frowns like I'm some sad fuckup. "*Wife.* And what the hell is wrong with you, anyway?"

"It's okay," says Deirdre. "Shush."

"No, I won't shush." Nelson tips his head, puzzled at me. "I know things are bad right now, Jen, but for Christ's sake, you're being unbearable lately."

Hands up again. Head down. Let it go.

"It's hard on everyone," says Deirdre, "with this war coming."

Fetzer says, "All the more reason to celebrate good news," and he gets up and goes to the wine cupboard.

"None for me, thanks," says Deirdre.

Fetzer swings around, his forehead crimped. "You sure?"

"I'm giving it up for Lent."

Nelson looks like, *WTF?*

Fetzer just stands there, bottle in his hand, surprise on his face.

I want to say, See? See? *See?*

59: NELSON

NELSON PUSHES OPEN THE tinkling diner door. It feels oddly incongruous to be visiting on Deirdre's day off. "Oh. Kate's already here," he says to Jen and Fetz behind him. She's at a booth, chatting with Mr. Nguyen. It almost looks staged, with Mr. Nguyen in his pink diner polo shirt, and Kate in a pink leather coat, sitting at the pink Formica table.

They say their hellos and sit down. Mr. Nguyen's baseball cap today has Bart saying, "Ay, caramba!" Ever cheerful, Nguyen takes their orders and trots away, leaving them to fall into an awkward silence. Nelson knows he should say something, but all that comes to mind is, *I'm a married man again.*

Instead he says, "No baby Adrian?" He keeps his hands under the table. Touches his thumb against the ring. The thrift store ring that Deirdre picked out for him and he picked one out for her, shoulder to shoulder over the scratched-up jewelry case at Goodwill. He doesn't want Kate to simply notice, he wants to announce it. To say the words he hasn't had a chance to say because hardly anybody knows yet. He considered calling his dad, and his brother in Malaysia, but what's the point? He'd rather tell people who actually care.

It's too bad the ceremony was so short. There weren't even flowers. But it makes sense to save the party for the church wedding later. Which is something he never intended to go through again after enduring that hymn-drenched fanfare Lise's parents orchestrated, but if it makes Dee happy, that's fine.

Funny that Dee went to church the next day, a Saturday mass. She hasn't been to church the whole time he's known her, but the marriage thing seems to have stirred something up in her. She says the church on Seventeenth Avenue is beautiful. He should go with her some time, if only for the windows, she says. "The windows are so lovely it's like they're doing the singing."

"Adrian's with a sitter," says Kate. Wherever she vacationed, it was sunny, because she has a tan. Then she says, "My god, I've hardly slept since I picked up this"—her eyes scoot around the diner—"*epic*. What have you guys been *doing*?" She waggles the fat brown envelope they'd given her. "This is incredible."

"Isn't it?" Jen says, fake-bored. "Good thing I had the girl-cojones to go the extra mile."

Nelson fiddles with his ring. Jen and Fetzer can barely talk to each other without arguing these days.

Fetzer pulls in a breath. "Developments since then are Reynolds took a sudden leave—for family reasons, according to his secretary—so the department is reshuffling. And President Wellesley is getting flack from conservatives for booting the military recruiters off campus."

Kate frowns. "I saw that, yeah. I was surprised HLU even had any."

"Briefly," says Nelson. "They were part of the reign of Reynolds. We hope things will get back to normal now he's gone."

Fetzer says, "As you've probably guessed, Reynolds really stepped down in exchange for all copies of that material."

"Thing is," says Jen, and she points a teaspoon at the envelope, "Reynolds thinks he has all six sets. Thanks to me, you've got number seven."

Kate looks at the envelope. "Okay. Next question. Why did you give this to me?"

Fetzer pauses, then says, "Times call for aggressive watchdog journalism."

"And to be honest," says Nelson, "we don't feel safe with it." He didn't feel safe at city hall, either, but the clerk was perfunctory with Deirdre's passport, didn't notice the expired visa, and they both were so relieved that as soon as they were out of the office they burst out laughing.

"You think I'm protected by invisible magic?" says Kate.

"No magic," says Fetzer, "just the establishment."

"Aha." Kate smiles and pulls the copies and the CD out of the envelope. "Well, I want to do a two-part feature. Reynolds, his Heritage Foundation ties, Wellesley, the perks, the blackmail. Pity you never saw the hard drive." She looks up, frowns, spreads her hands like Fetzer does sometimes. "How the hell did you get hold of this, anyhow?"

Jen rakes back her long hair. Stares at Kate. Says nothing.

"That would be telling," says Fetzer, and Nelson gives Kate a small smile.

Kate shakes her head and says, "Assholes," then, "Guess I shouldn't say that, huh, since you're giving this away."

Expressionless, Jen says, "Guess you shouldn't."

This morning Jen had kicked up another fuss. Nelson reminded her that getting the story out is what counts. At least she agreed. But she's making everyone miserable in the meantime.

Fetzer taps the pink tabletop. "This time, don't mention your source."

"Understood," says Kate. Mr. Nguyen brings their drinks, and Kate pours cream in her coffee. She says, "It's not great timing, though. If the war starts it'll dominate everything. On the other hand, Wellesley might resign. I want to preempt that."

For the first time, Nelson notices Kate wears no rings. Apart from amethysts set in silver wire dangling from her ears, no jewelry at all. A new baby, barely a year old, and not married. He hopes it wasn't one of those messy, dad-can't-cope-with-the-baby separations.

Jen says, "You heard about that godawful humongous rebuilding contract Bush is proposing?"

"Sure," says Kate. "The administration wants Iraqis to see fast results."

Fetzer rolls his eyes before closing them. "Winning hearts and minds."

"Fast results, my ass," says Jen. "They're bypassing the usual process and it's going to go to Bechtel or Halliburton or Fluor. You going to write about that?"

Kate looks Jen in the eye. "My beat's local, not international. And anyhow, if we're lucky, there'll be a last-minute exile by Saddam, or just a brief skirmish with minimal casualties."

Fetzer snorts.

"Yeah, well." Kate gazes into her coffee cup. "I agree. Things aren't looking lucky."

Nelson sips his tea. "I heard some of the human shields are coming home." His turn to receive Kate's steady stare.

"Good. No one gives a rip about ideals in a war zone." She goes, "Boom," and flings her hands apart.

Nelson prickles. He crosses his legs. "At least they're demonstrating that a few souls still have them."

Kate reaches to touch his sleeve. "Which is exactly why I don't want those few souls to get blown up."

His face flushes. The inclusion in her touch. Even though he didn't go.

Okay, it's time to tell her the good news. He presses his palms together and opens his mouth, but Jen says, "What about this embedding bullshit? If they sent you to Iraq, would you go?"

"No," says Kate. "And not just because I'd be embedded."

"You've got a child," says Nelson.

Kate's smile is tired.

He pulls his hands out from under the table. "So. I have some news. It's not really relevant, but—Deirdre and I got married."

Kate perks up. Stares at him for a second then says, "Congratulations!" and pulls his forearm closer. Peers at the ring. It's merely plated, and a dull, darker metal is showing through.

She gives his sleeve a playful whack. "You two are so cute!"

From the bed, their two pairs of eyes, frozen, staring. Then the naked women's limbs of them as they scrabbled to cover up.

Why is he even thinking about this? It's over. Over.

Kate sits back. "Didn't you meet just a couple of months ago?"

"June last year," he replies, trying to convey the lifetime he's lived between then and now.

Kate's eyes get crafty. "So, the reporter in me has to ask, how far along is she?"

"Funny, I asked the same thing," says Fetzer.

Nelson massages his knees. "Nobody's pregnant," he says, affecting weariness. "Yet."

Fetzer gives him a whack on the back. Jen sighs and signals for more coffee.

At least Jen made an effort to be nice at city hall. Smiled, somewhat, during the photos. Laughed, sort of, at Deirdre fussing over Fetzer using her camera. They asked a passerby to take a few, so Fetz could be in them. Dee's developing them right now—can't wait to see them.

Jen mutters a surly thanks to Mr. Nguyen as he pours more coffee.

If it wasn't for Deirdre in his life, Nelson would be as depressed as Jen.

60: FETZER

I WAS WONDERING HOW we were going to go on. In my mind's eye I saw Jen leaving, maybe joining the EFB. I saw Nelson leaving, getting a job. Not because he wanted to split, but if Dee had a kid, something was going to have to change, income-wise. It was going to take more than Franky's generosity and the occasional speaking gig to make that work.

And without them I'd be set adrift in middle age. And maybe that's exactly what I needed, I told myself, during moments of trying to look on the bright side.

But then things took a turn in mid-March. Part one of Kate Simms' story was published. She called at seven a.m., excited and swollen-headed. Some friend of hers in New York had read it online, told her she was going to land a Pulitzer if she wasn't careful. It knocked a small ding in my heart, but so what if we didn't get credit. The truth was out. That's what counts.

Kate had done a good job. We knew what was coming in part two, yet she wrote part one so well she left us wanting to find out. She called back and apologized for not saying thank you again. "This'll get some attention," she said, her smile sneaking through the phone. "It'll be a blow to HLU, but a healthy one. Liberal institutions have to work extra hard to maintain their integrity these days."

"So partisan of you, Kate."

She giggled in an un-Kate-like way.

Part two came out the next day. Franky visited, and we took turns reading the story out loud. We high-fived, made potato pancakes, and

Franky toasted his "natural" pop tarts. By the time we left for the peace rally, the house was filled with the smell of hot grease and strong coffee, and we were full and wired and united in a camaraderie I hadn't felt for weeks.

And together we joined our comrades, our friends, our brothers and sisters on the waterfront. Wispy new blossoms dotted the cherry trees and the sun eased out now and again. There were speakers and music, drums and giant puppets. The grim reaper rode around on a bicycle. Deirdre, with an excitement I attributed to being newly married, shot rolls and rolls of film.

We bumped into a girl we knew from the radio station, and she waved in the direction of the stage.

"You should say something," she said to Nelson. "C'mon." She snatched his hand and pulled him through the crowd, and we followed. She was mixed race, I'd guess Asian and Hispanic, and as we trotted along I thought, you're the future, young woman. Guys like me, time's coming when we step aside because you're the energy and the hope and you grew up with your feet in enough different worlds that it doesn't occur to you there's any barriers till some idiot reminds you he still believes in them.

"Look what I found," she said when we reached the stage, and there was Isobel like the last time, with her long gray cornrow braids and her clipboard, smiling like we'd made her day. She put an arm around Nelson's shoulder, and said, "Perfect. Can you say something for five minutes after Code Pink?"

And Nelson said, "Sure," as easy as if she'd asked him to mow her lawn.

The Code Pink lady looked more like a grandma than any grandma I've ever met. She had on a bright pink floppy hat and a bright pink jacket. She made the crowd laugh, and in the middle of that swell Nelson climbed the stage.

"This war will distract us," he said into the microphone, "from a far greater threat than the Iraqi regime. The greatest threat we face is global warming. Not terrorism. Global warming. The threat level is second only to all-out nuclear war. Right now, there are a thousand Pearl Harbors going on in the environment. We need to respond. And not just to the ones that tug our heartstrings, like pandas and dolphins. We need to respond to all of them, because everything is connected. And the response needs to be massive. Focused. Unambiguous. We need a mobilization."

The crowd loved it. He spelled out names of representatives to call and fax. Companies and institutions profiting from war contracts, and how to boycott their affiliates and subsidiaries. And people were writing it on their hands, on the margins of leaflets, on their signs.

As Nelson wrapped up, Jen jogged to the microphone. "All that info is on our website. Omniamundi.org. And check out the show, last Saturday of every month on your local community radio station. Next show's in two weeks. Third hour's all call-in." She pointed a finger at the crowd. "I expect to hear from *all* of you then." The crowd laughed. Jen stepped back with an electroshocked look on her face. Radio people aren't used to that kind of feedback.

Smiling faces were everywhere. I put one arm around Dee and the other around Franky. Nelson was going to be fine. And Jen was going to be fine, too. We'd get through just fine, I thought, and I was so damn proud of them my eyes were wet.

After that we all climbed the walkway to the Morrison Bridge. Nelson got handshakes and high fives all the way up the stairs, and at the top people made room for us at the railing. We looked out at the mass of humanity stretching along Waterfront Park into the distance.

I said, "Vietnam was going three years before the protests started. And look at this!" All those colored raincoats. All those fleeces. All those bicycles. All those bobbing signs, all those funny hats, the papier-mâché masks, the kids in black with bandannas over their faces. So many people that in the distance they blended together.

The organizers said 45,000—more than January's, even. The TV stations, 30,000. The *Oregon Herald*, 14,000. Our disgust at the *Herald* was complicated by our grudging appreciation of them letting Kate do the story.

But Kate never won a Pulitzer, or anything close. HLU's President Wellesley did resign a few days later, but by then the invasion of Iraq had begun, and the media was wall-to-wall war coverage. Kate Simms' exposé was probably the most ignored local scoop in the history of the *Herald*.

61: JEN

"YOU SERIOUSLY COUNTING?" SAYS Fetzer. He glares at the grid I'm drawing on the *Herald's* aerial photo of yesterday's crowd.

"Gotta prove the fuckers wrong," I say.

The door opens downstairs—must be Franky.

"Ask them for a better version of the photo," says Nelson.

"No kidding," I say. "One that hasn't been cropped."

Fetzer snaps his paper open. "They had to eliminate the other 29,000 people somehow."

"What the—" says Nelson, and he pulls his own paper closer. "Oh my god, we met this woman." He holds up the article for me to see. "Rachel Corrie? She was part of that workshop at Evergreen."

Franky comes in, drops the mail on the table. "Hi, guys." Deirdre says hi and shuffles her chair over to make room for him.

"Yeah, I remember her," I say. Had a crush on her for months afterward. "What happened?"

Fetzer snatches Nelson's paper and scans. "Oh, this is horrible."

And the first thing in my head is, *They cut out her tongue?*

"What the fuck happened?" I say, but Fetzer won't let me have the paper.

Nelson puts his elbows on the table, props his forehead against the tips of his fingers. "She was crushed to death."

The sweat on me's cold.

"By an Israeli army bulldozer. While trying to save a Palestinian doctor's house from being demolished."

Deirdre crosses herself and looks down at her toast.

"Wow. That's terrible," says Franky.

Fetzer drops the paper on top of his plate. "It's fucking tragic. I remember her at that workshop. She really stood out. Completely devoted."

The aerial photo is a mass of spots of color. It's pointless, really, counting all those tiny blurry heads. Even if I find more than 14,000, what good is it going to do?

Nelson murmurs, "No one gives a rip about ideals in a war zone."

When I look at Dee, she's staring right into my eyes. Her fingers touch mine under the table, then circle around and gently squeeze. Her hand is hot, like she's burning up. Like when she took my hand that day in that church. She's going to say, "Pray with me."

"Sorry you lost a friend," she says.

It's too hard to look at her, so I look at Fetzer. But Fetzer is frozen, staring out the window. I follow his gaze. Outside, the nose of a blue pickup inches into view, so slow it's quiet on the gravel.

The sweat on me's hot. "Who's that?"

Nelson looks up. "Huh?"

Fetzer keeps his eyes on the window. Real calm he says, "Everybody. Get down," then he's off his chair before I can blink.

Fetzer crouches, gestures like he's swimming with one arm. "Get down get down get down. Shut up. *No* noise. Follow me."

My chair jerks, snaps against the table. My hip hits the floor. Nelse and Dee on the floor with me. Nelse is pulling at Dee but she's holding onto a table leg like water's rising. Franky scoops her along. The table shudders across the floor. "Shhhh," says Fetzer. He's reached the top of the basement stairs. There's a thump on the porch, then another one. Two guys. Jumping the missing porch steps. The floor is hard on my knees. Franky's hand is over Dee's mouth. Her eyes like drowning. Someone's pushing my leg. My legs are being so fucking stupid. Okay we're all here. Out of sight. Oh fuck, they shot the door! Nelson grabs me, his eyes like drowning. Another shot, no, they're just whaling on it. Fetzer's pulling at us. "Outside," he whispers. Gotta get down the basement stairs first. He whispers, "When they're inside, we'll be outside." Another wham. The windows rattle. Franky picks Dee up and walks down. Another wham. My legs won't work. The handrail. Fetzer's yanking on me. The handrail, yeah. Handrail, holding me up. Another wham. They're cursing. Door's nailed shut, fuckwads. Franky's at the bottom. Basement door's open. Dee's there.

Nelson, too. Oh god. Outside air's like a wet slap. Fetzer's gone. No, he's on the path. Scouting. Our fearless leader. Will my fucking legs ever stop fucking shaking? Glass smashes. Thumping overhead. They're inside. They're running up to the top floor.

Oh god. The Crusher.

"Forget it!" hisses Nelson and he yanks me back, hauls me outside. Everyone's crouching on the path. Franky whispers, "My car's back that-a-way. Hard to see from the house," and Fetzer's already in the lead. We're crawling through puddles. A huge crash from inside the house and his hand goes up. I never noticed this moss on the path before. It's the greenest thing I have ever seen. We're crawling through the wet weeds. Avoid the gravel. Franky's car is like a whale from down here. He scoots around the front, opens the driver door super slow. Climbs in. Unlocks from the inside, and Dee crawls into the back. Another huge crash from inside the house. A laptop comes flying out of Nelson's window, and glass rains onto the street.

A face appears at the window.

"Get in get in get in!" yells Fetzer, and we're in and the car's roaring and we lurch through Franky's U-turn. I'm lying half on Nelson. Tossed around the corner. Dee's arm under me. The tires are squealing. We're on Division already. Telephone poles are rushing by. Franky runs a red, weaves around a honking bus, barrels up to Sixteenth, then swerves us left into Ladd's Addition.

"Good move," says Fetzer. He's facing backward, unblinking. On a map Ladd's looks logical, but the diagonal grid with those identical rose gardens is enough to throw anyone off.

"Pull into an alley," says Fetzer. "We need to think."

Franky squeals us around a roseless rose garden, veers off on another diagonal. Already I'm lost. He slows, opens his phone, presses three keys, puts the phone to his ear.

I say, "No fucking way you're calling the cops."

Franky pulls into an alley, cuts the engine. "Hi, yeah, I'm reporting a home invasion."

Everything is unraveling.

Yet it's so quiet. On one side of us is a row of trashcans, on the other an overgrown laurel. Fetzer's face looks like someone took out all the pins holding it up. He reaches over to the back seat, touches Deirdre's hair. "You okay?"

"Aye," she says.

"Southeast Novi between Eleventh and Twelfth," says Franky. "Two men attacked my friends' house. They're inside smashing it up right now."

"You okay?" Fetzer says to Nelson, and Nelson nods.

Fetzer looks at me. His face a suffer-the-little-children face. "You okay?"

"Five people," says Franky. "No, no injuries."

My hands are shaking. Taste of blood in my mouth. Mud on my palms. Holes in the knees of my jeans, and not in a good way. "No injuries," I say.

Fetzer touches my arm, then he faces forward. When Franky's done with the dispatcher, he closes the phone. "We should go back."

"No way," I say.

"How about just me?" says Franky. "You guys can wait at the diner."

"We're all going," says Fetz. "It's our fucking house."

I say, "What if they're still there?"

We sit in silence. In the distance, sirens. A tabby cat tiptoes from behind a fence, sees the car, stops in mid-tiptoe. Stares at us. We sit totally still. "Don't frighten it," murmurs Franky.

I don't ever want to frighten a living thing ever again for the rest of my life.

The cat decides we're okay and moves off. Franky turns the key. The laurel scrapes the car as he backs out of the alley.

On Division everyone's just driving along like it's all normal. We approach the diner. Turn the corner into Thirteenth. A cop car overtakes us and swings into Novi. Franky follows. There's a fire truck there already. Guys in uniforms. Smoke is coming out Nelson's window. Lights flashing like an epileptic Christmas fit. The fire truck is crazy red against the dust colored house, the gray street, the gray smoke, the gray sky. Not pretty. Just wrong.

The trunk of the Toro is caved in. The lights smashed.

A cop tries to wave us back. Franky leans out the window. "Sir, this is their house."

The cop bends to peer through the windows. "Pull over here." He waves Franky toward the curb like we're on some unfamiliar street and might not know what to do. "I'll need to ask you folks some questions."

PART FIVE

62: FETZER

WHILE FRANKY WAS PULLING over, I quietly said, "I think this is about Harry Lane. We helped Kate with the story, okay? We did some supplemental research. That's all. That's all we say." Knowing full well that it wasn't enough, and right away the cops would see we didn't have a consistent version of what that supplemental research was. But within seconds we were summoned out of Franky's car and led away from each other. Dee gripped Nelson's hand. "I need you to step over here, ma'am," said the cop. Dee just wound her hand tighter around Nelson's arm. The male cop went and got a female cop. I don't know what she said because by then I'd been escorted to the other side of the road, but she pried Dee from Nelson and led her away.

Jen was sitting on the ground near the house with a big tall dude standing by her. Nelson was in a cop car. Franky was in another cop car. Dee was taken somewhere behind the fire truck. Cops and firemen went in and out of our house.

Pretty much the loneliest I'd felt in a long time.

Turns out they were barely interested in our story. Had we ever seen these guys before? Nope. Didn't actually get to see them at all. Did we know why they'd do this? Possibly. But when I explained, my cop got fidgety and went back to watching what was going on around the house. They thought it was drugs. They brought in dogs. They searched, but didn't come up with even a seed. I sat, damp and coatless on the wet sidewalk, and prayed and prayed Jen didn't have a secret stash. Then I sat in a cop car and prayed thanks that she didn't, and for dry upholstery and that we'd decided a couple of years ago to clean ourselves up, substance-wise. And Deirdre's place was still clean, last I checked.

When the cops figured out it really wasn't drugs, they started treating us like victims instead of criminals. We were allowed back together. Some Red Cross folks turned up. Coffees were brought, and blankets, and soup in waxed paper cups with plastic lids. Chicken noodle. It was the best tasting soup in the world. Jen stared at the oily yellow broth for several seconds, then dipped in her spoon and ate. I was allowed to check out the Toro. The engine turned over but the network was zapped. Technically drivable, but illegal without lights.

The last of the cops went away, and we stepped inside our house. It smelled terrible. The thugs had emptied the fire extinguishers, and anything that wasn't broken was covered in white powder. There was nowhere to sit. For a while we wandered around and stared at broken shit. Deirdre sat on the floor, silent and dry-eyed.

After a while we got some plywood left over from doing Dee's darkroom. Boarded up the living room window, the kitchen window, and Nelson's window. We used big nails, and hammered them hard.

The brown velvet sofa was slashed, stuffing all over the kitchen floor mixed in with the food from the fridge. The chairs were in pieces. The green Formica table was a lopsided M shape, cracked right down the middle. The black living room sofas were smashed. Pieces of the TV were scattered all the way to the basement stairs. We broomed piles of debris out the broken front door, then we nailed plywood over that, too. Upstairs wasn't so bad, just clothes and bedding everywhere. Except Nelson's room was dripping wet from putting out the fire in his closet. His bookcase was tipped over, and the window was smashed. But the basement was the worst. So much crap on the floor it was like rubble. We had to clear a path to get from the bottom of the stairs to the basement door. The computers were smashed. The web server obliterated. The CD library lay in a stomped-on pile. Filing cabinets on their sides, and paper, paper, everywhere. Jen crouched on the concrete floor and hugged her knees, her face buried in her hair. "The Crusher," she whimpered.

That threatening hate mail we'd received? No one could remember where it had gotten filed away, and it was probably destroyed, anyhow.

By late afternoon a cop called and confirmed the two guys had not been caught. Naturally, we didn't want to spend the night. Not even at Dee's place, which they never touched.

Franky offered his place, but I knew it was tiny, and I suggested Isobel's instead. I had the phone open about to dial when it rang. It was Kate. Eager to share more feedback about the story.

I cut her short, told her what happened. And that I thought it was related.

A moment of silence on her end, then, "Oh, shit. You all okay?"

"We're fine. But Kate. Did you tell anyone at all about—"

"Are you *kidding?* I would never do that. No. Not a soul. But listen, two guys? What did they look like?"

"We never saw them. Why?"

"Then how do you know they were two guys?"

Irritated, I muttered, "We heard them. It was obvious."

"Sorry," she said. "But look. Last couple of days there's been this pickup. This blue pickup. I kept seeing it around. Never really close, but once I noticed it, it just seemed to be everywhere. It was creeping me out. Even outside Adrian's daycare. I was going to confront them. But when I started walking toward it, it left. Then this morning it was on my street. It drove away as soon as I stepped out the door. I never got the plates, but I could tell there were two young guys."

"This morning? What time?"

"About seven thirty. Then a half hour later I got a call. Blocked ID. It was a man, and he said, 'Soon you'll understand.' And I said, 'Understand what?' and he said, 'Not to believe anything so stupid again,' and then he hung up."

"Jesus. Did you make a report?"

"About what? That I keep seeing a blue pickup around? They never threatened me."

"What sort of guys?"

Kate shrugged. "Just ordinary guys. White. Youngish. Short hair, but casual—sweatshirts I think. Could have been students, I don't know."

"What about the call?"

"I don't know if it was connected."

"But it was."

She sighed. "I'd bet money it was, yeah. But I don't have anything useful to give the police. So what did they do? Is anything missing?"

After I described the state of our house, she insisted we come stay with her. I figured it was as much for her as for us. Under threat, you seek the company of those who understand the same threat. And seeing as she was a mom living alone with a kid, I said yes.

So we all grabbed a change of clothing and sleeping bags and went to Kate's. Turned out her apartment had about as much extra space as Franky's. Sure, it was two bedrooms, but the second bedroom was just big enough for her home office. Apparently we were going to sleep on the living room floor. But Kate's apartment was soft and bright, with oyster-colored sofas so deep that sitting in them might get you digested. And Kate was so kind with her hot coffee, fluffy towels, and ice packs for our bruises and sprains.

Six insomniacs crowded around Kate's kitchen table that night, and Kate brought out a half-full bottle of Scotch. Jen asked if she could borrow a laptop and if there was Wi-Fi. Yes and yes. Jen reminded us the website was mirrored elsewhere, thanks to some activist friends in the Netherlands, so even though our server was gone, the site was still accessible. Seeing our site come up brought a tear to my eye, and we drank a toast to at least being alive to the world. Jen drafted a notice for the home page explaining why we weren't going to be answering emails for a couple of days. It took the whole rest of the bottle and Kate insisting that Jen remove "fascist assholes" and "war-hungry goons" from the text. Eventually Jen posted a neutrally worded notice. And Kate brought out the second bottle.

63: NELSON

DEIRDRE'S MUTTERING SOMETHING. NELSON leans in close.

". . . and saints of God, pray for me."

Not the Catholic stuff now, please.

"How many is that?" he whispers. So much for Lent. He tries to pry the drink from her hand, but she says, "Fock off." Her elbow clips his chin, and whiskey splashes.

Jen yanks the laptop away. "Gah! Careful with that glass!"

Fetzer has the glass out of her hand in a second. "Quit wasting it," he says.

Deirdre sways, looks around. "Where's me drink?" Nelson rubs her back. She focuses on Fetzer, gasps like she was holding her breath. "Bastard, you took me bleedin' drink."

Before Nelson can catch her, Deirdre tumbles off the chair and squirms away. She balances on wobbly knees. Her eyes close and her hands clasp. Her face twists like a used tissue. "Holy Mary," she whispers. "Please forgive me. Please don't cast out this wretched sinner."

"Deirdre, come on, no one's going to cast you out," says Nelson. It's hard to keep the irritation out of his voice.

Her eyes snap wide. "I need to find the ocean." She pulls on the edge of the table and it tips and everything slides off and Jen shouts and Kate wails. Deirdre whimpers, "God have mercy."

They wrest the table upright. Now there's whiskey on the floor, and corn chips and cheese.

"Sorry," says Nelson. They barely know Kate and he's embarrassed to meet her eye. "I'm really sorry."

Franky says, "You get her other end," and together they pick Dee up. Her armpits are hot and damp. Franky has her under the knees. *"Mea culpa,"* she whimpers. *"Mea culpa. Mea culpa."*

"Put her over here," says Fetzer. They lay her down on a camp mattress, and Nelson straightens her thin legs.

"There you go." Fetzer pulls a sleeping bag over her. "Nice and comfy."

Nelson takes Deirdre's small hand. It's so hot. Their cheap, unmatched rings touch. Fetzer says something about all of them needing to get to bed.

"Need to get to the *ocean*," says Dee. Her head knocks against the floor.

"Relax," says Franky. He lifts her head, and Nelson slides a pillow underneath.

Kate kneels beside Deirdre. "You're going to be okay, hon."

Dee turns her face away. "God protects *your* baby."

"You'll feel better tomorrow," coos Kate.

Deirdre's face disintegrates again. "Thought I was forgiven. I really did."

Nelson takes Dee's meandering, gesturing hand, tucks it under.

"Where's the bleedin' *ocean*?"

"Deirdre?" says Nelson. "I'm going to be right here, okay?"

"I've ruined everything."

"Shhh, okay? You're not making sense." He hopes like hell she doesn't throw up on Kate's beige carpet.

Dee closes her eyes, gulps, opens them right away. Stares at the ceiling. "Normally—" she says.

"What, sweetheart?" His wedding-ring hand on her hair. The gold plate wearing off, a dull metal showing through.

"I'd ask you to hold me. So I don't fall. But now—"

"You're not going to fall, sweetheart."

A brief smile on her delicate lips. "Such an optimist."

He strokes her cheek. Her eyes close and her face relaxes. "But now, I should—"

Long slow strokes across her forehead and down her beautiful hair. "Should what, sweetheart?"

Her lips move, and he leans in closer. She's whispering, "God have mercy. God have mercy. God have mercy."

•••

NELSON OPENS HIS EYES. His mouth tastes foul. Fetzer's face is two feet away.

"Happy Monday," Fetzer mutters, and rolls onto his back. Closes his eyes with a sigh.

"Thanks, I'll do that," says Kate from the kitchen.

They're not camping.

"See you tomorrow," says Kate. Then the beep of her phone going off. The click of it being returned to its cradle. Past Nelson's feet Kate moves back and forth in her kitchen. Thick white terry robe. Naturally she owns a thick white terry robe. Her hair's looking flat in the back. Nelson has never seen her look anything but salon perfect before. The radio's on, but he can't tell the station. White walls, beige carpet. Blue-and-white-striped blinds in the kitchen.

Behind him there's shuffling. "You awake?" says Franky.

"Get your foot out of my hair," says Jen.

Franky says, "Sorry," then, "Is Dee in the bathroom?"

Nelson turns over. Empty space beside him.

"How should I know?" says Jen.

In unison Nelson and Fetzer sit up, look around.

A high, stinging sound fills Nelson's head and eats its way down his spine.

"Impossible," says Fetzer. "She was out like a light." He struggles up, grunting. Looks in the bathroom, peeks into Kate's bedroom, into her office.

"Hey, Kate?" he says at the kitchen door. She swings around, smiles sadly. Turns the radio down even lower.

"You know where Deirdre is?"

64: FETZER

THIS IS WHAT WE pieced together. She'd gotten her shoes on, gotten Kate's pink leather coat that was hanging by the door, and let herself out. You can see downtown and the river from Kate's living room; it's a twenty-minute walk down the hill.

She's done this before, we told Kate. Kate had planned a day off work. Planned to spend it at home with her kid, but in her ever-expanding graciousness, she dressed him up warm, and in her car and Franky's we drove up and down the steep winding streets of Southwest Hills and Goose Hollow. Drove around downtown. Crossed the river and looked in the bars and cafés on Grand and MLK, starting with the crab house. Went back to our house, which still smelled bad. Looked in at Deirdre's place. Went to the diner.

"I hear what happen!" said Mr. Nguyen as soon we walked in. He gave me a quick up-and-down like he was checking for wounds. "Terrible!"

"It gets worse," I said. "Deirdre's missing. Did she come by here?"

Mr. Nguyen's eyes went straight to Nelson. Nelson stared back, his face still and sleepy. He'd panicked, of course. Hands in his hair, pacing, bumping into things. We couldn't leave him alone like that, but we couldn't take him with us, either. Kate had some Percocet left over from an oral surgery. She told him they were ibuprofen.

"Where she go?" said Mr. Nguyen.

"We don't know. Last time she did this she came back in a cab. Very drunk."

Mr. Nguyen looked at the floor. "Sorry to hear. You eat?"

Which we hadn't, so the cereal and eggs and coffee were welcome. Whenever he wasn't with a customer, Mr. Nguyen was at our table, but the rest of the time we ate in silence. When we were done Kate pulled out her purse, but Mr. Nguyen waved her away.

"No, is on house. You need to rebuild." He emphasized *rebuild* like a man who knows what that means. "Any time you need to eat, come here. Is on house from now on."

His ball cap that day showed bug-eyed Bart Simpson and the words *Eat My Shorts*. I got up and hugged the guy.

But Kate didn't put her wallet away. She stared into the empty billfold. "I had fifty dollars in here," she said.

My heart dipped further.

We kept looking. By late morning the calls started coming. Isobel from the station. People from the infoshop. Indymedia. Strangers who'd gone to the website. Shock. Sympathy. Curiosity. Anecdotes about home invasions. Police horror stories. Police hero stories. Offers of food, a place to crash.

Early afternoon Kate pulled into a Taco Bell parking lot and turned off her car. It was just her and me, and the baby asleep in the back—the others were in Franky's car. It was raining, and the sky was flat gray. Kate said, "I'm exhausted," and dropped her face into her hands.

"Let's get you home," I said. There was a cut on my palm from crawling down the path the day before. It was starting to swell.

Kate's hair was limp at the back, and it occurred to me she must curl it every day to get it looking bouncy. She fished in her purse for a Kleenex, honked into it. Then she twisted around to gaze at her son. "Fetzer. I have this feeling. I hate to say it, but I have this feeling that all this driving around is futile." Adrian was waking up and gurgling.

I said, "Yeah."

Kate got up on her knees and had a one-way conversation with Adrian about his diaper. Then she said, "I think you should report her as missing."

It was a wall I'd walked up to and kept hitting my head on: I didn't want Deirdre to be "missing." For all the times I'd wanted to throw her out of the house, I absolutely did not want her to be gone.

"Isn't there a time delay on that?" I said.

Kate sat back down and shook her head. "Not if you suspect the person might—" She squeezed the Kleenex into a wad. "Oh god, what about John?"

"I don't know. Right now, I'm stalling, because I have no fucking idea what to do."

Franky had pleaded with her to file a report about the stalking. "Police'll take it seriously if they know they did it to a lady with a baby," he said.

There was a warrant out on the two guys, but as Kate pointed out, Portland has thousands of outstanding warrants, and we had no real description and no useful evidence.

Sitting in her car with me, she must have been wondering what the hell she'd gotten herself into. After a minute of us staring at the rain, her phone rang.

"Yeah?" she said, then, "I arranged a day off. No. No, I'm dealing with a situa— No. When?" She looked at her watch. Mouthed *Fuck*. "Yeah. Okay." She closed the phone and groaned. "Some bullshit urgent meeting with the senior editor. Maybe Saddam's resigned. He gets all 'mission control central' when something big unfolds. You want me to drop you off at the diner? Maybe I can connect you up with the others."

"I'll go with you," I said.

"You don't want to do that. I might be an hour or two."

"I'll wait in the lobby."

She laughed without smiling and turned the key in the ignition. "Why?"

I didn't say, *I just have this feeling*. "I'll watch Adrian."

"Bless you. But the lobby's horrible. I'll get you a pass and get you into the staffroom. There's a sofa in there, and coffee. I'll need to feed him before I go in, though, or he'll cry nonstop."

ADRIAN CRIED NONSTOP ANYHOW. And lacking the requisite soft parts, I apparently wasn't much comfort. After ten minutes of incompetent rocking, I put him back in his stroller. I was stirring cream into my coffee when Kate returned to the staffroom.

"Let's go," she said. Her face was blotchy. She swung the stroller around and marched out. Thinking I must have screwed up the childcare in a really big way, I tipped the coffee down the sink, rinsed the mug, put it upside down on the dish drainer. I caught up with her at the elevator. Eyes forward like strangers we descended to the lobby.

"Look," I said. "I wasn't sure exactly what to do—"

Kate marched out through the glass doors. I handed back my laminated pass with the big green *V* on it. Signed out. Joined Kate on the sidewalk. She had her arms folded. I lifted my eyes away from the extra cleavage it made in her robin's-egg-blue fuzzy V-neck sweater.

"Under tremendous pressure," she said. She made air quotes, and her voice was singsongy with rage. "Jeopardizing relationships. Unpatriotic. Unprofessional. Bad timing." Her eyes came down from the sky and clamped onto mine. "Swear to me, Irving Fetzer, there was not one word in what you gave me that wasn't true."

Trying not to sound relieved it wasn't about Adrian, I said, "Everything was exactly as we found it."

She hugged herself tighter and looked up at the building that housed her office, her career. "I pushed hard to get it published. He warned there'd be backlash. I said I'd take it. But I *never* said I'd write a follow-up whitewash."

LATER THAT EVENING WHILE Nelson was asleep on Kate's sofa and Franky was out getting Thai food, me, Jen, and Kate sat in her kitchen. Jen poked around the internet, and we learned that Nate Junior, president of Nathan Dobrin's department store, the *Herald's* biggest advertiser, was also a Harry Lane alum and generous donor. His wife's brother was a fellow at the Heritage Foundation. The Dobrin auditorium at Harry Lane had been donated by the late Nate Senior. Nate Junior was probably pissed off. Nate Junior had probably threatened to yank his advertising.

But before that evening's digging, and after I dropped Kate off at her place, I borrowed her car and went to the police bureau to file a missing-persons on Deirdre.

What was my relationship with the person in question? Friend, housemate. Next of kin? Her husband. Where is he? Sick. Any reason I could think of why she might go missing? She's pretty shaken up, I said. Our household was attacked yesterday.

The officer said, "Southeast Twelfth and Novi? I heard about that, yeah." Then he walked away. I didn't know whether we were done or not. The paperwork wasn't completed, so I figured I should stay. I was standing at a counter. There were no chairs. My feet hurt like hell. Could smell the anxiety coming off me. About five minutes later the officer came back with a detective I recognized from the day before. He was white, about my age, crew cut, gray mustache. "Oberlinder," he said. The guy was nice to me. Didn't exactly say *sorry we made you sit in the drizzle for hours like you run a meth house.* Instead he took me to a small room with hard chairs. Brought me coffee. Said he's real sorry she's run off. Said she looked pretty traumatized at the time, so it's no surprise. Said he'll take the case on personally.

So, when he asked if I have any other concerns, my mouth articulated what I hadn't shared with a soul up till then. "She's been clean for the last nine months," I said. "I'm pretty sure. But she has a—history of hard drug use. And she's been drinking heavily lately."

And suddenly it turned into a debriefing. Oberlinder's questions came like gunfire. Finally he got to the part about how it might turn out to be "a fatal."

"Oh, Christ," I said, and swallowed.

Oberlinder lifted one eyebrow. The light hummed overhead. It was way too bright. My eyes had gone wet.

I said, "Up till now it's just been this nebulous possibility."

Oberlinder looked away and I mentally thanked him for the privacy. "More coffee?" he asked.

"No. Thanks. Thing is, he doesn't know."

"Who doesn't know what?"

"Her husband. He doesn't know about her history."

Oberlinder scanned the first page of the form. "Mr. Nelson? You said he's sick right now?"

"Yeah."

"We need to deal with next of kin."

"Please," I said. My hands face up on the desk. The cut on my palm swelling red. For the first time I understood what I might be losing. "Please. She's become like a daughter to me. If you learn anything, talk to me first."

"How sick is he? Is he incapacitated?"

"He's . . . he's sedated right now."

Oberlinder put down his pen and touched his fingers to the edges of the form. "You folks had a rough time yesterday. This can't be helping."

I had to swallow, and swallow again.

"She have any relatives?"

"She's Irish. She . . . her mom's apparently dead. Didn't know her dad."

Oberlinder nods for a while. "If I call, and he's still sedated, I'll ask for you."

I wanted to tell him how much that meant to me. "Thank you," is all I said.

"HE'S NOT GOING TO stay stoned much longer," said Kate.

"And we can't stay here much longer," I said. "We'll head home tomorrow."

We looked down at Nelson lying on Kate's poufy sofa. His face was soft with sleep. I wanted him to stay that way until Dee turned up and then he'd smile again.

Adrian threw a red plastic fish and shrieked. Franky was in the kitchen helping Jen return the pile of calls and emails.

Kate shrugged. "I'm on probation. I'll come by tomorrow and help you clean up."

On the TV news behind us, the anchor said that since Saddam hadn't surrendered, the beginning of a seventy-two-hour window for invasion had begun.

65: JEN

"LISTEN TO THIS," I say. It's just a crappy Dell laptop Franky got me, and it's on the one basement desk we've cleared the debris off, but with a wireless card it's our connection to the world. Because the goons never found the router. Because it's mounted high on the wall, suckers! "Email from Isobel. This is so fucking rad!"

Fetz looks at me with tired eyes.

"They want to do a fundraiser for us!"

Fetzer blinks. "That's good."

"Good? Do you know how many calls and emails we've gotten?" I unpin the envelope off the wall and wave it at him. "And look, checks! Four unsolicited checks! From people who love us! It's only, like, a hundred and ninety dollars, but already people are helping out. And even more have pledged money, right, Frank?"

Franky says, "Yep." The guy doesn't have the best grip on political complexities, but he's damn good on the phone.

"It's awesome how much people care," he says, then he draws in a shaky sigh before he dials the next number.

"Dude. She'll roll home in another cab," I say.

Franky says, "Hi," in a perky voice. Even puts on a smile. "This is Franky Moore from Omnia Mundi, and I'm returning Ms. Jensen's call."

Good thing operators are standing by.

"And check it out," I say. "Brian brought *another* casserole." I lift the lid and inside is curried rice and lentils and it smells amazing. "He is being so damn cool."

The phone rings, but it's our landline, upstairs. Which for some reason the fuckers also left alone. We both head for the stairs but Fetzer pushes in front. "You're eager," I say, but he just motions me to follow.

He catches it right when the answering machine clicks on.

"Omnia Mundi," he says, then, nearly whispering, "He's not well enough to come to the phone right now."

Nelson? He's well enough. Maybe not. Poor fucker's lying on my bed 'cause his is still damp. Are any of us well? Nowhere to sit down. The floor's still sticky even though we cleaned up the food. All the dead furniture in a stack by the door. Just a big empty space like the day we moved in, except for the trash. And the boarded up windows. It sucks not being able to see outside.

Fetzer rests his forehead against the wall. His voice is so soft I can barely hear his "Thank you." He puts down the phone. Presses his hand to the wall. Starts to slide. Jesus, he's going to fall over.

I grab his arm. He grips me tight.

"There's a Jane Doe in the county morgue," he says. He holds up a scrap of paper that he's scrawled an address on. "Pink leather coat."

No way.

Fetzer's fingers burn into my arm.

"So someone stole the coat," I say.

Fetzer lets go. He walks off. Only thing to do is follow him down the stairs.

"Running an errand," he says to Franky. "Take your car?"

Franky puts a hand over the mouthpiece and nods at his keys by the door. I follow Fetz out into the light rain.

In the car I say, "Dude, it's probably not her." Morning commuters clog the roads. He drives like I'm not here. After a while he says, "I miss the GPS."

"No kidding." All that effort we put into the Toro. Don't even want to think about it.

"Turn on the radio?" he says.

But there's just ridiculously happy Latin music on our station, so I go to NPR. Another retired general pontificating about the necessity of invading Iraq. "Fucking collaborators," I say. "You ever hear them interview anyone from the peace movement?"

Fetzer shakes his head. "Not without redbaiting them."

I turn it off.

Someone definitely stole the coat. In fact, she probably gave it away.

The traffic in front of us slows. I turn the radio back on. Some paleontologist doing CAT scans on fossils.

Couple miles later, Fetzer pulls left, goes a few blocks, and stops. He turns off the car and the radio dies.

"So," he says. He looks across at a white building with columns. "This is it."

A sparrow hops along the sidewalk, pecking at invisible specks. Fir trees sway in the wind. Can't check email in this car.

Fetzer's door clicks open. The car rocks from him getting out. The door whumps closed. His footsteps fade. The building swallows him right when I look up.

Should've gone in with him.

Should've kept searching. Franky wanted to. Nelson wanted to. Fetz and Kate and I outvoted them. The look on Nelson's face, even through his daze. Betrayed.

Fuck it, too many lies. I even lied to him the day after they got married. Going out for better coffee, want some? Knowing he wouldn't say yes.

She was happy at city hall. And I'm thinking, cool, she's back to normal. But next morning, no Deirdre, and Nelson's working on the newsletter. Fetzer says something about not even one day off for a honeymoon? "She's gone to church," says Nelson. Normal as can be.

"Going out for better coffee," I say to him. When I should have said, "Dude, there is something seriously wrong with this picture."

The door to the building opens and my heart goes ka-bang. But a young guy comes out, scans the scene, opens an umbrella. Wuss.

Should've gone in with Fetzer. Should've gone in. I'm going to get out of the car and go in there. I'm going to do it.

Wind in the fir trees, bending the branches.

Maybe I should've knelt and prayed with her. Maybe I would've felt better, like she said. Maybe she would've felt better.

Would it have hurt to do one little thing to make her feel better?

It has to not be her. Please. It's some other chick who stole the coat. Deirdre's coming home. She'll sleep it off. Wake up tomorrow. Take more photos. Nelse'll be happy. We'll put all our shit back together. Dee'll get that book published. Maybe we can make it be a fundraiser, too. A percentage of the proceeds.

Holy cow, we haven't even started anything for next week's show. We *have* to put everything back together; we've got a show to produce.

The door to the building opens and my heart goes ka-bang again. A woman in a long brown coat steps out. Fetzer comes out behind her. Who's the woman? But she walks in another direction and Fetz comes toward the car.

He's a weird color.

Please, God, or whatever you are, I have never asked you for much.

Fetz opens the door, sinks into the seat. Drapes his pudgy hands over the bottom of the steering wheel.

"It's her," he says. A sound like a flock of bats rises up, screeching pins into my shoulders, my brain, beating me down.

His arm rests across my back. "It's going to be okay."

"That is a totally insane thing to say. It is never ever going to be okay."

He rubs my shoulders. The bats subside enough that I can sit up, but it's like pins are being driven through my muscles, making me twitch.

Please. Just don't let her be raped.

"How?" I say.

"They haven't done the autopsy yet. But she was pulled out of the river."

"Drowned?"

That weird shit from *Peter Pan* she was talking about. The tide is rising, or something.

Fetz shakes his head. "They're not going to say till the autopsy."

"Was she, like, beat up or anything?"

Fetzer keeps shaking his head. "No immediate evidence."

"Meaning, what?"

"Meaning they haven't done an autopsy, but there's no immediate evidence she was assaulted."

Oh, thank god.

Fetzer stares out the window. I should offer to drive.

My whole body's gone twitchy. Like hell I can drive right now.

"Sorry I didn't go in." It comes out in a whisper.

He looks at his hands. "Wish you had."

"I should've."

Fetzer turns over his hands and there's a gash in his palm, all swollen and nasty looking.

"You need to do something about that," I say.

"I guess," he says. Like it's some random thing that doesn't belong to him.

"What—what'd she look like?"

"Asleep. Grayish." He turns to me and his eyes are watery. His mouth turns down and he shrugs. "Peaceful."

It is never going to be okay, and it is never going to be peaceful.

"Fetzer," I say.

His eyes on me, watery.

"Fetzer," I say. His eyes on me, red rimmed, the folds of skin uneven. He's seen way more dead people than I ever have. Breath falls out of me, rainy day car air fills my lungs. "I need to ask you something."

"Sure," he says. His face sad and kind and patient.

And the fucking phone buzzes in his pocket.

His eyes pull away like he doesn't know what the noise is. The phone buzzes like an angry bee.

"You going to get that?" I say, and reach for it but he flips it open.

"Franky?"

Only barks of excitement make it through the rain on the car.

"Okay," says Fetz, and his palm pats air. "Okay. Calm down. You're where?"

Ka-bang goes my heart. They found her?

Fetzer's eyes close. His fingertips touch his forehead. Rain pebbles the roof of the car, sheets the window. "We're fifteen, twenty minutes away, be home as soon as we can."

They *found* her?

"Nelson took the Toro," says Fetzer. He snaps the phone closed. "Probably went looking for her." The car hums into gear. Wipers slice away the rain, and the road appears, and buildings, sky, telephone wires. Everything is gray. "Franky's got a bad feeling. He tried to follow him on your bike." The road moves, comes toward us, wipers sweep away fresh rain. "Didn't get far in this weather."

Out of the corner of my eye Fetz is looking at me. "You're shivering," he says. He punches a finger at the heater controls. Freezing-cold air blows onto my ankles, my face. By the time we're on MLK, it's too hot.

THE MOSS ON THE path.

Fetzer stops and turns. "For crying out loud, whatcha doing down there?"

It's so goddamn unbelievably green. And all the tiny stalks sticking up, with the tiny cups on the ends. A colony.

Shit, I'm crushing it. *Sorry, moss.*

"Don't stand on it!" I yell, and Fetzer steps back.

The tiny cups bend under my finger, transfer droplets to my fingertip.

Fetzer crouches beside me. "Lose something?"

"The moss." My knees in a puddle, rain trickling down my collar. "We're all so full of shit. *All* of us. Me, you, our stupid shows. Stupid fucking rallies, stupid politics. Stupid war, stupid killing. Stupid—"

Fetzer's hand a warm patch on my back.

"And this moss. It's just growing."

Fetzer reaches forward, touches his fingertips to the moss cups. "Come inside," he says. But the only thing to do is put my arms around him. Like I never did right with Dee. And Fetz is holding on tight, my chin hooked over his shoulder, huge sighs going in and out of me, huge noisy sighs, crazy noisy breathing I can't stop.

66: FETZER

AGAIN WE HAD TO piece things together. In a fit of urgency Nelson had stormed out to look for Deirdre near the river. He ran a stop sign, got clipped by a truck, and smacked the Toro into one of the old concrete supports under the Hawthorne Bridge. Smashed two fingers, cracked a rib, and he still gets tinnitus from when his head hit the side window.

The truck was fine. The Toro got towed. Nelson got a citation for reckless driving.

Detective Oberlinder called me himself. Seems our troubles were becoming known down at the station. "Melodrama du jour," he said. But he was sorry, he said. "Hope it's the last of it."

We caught up with Nelson as he was being released from the emergency room. His jacket was missing, that tan corduroy jacket he'd lived in since I first knew him, back when Jen and I noticed him at town hall meetings in Salem. Back when he was a young Forest Service rank-and-filer. Back when he still had puppyfat on his face. He limped across the hospital linoleum and my heart just about cracked in two. He hadn't shaved since the attack. There were bandages. Blood on his shirt. His glasses mended with tape. And nine months of ups and downs with Deirdre had left him gaunt. His pants hung off his hips.

We couldn't hug him because of his ribs. And we had to break the news.

•••

WE GOT SETTLED IN at Kate's again. To get through the next twenty-four hours I knew we were going to need soft furniture, windows with glass, a working coffee pot, and Kate herself.

Dry clothes for us all, and hot drinks. I'd told Kate already, and she was doing her ultimate to keep it together while we got Nelson clean and dry and some hot tea in him.

It was the five of us plus the baby crowded onto her sofas. Nelson was stiff with pain, cupping his tea in his hands, two fingers fat with white bandages.

My heart was just about coming out of my ear. Franky's panic eyes flicked to me, to Nelson.

Nelson kept his eyes on his mummy fingers. In a croaky voice he said, "I know. What you're going to say."

It didn't make it any easier.

THE NEXT DAY JEN and I borrowed Franky's car and went to check out the Toro, but she'd already been stripped of the hard drive, the second battery, the GPS system, the monitor, and the Ear. And Nelson's jacket was nowhere in sight. Back in the unheated tow company office the old guy there denied any knowledge. We walked out of that office with the black fingerprints on the door and the faded *United We Stand* flag poster and took another look at the Toro. The smashed lights. The wiring ripped and poking out. The crushed passenger side. I put my hand on her dull white hood and said thanks for the ride.

On the way back we dropped by the house. I thought we should try and contact someone from Deirdre's past, but no one could remember Deirdre's other name, the married name that was on a credit card, or even the name of her hometown. We needed her passport.

Deirdre's place was cold and smelled sour. Water was trickling in her bathtub, a half dozen prints slowly spinning on top as the siphon drained to the sink. She must have set them in there to rinse before she came over for breakfast that morning.

Prints of their wedding. One I took of Dee and Nelson before the ceremony, sitting on the benches outside the judge's office, holding hands and looking in different directions like wide-eyed refugees. And then the five of us afterward outside City Hall, in front of the pink granite colonnade. Deirdre had smiled so much after the ceremony I thought her face would split.

Jen crouched by the bath, the corner of a print between her fingers. A picture of her, moving past a window. A silhouette with motion blur.

I disengaged the siphon and Jen turned off the water. She pegged the prints to the wire with such tenderness I had to step out of the bathroom. Near the bed was Dee's dresser, and under some T-shirts was her passport. Burgundy cover with a gold harp and gold words. Eire. Ireland. And the European Union. Inside, there she was, younger, brighter, ready to take on the world. Deirdre Assumpta O'Carroll. "Edenderry," I said to Jen when she came out of the bathroom. The inside pages had stamps for England, India, Australia, USA. "And it's in her maiden name."

Edenderry. A place I didn't know the size of, the smell of, the look of. So many things about Deirdre we didn't know.

Jen sat down on Dee's bed and scrunched the sheet in her hands. I couldn't see her face for her hair.

NELSON SPENT THE DAY lying on Kate's sofa, his broken glasses on a side table, the unbruised side of his face in a pillow. At one point Kate put Adrian in his arms and they both slept hard. Years later Franky told me he and Kate made out in the kitchen. Nothing came of it and they were both embarrassed, more so afterward, because at the time there wasn't much to feel except numb or gutted. But like I said to him, people do weird things when their world turns upside down.

And on the way back from getting Dee's passport, Jen told me what she'd tried to tell me the day we went to the morgue. That she felt responsible. That Dee had never gotten over her show closing. The goons wouldn't have attacked if Jen hadn't bugged Wellesley's phone. She'd driven Dee to suicide.

"Jesus," I said, and slowed the car.

"I'm the lowest life form on earth," said Jen from under her hair. "I'm going to leave. Get out of you guys' way. 'Cause you're right. My impulsive shit is fucking everything up."

"Are you out of your goddamn mind?" I pulled over so I didn't do something stupid with Franky's car like drive it into a pole. Undid my seat belt so I could face her. "You are so not responsible, you don't even know." I slapped her knee and she lifted her broad pale face and stared into my eyes.

"You are not responsible. If it wasn't the show and the goons, it would've been something else. And what the hell is this 'leave' crap? You gonna go save the world on your own?"

A pitying frown crimped Jen's forehead. "No one can save the world, Fetzer."

I had no response to that. Instead I asked, "You think it was *suicide*?"

In my mind's eye Dee was simply drunk, and had slipped. And the Willamette is very cold that time of year.

Jen shrugged. "She said some *really* weird shit to me the last few weeks."

"What kind of weird shit?" Then it hit me in the gut: Jen had tried to tell me, and I hadn't listened. "That religious stuff?"

Jen's eyes were pouchy. "It was freaky, Fetz. Half of it I didn't even understand."

"Did Nelson know?"

Jen shrugged. "You'd think so. But I dunno. He seemed totally unfazed."

"It was weird how she suddenly started going to church."

"I *know*," said Jen, and she gripped her head. "I mean, what the fuck?"

"And I did see she was wearing a crucifix."

Jen's hands became fists, clutching at nothing. "Fuck. See? Why didn't we *say* anything?"

"Well, plenty of people wear crosses and go to church, Jen. It doesn't bear remarking on."

"Dee was losing her shit. She was losing her shit because of her show closing, then the attack tipped her over the edge." Jen's hands splayed, rigid and trembling. "And we didn't stop her losing her shit. I tried, dude, I tried to make it up to her with the website, and I was trying to be nice and everything. But she was sliding away. And I just made it worse." Jen dropped her head on her knees. "And I just let her go."

Like I was doing so often lately, I rested a hand between Jen's shoulder blades.

Deirdre had made me promise never to tell about the drugs. If I told Jen, then it would be two of us knowing and Nelson not knowing. Somehow that seemed wrong.

"Nelson needs every ounce of support," I said after a while. "He needs you. *I* need you. So don't you dare leave, okay?"

Jen nodded against her knees.

"And don't give him any reason to think suicide. Or that she was losing her shit. Okay?"

Jen sat up and her face was so twisted it hardly looked like her. "But she *was*."

I pointed a finger and spoke slowly. "We can't let him think—that there might have been— something more—he could've done—to save her."

Jen stared at me, desperate. "But maybe there *was*."

I shook my head. "There wasn't."

67: NELSON

"WE'LL BE BACK SOON," says Fetzer.

Nelson's inner eyelids are hot orange. His stubble rasps on the pillow, loud through the angry insects in his head. Franky and Jen's footsteps pad down the hall carpet. There's a tiny creak from Fetzer's coat as he pauses in the doorway. The clock ticks.

"We'll be fine," insists Kate. Adrian hiccups. The elevator dings in the hall. No one calls for Fetzer to hurry up. Everyone is patient now. The only thing to do is wait for the next thing to do. Nelson keeps his breath shallow. His bones press into his muscles in abrupt ways. Kate's door closes. The sound of Kate bending, putting Adrian down. Adrian's knees on the carpet, little thumps. His hands hitting the door. "Shhh," says Kate.

Adrian whimpers. He hasn't learned that the only thing to do is wait.

Nelson's ribs ache. He will have to turn over soon. It's too bright to open his eyes. The headache zings in waves. "Look, Uncle Nelson is still here," says Kate.

He is still here.

But it hits him again, in a percussive, ringing blast: Deirdre is not.

The blast fades. Adrian's gaze is on him; he can feel the striving eyes. Nelson stretches out one arm for the boy, but his shoulder cramps, and he has to shift onto his back. Carefully, carefully, like an old man. His clothes scrape across his skin.

This is me as an old man.

"C'mere," he says when he's settled. His eyes still closed. Adrian thumps in a fast crawl across the carpet, then his sticky hands are on Nelson's arm, his face.

"Kate?" says Nelson.

"What, hon?" She pushes his feet over and sits on the sofa.

She has put up with so much already. He says, "Would you mind closing the curtains?"

A tiny, this-is-the-first-real-sun-for-days pause before she says, "Sure," and gets up. "Your head bad?" she says.

"Yeah." He pulls Adrian close, infant breath and spit and a small finger poking his ear. The curtain rings drag along the rail. The orange of his eyelids turns sepia, and the squealing in his head softens to a drone.

"I'll get you an ibuprofen," says Kate.

"Promise me it's just an ibuprofen."

"Promise," she says, and squeezes his socked foot on her way past.

It's nice to be touched.

68: JEN

KATE SAYS, "WE SHOULD eat something."

Weird how she just took us in and we're all practically living together. Hardly know this woman but she's turning out to be very cool.

Franky says, "I'll go get some Thai. Anything else we need?"

"Justice," I say. And Deirdre back.

"Band-Aids," says Fetzer. He peeks under the one on his palm. "Big ones."

Kate goes into the living room and steps over the sleeping bags, looking for something. "How are you doing?" she says to Nelson on the sofa.

"Ibuprofen's helped," he says. He has an arm over his eyes.

"Whatcha looking for?" I say.

"The remote."

"Adrian hid it again," says Fetzer.

It was actually me that hid it, but I'll let them blame the baby.

Kate turns over my pillow by the stereo. "Here it is."

Crap.

She aims it at the TV, and a green-and-black night-vision cityscape appears. A voice says ". . . fragmentary reports of explosions in the suburbs of Baghdad just before sunrise."

Fuck. It's started.

Those poor people.

Then it's fuckhead Ari Fleischer acting all serious in front of the blue curtains of the White House press room. "Opening stages of the disarmament of the Iraqi regime have begun," he says. Text below him reads "Operation Iraqi Freedom."

Freedom my ass.

And the words, "Terror Alert: HIGH." The green-and-black Baghdad cityscape looks like the X-files. Iraqi birds fly across the screen. For god's sake, *fly away*.

A burst of antiaircraft fire flutters in the dawning sky like fireworks. A disembodied voice says, "We've been told authoritatively from the Pentagon that the massive air campaign we have been anticipating has yet to begin." Then the screen splits in two, and on the other side is one of the retired generals the media's dragged in to explain to the masses how necessary it is to kill people. People who have left you alone all your life and would likely leave you alone the rest of your life if they had the opportunity to live that long themselves.

"You'll see the lights are still on," says the general. "We want every Iraqi citizen to know that we are not going to turn the lights off on him. We're going to turn the lights off on Saddam. We're going after the weapons of mass destruction."

Fuck you, you smug lying bastard.

The ticker spells out, "Police . . . prowl . . . NYC . . . with . . . bomb-sniffing . . . dogs . . ." Bottom right is a mysterious three-letter word, NAS, with some numbers.

"Can we turn that off?" says Franky.

But Kate stands there, the remote slack in her hand, her gaze trapped by the screen.

Write the follow-up whitewash, we said. Keep your job, we said. Enough's been lost already. But instead she resigned.

She is one righteous woman.

"Nelson?" Franky's voice is tight. "You don't want to listen to this, right?"

Nelson keeps his arm over his eyes. "Doesn't matter. But could you turn it down?"

Franky wrenches his shoulders into his jacket. His keys jangle. He's gone and the door slams closed. Never seen him so ticked off.

I catch up to him outside the elevator. "Dude."

He shakes his head at the elevator doors. "War's the last thing I want to think about."

The elevator dings. The doors open. Franky steps in.

"It's the last thing I want to think about, too," I say.

Franky looks up at the fluorescent elevator ceiling. The doors start closing. I don't want him to go so fast. His hands lift up, then drop and smack loose and helpless against his pants. Then the doors meet in the middle and he's gone.

The metal of the doors is cold on my forehead. Through my skull comes the vibration of elevator machinery.

He's got no reason to hang around with me. I've been mean to him all these years he's been helping us out.

I am such an asshole. In a world of assholes.

Back at Kate's the lights are off, and the TV's the biggest thing in the room. And there's Rumsfeld himself. "What will follow will be of a force and scale never seen before."

If there is a hell, you are going there, dude.

Kate and Fetzer are side by side on the sofa. Glued. Nelson on the other sofa, maybe asleep. Adrian crying in his bedroom. Kid doesn't like being left out.

Bottom right it now says DOW instead of NAS.

The markets. The fucking *markets*. And the DOW is up 16.49. It changes back to NAS—also up, 6.20. Rumsfeld's gone and the anchor says, "The Pentagon now confirms that in fact cruise missiles have hit strategic targets in Baghdad . . ."

Bottom right it changes to S&P. Up, too, by 1.15.

". . . targets of a surgical strike . . ."

Nelson's watching me through slits.

Can't figure this guy out. We've been expecting him to completely unspool. But he hasn't cried, hasn't flipped out, hasn't done anything stupid. Well, except total the Toro, but that was before he knew. Instead, he's just all quiet and tired. He draws up his legs to make room for me. The anchor says, ". . . as we continue to watch these pictures come in of the sunrise in Baghdad . . . "

"Tomorrow," I say, and drop my ass on the sofa. "This city's going to go ballistic."

69: NELSON

NELSON LETS A SLIVER of light into his eyes. Kate's sitting at the kitchen table, doing bills or something. It must be after midnight. The sound of the others' breathing surrounds him. Faint traffic noise bleeds in from outside, and a muffled TV is on next door. Even through the wall he can tell it's the blow-by-blow bombing of Baghdad. Shock and Awe.

Nelson's chest is heavy and uneven like it's stuffed with dirty damp towels. His head seems only partially connected. Moving so slowly it takes him nearly a minute, he turns his feet and lowers them to the floor. He holds his bandaged hand away from the cushions and uses his other hand to push himself up to sitting. Somehow his head follows.

His sleep has been dreamless. Each time he wakes a memory comes to him. A thing whole and complete that he can review and process. Then he sleeps again. It's as if his brain is feeding him bite-sized chunks and letting him rest in between. He needs to take a piss, but he has to get used to sitting up first, so he waits for the pain in his chest to ease, and a memory to present itself.

Kate turns over a page and moans in a small private way. In another context the moan could sound sexual, but over bills it's just a moan of resistance. With Deirdre, sex sounded like grief.

He closes his eyes and an image comes. He's kneeling before her, crying into her belly. How did he get there? That's right, it was their first big fight. The others don't know about the fights. They mostly happened quietly. They mostly happened inside his head. But this one happened on the outside.

It had come from above, behind, he didn't know where. Not his usual righteous anger at the world, no, this was different. A flash that overtook him, made him backhand a bottle of photo developer off her darkroom table. It was blinding and strangely neutral. No thoughts or words, no rationalizing. A pair of wooden tongs flung at the wall. He'd hoped they would shatter, but they merely bounced off.

She stared. Then she ran, and his skin washed hot with fear.

He stopped her in the foyer. Her hand gripped the doorknob, already open to the metal stairs outside. He wanted her to notice how hard his knees hit the floor. How tight his arms wrapped around her waist.

It was sunny outside. The sound of crows poured in. He lifted her T-shirt and kissed her stomach. She couldn't leave. He couldn't live without her. His vision was full of her smooth belly, the shine of his tears on her smooth belly. Her hand dropped from the doorknob. His voice was messy on her skin. Then her fingers were in his hair. The crows cawed. He had to focus. He didn't feel nearly as horny as he was behaving, but she was liking it. He nipped at her belly and his fear ebbed with every little responsive movement from her. In a minute she would be moaning like it hurt. With his foot he pushed the door. The light muted and the crows faded. The door didn't click closed, and he worried that someone might come up the stairs. And then, with his face on her skin, his toe pressing the door trying to get it to click closed, his focus stuttering, but his fear diminishing, she sank to her knees and her mouth bit into his. Her hair was like the crows: sleek and black. Desire tossed him up and over, and he didn't have to pretend anymore.

Nelson opens his eyes. In the glow from the kitchen his hands are thinner than he remembers. Older looking.

She was easy to seduce.

He was eager to seduce.

That is over now.

70: FETZER

First thing I saw when I woke up was a hairy Nelson gazing down at me. *This is it,* I thought, *the part where it sinks in and he freaks out.* Instead he asked, "How are you?"

Sleeping on a one-inch air mattress wasn't doing me any good, and my bones creaked on the way up to sitting.

"Uh, okay," I said. His taped-up glasses sat crooked but his eyes were clear. Jen and Franky were in the kitchen, and from the bathroom came the sweet sound of Kate singing to Adrian. "What the hell time is it?" I said.

"After nine," said Nelson. He put his good hand on my knee. "You needed it."

"Shit. I was supposed to call Nancy by now."

Nelson sat back on his heels. "Oh god, she knows, right?"

"Yeah. Yeah. I told her a couple of days ago."

Nelson shook his head. "Ugh. Sorry. You shouldn't be doing all this."

"Sure I should. And bless that woman, she's arranging the funeral."

Nelson closed his eyes. "What about Sylvia?"

Damn, what's he on? I wondered. "Uh, Franky told her."

Nelson's eyes opened, clear, unblinking. "I want her to come to the funeral."

By now Franky was craning backward to listen from the kitchen. He gave me a quick thumbs-up. "She'd really appreciate that, Nelson," he said.

Nelson stood up and put his good hand on his hip. "When is it?"

"Friday morning," I said. "At the church on Seventeenth. The priest there got to know her a little bit, apparently."

"Good," said Nelson. "Good, thank you. And how are we paying for it?"

By now Franky and Jen were edging their way into the living room, warily watching this upright and businesslike Nelson. Franky said, "I'm—some of it."

"And Kate's helping out," I said.

"That's nuts," said Nelson. "We're already living off her. We can't possibly accept that."

"Sylvia's, uh, helping out too," said Franky. Something we'd planned not to tell Nelson, but now that she was invited those rules were history.

"Mostly Sylvia," said Jen.

Nelson's hand went to his mouth and his forehead crumpled. "Oh. That's really good of her."

Kate came out in her white terry robe, laughing baby in her arms. "Aieee," yelled Adrian, and he kicked his legs.

Nelson dropped his hand. He gave Kate a polite half smile. "Are you done in there? I really need to shave."

OVER GRANOLA WITH ME and Kate and Jen, Nelson asked, "What about the emergency room bill?" The bruise on his face was going yellow.

"Payment plan," I said. "Don't worry about it."

"Payment plan out of what?"

"Don't worry about it."

"I have to make things right," he said.

In the living room, the TV was all Baghdad. Jen muttered, "There are bigger problems."

I said, "Tell you what. Today you could go meet Nancy at Deirdre's place. Pick out some clothes."

His spoon paused. "For Nancy?"

"For Deirdre."

"Oh. Of course."

"I was going to do it, but I figured you'd know better. Like, Dee's favorite dress or something. Nancy said maybe what she got married in."

Wrong thing to say. Nelson went pale, and I kicked myself for trying to offload the dreaded chore onto him so fast.

"On second thought," I said, "I need to go over there anyway, so I may as well take care of it myself. Then drop in on the protests downtown. Normally I'd pass, considering the circumstances, but this is, well, historic."

"I'll go with you," said Nelson.

"You're all bandaged up!" said Kate.

"I'm up for it," said Nelson.

Jen said, "Nelse. It could get crazy."

"Not nearly as crazy as it is in Baghdad right now," said Nelson. "We can't just sit in our comfortable homes as if this isn't happening. *I* can't." He shoveled granola into his mouth and mumbled, "I *won't*."

71: NELSON

FETZER TURNS OFF THE engine and the street is quiet. Nelson sits still. It's the same old street. Except for the boarded-up windows. Before Fetzer can repeat, "You sure you're okay with this?" Nelson gets out of the car. The camellia is bigger this year, and he hadn't noticed until now. Dark ruby flowers the size of coasters. Deirdre had talked about trimming it after it bloomed. They'd talked about starting a real garden. The single *Narcissus papyraceus* has come up again where the path turns. Last week, when life was normal and it was a paintbrush-like bud, he'd imagined her kneeling down to smell it when it opened.

Nelson looks skyward. The silver maple towering up from the back yard is covered in brick-red flower buds. The metal stairs are dark against the white of the sky and the tangle of branches behind the house.

There's the clang of their feet on the stairs. The squeak of her door. The dusty wood smell of her foyer. For a second Nelson expects Dee to call out, "That you, John?"

Fetzer has his hands in his pockets, waiting for Nelson to move forward.

There's her second door, the way it sticks. And oh, god, the tang of photo fixer, and the musk of unwashed sheets. The smell flows into Nelson's pores.

There's their rumpled bed.

The space around him like a whirlpool, rushing, swirling.

There's the wall, half-filled with new photos. There's the pistachio-green sofa they found on the corner of Harrison and Twenty-Second. There's the three windows, one of them with newspaper stuffed in the gap where it won't shut right and winter air leaks in. There's her dresser. Her narrow clothes rack. Empty dresses that will never feel her body again. Empty jeans. There's her boom box, the housewarming gift. Her tiny stack of CDs.

Fetzer stands by one of the windows, his face turned away.

Nelson steps toward the dresser. He picks up her hairbrush. The handle is purple plastic, the bristles are blue plastic with tiny rounded tips. Wrapped around the bristles are dusty fuzzballs, and her hairs. Black and smooth and long.

"Nancy's just pulled up," says Fetzer. He goes out to the top of the stairs. Shouts, "Up here, Nancy."

The hairbrush smells of her, but stronger. A shock reverberates through Nelson with each breath he inhales.

The slow clang of Nancy climbing the stairs. Fetzer is back beside him. He murmurs, "Nancy's here, buddy." Nelson breathes in deep from the brush. Fetzer puts his hand around the brush. He pulls. Nelson lets the brush go.

Fetzer has the hairbrush.

The clack of Nancy's shoes in the foyer. Dee's long hairs, in that brush. Like she'll pull it through her hair tomorrow and a few more will get caught. Nelson looks up. Nancy pauses, then comes over. Her sweater is turquoise. Her raincoat is pale blue. She's wearing turquoise heels. Her arms open and she wraps him, and despite the pain in his ribs, he doesn't want her to let go.

But she lets go and touches her cold fingers to his cheek. "The saddest damn thing that could happen," she says. He wishes she would hug him again.

"Thanks for coming," says Fetzer. "I don't want to keep you. Maybe we should pick something out?"

Nancy turns to him. "Why you in such a hurry? She isn't going to get any colder."

Fetzer's eyes bug out. *"Nancy,"* he says, and he looks down at Deirdre's hairbrush in his hand. "For crying out loud."

But Nelson is washed in a flood of gratitude toward Nancy. Toward them both. "It's okay," he mumbles.

"Oh, you poor men," says Nancy. She takes the brush from Fetzer and points it at the clothes rack and dresser. "This all she had?"

Nelson nods.

Nancy lays the brush on top of the dresser, almost exactly where Nelson had found it. "Bring that sofa around to face the bed," she says. "Uh-huh. Now sit on it. Both of you."

Beside him on the sofa, Fetzer's back is straight. Nelson's back is soggy cardboard. More than anything he wants to lie down on the bed. Bury his face in the sheets.

Nancy's long fingers make the clothes hangers go thwack, thwack, thwack like she's counting. "Okay, John. Which was her favorite dress?"

"Uh. The, uh, flowery one." He wants to hold the hairbrush.

"Now, see, that's a fine dress." The floral fabric stretches taut as it's pulled from between other clothes, then drops back into the Deirdreless shape of the dress. Nancy lays it on the bed. "That what she got married in?"

"Uh, no. The blue. Yeah, long sleeves, yeah, that one."

Nancy pulls it out. "Huh. Why?"

"It was a cold day. And she didn't want to wear jeans."

Nancy lays it on the bed. "What's *your* favorite?"

That's easy. "She has a blouse," says Nelson. "Middle drawer. Sea green. With ruffles. Yeah, that's the one."

Nancy holds up the blouse. Light shines through it. It was the sexiest thing he'd ever seen, the first time he saw her in that blouse. Dancing.

"She's got to wear more than a see-through blouse," says Nancy.

Fetzer nods. "I remember that shirt."

Nelson's face feels odd. It's hard to know what size it is.

Fetzer's smiling a little. "Yep. And Joe Cocker. And them dancing around."

"I'll never forget that song," says Nelson. A tremble starts under his breastbone.

"Me neither."

"I love that shirt," says Nelson. He feels a little dizzy, like he's drunk. "Blouse, I mean. Dee liked it too."

"Then that's what it'll be," says Nancy. "Now, there's a skirt she wore with it?"

"No," says Nelson.

"No?"

"I mean, no, she can't wear it. I want to keep it."

Fetzer shakes his head. Nancy shakes her head. "Bad idea," says Nancy.

Nelson needs air. His cardboard back sags. "The long-sleeved dress," he manages to say, "would be more appropriate."

Nancy wafts the gossamer ruffles through the vacuum of the room. "Maybe. But you're not keeping this."

He'd asked Dee to wear it a few days after they had first gotten close. She didn't associate it with that night, she'd forgotten. It was stretchy. It was tight on her. She was still doing up the buttons when he took her in his arms and pushed her down onto the camp cot. He landed on top of her. Afterward they found bruises on his knee, her shoulder. The cot's metal edges often got them that way.

Nancy frowns at the translucent fabric. "She'll need a camisole."

He's never going to love anyone like that again.

Which, in a strange way, is good to know.

His chest relaxes. His back firms. "There's one in the top drawer," he says. "And there's a plain black skirt." He gestures and his arm is stronger than he expects, and he nearly clips Fetzer. Nancy flicks through the rack and finds the skirt.

"That's it," he says.

"Uh-huh," says Nancy. She lays the blouse and the skirt on the bed, and with her long nails flips the frilly bottom edge of the blouse over the waistband of the skirt.

These are the clothes that will go into the ground with Deirdre, and stay there.

Nancy pats the ruffles into place. "Pretty. Now, shoes."

72: JEN

"ME AND FRANKY WALKED," I yell. I have to stick my finger in my other ear, the drums are so loud. "We're in the unpermitted march. Where are you?"

Fetz says, "Fourth and Taylor. There's thousands."

"Cops?"

"Just watching."

"Same here." Franky films me. "We're on Second near Burnside." Franky points the camera at a guy carrying a giant upside-down flag. Don't drift away on me, Frankyboy. Last thing I need is to lose you if the crowd gets wiggy.

The sun's going down and the crowd's getting thicker. I say, "Hey, um, how's Nelson?"

"Doing okay," says Fetzer. "Doing okay. Taking photos."

"With Deirdre's camera?"

"No, dumbass, ours. And Nancy was great. She sorted things out real fast."

"What—what'd you pick?" Then a guy stands up on a trash can and yells through a megaphone, *"Steel Bridge, Steel Bridge,"* and it drowns Fetzer out.

". . . and a black skirt. And black heels. It'll look nice."

Some daffodils are blooming in a city planter. Seems weird and uncool that nature keeps doing flowers at a time like this.

I say, "It's so fucking strange, Fetzer. That we'll never see her again?

Like, not even one last time? Doesn't that sort of freak you out?"

"What's weird? Someone yelled right when you spoke."

No more Deirdre photos, ever.

"Looks like people are staging a sit-in on Burnside," I say instead. "The lanes going onto the bridge are blocked. Awesome. Traffic's doing U-turns."

"Okay. We're nearly at Alder," says Fetzer. "It's jammed. But I need to get Nelse home soon. He can barely hold the camera straight with his one good hand."

"Man, get him out of there, will you?"

"I intend to. We'll head your way first."

I tell Fetz that we're walking across the bridge and we'll come back and meet them at Second, then I close the phone.

Heh. This is very cool. Five lanes and no cars—just lots of people. Franky zooms in on the barricade. He never would have participated like this before. Something illegal like an unpermitted takeover of a bridge.

Halfway across, we stop and look over the railing. Below us the Willamette is dark and wide. "Salmon swim up every year," I say to Franky, for the sake of saying something to Franky. He's been so quiet, since.

"That's cool," he says. The camera is off and cupped in his big hand. "But this river's never going to be the same."

We look south, past the Morrison and the Hawthorne bridges, toward the marina in front of the condos where they think she went in. The sun has set, and down there the water is darker. At least, it's where they pulled her out. The strap of the pink coat snagged. Half hidden under hanging foliage. No one saw, no one heard.

We start walking again. I call Fetz back. Weird how I want him nearby. A woman walking next to us yells, "We're liberating the bridge!"

"You hear that Fetz?" I say into the phone. "We're liberating the bridge."

Fetzer snorts. "What's it going to do now that it's free?"

Franky films people flying past on bicycles. "Become a park, maybe," I say. "Hey, community ownership of public spaces, man. It's so wide and the view is so great, it would be a cool place to hang out if there was grass and trees and—Oh, wow!" I grab Franky's sleeve and point over the railing. Right away he's filming the people climbing the fence below.

I yell, "Fetz, the fence between the esplanade and I-5 is breached! People are climbing it. Wow. They're spreading out across the interstate. Dude, the freeway is stopping. It's, wow, it's *stopped*."

Fetzer goes "Hah!"

"Wow. There's a chain of people sitting down across all the lanes. Facing the cars. And traffic's backing up for miles."

I-5. A river of gas consumption from Mexico to Canada, and here it's stopped like a finger on a guitar string. Put a finger on the string and it plays a different note.

We should do this more often.

BACK ON SECOND THE crowd is bigger. And there's Nelse and Fetz outside the Salvation Army and we're all hugging. The low clouds are lit up brown by the streetlights. Everywhere it's faces flashing by, bobbing dots from candles, folks sitting in the intersection. And a girl seems to be hanging on to my arm.

"Heyyy," she says. I'm flipping the mental Rolodex but nothing's coming. "It's Emma," she says, then murmurs, "Maryville," near my ear.

"Course," I say, and there's greetings all around. She spreads her arms wide. "Isn't this beautiful?"

"Yeah!" yells a guy nearby, and he pumps his fist. "All power to the Burnside Free State!"

Emma tugs at me. "You guys should come meet Kashan."

"Kashan?" says Fetzer, but Emma just pulls us through the crowd. Why do girls like to pull us through crowds?

A big old guy is sitting on a blanket with Brian. Brian says, "Dudes!"

It's good to sit down. On a blanket, in the middle of Burnside Street, surrounded by singing and drumming and candles.

Turns out the old guy is Kashan. After the introductions, Fetzer says, "Jen and Franky saw people stopping I-5. And I heard Critical Mass stopped traffic on I-405."

Kashan is wearing a long heavy coat and an old-fashioned brimmed hat. He sits cross legged with his hands cupping his knees. "What is critical mass?" he asks, with an accent.

"A cyclist group," says Nelson in an uber-respectful voice. "They do alternative transportation advocacy work."

"So they stop the vehicles," says Kashan, and he waves his hand like you don't see people do here. "It is a gesture."

I'm about to say, *It's awesome,* but Nelson looks down at the blanket. "Yeah. Just a gesture."

"Don't give the police your name, okay?" says a woman as she walks past. "Jail solidarity."

Nelson leans toward Kashan and asks quietly, "Where are you from?"

"I am Iraqi," says Kashan.

Whoa. Instant goose bumps.

"This must be extremely hard for you," says Nelson.

Kashan stares out at the crowd. "Saddam was hard. This is also hard."

"Mr. Kashan," I say. First Iraqi I've ever met and on the day my country invades his. How fucked up is that? "I don't even know what to say. This is the worst shit my government can do to your people."

And I don't have a minidisk recorder, either, dammit. The jail solidarity woman is still walking around saying, "They can't hold you without due process." Nearby someone starts singing in Spanish.

Kashan looks at me with eyes even shinier and sadder than Nelson's. "Maybe not the worst," he says. "Under Saddam, my brothers—" He grimaces and draws a finger across his throat.

Goose bumps again.

"Mr. Kashan," I say, "would you be willing to be interviewed? We do a radio pro—"

"I see the people with the signs: 'Not my government, not my war.' I understand it is not American people's fault."

Nelson shakes his head. "Yes. And no." His voice gets breathy. "We can't abdicate responsibility. America supported Saddam. Then this war. We didn't do enough to stop it."

Brian and Emma shake heads in unison. It would be funny if it wasn't so fucking tragic.

"What can you do?" says Kashan, and he lifts his shoulders, his hands, like he's emoting to the back row. "When it is not a true democracy?"

Nelson breathes in hard. He looks up at the brown sky. Then his eyes close and his mouth opens and he starts sobbing. For the first time since. He covers his face with his hands. His wedding ring glints in the streetlight. The noise he's making is cutting me up. Brian is on his knees, his hands butterflying around Nelson. Kashan shifts away a few inches.

Fetzer pulls himself up, says to Nelson, "Let's get you out of here."

It's like Nelson's trying to cough out something huge. Me and Franky coax him up. He touches Kashan's shoulder. "I'm so sorry," he gasps at Kashan. "I am *so sorry*."

Kashan looks kind of disgusted. "Don't waste your energy this way."

All around us is drumming. Dancing. Candles. An older woman behind us says to her friend, "That's bullshit. They keep you longer if you don't give your name."

"Thanks for sharing your blanket," says Franky. "I, uh, hope the rest of your family is okay."

There's tears in Brian's eyes. Kashan just stares out at the crowd.

Fetz and I each take one of Nelson's arms and lead him away. Nelson's bandage is dirty, even in the dark. The edge is wet. We're leaving. We're taking Nelson back to Kate's. The drums are tireless. We stopped I-5. We stopped I-405. We stopped downtown. We stopped the Burnside Bridge. Put your finger on the string and it plays a different note. If enough people put their finger on the string, everything around them changes.

"I have to stay," I blurt out.

We all shuffle to a halt. Fetzer rolls his eyes. "Figured you would."

Nelson's crying is quieter.

I say, "One of us should stay, right? It's only a gesture, but what else have we got?" I hand Franky my wallet. "Rachel Corrie stood up to a fucking bulldozer. Least I can do is help keep this one stupid bridge closed."

"Funeral's at nine o'clock tomorrow," says Fetzer. He points a finger at me. "*Don't* get arrested."

73: NELSON

IN THE LIGHT OF the street lamp, his own bed, the blankets off, still drying out. A twin bed. The bed of someone not expecting to share.

His books. Dried out too, but they're swollen, some with pages stuck together. *Annual Review of Plant Physiology and Plant Molecular Biology: 2000. Green History: A Reader in Environmental Literature, Philosophy and Politics.* Then, *Five Greek Plays*. The Greek mask on the cover. Mildewed paper smell. *Timeless*, it says on the back. He sees Deirdre lift her head the way she did when quoting from the classics, but her mouth stays closed.

Unopened, *Five Greek Plays* makes a soft thunk back into his bookcase.

His clothes rack. The dangling arms of one of his two surviving shirts. A white shirt, a little frayed at the cuffs. The shirt of someone not expecting to impress. His tie-rail, empty. Two remaining pairs of khaki pants on hangers. His fleece melted, but his down jacket survived, and his one gray suit. The only shoes he owns are the ones he was wearing the day they ran from the house.

The floor is water-stained and dark. On the far wall, above the desk, are his four framed Ansel Adams photos. And the map of the Milky Way that came inside a *National Geographic*. Puckered where drops of water hit, but otherwise unscathed. He sees Deirdre put her finger on the arrow that marks "You are here." He sees her hand fall to her side.

In college he'd switched majors and gone into science. But Pastor Dortmund got wind of it and sat him down, probed him on his faith.

He'd told Dortmund he loved nature too much. He couldn't have faith in an abstract god any more, he had to follow nature, wherever it led him.

"And if nature turns out to suggest you are alone in a universe without purpose, what then?"

"I don't know," he'd said, unsure but stubborn in front of the big man who'd spoken to him every Sunday from the pulpit.

His sash window, already repaired, the new glass still with a sticker. The window squeaks as he opens it. It's still drizzling. He's twenty feet above the overgrown front pocket garden and Novi Street. Dusk, the falling hour. From this distance, he'd hit the ground at twenty-five miles an hour.

McLoughlin rumbles, flickering headlights in the sliver of space between warehouses. Wet halos cling to streetlights.

On the other side of the world is shock and awe, terror and pain.

He thought he could change things. Boy, was he wrong.

Maybe it was when he left the Forest Service. If he'd stuck around, his dad would still be speaking to him. And besides, he might have effected change from within. Instead he exiled himself to the margins.

Maybe it was when he left Lise. If he'd stuck around, they'd have kids by now. Old enough to be in school by now.

With Deirdre he thought he had another chance.

All this restlessness. He called it "making sacrifices." What a crock. Misguided egoism, more like. That left a wake of disappointed people and got him nowhere.

So far Deirdre's come to him only in his memories. With his elbows on the sill and damp air pouring in, he tries to sense if she is there.

"Deirdre?" he whispers.

Far away he can hear the helicopters.

He scootches over to make room. "Why were you so unhappy?"

On Twelfth tires hiss in the dark. A drop of water hits the back of his head like a cold pellet.

"Why did you leave me?"

Because you're pigheaded and pathetic, says a voice.

His, not hers.

Steps behind him, and it's Fetzer, his hand on the doorknob, his eyes dots of shine in the dark.

"Want some tea?" says Fetzer.

The window squeals as Nelson closes it. Now the rain and night are outside, and they are inside. The distinction seems important. But Jen is still outside. And Deirdre is nowhere.

Fetzer stands back to let Nelson through the door. He turns on the landing light, and everything becomes heavy and bright.

Nelson says, "Jen's going to get arrested."

"She better not," mutters Fetzer.

"She can't help herself."

Fetzer gives him a funny look and snaps, "Course she can."

"Deirdre couldn't help herself," he says.

Fetzer folds his arms. "So, you're what, extrapolating because Jen's female?"

"No," says Nelson. The hall light is the color of clay. "Forget it. I don't know anything."

Fetzer unfolds his arms. Slides his hand over his freshly shaved head.

"Thanks for bringing me back here," says Nelson.

"Sure. No problem."

"I didn't want Kate to see me like that."

Fetzer lowers his hand. "Sure. Come and have some tea."

"But I want to go back to Kate's tonight."

Fetzer cocks his head. "Okay."

Nelson gestures toward the spare room. "This is going to sound weird, but I don't want to sleep alone. I want to be with you guys."

Fetzer's arm rests across Nelson's back, and he steers him down the stairs. "Not weird at all. And I know Kate's out of Earl Grey. Let's make up a thermos."

They could just take the box of tea over there, but a thermos sounds so nice.

74: JEN

CHECK IT OUT: IF I rest my elbows on my knees and hold my hands up, the throbbing dies down. Who cares how dumb it looks. No one here I recognize, anyway.

"Robbins," calls a cop at the counter, and a guy gets up, goes over.

I'm so damn cold. And my wrists are still weeping that fluid. Asshole wrenched my arms back like he was tightening fencing wire. "Idiot," he'd spat into my ear. "What did your theatrics get you? Huh? Nothing."

Then when they were diddling around processing the crap in my pockets, stupid female cop said, "What is this, anyway?" and she waved the cable in my face. That I'd picked up off the basement floor.

"That's an Ultra ATA IDE ribbon cable to connect your hard drive to your controller card, and it was ripped out of my computer when my house was trashed by two violent criminals. But you arrested *me* for peacefully protesting. Can you tell me how that makes sense?"

Bitch was already pissed off I didn't have ID. She squished her mouth. "You and your friends are costing the city a lot of money."

"George Bush cost the city a shitload of money in August. Arrest him."

The cable went in the clear plastic bag, and she shoved the possessions form into my handcuffed hands behind my back.

"Basso," calls a cop at the counter. Another guy gets up. Got a giant circle-A painted on the back of his jacket. Huh, they're making him turn it inside out.

My shoes are soaking.

Been maybe three years since I danced and sang like that, and there I was despite everything, despite Deirdre. It was like I was dancing *for* her, or something. Then Brian and the others moved on, and for some stupid fucking reason I decide to stay.

My impulsive shit.

"Don't bother with the 'jail solidarity' thing," said a cop when they took my details. "We got plenty of room for all of you in here, and we can keep you over the weekend if we want." And now we're sitting in rows in plastic chairs like we're at the DMV.

"Henderson," calls a cop. A woman in red-and-white-striped tights stands, picks up her red-and-white-striped sweater.

Clock says 3:16 a.m. Funeral's in less than six hours.

"Hey," whispers a girl next to me. "It's gonna be okay. We accomplished a lot. We shut the city down."

She's about twelve. No, make that eighteen. Everyone's getting younger these days. And perkier. I whisper back, "I have fucked up so badly you don't even know."

Across the low barrier to the men's section, a guy whispers, "Yeah. There was so much love on the streets tonight, it was totally inspiring."

"Yeah!" says another girl. She's got long blond hair and beams like a cult follower. "It was so beautiful." She clenches her fists. "We're living the behaviors we want to see in the world."

"Quiet down!" yells a guard, but I'm already on my feet and walking toward her and yelling, "You people got *way* too much praise from your parents or something."

"*Sit* down! *No* more talking!"

I sit down. It's a different chair and it's cold. The guards go back to wherever they came from. One by one the staring heads turn away.

Burnside free fucking state is dead, kids. It wasn't a free state, it was a few hours when the cops were probably too busy clearing the interstates and shit to make our little takeover a priority. And when they got around to us, they got around to us good and hard like we wanted them to. Tear gas and pepper spray and flashbangs. And we feel good because we resisted something. Meanwhile, bombs are still dropping on Baghdad because what we did had absolutely zero effect. Bombs are dropping on people just like Kashan.

What's my point? Beaming cult-follower-girl doesn't say it, but it's like she's in my head and she wants to know.

My point is. My point is. I don't know. I was all psyched to be in the sit-in. Then a ton of people left and they picked the rest of us off one by one and we're like, *come get me, fascist oppressors.* And we're all white, right? So like Nancy says, apart from a little roughing up, it's basically a risk-free adventure for us. And while we're feeling good about our token resistance, people are seriously dying and losing their legs and shit in fucking *bomb* blasts in Baghdad. And I'm going to *miss* her *funeral* and what the *fuck* was it *for*?

"Quit that," says a guard.

"Quit what?"

"Quit fidgeting."

7:09 ON THE CLOCK. Jesus, must have dozed off. Shit, my neck hurts. And my injury liquid has stuck my wrist to my coat. Christ, that stings. Least it's not bleeding. Damn, I'm hungry.

"*Owens*!"

That guard's getting closer. I stand up. "Just woke up," I say.

More questions at the counter. Then a female cop with straight brown bangs leads me out the room and down a black stripe on the floor in the hallway, down another hallway, black stripe, black stripe down another hallway, through mechanical buzzing doors and up an elevator to yet another officer behind yet another counter. The man has a plastic bag by his elbow. The ribbon cable and my other junk.

Goose bumps.

"Sign here," says the officer.

Hot tears in my eyes. I'm going to make the funeral.

"And here. Your arraignment date is on this form."

My flimsy papers. My plastic bag of possessions. It's seven in the morning. I'm going to make it.

I walk out the door into drizzle. Sweet fresh air and freedom. First find a pay phone, got change for a pay phone.

"Jen!"

Christ, it's Fetzer. Leaning against Franky's car with his arms folded. He says, "Posts on Indymedia about folks being released this morning."

Goddamn tears get too much. Goddamn Fetzer waiting for me in the goddamn rain. He's hugging me so tight I can't breathe, and I'm going to make it to her funeral. Going to have breakfast. Going to put on some clean clothes. Going to be there for Nelse, for everyone.

75: FETZER

AFTER IT WAS OVER, we crunched across the frost-covered grass back to the cars. The sun started to come out, and the world had color, with far-away blue patches in the sky, pink cherry trees in the distance, and the deep green of the cemetery lawn.

Nancy walked arm in arm with Nelson. The bruise on his face had gone yellow, but he had a fresh bandage and new shoes. Nancy wore simple black, and antique jet bead earrings that swished back and forth across her shoulders. I knew they were antique jet because I heard her tell Kate and Sylvia when they admired them.

Nancy was an angel. She and her startlingly grown-up daughter, Clarissa, gathered us, spoke softly to us, handed us small cards with Dee's full name and the beginning and ending dates of her life. She would have been thirty-one in April.

Mr. Nguyen looked so thin in his suit and without a funny ball cap. Brian kept his eyes down and his hands in the pockets of what looked vaguely like a ninja outfit. Sylvia walked beside Kate, Kate holding the baby, dabbing a tissue into her eyes.

What moved me the most was not Nancy's short and powerful eulogy, nor the prayer at the graveside. It was when Nelson and Sylvia wordlessly fell into a long hug.

He endured hugs all around, despite his ribs. Kate stood next to me, watching. "Look, his jacket's all crooked," she said, and dabbed at her eyes again. "I think my heart's going to break."

The casket was open, but Nelson got agitated, said he couldn't look.

"You'll regret it if you don't," said Nancy, and she and I guided him up there. The church walls were white. The stained-glass light was red and blue and green. There were gladioli.

Nelson's eyes journeyed over the waxy woman lying there with opaque eyelids and doll-pink cheeks and the ends of her hair turned up in a curl. He calmed right down.

The night before, on the way back from the sit-in on Burnside, he had stopped, grabbed a parking meter, and leaned over like he was going to be sick. Franky and I waited, a light rain falling on us. A newspaper box said, *ALLIES STRIKE WITH DECISIVE FORCE.* A police crowd-control vehicle passed by, a dozen black-clad riot cops standing on its runners. Helicopters throbbed overhead. Deirdre was already lying in her padded box, beyond sleep. She'd left us with our eyes pinned open, forced to look out on our chaotic world.

Now, in the morning light, as we walked away from her grave, the air was quiet. Just the sound of shoes on frost. Deirdre was laid to rest, as they say, in the earth of Portland. And it struck me why we use the word *rest*.

I turned and walked backward, watching the headstones recede. The lawn was marked with dark swaths where our shoes had broken the frost. Clarissa and Jen caught up with me. Clarissa smiled, her eyes full of love and care, and I knew my old friend Nancy had done a good job of raising a fine young woman.

Jen's face was still puffy from crying. Head down, she'd been quiet, contrite. Didn't make a peep about embalming, or the resources that went into the coffin, or the wasted space of a burial plot. Nancy had explained that the church was conservative. For the sake of making it easy on everyone, she just went with their suggestions. We nodded and proceeded to participate in a ceremony that seemed foreign and strange. But then life had become foreign and strange, so we rolled with it.

By the time everyone was climbing into the cars, the frost was melting where the sun touched, and the lawn was covered in sparkling drops.

NANCY AND CLARISSA, BLESS those women. They'd cleaned up Deirdre's apartment and brought in rented chairs—the nicer, padded kind—plus tables, food, burner things to keep food hot—you name it, it was there. Except alcohol. Turns out Nancy doesn't drink. Didn't occur to her that we might want to approximate an Irish wake for Deirdre. Sylvia—bless her, too—went away and came back with good beer, better wine, and a bottle of smoky Lagavulin. It was before noon, but we needed to mourn, and getting maudlin was the route of choice. Sylvia poured with a heavy hand.

The scotch stood me up and opened my mouth to tell the room what had hit me like a goddamn rock when I had looked down into Dee's plate-still face.

"She gets to *lie* there while the rest of us run around like headless chickens," I said.

Jen emerged from under her hair, and watched.

"She gets to take *off,* while *we* stay behind and pick up the *pieces*."

Everyone looked at Nelson. Nelson looked into his glass. Nancy flapped around me, shushing.

My feet took it upon themselves to sidestep Nancy. "She gets to *rest up,* while we reconstruct our *lives*."

Nelson nodded at his glass.

"She gets to be at *peace,* while we watch a *war* we tried to prevent."

Kate put an arm across Nelson's shoulder. Sylvia had her chin in her hand, her sad eyes on me. Brian said, "It's normal to be angry."

"I'm not just *angry,*" I barked, and scotch splashed from my glass. "I'm fucking *jealous*."

That's when Franky took the glass out of my hand and sat me down hard on the sofa. "You're on a time-out."

Sylvia giggled.

Nancy swung around to face her. "What is *wrong* with you people?"

"We're fucked up," said Jen, like there was nothing to be done about it. "We are seriously fucked up."

Nelson nodded at his glass again.

Mr. Nguyen stood and raised his beer.

"Miss Deirdre was a beautiful lady." He smiled at Nelson. "And when she met you, she was a lucky lady. But she was a sad lady. And now, she is free." Then he said quickly to me, "Don't be jealous. Your turn coming."

"We all got our turn coming," said Nancy. She lifted her root beer. "To freedom, whether you find it in this life, or some other."

We raised our glasses, drank to that.

There were more toasts. There was reminiscing. Nelson listened, wiped at the corners of his eyes. Clarissa kept Deirdre's CDs spinning on the boombox. Nelson opened up boxes of photos and we each found our favorites to keep. There were no hours passing on the clock, just food and talk and drink and pictures. At some point Mr. Nguyen left. Later I noticed Brian wasn't around. Nancy and Clarissa left in a clattering parade of burners and bowls and serving spoons. Kate took Adrian home to sleep. Franky left for a work gig he had to get to. Dusk was in the sky, and it was just us and Sylvia, and a room full of quiet.

"Sorry I lost my cool earlier," I said.

Nelson shook his head. "It was all true." He was stretched out on the sofa, his hands under his head. There was a wistful note to his voice. "She doesn't have to worry about anything anymore."

"Sunny side of the street," said Jen.

Sylvia sat on a folding chair, her feet up on another. Her drink was clutched close to her chest, her chin tucked in so hard it was doubled. I'd never seen her so inelegant.

"Well," she said, "If the heaven stuff is true, which I don't think it is, but if it was, she'll be with Sophie." Sylvia burped. "Oops. So that's good."

Nelson looked up from the sofa. "Who's Sophie?"

Sylvia slowly lowered her feet to the floor. "Oh, god. I thought—I assumed you knew."

Nelson stood up. I didn't particularly care who Sophie was. What hurt right then was the betrayed confusion in Nelson's face.

"Was this another girlfriend?" he demanded.

Sylvia shook her head. Sophie, said Sylvia, her eyes everywhere but Nelson's face, Sophie, as far as she could tell because she'd never seen a picture, didn't know a lot of details, Sophie, said Sylvia, was Deirdre's daughter.

76: JEN

"DUDE," I SAY, "IT WAS BAD."

Franky takes the freshly burned DVD from me, tucks it into its case. "I kind of wish I'd been there, but I'm kinda glad I wasn't."

"Uh-huh." I put in another blank DVD. "We were, like, blindsided."

"Did Sylvia say how old it was, the baby?"

"Nope. She doesn't know much. Just that she thinks it was an accident."

Franky's hand pauses above the address label. He looks up. "Hey, what about those diaries? Remember when she first moved in, you guys looked through her stuff, and there were those diaries?"

"Yeah," I say. "She apparently burned them. In a fit of wanting to 'start over.' She and Nelse did a little 'ceremony' in the back yard one day. He never saw inside them."

Franky peels the label from its backing, positions it across the mailing box. "Does Nelson know anything about it?"

"Nothing. There was a credit card, too, remember? In probably her married name. None of us can find it."

The crossing bells start up again. Jeez, some days it's almost no trains, others it's like one an hour.

"Did you check the internet?" says Franky.

"Yes." Pause for effect. "I checked the internet."

Franky makes a face at the address label. "Just asking."

The train shrieks. The house shakes. The DVD burner chugs away. "Shoulda done this years ago," I say.

"DVDs?"

"Yeah. People who were at the San Francisco conference want them. Not a bad profit at ten dollars a pop."

"Cool." Franky's marker squeaks block capitals across the label. "So Sylvia was the only one she told?"

"Looks like it. She ever say anything to you?"

Franky shakes his head.

"What a secret to carry around," I say.

Next thing I know, Franky's got his fingers pinched into his eyes.

"Dude. It's okay." His shoulder is square and hard under my hand. He keeps his fingers in his eyes and draws sharp breaths through his teeth.

"It's okay," I say again.

"The father. He'll never know," says Franky. "Even if they split up, he should know."

"Yeah," I say. Don't know what to say. Never in my life have I comforted Franky about anything. The main thing is just not to fuck it up.

After a minute, he does a big sniff and straightens up.

"I really miss her."

"Me too," I say.

"Funny. The way you hated her when she moved in."

It burns all around my chest. It's not even a little bit funny.

"I wouldn't say *hated*. It just took me a while to adjust."

He looks at his watch. "Yeah. Hey, I need to get going."

"Sure. Thanks for helping out."

"No problem."

He sits there with his hands on his knees. "Hey, uh. She had an email address, right?"

"Yeah. I guess I should delete her account." Something about that seems extra sad.

"No, leave it open. Like, it could become a memorial guestbook or something."

My knee-jerk response is to tell him that an email address is not remotely the same animal as an online guestbook, but I say, "Yeah. I could set that up."

Franky slides his palms down over his knees and back up again. "Do you think she's got any emails, you know, since?"

The idea gives me a chill. "Probably. She was getting random emails from time to time. Oh shit, and I should check on those New Western Light people. I was thinking, with the DVDs, the fundraiser, and if there were book royalties, maybe all together it might get us going again."

Franky looks up. "That photo book. Yeah. That has *got* to happen."

He watches over my shoulder as I open Deirdre's mail window. Four unread messages, and one's from New Western Light, wanting to discuss moving forward with the book project. The other emails are from random people liking her photos.

"Nice," I say. "Going to gather these puppies into a mailing list for when the book comes out." And for some dumb reason Franky and I high-five.

Then we're just staring at her mail window for a while.

"I looked everywhere," I say.

Franky says, "Huh?"

"I went though all these Australian newspaper archives. Searched all these different spellings of her name. Irish news archives too."

I close the email window. Nothing to do but shake my head at the strangeness of everything.

77: NELSON

THE SUN IS WHITE; the air is blue. Johnny-jump-ups—*Viola tricolor*—nod from cracks in the concrete, and Jen seems to be taking care not to step on them. The world is clearer, thanks to his new glasses. He hadn't even realized he needed a new prescription.

The bandage is finally off, but the fingers were set a little crooked. That's what you get with no medical insurance—a rush job. But they still work fine, so it doesn't matter. He brushes his hand over the weeds and they caress his wrist. His basement-pale skin feels the sun. The Cecile Brunner rose by the porch is bursting with soft new leaves. Jen spins around, walks backward till he catches up.

"Better today?" she asks.

"Today's a good day," he says. On bad days he stays in his room, swamped with tinnitus from the car accident and an overwhelming sense of the futility of everything. Those days are coming less often. And today there's something satisfying about climbing the chain-link fence with freshly healed fingers and landing on the other side in donated thick-soled boots that feel sturdy enough to last the remainder of the century. In the long grass there's a cigarette packet, a smashed pencil, and a tangle of heavy wire.

"Shortcut," says Jen, and she leads him between two buildings until they're under McLoughlin and trucks are roaring overhead. "I brought Dee here once."

"Yeah? When?"

"Near the beginning. She was still sick. Well, not all the way well."

He's become a pig for details about other people's experiences of Dee. "Anything," he'd say. "Even if it seems trivial. I want to know." So now they tell him little things, and he tucks them away like treasures. Because it means she wasn't just a dream, a figment, a prolonged hallucination. Other people saw her too.

"She told me she grew up near peat bogs."

"Uh-huh?" The river is getting close. He can see the city on the other side.

"It would be cool to visit one," says Jen.

"I looked up Edenderry on the internet," Nelson says. "It's just a small town with these little houses. A canal. She always said it was nothing special. Nothing for the tourists."

There's a faded stencil on the sidewalk, the red paint wearing off. He stops, scrapes his boot over what's left. "The peppers—The pepper spray babble? Oh. 'They pepper-sprayed babies.' God, that seems so long ago."

Jen stares at the stencil, her hands in her pockets. Whispers, "Yeah."

She turns, and he follows her past a flowering cherry tree in a lumpy parking lot labeled *Bridge Employee Parking ONLY.*

At the river they scramble down a steep track to the water's edge and sit on boulders. The smell is moist and weedy. The water is a dark, impenetrable olive, and floating on top are clusters of tiny bubbles and the occasional stick or leaf. Flakes of something white hang suspended just below the surface. The stereo roar of traffic on the freeway and bridges fills the air like fog, obscuring the smaller sounds they would otherwise hear, like the lap of water on stone, the grit crunching under their shoes. Across the river is the condo development and the marina. He can just make out the alternating colors of the condos: a dusty apricot, a beige, a taupe. The river is high from spring runoff. They pulled her out of the water near the north end. He visited the spot, and it became clear that she would've been found a lot later if a guy hadn't fished his dog's tennis ball out from under overhanging bushes. The ME said she'd only been in the water an hour or so. A clerical error meant the news came to them late.

"You have a choice," Mr. Nguyen had said to him last week. "Every moment. *Every* moment."

Nelson had been drinking Nguyen's weak diner coffee, sitting on a stool in the diner kitchen while Mr. Nguyen cleaned up, and the new girl was out front taking care of customers. Nelson imagined Deirdre loading the giant dishwasher and filling the glass-doored storage fridges.

Mr. Nguyen had wiped a cloth along the stainless-steel counter. "You can let it rule your life. Like her baby die rule her life. Or you take a different road."

"I can't see any roads," he'd said.

"You walking in dark. But road is there. You take a jump of faith. Then light comes."

"Leap of faith?" He'd smiled, and Mr. Nguyen smiled back with his long gray teeth.

Nelson had said, "I used to scoff when Deirdre talked about fate. But now I'm humbled by the idea. I don't know anything. I don't understand anything."

Mr. Nguyen rinsed the cloth in the sink. "Good."

"Are you married, Mr. Nguyen? I hope you don't mind me asking."

The cloth stopped halfway across a countertop. "Yes. Mrs. Nguyen die, nine year ago." He finished the countertop, then started on the microwave.

"I'm sorry to hear that."

"I glad she die," Nguyen had said, and it sent a jolt through Nelson.

"Her pain over and my pain less."

"I'm so sorry," was all Nelson could manage.

"She burn by napalm when she was young woman." Mr. Nguyen wiped the microwave window in fast circles. "Hospital in Vietnam not good then, too crowded. She suffer whole life from burn. Her thumb stuck to her hand. Then cancer. Doctor here try to help, but she too damage. She in bad pain. But most peaceful person I ever know." Mr. Nguyen then opened a fridge and started rearranging sodas. "She with God, even before she die."

Nelson's coffee had gone cold. The dishwasher rumbled. When he looked up, Mr. Nguyen's dark eyes were staring into his.

"Don't be sad, Mr. Nelson. Is only life. Only one life." The old man's hand moved like he was pushing away the idea. "Many million before, many million now, many million in future. Important not to take life too personally, eh?"

Nelson gripped his coffee cup.

Mr. Nguyen said, "Heh heh. We get so many, job is to learn right lesson to prepare for next one coming."

"You make it sound easy."

Mr. Nguyen chuckled again, then made his voice deeper. "Your mission, should you choose to accept."

Now, on the rock next to Nelson, Jen says, "It was at sunset." Jen wraps her elbows around her jutting-up knees. "She was so new she didn't even know the name of the river."

Nelson says, "She was so alone."

Jen gazes across the water. "I wish I'd been nicer to her."

"Yeah," he says. "But maybe—" The words have a hard time coming. But there's no sore place now. It's like there's been an all-out fire in there, and the coal burned to ash and blew away.

Jen turns. "Maybe what?"

"We should have listened to you, too."

78: FETZER

THE LANDLORD'S INSURANCE FIXED the windows and also got the porch replaced. Franky and I were sitting out there on a balmy evening, munching on corn chips, swigging beers, watching the crows fly over, and wondering why the landlord had chosen sunflower-yellow paint.

The next show was coming up, and Franky asked if he should start researching news items.

He's such a great kid. A few weeks earlier I'd suggested that he didn't need to stick around out of a sense of loyalty. That if he wanted to move to Seattle, be with his new girl, steer his life onto a different track, he had our blessing.

He looked so hurt, and I spent the next half hour reassuring him that I wasn't trying to get rid of him. I just didn't want him to feel trapped with us fogies. Turns out he was tired of the girl, her friends, and their callow lives. He wanted to save the world more than ever, he said. "And I was thinking, if it's okay with you, what if I, like, moved in?"

Of course we'd said yes.

And on the porch I said to him, "Some extra research would come in handy, thanks. Nelson might sit this one out, too. But boy, people want him back. The emails, sheesh."

"I know, Fetz. I've been replying to most of them."

His profile was clear and sharp in the golden light. A classical face, Deirdre said once. "Praxiteles could have carved him," she said. I remember because I Googled Praxiteles and saw what she meant.

"Of course you have. Sorry."

Franky waved a hand and smiled at the street. "Don't worry about it."

"No. Really."

He looked at me with those classical eyes.

"You have to understand," I said. "We appreciate everything you're doing. Everything you've ever done."

"Gee, Fetz," he said. He looked down at his beer. "Thanks."

"Please tell me that isn't a surprise."

He smiled. "Nah," he said, and lifted his bottle, and I clinked mine against it.

We went back to staring at the street. The sun raked deep shadows off the overhangs and pallets, and drifts of pink cherry petals gathered in the gutters.

He said, "You know, when I first saw her there?"

"Deirdre?"

"Uh-huh. At that bus stop. I had to stop, you know? My body said, 'turn the car around,' you know? It was sort of a big deal, but it was no big deal, too. It was easy. Natural."

"Okay."

"And even though things turned out so bad—it was the right thing to do." He turned to me, that classical, straight nose, those curvy lips that've always looked girly to me, but then I'm not an ancient Roman.

"Right?" he asked in a voice so quiet I thought it had come from somewhere else.

"It was," I said.

His face hung there. He whispered, "Do you think she killed herself?"

That took the wind out of me for a moment. "I don't know. Maybe. Jen thinks so."

Franky leaned sideways toward me. "Does Nelson?"

"I hope not, and I don't want to put the idea into his head."

A rattling sound started at the end of the street.

"It's so incredibly sad," insisted Franky. "Didn't she know we all loved her?"

"She tried real hard to keep herself together, but it's like rust. You can wire brush it till it gleams; you can sand and you can prime. But the rust is still there, and it starts eating away again. After a while there's nothing solid to hold the chassis together."

"That's so damn ni—nile . . . what's that word?"

"Nihilistic?"

"Yeah."

Right then the three homeless guys rolled up with their rattling cart and stopped.

"Got a smoke?" asked the vet in fatigues. Deirdre had told me their names, but I couldn't remember.

"Sorry, man, not tonight."

Franky gave me a funny look.

I held up the bag. "Want some chips?"

As they left their cart on the sidewalk and shuffled up the cracked front path, I realized there was no way I was putting my hand back in the bag after they'd helped themselves. To my relief Franky said, "I'll get a bowl," and he sprinted inside. When he came out I poured most of the chips into the bowl, and the three guys arranged themselves on the brand-new bottom step and started to eat. That sour odor of neglect wafted up.

"She gone?" asked the black guy with impossible cheekbones. "Deirdre, the donut lady?"

"Yeah," I said. "She's gone." I was going to leave it ambiguous, an implied move to another city, but the guy nodded. "Yeah. Her soul was half floating away, anyway."

"Aw, shit," said the vet. He shook his head. "That's real sad."

The one with the shakes concentrated on conveying chips into his mouth.

"Yeah," I said. My heart was thudding at the cheekboned guy's prescience. "It is. Franky, can you get these gentlemen some juice?"

Franky took his cue.

"How'd she go?" asked the vet.

"Drowned." I nodded in the direction of the river.

The vet slapped his thigh. "Shit. She was so fucking nice, too."

The high-cheekboned guy swallowed a mouthful that bounced his bony Adam's apple. He took another chip. "It's a clean way to go."

Volumes of understanding opened up between us. "Yeah. She stayed clean. Relatively."

"That's good," he said.

Franky reappeared and handed out three bottles of sparkling pink grapefruit juice. Something Nelson had gotten a taste for, and when Sylvia found out, she bought him a case.

The vet opened a bottle for the guy with the shakes and he clamped both his dirty hands around it tight.

"I'll drink to that," I said.

"Drink to what?" said Franky.

"Deirdre's kind heart."

"Yeah," said Franky.

The crossing bells started up, and our bottles clinked together over the yellow paint of the porch.

79: JEN

"KATE'S HERE," I SAY, and I step over to our new front door. It opens so smoothly in my hand. "Hey, Kate."

She's all dressed up in a skirt and heels, ready for the big interview. "Hi Jen," she snaps, and she hands me Adrian. "Can you hold him?"

Right.

Over in the kitchen, Fetzer holds up the coffee pot. "Just in time."

What am I supposed to do with this small human being wiggling in my arms?

Kate throws an *Oregon Herald* on the new coffee table. "They finally wrote a whitewash." Then she turns and puts a hand on her forehead. "Sorry, Jen, I'm just—"

"It's okay," I say, because Adrian's now teetering on his own two feet, holding on to my hand, and the look of astonished concentration on his face is the best thing ever.

"He's standing!" I say.

"Yes." Her voice says he's been driving her insane all morning. She drops her butt onto one of the new sofas.

New to us, that is. They're pretty nice, for donated.

Nelson sits next to her, picks up the *Herald.* She stares up at the ceiling. "Bastards. It's full of distortions."

Adrian take a step, wobbles, regains his balance. Wow. Imagine learning to walk.

"You wanna go to the table?" I say. Our brand-new kitchen table, thanks to the awesome fundraiser. But his eyes don't follow where I'm pointing. They're caught by a cat on the TV, an ad for cat food with the sound turned down.

Nelson hands the paper back to Kate. "It's unconscionable."

Fetzer and I agree, and he brings her a coffee, starts reading the story.

"Wanna say hi to Nelson?" I ask, and Adrian takes a step in Nelson's direction.

"Thank you *so* much for minding him," says Kate. "You guys are lifesavers."

"No problem," says Nelson, and he crouches down. Adrian lets go of me and reaches for Nelson's open hands. Kate's watching through half-closed eyes, and the soft mom in her comes back and she smiles.

"Wow," says Nelson. "You are such a big boy. You are *such* a big boy," and Adrian giggles like crazy from the tickling.

"Anyhow, dudes," I say, "It's like, getting worse everywhere." I turn the laptop around so they can see the news headline. "A cell got raided in Idaho. Three taken into custody. The Bush administration's treating the EFB like some homegrown equivalent of Al-Qaeda."

"Oh. Crap, yeah," says Fetzer. He pulls a scrap of newspaper out of his back pocket. "And listen to this. 'A patron logging on to an internet chat room from a college library computer was handcuffed and detained by local police for five hours after Secret Service agents accused the forty-year-old man, a federal polygraph instructor, of making threatening remarks about President Bush.'"

Kate winces. "God help us."

Adrian's tugging on Nelson's tie. It's the first time he's worn a tie since the funeral. It's purple-gray and it goes with that new gray shirt in a way that I would not normally notice or if I did, approve of, but it's good seeing him getting his shit back together.

On the laptop the IM box pops up. It's VioletFire.

`>Jen, what's UP? It's been WEEKS. You okay?`

"Oh, and you know what?" I say. "Maryville—the wild horse and burro facility? Brian told me it's been rebuilt."

"With horses?" asks Fetzer.

"More likely with wood," I say, and Kate grunts out a laugh.

"Well, that was a complete waste of time, then," mutters Fetz. He gets up to pour himself more coffee.

"It's the prevailing trend," says Nelson. He plops himself down opposite Kate. Arranges the kid on his knee. "The Taboose ranger station was rebuilt. And so was Vail."

"Was that the ski resort?" asks Kate.

"Yeah, Colorado," I say. "They tried to save lynx habitat. Bye-bye, lynx."

Nelson jiggles Adrian on his knee. "These places always have good insurance."

Okay, I *have* to get back to Vi. Been putting it off too long.

`*** TheJenerator has joined #rezist`

`<schrodingers_cat> Yup. Trapping IO calls to and from isatty(3) file descriptors, in realtime, saving them on file along with a timestamp.`

`<VioletFire> It's alive!`

`<schrodingers_cat> Jen?! Where've you been?`

`<ignite> hey, wb Jen!`

`<TheJenerator> Hi everyone. Yeah it's been a while. I'm fine. Shit went down, but we're okay.`

`<VioletFire> What kind of shit. Mustve been major.`

`<TheJenerator> That girl who moved in? She died. Plus our house got trashed.`

`<ignite> OMG that sux.`

`<VioletFire> Wow. Sorry to hear that.`

`<schrodingers_cat> Who the fuck trashed your house?`

The silent TV flickers with another commercial. A grinning peach slices itself into a bowl of cereal. Kate's watching Nelson over the rim of her coffee mug. Nelson and Fetz are talking about sabotaged shit getting rebuilt. Stuff we'd never normally mention in front of someone like her.

But she's not Kate, *Oregon Herald*, anymore. She's Righteous Kate.

The TV weather comes on. Silent maps. Silent, happy weatherman predicting silent spring weather.

Nelson finds a label sticking out of the back of Adrian's tiny jacket. Kate watches him tuck it in. The guy's been through so much. Come so far.

"Nelse," I say. "It's hard to believe you're the same guy as six—no, nearly seven years ago."

Nelson smooths a hand over the kid's blond hair. "Yeah?"

"Dude, you were such a noob. But you jumped right in."

Over in the kitchen Fetzer yelps out a laugh. "Remember that first time you worked on a roadblock?"

Nelson snorts. "Yes."

Fetzer comes over and says to Kate, "I decide to check up on the new guy, and what do I see? These branches, like, fallen rotten-wood branches, dragged across the road!"

Nelson's blushing. "I didn't know, sheesh." He glances up at Kate and his smile drops.

The look on her face. "*You* made roadblocks?"

"Several," he says, nodding. "Many."

Fetz scratches his ear. "We haven't done anything like that since '99."

Kate's eyes travel across the three of us.

The look on her face—if I'm not mistaken, there's a little bit of admiration in there, too.

"Not that I'd ever share that with someone from the mainstream media," Nelson says, and she grabs the newspaper and swats it toward his head while he ducks and laughs. For the first time since, well, a long time.

"But seriously, guys," says Nelson, "when I look back at the things we used to do, and the things we report on, it's been a lot of effort. A lot of risk. But so much of it seems so . . ." He smooths his hand over Adrian's hair again. "Ineffective."

My stencil down near the river. The only one left 'cause it gets the least traffic, and it's already unreadable. And the event itself has fallen into the memory hole.

"Protest in general," says Fetzer, and he throws up his hands. "Look at how many people turned out before the invasion. Millions around the world. Month after fucking month. Dissed by the mainstream media. And now it's millions of people feeling totally cynical."

In chat, Vi and the others are still throwing me questions.

`<TheJenerator> Too many details to go into, guys. But I'm going to take an extended break from the group. Got my work cut out for me here in RL.`

`<ignite> Whaaa? We need you!`

`<VioletFire> Crap. Glad you're ok, though.`

`<TheJenerator> I'll be baaaack`

`<TheJenerator> Vi, thanks for checking in. You're great. All of you.`

`*** TheJenerator has left #rezist`

The laptop clicks closed. Out the newly glazed living room window is the new yellow porch. The gravel street. Kate's car.

Kate touches Nelson's foot with the toe of her shoe. "I'm glad you're back at the rallies," she says.

"Thanks," says Nelson. "I was nervous getting up on that stage again, but, it turned out okay."

"You were *great*."

"And I got most excellent footage to prove it," I say.

"But that saying," says Nelson, "about a tree falling in a forest keeps coming back to me. If dissent rises on city streets, and the media isn't listening, does it make any sound?"

Kate raises her eyebrows. "Cute."

"Seriously," says Fetzer. "Saving puppies would be wall-to-wall news, but the reasons why thousands of people are blocking city streets every week? Nah."

Nelson picks up the VCR remote. "You saw what they said about it on Channel 8?"

Nelson rewinds and the sound comes up. The Reporter We Loathe has short curly hair and a red rain jacket. Behind him the street is thick with protesters in the rain. The reporter says, "These kids are chanting the same thing over and over again. It seems to be the only thing they know how to say." Then it cuts to the studio. "Timed to coincide with this was another Support Our Troops gathering in the Park Blocks," says the anchor, and it cuts to a crowd on a street corner. Even with careful cropping, they couldn't hide the fact that it's only about two dozen strong. "We need to trust our president," says a man.

"Turn it off," says Kate. She's closed her eyes. Nelson turns it off. Wraps his arms around the baby.

"Which one is it this morning?" says Fetzer. She opens her eyes like it's a relief to change the subject.

"OIT Journalism department. Summer classes. With a possibility of more in the fall."

"You'll do great," says Nelson. Then he says to Adrian, "Your mom's going to be great. Before we know it she'll be inspiring a new generation to replace these cowards."

Kate sips her coffee. "Never thought I'd go into teaching. But, I never thought I'd trash my career, either."

I hold up a headline: *IRAQ IS ALL BUT WON; NOW WHAT?* "Put a stop to crap like this. We beg of you."

Kate looks away. Her soft mom voice is gone when she says, "Supposed to be a cornerstone of democracy. Only private business protected by the Constitution. And they go and violate that trust."

"These are seriously dark days," I say.

Nelson rests his cheek on Adrian's blond head and murmurs, "Yeah."

80: NELSON

NELSON LOOKS OUT ACROSS the crowd filling Pioneer Square. Helicopters throb in the hot August sky, but he isn't angry. Riot cops bristle on the corners, but he isn't afraid. The crowd is cheering, and the sound scours through him, rough and clean.

"Four months ago," he says into the microphone, "President Bush declared 'Mission Accomplished' and that 'major combat operations in Iraq have ended.'"

Boos from the crowd.

"Since then, a hundred and fifty more US soldiers have died in combat. And altogether more than *ten thousand* Iraqi civilians have met violent ends. *Nothing* accomplished but suffering and waste."

More boos.

"But we can accomplish something here at home. We couldn't stop the war, but we can build peace. Peace here at home."

A smattering of claps from the crowd.

"Let's not be distracted by this war. Together we need to prepare for the changes that global warming will bring. Our lives will be altered in ways we can barely yet imagine, and we need to get ready. And not in fear and isolation, but together. We need to convene; we need to learn from each other. We need to examine the threats and the opportunities. We are poised to make decisions that will reverberate for decades to come."

A thousand faces watch him, but he's most aware of the people he loves who are close by. Jen, manning the video camera. And at the bottom of the steps, Fetzer and Franky. Kate and Nancy's daughter, Clarissa. And their new director of development, Sylvia.

When Sylvia had come to their house last month and offered her services pro bono, Jen shook her head. "What you're saying sounds insane. Brand? Positioning? Who are you, Karl Rove?"

Sylvia spoke slowly. "I'm talking about long-term plans to make Omnia Mundi financially viable. Enable everything you've done together to grow and become a powerful voice in the public conversation."

Franky had slapped his knee and pronounced the idea "Awesome!"

Nelson had said, "Strategic development, Jen. We're long overdue."

Fetzer had said, "Jen, we've been stripped down to the studs. It's a good time to remodel."

It wasn't until Sylvia revealed that she'd fired most of her clients to make room for working with them that Jen unfolded her arms. Started to ask reasonable questions. Started brainstorming ways to connect with other communities. And the forums idea was born.

A thousand faces watch Nelson as he announces the forums. How they'll reach out to underserved and isolated communities. How together they'll search for ways to move forward despite this administration.

"*Despite* a war that's not in our name," he says. "*Despite* the anger. *Despite* the shame." The crowd cheers.

"There's a chant being used a lot lately," he says. "What—does—democracy look like?"

The crowd yells back, "*This* is what democracy looks like," and cheers. Nelson holds up his hands until there is quiet. Then he points to himself, to the crowd. "This isn't what democracy looks like. This is one person, standing in front of a thousand. Democracy isn't listening to people on stages. Democracy is getting together in dialogue. It's taking turns at the microphone. It's *all of us* asking each other for help. It's *all of us* offering what we're able. It's *all of us* taking action. That, my friends, is what democracy looks like."

A ripple moves through the crowd and the clapping is stronger.

"So who's coming to the first forum?" he asks. "Raise your hands. I need to know how many chairs to put out."

Laughter from the crowd, and a sea of hands goes up. Someone yells something unintelligible, but it causes more clapping.

"Great," says Nelson. "And between now and then, ask yourself what is *one* good idea that will benefit your community? It can be big or small. Bring an idea to share."

A guy in the crowd yells again, sounds like "unform error." Heads turn. A heckler? But people around the guy cheer, so probably not.

Nelson says, "It's unconscionable what the Bush administration has done. But we can't turn the clock back. The future is coming, and there's work to be done."

"Run—for—mayor!" From someone closer this time.

"Run for mayor!" yells a woman near the front row.

Nelson gets a small kick in his stomach. Not entirely unpleasant. He pinches the top of his tie. It's the dark olive silk. Deirdre always said dark colors suit him, better than the tan of that old corduroy jacket. He worries that he looks too conservative in darks, but Kate also says they look good on him.

"Thanks for your confidence," he murmurs into the microphone. "Ah, bring it to the forum, okay?"

SYLVIA TURNS HER CAR onto the Hawthorne Bridge.

Nelson says, "I can't keep asking you for rides."

Sylvia smiles. "Get one of those Priuses."

Nelson keeps an eye on Kate's car in the side mirror. Kate's Honda carrying Kate and Franky and Clarissa, and Adrian strapped into his little safety seat. He says, "But Fetzer wants to stick with biofuel."

"You can't agree?" says Sylvia.

"We can't agree," says Fetzer from the back.

"They can't agree," says Jen next to him.

Last week in the kitchen, Fetzer pulled up a chair. Sat down. "So."

It was time for the talk. Nelson was ready.

Fetzer had tilted his freshly shaved head to the side. "How're you doing?"

"Fine," Nelson had said. "Really."

Fetzer leaned closer. "How come?"

"I feel very supported. You guys are the best friends I will ever know."

Fetzer winced. "That's extremely nice, but, I don't buy it."

Dear Fetzer, as Deirdre would say.

Fetzer circled a finger near his ear. "What is going through your head? You're planning, planning, working, working."

Nelson had smiled at him. "Future's coming. There's work to be done."

"Don't give me your little catchphrase." Fetzer propped his hands on his knees. "Don't you miss her? I miss her all the time."

"Of course. All the time. But I get to start over, don't you see? Isn't that amazing?"

Fetzer's mouth pinched, searching for words. "It's—no, I wouldn't say 'amazing.' But then, I rarely do."

The kitchen floor was solid under Nelson's feet. The air was very still.

There are gifts that come and we can't even explain it.

"I was greedy for her, Fetz. I was addicted. And now I'm not."

Fetzer's eyes opened a little bit wider, then for some reason he snorted. Put his hands over his face.

Nelson said, "Don't you see? I get another chance."

Fetzer moved a hand to Nelson's shoulder. He nodded. "That's good, John." And at that moment love flowed across Nelson like clear water on white sand.

Sylvia turns the car onto Thirteenth and looks into the rearview mirror. "Hybrid or biofuel?"

Jen says, "I could go either way," and Nelson smiles to himself. Dear Jen. How hard she's trying.

Sylvia says, "Do you think Franky could be persuaded to trade his in for something diesel?"

Nelson turns to Fetzer and Jen in the back seat. "Now that's an idea. Franky gets a new car, and you convert it. Think he'll go for it?"

"I don't see why not," says Fetz.

Nelson faces forward again. "Excellent idea, Syl."

Sylvia pulls to a stop outside the house. Most of the top story is a deep forest green. It looks really good for recycled paint. Makes the house look more solid.

Fetzer looks up at the paint job. "We got pretty far on Friday. Should be finished end of next week." He slaps his knee. "Crap. I forgot to get more window putty."

"You need a pen?" says Nelson.

"You need one of these," says Sylvia, and she holds up her Blackberry.

"I kinda covet that thing," murmurs Jen.

Nelson fishes in Sylvia's glove compartment for a pen. He used to fantasize about the house he'd live in with Deirdre one day. How they'd pick out colors together. He was so blind.

"I heard another good idea today," says Fetzer. He opens his door but doesn't get out. "Run for mayor."

Nelson gets the small kick in his stomach again. Turns around to Fetz and Jen. "That sure came out of left field."

"Mayor's a stretch," says Fetzer. "But what about city council?"

Sylvia rests her forearms on the steering wheel and looks up at the sky. "A political campaign. Now that would be an interesting challenge."

Jen rakes her hair back from her face. "You guys are asking this anarchist to adjust to a *lot*."

EPILOGUE: FETZER

BY END OF SUMMER Nelson was back on air. The community forums were proving a success, and we were learning to listen without inserting ourselves in every conversation. A hard lesson for radio folk, who are used to talking, talking. But slowly communities opened up to us, and we heard things we hadn't heard before. It drove us into even deeper commitment. And it changed our show. The term *radical heterogeneity* is getting tossed around lately, and as much as I hate buzzwords, that's one I can get behind.

Meanwhile, Sylvia worked her magic—or paid her penance, if you look at it that way—by setting us up as a foundation and shifting our paradigm. Franky was now our official receptionist and liaison, and our new assistant? Nancy's daughter, Clarissa.

"Despair is a sin against the holy spirit," Nelson said to me one day. He and I were sitting in the kitchen, drafting a budget for '04. The topic of hope came up. Or lack of it. That day's bad news was the White House's hatchet job on the official EPA assessment of climate change, to suit el Presidente's skepticism about global warming.

"Deirdre brought it up a couple of times before the end," said Nelson.

"Yeah?" Neither Jen nor I had mentioned the religious stuff to him.

"She started going to church. And wearing a crucifix. I thought it was endearing. Like she was reconnecting with her heritage. She must've been in such despair. I don't know why I didn't put two and two together."

"She hid it well," I said.

Nelson shook his head. "She seemed happy. I mean about being married, starting a family."

"You loved each other," I said. "You get to remember it that way."

Nelson picked up the paper he'd been reading earlier. "We're all so lost in our own issues. But we're so tightly woven into so many networks and systems, and so dependent on them not just for our survival, but for the continued ongoing creation, moment to moment, of our selves, that self-centeredness is just petty. Don't you think?"

He looked up at me, those big eyes. And right then I got an inkling of what he was becoming.

"It also creates fear," he continued. "Something's got to change. It just has to."

I felt like I was no longer on terra firma, but I nodded.

He scanned down the article. "Jeez, they even removed a graphic showing rising global temperatures compared with the previous thousand years. Replaced it with a study, partly sponsored by the American Petroleum Institute, that disputes those findings."

Feeling grounded again, I replied, "At least someone in the EPA had the stones to leak it."

Nelson gazed past the paper. "We will head for ruin or we will aim for hope."

"Is that one of those classical quotes of hers?"

He folded the paper, put it down. "No, I just thought of it. We will head for ruin or we will aim for hope. And despair is a sin against the earth."

Hope was the theme of the next show. Themes were a new thing, and people loved it. Each month we called for submissions in the form of anecdotes, photos, essays. Thank god we had an assistant to handle what poured in.

WE HAD AN INTERN program rolling by the winter. Kids were falling over each other to work with us, which was pretty cool. Well, our internships pay better than most student jobs, so that might have something to do with it. And we get to pay interns thanks to a big old grant Sylvia wrote for us.

We've got three areas of training: Biofuel Technologies, Radio Journalism, and Open Source Computing. That one was Jen's idea. And it turns out she likes teaching a whole lot.

A couple of years later we bought the whole house off the landlord and fixed up both sides. Luckily it's a big house. Kate moved in. Adrian is nearly seven, and in school. Nelson's a great dad, naturally. And no one can deny that he and Kate are good together. She doesn't need rescuing, and neither does he.

Nelson's also going to be a good city councilor. We're still dusting off the victory confetti (the biodegradable kind, of course) and packing away the lawn signs. He was swept in on a wave of political change. Expectations are high. We don't know what the next few years will hold, but like he says, he comes with a team, and we'll do our very best.

Every so often I pour myself a nice glass of wine, pick up a copy of Dee's photo book, and look through it cover to cover. It reminds me that the year everything went up in flames had some good parts, too. And Dee's original photos, the ones from her show, Sylvia's planning an exhibition of them early next year. To coincide with Nelson stepping into city hall.

We stopped working directly with folks like the EFB. Jen misses it, I know, but sneaking around at night just doesn't mix with a public position like city councilor. Besides, cameras and editing technology have gotten so cheap, folks like the EFB don't need us to do the legwork anymore. But we still include their material on the Omnia Mundi website. All still means all.

When Nelson announced his candidacy, he got flak from direct-action radicals for selling out. But he's been working hard to convince them we're still going to keep the issues front and center on the radio show. He's also adamant he's going to bring a radical perspective to city hall. Personally, I have no idea how he's going to pull that off in an environment that'll force him to compromise. We'll see.

Meantime, the planet's still being ransacked. The Pentagon keeps gobbling up universities. Kids are still being sent into the meat-grinder of a pointless war—justified by a fiction crafted to make the voting public afraid and compliant. And the Green Scare has removed some of the bravest activists from society.

In this context I'm thankful for the simple pleasures of my life: I teach Biofuel Technologies half a day each week. Students bring their old cars and we have a good time. Sometimes I show them pictures of the Toro, and their eyeballs almost fall out. And I never have to make fuel anymore, since there's always someone around who needs the practice.

Another change? Nelson got himself a violin. Nothing fancy, but it's a real pretty instrument. Shiny burled wood stained a clear dark brown. It's hard to find a quiet space in our house, so he practices alone in the archive, the big room upstairs on the west side that used to be Deirdre's space. And sometimes, if you're outside and he has the west-facing windows open, you can hear him start and stop, start and stop, some Irish reel or other.

About the Illustrator

GABRIEL LISTON is an artist and illustrator of domestic scenes and water history. He was born in Texas, raised in Colorado, overheated in Iowa, and lives in Oregon. He has children and the children have chickens, a rabbit and a Newfoundland dog.

About the Author

Julia Stoops was born in Samoa to New Zealand parents, and grew up in Japan, Australia, New Zealand, and Washington, D.C. She has lived in Portland, Oregon, since 1994. She has received Oregon Arts Commission fellowships for visual arts and literature, and was a resident at the Ucross Foundation in 2016.

Acknowledgments

With gratitude I thank the many people who helped get this story into your hands.

Stevan Allred and Joanna Rose, my insightful, deep, and patient teachers at the Pinewood Table, whose mentorship was powerful and profound. Without them this book would not have made it past the first draft.

Harold Johnson, who showered attention onto single words, sentences, fragments, silences, and whose Private Birdsong was an inspiration.

Laura Stanfill: friend, reader, fellow writer, community-builder, and brave publisher. Our meeting was fated!

Jackie Shannon Hollis, Sarah Cypher, Christi Krug, David Nishizaki, Christian Gaston (twice!), Julie Perini, Hope Hitchcock, Scott Sparling, Amy Harwood, and Gabriel Liston, who at one time or another read the whole manuscript and provided honest feedback that helped me take it to the next level. Also Suzy Vitello, Mark Lawton, and Kristin Kaye, who read large chunks and provided more invaluable, honest feedback. Then there are the many fellow Pinewood Table writers whose insights over the years helped shape the story. Your thoughtful support means more than you'll ever know.

Gabriel Liston, the illustrator, the demiurge who brought these characters to life with such grace and humor and depth. You see dark and light with the same eye— and I'm not talking about photons. And Kristi Wallace Knight, fellow Pinewood Table alum and long-time writing peer, who generously helped Gabriel and me run a successful Kickstarter for the illustrations.

Many thanks to the inimitable Gigi Little for her artistic vision and boundless patience designing the cover, and to Forest Avenue Press intern Samm Saxby for her energy and enthusiasm in getting the word out.

I strove for accuracy across the board, and where I dared to dip my toe into subjects about which I have little first-hand knowledge, I sought help. Shannon Lee, Mark Keppinger, Andrew Clapp, David Severski, and Forest

Basford helped me communicate the nuances of certain technical aspects. I am grateful for their generosity and expertise. Any remaining errors are my own.

I also gratefully acknowledge that Nelson's address to the (fictional) Science and Sustainability conference was inspired by an eloquent book review by Anna Lappé in *The New Scientist*, July 12, 2006.

And a big thank you to the 82 people who backed the Kickstarter:

Andria Alefhi
Stevan Allred
Anonymous
Anonymous
Anonymous
Anonymous
Anonymous
Anonymous
Anonymous
Anonymous
Anonymous
Another Read Through
Bruce Barrow
Pollyanne Faith Birge
Ness Blackbird
Pat Boas
Jack Boas
Sven Bonnichsen
Oliver Brennan
Yolanda Brown-Burnstein
Cath Carrington
Jeffrey Jerome Cohen
Anne Connell
Olivia M. Croom
Beth Curren
Jennifer Curry
Cesar Delgado
Steve Denniston
Jody DiLeo
Al & Christine Downs
Leslie Durst
Cai Emmons
Sandra Fitzgibbon
Liz Fuller
Moses Gunesch
Justin Hocking
Mark Humpal
Beth Hutchins
Jennifer Jako
Harold L. Johnson
Deb Jones & John Katzenberger
Vinnie Kinsella
Doug & Linda Knight
kollodi & Roger
Jen & Levi Kruch
Jude Kujanson
Smyth Lai
Mark Lawton
George Mandis
Judith Margles
Bryan Markovitz
Thomas Martin
Allyn Massey
Jim Neidhardt
Mark Penlington
Julie Perini
Chris Piuma
Brett Cody Rogers
Jenna Rose
Sheryl Sackman
Madeleine Sanford
Jackie Shannon Hollis
Colleen & Larry Sibelman
Lynn Siprelle
Laura Stanfill
Karl Steel
Denis & Noeline Stoops
Mike Strathan
Sharon Summers
Ann Talbot
TSFPLTMT
Kristi Wallace Knight
Shu-Ju Wang
Greg Ware
Lyn White
Ryan White
Joy White
Jon Wilson
Theresa Wisner
Jill Wollack
Christy & Laura Wyckoff
Yuvi Zalkow

PARTS PER MILLION

A NOVEL

READERS' GUIDE

Afterword

I HAVE BEEN ASKED, "How much of your novel is fact and how much is fiction?"

The characters are entirely fictional, as are their activities. The university they investigate is fictional too, and I strove to make it not match any particular local institution. No, it's not Reed College, even though it's private, and it's not Portland State University, even though it's downtown. I hope my skewering of the fictional Harry Lane University is interpreted as a criticism of the influence of the military on higher education, and not a veiled attack on any local institution.

Harry Lane, 1855 – 1917, was an Oregon doctor, mayor, senator, and Progressive Era reformer. He stuck to his ideals throughout his life, championing public health improvements, campaigning for women's suffrage, and advocating for Indian tribes. He battled injustice, special interests, corruption, and the U.S. entrance into World War I.

The inner Southeast industrial neighborhood the characters live in is real, but some streets are shuffled for the sake of narrative flow. The characters live on Southeast Novi, which is a fictional street between Southeast Ivon and Southeast Clinton. (Novi is Ivon backward.) That neighborhood has gentrified dramatically since 2002 and no longer looks the same.

The characters' radio show is fictional but is not unlike something you might hear on KBOO, Portland's independent community radio station, where I volunteered in the news department during 2002 and 2003.

Every word the characters read in a newspaper or hear on the TV is verbatim from news reports during the fall of 2002 and winter/spring of 2003. However, the exact date was sometimes nudged or the source was renamed for aesthetic reasons. The one exception is the report of the Maryville firebombing heard on the car radio in chapter 2. That is entirely fictional.

The descriptions of rallies and protests are closely based on my experiences, as well as interviews with fellow protesters. (Indeed, they did pepper-spray babies at the Bush protest in August '02. You can see a picture of the family in distress on the partspermillion.net website.)

The story follows historical events, but I sometimes embellished the weather to underscore the mood of a scene.

Thanks to the generous help from several experts mentioned in the acknowledgments, I hope the scenes of hacking, wiretapping, and the tricked-out Oldsmobile Toronado bear at least a passing resemblance to how these things might actually go down.

—Julia Stoops, January 2018

A Short Note from the Illustrator

I'M HERE BECAUSE OF JEN.

I drove to Portland in 1995. Its downtown art school had accepted my portfolio and I hoped the city would be small enough for me (hometown: 8.5k humans) to negotiate with a toddler. On Southeast Clinton I found a tiny cafe where I could check email, watch my child nap in her car seat, and, surrounded by people sitting at terminals and chatting IRL with the same geeks they were simultaneously in chat rooms with, feel less alone.

Jen stepped right out of the Habit Cafe, just a few blocks from the HQ of Omnia Mundi.

On the other hand, Omnia Mundi itself will, in my head, always resemble North Portland's Chicken House, a neighborly palace once the home of deep heartblood like Moe Bowstern and Marisa Anderson and Ben Haile and the Amalgamated Everlasting Union Chorus Local 824. Julia and I redrew the house plan for OMHQ in my *Parts per Million* sketchbooks (1 and 2) again and again. The sun comes in a different window and it's Fetzer, not Dwayne, distilling veggie diesel in the shed, but the smell remains the same.

Julia was my Art and Ideas professor that first year in Portland. As a studio artist, she showed how we could visualize our understanding of the world through interlocking ellipses and vortices and plenty of color. Two decades later when she asked if I would read her novel I assumed it would be something equally woven and complex. It was, but what caught me was Jen; Jen was funny, familiar. And there was the frustrated self-knowledge that Portland was not super-diverse, super-radical like Oakland, but we had to, and could, make do, and learn. My scalp burned with all the people I suddenly needed Julia to share the novel with, talk to, harass.

And I was caught by that same question that must have haunted Julia: "How do I take this time and place I knew and loved and remake it with people I've never met before?" Except I had the advantage of Julia herself making all the introductions.

—Gabriel Liston, January 2018

Book Group Questions

1. Who is your favorite character, and why? How does that character grow from the opening of the novel to the epilogue?

2. Of all the characters, major and minor, who do you think gets what they really want by the end?

3. Why do you think Nelson's chapters are in third person, whereas the Jen's and Fetzer's are in first person? How does this influence your understanding of the characters?

4. The author wrote about a particular time in the history of the United States. In what ways does the telling reflect how you remember that time, and in what ways does it differ?

5. Would you characterize this novel as more character driven, or more plot driven?

6. Why do you think *Parts per Million* is told from three points of view? What effect does this have on your understanding of the story as it unfolds?

7. Nelson is a rational optimist, whereas Deirdre is a pessimistic fatalist. Do you think their relationship could have survived long-term?

8. Imagery is repeated throughout, such as Deirdre nearly tipping the table over during her first breakfast with the crew, then actually tipping the table over during her last evening with them. Can you think of other examples of images that are used more than once?

9. Identify some similes and metaphors used in Nelson's scenes. Is he really such a rationalist after all?

10. Jen is the youngest activist of the trio, and the one who pushes back the most when Deirdre joins the household. How does her social interaction with the other characters, and with #rezist, change?

Learn more about *Parts per Million* at partspermillion.net. Discover more details and characters sketches about Nelson, Jen, Fetzer, and Deirdre at the Omnia Mundi website, omniamundi.org. Forest Avenue Press publishes literary fiction on a joyride from its Portland, Oregon, headquarters.